Sea Trials

Alaric Bond

for Joan and Ron
(WR)

Contents

Sea Trials

Chapter One

"Really, Tom, I don't know what you have to complain about."

King blinked and sat back in the only chair that fitted into their tiny cabin; he supposed she was right. After all he was at sea, the element where he felt most at home, and aboard a new and sprightly warship. Furthermore, the elegant young French woman currently combing out her hair before him was now in almost every sense his wife and seemed determined to remain so, despite the many disadvantages in having an English sea officer as a companion.

"It's being a passenger," he explained vaguely. "I cannot become used to having no duties to perform."

"A passenger?" Aimée repeated with a scowl as she withdrew her comb and turned to him. "But we have been aboard this ship for so long!"

"Indeed we have," King agreed. "Though with a fellow like Johnston in command..."

"Ah, that is the problem." She grinned in triumph before returning to the tiny mirror. "Our famous captain – what is your English expression: he rubs you the wrong way?"

"Something in that manner."

"Well I think it is the same for him," Aimée continued while, stooping slightly to avoid the low deckhead, she began to plait her thick mane of hair. "I think you rub Monsieur Johnston the wrong way also. *And* it is his ship, *and* you are merely a passenger."

"I would mind less were he a true seaman," King insisted. "As it is he relies too much on his officers; it is fortunate they at least know what's about."

"You, too, have good officers," Aimée reminded him. "Many's the time you have spoken well of them."

"I do," he agreed, "though fancy I can do their jobs as well as my own, whereas Johnston would struggle to replace one of his midshipmen."

"Then why was he given this ship to command?" she asked.

"The Dear knows," King shrugged. "Besides, the *St. George* isn't strictly his ship, he is only taking her as far as Bombay."

"But you are still jealous perhaps?"

"Not of the ship." King was emphatic. "This is naught but a sloop, whereas a fine frigate awaits me in Cape Town."

"And that is larger?"

"Oh, much," he assured her, "and far more powerful. Johnston's *St. George* mounts nine-pounders and barely enough to call a true broadside whereas my frigate carries eighteen-pounder carriage pieces in addition to her carronades so is a different proposition."

"Ah, and a man will find such a thing important," Aimée agreed lightly as she dabbed at her hair with the edge of her comb.

"It is normally considered so," King replied with just a hint of doubt. "But there is more," he added quickly. "*Mistral* is a King's ship."

"But of course!" She turned to him and beamed.

"No, I mean she sails on behalf of King George," he flustered. "She belongs to the British Navy – as do I – whereas Johnston is merely a John Company officer."

"And that must also be important," she supposed gravely.

"The Honourable East India Company is a commercial enterprise," King explained. "So the *St. George* is a private warship."

"Well, I don't know about your royal ships and private navies; when both fight the same war it surely makes no difference?" The hair, though not perfect, was sufficient for a day at sea and she turned her attention to one of the small pots of cream that currently lined their washstand.

"Some would say there is no difference," King continued with a little more care. They were as close as any married couple, yet Aimée remained French, so technically his enemy. "But truly the Honourable Company is less interested in fighting and more concerned with trade."

"Then why do they need warships such as this?"

King pursed his lips. "To protect their shipping. The Royal Navy does their bit but cannot be everywhere. The Company occasionally needs additional escorts for their Indiamen, which is why we were able to take this passage to The Cape."

"Ah yes, the Indiamen..." The woman now adopted a slightly wistful look. "They are fine ships are they not?"

"They are, for their purpose," King agreed hesitantly.

"From what I hear, the Indiamen serve excellent meals and have much space for their passengers. And they carry so many! Plenty of interesting people to talk to." She had finished applying the cream and stepped back as far as she could to gauge the result. "It must be why most who travel on long journeys choose to go aboard such wonderful vessels..."

King eyed her warily but made no comment.

"And this private warship that we are aboard, where we are the only passengers, she is escorting three such Indiamen, is that not so?"

"It is," King agreed dutifully. Their conversation was fast acquiring the hallmarks of one already repeated many times during the long journey from England and would probably end in much the same way.

"Ah, those Indiamen must be so much more comfortable than this, what did you call it, a sloop?" Aimée finally abandoned the mirror and, turning only slightly in the narrow space, ran her finger down his cheek with affection.

"They are more comfortable," King agreed, taking her hand and kissing it gently. "And I know, I should have booked our passage aboard one," he conceded. "It just seemed better not to at the time."

"You do not like comfort, perhaps?"

"I do not care much either way," he shrugged. "Though have encountered enough John Company passengers to make me wary. To my mind the type who journey so far through choice make poor travelling companions. Most are men, though their wives can be as hearty, and much time is spent drinking and gambling."

"Much time?"

"Some," King allowed. "But because of them I felt us better taking passage in the escort."

"Yes, in the tiny warship," Aimée agreed as she glanced around their cramped accommodation. "Where perhaps you are more comfortable?"

King made no response, preferring instead to study the washstand which had unaccountably caught his attention.

"And with that nice Captain Johnston in command whom you admire so much," she persisted. "So tell me, Tom, was that truly a good idea?"

* * *

The *St. George* was indeed not intended to carry passengers so the presence of Captain King and his French companion had forced Scott and Salmond, the sloop's second and third mates, to share the adjoining cabin. Not that either minded particularly, they were good friends and often on duty at different times. And there was certainly no resentment against their guests; both men had a measure of respect for the Royal Navy while the presence of a pretty young woman at mealtimes was an unspoken bonus. Especially for Salmond who, though barely in his twenties, was already making inroads into what some would consider the life of a rake.

It had begun at the age of twelve with a girl in his village. The pair had truly been little more than friends but her association convinced him of the pleasures of female company. And it was something the intervening years, along with later spells of celibacy while at sea, had been unable to dispel. For even the longest stretch of desert cannot continue indefinitely and when whatever ship he happened to be aboard finally touched land Salmond's interest revived like a cactus in the rain.

In this the sloop's third mate differed little from most lower deck seamen, even if he shunned some of the places they frequented. For it was not the intimacy of physical contact Salmond craved, he simply enjoyed female company. With a dashing smile, a smart blue uniform and an ever-growing fund of stories, the young officer made attractive company and usually found enough daughters of local factors or shore-based officers' sisters to make his visits a recurring, yet totally innocent, pleasure.

Women were not his only diversion, however; Salmond was

enthusiastic about other matters. There was the sea and all aspects of seamanship, as well as foreign travel; in his view the three combined to provide the best that life could offer. He was also an insatiable bookworm, having already consumed and assimilated all he could on Company law and the principles of trading; an activity that had directly led to his present position at what was quite a young age. And his current responsibility for the ship's guns had awoken yet another distraction. Little in the way of intelligence was required to command a battery of nine-pounders, but Salmond's innate curiosity found the science behind the weapons' performance fascinating and he was steadily amassing a considerable library on the subject.

But none of his professional duties were occupying him at that moment. Salmond was off watch and the convoy had run across a packet ship the day before. The craft, a sprightly little thing that immediately caught the young man's eye, had overhauled their untidy clutter of a convoy at speed, yet paused long enough to transfer post due to be delivered in Cape Town. And so with several hours of free time and a pile of mail to digest, Salmond's original interest had reclaimed him and when Scott barged into their cabin he was deeply immersed.

"Upon my word," the second mate exclaimed taking in the pile of papers perched on his friend's chest. "Would they all be for you?"

"From my sister," Salmond replied levelly from his bunk. "She is the very devil for correspondence."

"And has a fair hand," Scott remarked, collecting one of the closely written sheets. "Though it does tend to vary from letter to letter. As does her choice in ink..."

"She keeps me entertained," Salmond sniffed, snatching the paper back. "But what calls you here? Does not our respected master require your assistance?"

"Our respected master remains snug in his quarters on account of the hour and a slight chill to the air," Scott explained, adding, "while mortals such as us must rely on an extra waistcoat when we can find the time." So saying he hauled his sea chest out from beneath his own bunk and began to rummage through it.

"Busy on deck is it?" Salmond enquired with a notable lack of interest.

"Weather is clear and bright though methinks there to be a storm brewing," Scott replied while sorting through his clothing.

"Just what I need to keep my trick entertaining," his friend sighed before listlessly collecting another letter.

"Oh, you'll be enthralled," Scott confirmed. "Captain King has just come up; once the old man appears they'll be needling each other as always. Having the two on board is like sailing with Punch and Judy."

"Captain King is well thought of in the Royal Navy," Salmond mused.

"Maybe so." Scott stood once more. "But not this one, or at least, not by our own dear captain."

Salmond made no comment. At the back of his mind were thoughts of leaving the HEIC. Like all the sloop's senior officers, he was only employed to see the warship safely to Bombay. Once there he might well seek a position in the Royal Navy, a Service that took the science of gunnery far more seriously, and the recommendation of an officer like King could be useful.

"So where are these from?" Scott asked glancing back at the letters.

Salmond shrugged. "Here and there," he said. "Folk I've met along the way and seem keen to keep in touch."

"Folk?" Scott questioned as he made to leave. "Would that be of either gender?"

"Mainly the fairer," Salmond allowed. "In fact I should say exclusively."

Scott laughed, "I've several years on you and a measure of seniority, yet the only woman who writes is my mother and that is to advise on laundry."

Salmond adopted a look of apparent concern. "But that is terrible, Sam, and a situation we must surely address. Why every young man should hear from a pretty girl occasionally. What say I lend you one of mine?"

But Scott had already left.

* * *

King was taking in deep draughts of clean sea air. There was something about the scent of the South Atlantic that distinguished it from northern waters. The weather, though more intense, was also easier to predict while a comparative lack of land suited his temperament perfectly. His previous commission had been at The Cape and he was pleased to be returning; according to the first officer's most recent report, his ship,

HMS *Mistral,* should be free of the dockyard soon and be ready to commence her sea trials on his arrival. Once back in harness, his immediate superior would be Commodore Sir Richard Banks, an officer he had served under for much of his professional life and one he respected more than many, while the station itself promised sufficient action and prize money for the most restless of souls.

Not that King needed much in the way of additional income. His wages and allowances as a post captain easily covered all living expenses for him and Aimée while also allowing the extravagance of retaining their small leased house in Alton while away. And that was ignoring his other funds; the considerable pile amassed during several fortunate engagements. It was a figure most serving officers could only dream of and all but guaranteed them both a comfortable living for the rest of their lives – assuming, of course, that money alone could provide such a thing. He was fortunate to have earned so much although King privately considered it no more than his due. For he had also seen more combat than most and been held prisoner on more than one occasion, while the loss of his left arm surely confirmed him as equally prepared to give as to take.

But, despite so much being to his advantage, and even with the slight feeling of guilt that remained after his last conversation with Aimée, King still felt vaguely discontented and probably would remain so until Table Mountain came into sight. Only then might he quit this passenger caper and start proper work. More than that, only then might he choose with whom to mix. The other officers aboard the *St. George* were decent enough but he simply could not abide Captain Johnston. And it was at that moment the cause of his discontent made himself known.

"A pleasant day, Mr King."

Johnston's appearance actually gave him a start; the man must have emerged from his quarters in studied silence and his sudden approach forced King to step aside to allow him access to the binnacle. To disguise both the movement and his reaction, King took a couple of paces fore and aft as if merely pacing. As so often, there was nothing inherently wrong in Johnston's action – it was his ship after all and every captain had a right to come and go as he pleased, yet the irritation remained and each time dug a little deeper. He was sure Johnston went out of his way to be objectionable and was the only one aboard the *St. George* to determinedly ignore King's proper rank and refer to him as plain Mister.

"Indeed, Mr Johnston," King replied with equal disregard as he came to a halt. "Though it will rain afore dark if I'm any judge."

"Think you so?" Johnston sniffed while collecting the traverse board.

King briefly considered the man. He was slender and excitable with pale pockmarked skin that reddened at the first hint of strain. Though in his early forties, an age when most Honourable East India Company masters had a regular command, Johnston remained a jobbing captain, taking short and irregular commissions such as his current placement. But then he so clearly lacked the attributes of a regular HEIC commander; most were experienced, mature seamen who were equally expert in handling important passengers and negotiating for cargoes. King had no idea how Johnston might fare with commercial trade but could vouch for his lack of personal charm and was equally contemptuous of his abilities as a seaman. Yet Johnston had been given charge of a warship; something King was still coming to terms with even this deep into the voyage. It was a temporary appointment for sure but even stiffer requirements were expected of those filling such a role. A man-of-war's captain must be alert and active with an agile mind: a fighter and a leader of men. Qualities that Johnston so obviously lacked.

But he was fortunate in having competent officers to support him. These were led by an unassuming older man named Casey. Although stouter in build and with a wrinkled skin that betrayed his age, Casey reminded King strongly of Croft, his own first officer. Quietly spoken but supremely capable, the man absorbed the problems of running a ship, as well as his captain's erratic attempts to correct them, with equanimity.

Casey was backed by an equally able second mate named Scott who carried out the duties of navigation officer with unhurried ability, and a third mate, Salmond, who, though young for his post, seemed equally capable and had totally fallen under Aimée's spell. Apart from these there was a sound body of conscientious midshipmen, any one of whom would have been welcomed into the cockpit of a government vessel. Even the sloop's lower deck was of a good standard; blessed with generous wages and considerate living conditions, every hand was a volunteer, content in their work and genial whenever King had cause to speak with them. Yes, it was only Johnston who seemed out of place but, being that he was captain, the fact rather set a seal on the entire vessel.

After several minutes of silent yet ostentatious study, the man finally replaced the traverse board and inadvertently caught King's eye.

When alongside a fellow professional it would be polite to comment on their position, the possibility of encountering enemy forces or maybe the distant prospect of raising Cape Town. Both men were equally disinclined to do so, however, and, after spending so long forced into the other's company, felt little need to disguise the fact. But fortunately Aimée's appearance at the head of the aft companionway was enough to break the tension.

The couple had been together a good while, yet King could never rid himself of the feeling that his companion's nationality would cause problems. Their two countries had been at war for most of his adult life and, however much her English improved, the accent would always be hard to ignore. But Aimée's beauty was far more than physical; she had a natural charm that transcended politics and it was rare for even the most strident patriot not to be entranced by her. That Captain Johnston was totally enamoured was a clear example of this, and something that hardly made King like him more.

"Good day to you, Ma'am." He greeted her now with a pretentious flourish of his hat and Aimée rewarded him with a radiant smile.

"Good morning, Captain. It is indeed a fine one, if a little chilly. And I should like to thank you, once more, for the splendid meal yesterday." Aimée flashed a stern look across at King before adding, "We both would."

"Ah yes, a memorable occasion, Mr Johnston," King agreed obediently although his main recollection was of the vast amount of wine the captain had consumed.

Johnston granted King the merest glance before returning to Aimée. "It were a pleasure ma'am," he enthused, "and one made the greater by such enchanting company."

Then it was her turn to nod and, as she did, King realised with horror that Aimée was blushing. Quite how someone so intelligent could respond to such flattery was beyond him, especially when delivered by a man who would be lucky to receive a commission aboard a true warship.

"I am only sorry the occasion had to be postponed," Johnston continued, gazing into her eyes. "We are now many leagues south of the line, so the event had somewhat lost its relevance."

"There need not always be a reason for friends to meet in company," Aimée replied easily as she cast a glance at King.

"Indeed not," Captain Johnston agreed. "Though I think we might have cause to celebrate again before very long."

"*Est-ce vrai?*" Aimée exclaimed, the excitement sufficient to awaken her native language, and Johnston was about to reply when King interrupted.

"I assume you are referring to our arrival in Cape Town?" he asked, pleased to break into what was fast becoming a private conversation. "Do you intend to make for the African coast and follow it south?"

"Certainly not, sir," Johnston sniffed. "The Honourable Company prides itself on a high standard of navigation; I have instructed Mr Scott to bring us in plumb at the entrance to Table Bay."

King said nothing. The sky had been clear since the bad weather encountered while crossing the Equator and they had made good progress since. Oncoming storm or not, he fancied Scott's abilities equal to such a feat although attempting to raise land exactly at the destination port seemed an unnecessary test of anyone's talents, especially with three merchants in tow. Reminded of their charges, King turned to consider the Indiamen as an agreeable alternative to continued conversation with Johnston.

They rode in a ragged column to leeward; all were eight hundred-tonners and had been competently handled throughout. Currently their holds would be filled with anything from Manchester goods to pig iron while each would also be carrying a fair amount in specie. It was a cargo decent enough by anyone's standards and much in demand at Eastern ports although its true worth lay in what could be taken in exchange. Once spices, silks, tea, and other riches of the East were aboard, each ship would be worth a small fortune with all profits going to line the pockets of Company shareholders. And if the drunken claims of yesterday were to be believed, Captain Johnston was just such an investor, which probably explained the man's current position and appalled King more than he could express.

He had little need for money and certainly did not begrudge an income made by free enterprise, especially if it were attained by skill and ability. But King's pile had been earned through a series of hard-fought actions, one of which had cost his left arm, and the idea of men like Johnston becoming rich with ease and little physical risk was mildly repugnant.

"Captain Johnston believes we should be in Cape Town within the month," Aimée spoke in a tone of mild reproach.

"I am glad to hear of it," King replied flatly as he returned to them.

"My husband is keen to take up his new command," Aimée explained and King bit his lip. Her habit of referring to him so had become well established and many, even those who knew better, had taken to addressing her as Mrs King. Not that he had any objection; there was nothing he would have liked more than to find himself securely wed, which only made the practice more annoying. When last heard of, his true wife had fled her London lodgings leaving behind a list of creditors and almost as many rumours. One, the strongest, spoke of a captain in the Guards who was supposed to have taken her in, although a considerable stack of guineas spent on enquiry agents had failed to reveal more.

The ship's bell rang out seven times and the first of the new watch began to appear on deck. King gave a polite nod to Scott, who would be taking the noon sightings before handing over to two midshipmen who were currently studying the traverse board. Below, in their cabin, King had been keeping track of the ship's progress on a borrowed chart; he would very much like to confirm their exact position and knew Scott would share the information later in the privacy of the sloop's tiny wardroom.

"Perhaps we might take some refreshment below, my dear?" he suggested. In a vessel the size of the *St. George* there was little room for exercise; the quarterdeck and waist were too crowded for proper pacing while, for decency's sake, only men were permitted on the forecastle. But the pair could find a measure of comfort in their cabin and King would be on hand to ambush Scott when he went below. Aimée smiled and was about to reply when one of the midshipmen let out a high-pitched cry.

"Signal from *Earl of Dalkeith*," the lad piped, pointing at the nearest merchant. Several glasses were turned upon the larger ship and soon the second youngster was flipping through a small book.

"Sail in sight to the south, sir," he said.

"Acknowledge," Johnston commanded.

There was silence as the reply was hoisted. The *Earl of Dalkeith* had several hundred tons on the sprightly *St. George* and her lookouts were positioned on correspondingly taller masts; it might be half an hour before the warship could make the sighting and in that time they would have closed considerably.

"She's signalling again," the first midshipman observed as a series of black balls broke out amid the merchant's tophamper.

"Now two ships," the second lad reported, "bearing sou-sou-west and making for us."

That might mean something or nothing. It was still early in the shipping season but not impossible to have run across a homeward-bound convoy. Either that or they could be steering straight into the path of enemy raiders, but in either case King was suddenly reluctant to quit the deck. Johnston had other ideas however and, as the second signal was being acknowledged, turned to him.

"Perhaps you would indeed be more comfortable below, sir," he suggested pointedly.

"Yes of course, Captain, we must leave you to your duties," Aimée agreed adding, "Come, Tom," as she took him firmly by the hand. A third signal was now being run up on the *Earl of Dalkeith* but King was not to hear of it as he was led determinedly towards the aft hatch and away from any chance of learning more.

Chapter Two

HMS *Mistral* was almost ready for sea, or almost as ready as Croft could make her before the ship's true keeper returned. But as he gazed at the graceful form secured to the quay he had no thoughts for Captain King.

Topmasts were down, giving the frigate a slightly stunted look and destroying her natural symmetry although the sight was quite acceptable to anyone familiar with shipping. She was also riding unnaturally high; a strip of fresh copper gleamed above the oily waters of Table Bay revealing her to be unladen. But few could ignore the beauty of the subtly curved stripe of ochre that ran down her hull, nor the fresh shrouds sweeping up in graceful lines to her fighting tops. When first released from dry dock, *Mistral* had appeared frail and weak; leaning on the hawsers that tethered her for support. But since Croft and his men had done their work those same cables now acted as restraints, keeping a captive beast from the freedom of its natural element. In three days – four at the most – she could be let loose to cut about the wide Atlantic ready to do battle with anything foolish enough to offer combat.

It was the image Croft had envisaged throughout the long months of rebuilding. Teams of *Mistral*'s own men had supplemented the dockyard force with many working double tides in an effort to maintain his own strict schedule. And while they toiled, he and his fellow officers had been equally busy prising stores and supplies from a dozen different sources to see their hungry charge's needs were met. When, still apparently smoking from battle, *Mistral* had been deposited in Cape Town's only dry dock, Governor Baird had rashly promised the best equipment and materials for her refit, and it was a commitment Croft felt no qualms about enforcing. Especially as the dockyard was supervised by an indulgent sop of a post captain who he strongly suspected of embezzlement. Extracting even usable supplies soon became a major occupation which at times had led as far as Sir David Baird's office although now, as Croft considered the sound and viable phoenix that had risen from the ashes, he judged the effort worthwhile.

Turning from the sight, he continued along Strand Street, one of Cape Town's characteristically wide roads, towards the Castle where the last of *Mistral*'s crew were still accommodated. Captain King was due to arrive in the next week or so and Croft's commitment to having all in place when he did extended as far as the hands. There was little he or Foil, the purser, could do to order consumable stores as such requisitions must be countersigned by the captain but Croft saw no reason why the people should not be embarked. For there was still a deal of finishing to be done and having the men aboard would see it attended to more conveniently. Bringing them back early would not be a popular move; even some of his officers had baulked on learning there was to be no reprieve after their efforts. The previous day Croft had also received a deputation from the lower deck: a pair of petty officers respectfully requesting a period of rest and for women to be allowed on board. But he was not the kind to let up, either on himself or others. All they had achieved so far was surely a testament to his determination and Croft had no intention of spoiling anything by relaxing now. Besides, the last thing he wished to present to his captain was a floating brothel.

There was a group of *Mistral*'s hands in the distance; he could see them as they rambled down the street with the typical rolling gait of seamen ashore. They were under the notional direction of Greenwood, a boatswain's mate, and must be the working party sent ashore to return the borrowed cauldrons. These had been required when the waist had been re-caulked following a less than acceptable effort from the dockyard. Croft remembered with pride that, despite being performed by regular Jacks, the work was completed in approximately half the time needed by professional caulkers, and with far superior results. Now the men would be heading back for the ship and, by their demeanour, Croft guessed they had encountered at least one pot house on their journey.

At the sight of him, and a muttered command from the petty officer, the men smartened their step as much as they were able and Greenwood acknowledged him with a smart, if gnarled, knuckle to the forehead. Croft returned the compliment and passed in the stony silence that would be expected of him. Strict though he might be, the elderly lieutenant was no fool and considered it prudent to ignore the men's mild inebriation. His tolerance even stretched to not hearing the muttered comment that was followed by a deep rumble of laughter. He would be the target of the jape as denying the wedding garland had not been a popular move. But then esteem had never been one of Croft's ambitions, while the men would survive without female company and probably be the better for it. As would his officers, some of whom had also made what they fancied to be romantic connections ashore, despite the heavy work schedule. As for himself, he needed no such comfort and had an object of affection far more reliable than any passing attachment. He paused now and, turning back, enjoyed the view of *Mistral* once more. It was just a shame he would shortly have to hand her over to the whims of another man.

* * *

The view through the scuttle was confined indeed and showed King only the vast, empty ocean to windward although a blind man would have known what was about when the *St. George* began to clear for action.

"We are going to battle perhaps?" Aimée enquired from her seat on their narrow bed.

"I believe so," King confirmed, drawing away from his viewing point and half standing under the low deckhead. "In which case you cannot stay here, we must find a place below the waterline."

"For me, or us both?" she asked with a knowing smile.

"For us both," King replied. "This is not my fight; I can take no part in it."

"Of course not, *mon cher*," she agreed, her expression unaltered.

* * *

Peter Casey, the sloop's chief officer, had come onto the quarterdeck after the sighting was reported and several hours later, when the vague images of topmasts developed into four solid warships bearing down on them, had barely moved. Beside him Captain Johnston was fidgeting uncontrollably while his tendency to chatter steadily increased. But Casey remained still and apparently composed, even if inwardly he was in turmoil.

Quite why Johnston had ordered the ship cleared for action was beyond him, especially as a turn to starboard might yet see the precaution unnecessary. There was still doubt about the oncoming ships' identity; were they to be friendly – a possibility the captain repeatedly proposed – all they would have lost was a day in raising Cape Town and no one could blame a single escort for taking such precautions. As it was, and in some misguided effort to appear efficient, Johnston had stuck to his course and, in doing so, was placing them all in very real danger.

"Are we not cleared yet?" the man was now demanding of no one in particular. "Why we should have been beating to quarters these ten minutes past!"

Casey made no response as none was necessary. Although their nationality might be in question, there was no doubting the oncoming vessels were warships. It would be an hour at least before they closed sufficiently for shots to be exchanged but that time could be stretched considerably if only Johnston ordered that turn. With the wind in their favour and less than three hours before nightfall they might yet keep the convoy safe.

But the captain would have none of it. First he had clung to the belief the oncoming squadron were merchants. Then, when one frigate at least had been identified, claimed them as a homebound convoy. But now it was clear all sported gun ports and the heavily sparred masts that could only belong to men-of-war, his hopes were turning to their being British, or at least from a neutral country. Earlier, Scott, the second officer and another who had been on deck as long as Casey, had mooted the possibility of evasive action, only to have the suggestion publicly ridiculed. With no prominent French bases nearby, Johnston refused to accept such a squadron would venture so deep into the Atlantic. Besides, Frenchmen were known to raise their colours early and, if not an ensign, some form of commissioning pennant was usual, yet no flag of any variety could be made out on the oncoming shipping.

Casey's thoughts went back to the start of the voyage when an encounter with supposed privateers had almost seen the loss of one of their company. Just as they were passing Brest, two small vessels were sighted and, though there was no further evidence to identify them as pirates, Johnston promptly ordered all to scatter. Consequently they had lost touch with the *Earl of Dalkeith* for one night. Dawn found her safe with no sign of attackers, but the incident had undoubtedly left an impression.

Since then the man had sheered away from any move that could be avoided, a policy that was not without its merits although clinging to the steadily decreasing chance of the approaching ships being benign was surely asking for trouble. But then the order to clear for action suggested he might be having doubts; perhaps a further suggestion to turn westward would be better received or at least acted upon? If so, it could only come from him; Scott had already done his duty on that count. As a young and aspiring officer, a detrimental captain's report might easily blight his career whereas Casey had nothing to lose. He cleared his throat in preparation for the act, then took the plunge.

"If you would forgive me, sir, might we now make for the west?"

The elderly officer stood open-mouthed; once more it was Scott who had spoken, from his position on the opposite side of the binnacle. The second mate must have beaten him by a fraction of a second and Casey briefly closed his eyes.

"The west again is it, Mr Scott?" Johnston questioned as he turned upon him. "We surely dealt with that suggestion some time ago! As I made perfectly clear then, there is no reason to turn, not when we have the wind in our favour. The enemy – if that's what they truly be – are not so well set."

"Then steering west will force them to beat into its very eye," Scott persisted and, once more, Casey was about to give support when again he was beaten to the mark.

"And a change of heading might settle matters once and for all."

This last voice had come from behind and caused all by the binnacle to look back.

"If they turn also, it will show they have designs on us," Captain King continued as he approached from the aft companionway. "And if not, we might relax and continue our journey in comfort."

"I had considered you to be below, sir!" Johnston snapped angrily.

"You will forgive me, but I may have more experience of such matters," King replied. "And Mr Scott is quite correct; maintaining our present heading only invites trouble. Why you surely cannot believe we are facing anything other than French ships of war?"

"What I believe is of no concern to you, Mr King," Johnston retorted, his voice now approaching a screech. "You are interfering with the working of my ship and I will say as much on reaching The Cape. Now kindly quit the deck."

"Unless you look to your station you will not make The Cape," King maintained. "There remains time to take evasive action. Night is coming and the moon will be new and barely waxing; a change of course might still allow us to slip by during the dark hours."

"I say again, Mr King – you will go or I shall have you removed!"

King glanced uncertainly from Johnston to his two senior officers and, on finding nothing other than sympathetic looks from the latter, nodded silently before making his way back to the aft hatch.

"Ship is cleared for action, sir," one of the midshipmen

announced with a crisp salute.

"Very well, Mr Kelly," Johnston grunted. "Then, with that troublesome Navy man out of the picture, I might continue. Make to convoy; 'turn six points to starboard on my signal'."

"Six points, sir?" Scott spoke before he had given himself chance to think. "That will take us to a heading of west-sou-west."

"Indeed, Mr Scott," Johnstone agreed with a hint of triumph. "So we will still retain some degree of wind." He allowed himself a slight superior chuckle. "Whereas to turn fully west – as some would have – must leave us in irons."

"B-but I did not mean for us to head directly west, sir," Scott stammered. "And neither did Captain King – just a turn in that direction."

"So you say, Mr Scott," Johnston allowed far more coldly. "Though you will forgive me if I believe otherwise."

* * *

"The man's a fool," King told Aimée in the relative privacy of the orlop deck. "Unless something is done he'll have us all taken prisoner."

They were seated as far aft as could be. Before them, in the cockpit, the surgeon and his assistants had set out an improvised sick bay while a gentle glow from the magazine's light room told how the gunner and his mates were ready to do business with their deadly wares. Indeed, the entire ship was prepared for action and it was likely to be a vastly unequal fight. So, with a fool for a captain, King decided he had a right to feel uneasy.

"But what can anyone do?" Aimée asked, her eyes bright amid the darkness. "He is in command while you are merely a passenger – not even one of his crew."

"In which case he has no power over me," King snorted.

"But surely Captain Johnston must be in charge of his passengers as well?"

"Perhaps – to some extent..."

"To some extent?" Aimée questioned with a grin. "Well he did order you below, *mon cher* and are you not here?"

"We're turning," King announced as the ship began to list. "And to starboard – so he has finally seen sense. That might keep us out of trouble for a while."

"But not for ever?" she asked more seriously.

"No, not for ever," King sighed. "An hour or two earlier, perhaps but, though harder to reach, we will still not be free of the Frenchmen's grasp."

"And you are quite sure they are Frenchmen?" she added, now with a hint of sadness.

"There is now doubt of it," King replied before the full implications of her question occurred. He drew breath and softened his tone slightly. "Do you think that will present a problem, if we are taken, I am meaning?"

Aimée shrugged. "I truly do not know. There are many French who do not live in France and this is not a British Navy ship – it can hardly be said I am fighting against my country."

"And I am not your husband," he added.

"No, Tom, you are not," she agreed. Then the grin returned, "Though if asked I shall not renounce you."

* * *

On deck, things were developing further and, though he had still not moved significantly, Casey was starting to notice the growing stiffness in his joints. The *St. George* had led the merchants in the turn and, still on the starboard tack, all four Company ships were now in line of column. They were sailing as close to the wind as they could bear while to larboard, and still in plain sight despite a darkening sky, the warships had also altered course. It was an act that revealed their intentions better than any flag and banished all hope of them having no interest in the convoy. But now at least a firmer assessment could be made of their size; two were heavy frigates accompanied by what looked to be corvettes. Currently they seemed content to keep pace although King's predicted storm was starting to materialise and, with the sun well on its way to the horizon, it could not be long before they made a move.

Casey shuffled uneasily and tried to stretch his protesting legs. He knew he had several years on his captain and accepted the thoughts of an old man were inclined to repetition. But still the fact remained: if Johnston had ordered the turn earlier the convoy might be out of danger by now. As it was, the hours of indecision could cost them dear.

At first glance the two lines of shipping were on the same course, but careful study and years of experience told him the warships were managing a point or so closer to the wind. That, combined with their sleek hulls and obvious manoeuvrability, would give them a considerable advantage against the merchants if it came to a close action. But Casey was still hoping not; even though it went against all evidence before him, there remained a chance that a combination of storm and nightfall would grant them safety.

He turned for the first time in several hours and, acknowledging young Scott with a subtle nod, strode stiffly towards the break of the quarterdeck. The sun was definitely preparing to set and, as he glanced down at the waist, there was a perceptible chill to the air. Once the ship was cleared for action, Captain Johnston had sent the hands to their battle stations. That was some time ago and now, as they squatted amid the smoking tubs of burning slow match, some were showing signs of restlessness. Casey turned back, his eyes naturally falling on the nearest Indiaman several cables astern. It was the *Bodiam Castle* and Dick Kennet, who had command, would have more to concern himself with than a few fidgety hands. There were at least four senior Company officers aboard the Indiaman, along with their families and households. Captain Kennet could take comfort in being under the direction of the escort commander although, should any of the merchants fall to the French, it would reflect badly on all aboard the *St. George*.

But, even if the convoy were seized, it would be of little concern to Casey. Rumours from France were now too common to ignore; life for a prisoner need not be one of hardship, providing they had funds to support them. With no family or dependants, he had long since bidden farewell to his country of birth and, once the *St. George* was delivered to her new captain, would be heading for a peaceful retirement in Bombay. With a substantial pile built up from a lifetime of private trade and investment, Casey had enough to see himself comfortable for several years and it mattered little to him where the coin was spent.

There remained the trader's inherent desire to avoid capture, however. He had served the HEIC for almost forty years and in that time faced dangers from pirates, privateers and enemy national ships alike, yet survived them all. So to find himself in danger of capture on his last voyage and, ironically, first posting aboard a warship, was mildly galling and it was a feeling made so much worse when all blame lay squarely with his current captain.

The man had retired to his quarters some time ago but chose that moment to appear at the head of the aft companionway. Mildly dishevelled and carrying his hat, Johnston stood for a moment with obvious uncertainty before making his way to the binnacle.

"No movement from the enemy, sir," Casey said as he approached. "Though I fancy they are gaining on us."

"Indeed, Mr Casey." Johnston's voice was thick and he seemed unable to focus properly on his first officer. "Though we have made good progress so far, what? How long before nightfall?"

"Just under two hours, sir," Casey replied. The subject had been on his mind a good while, in fact he had been unconsciously counting off the minutes, yet the captain seemed oddly uncertain of the exact time. And there was more in the man's demeanour to cause concern. He was blinking as if staring into a strong light and seemed unsteady, despite the motion that was gentle and predictable.

"Are you quite well, sir?" Casey chanced, and noticed how Johnston's usual pallor suddenly reddened.

"Well? I am perfectly well thank you, Mister Casey!"

The mate took a step back.

"Under two hours you say?" Johnston fumbled for his watch which he promptly dropped on the deck. Casey bent down stiffly, collected the timepiece and handed it back without a word. There was now no doubt in the older man's mind; it was hardly the first time Captain Johnston had let himself down so, but certainly must be the worst occasion. Casey considered him as he peered myopically at the watch before struggling to replace it in his pocket; the man was as drunk as a lord, and that was the last thing they needed.

Chapter Three

"If you will excuse me, my dear, I shall see what's about on deck."

"Do you think you will be welcomed?" Aimée asked, looking up.

"Not by some," King replied.

"Be careful, won't you?"

"Of course," he promised, then was gone.

For a moment Aimée sat in the relative darkness of the orlop. In some ways she was not sorry to have been left alone. The claustrophobia of being aboard ship was still new to her and there was so much she missed that had never before been held precious: things like privacy and silence. But most of all she yearned for the chance to just go; to walk, or run, for as long as the need remained. Being at sea gave the impression of freedom but it was an illusion: despite an almost constant view of infinity, she remained pent up in a space less than thirty metres long and nine wide and it was a confinement shared with so many similarly imprisoned. So, despite the circumstances, the time to be private was welcomed, especially as she had matters to think about which were far more important than any battle.

She was to be a mother; the signs had been clear for some while and soon Thomas would have to be told. But for the time being she almost relished the private knowledge. Motherhood was something Aimée had never felt in need of, yet, now it appeared likely, could not come too soon. And a child; the three of them a family. The concept was far more vital to her than any paper proclaiming them to be wed.

A movement forward caught her attention. Mr McIver and his assistants had set up a sick bay in the junior officers' berth. She watched them for a moment; all was very organised and planned although it still came as a relief to remember they should be in Cape Town when she needed medical attention. The thought brought her mind back to her own family, so many miles away in Verdun. They would have cared for her without the need of outside assistance; her mother was an expert at tending the sick and had helped several neighbours' children into the world. Thinking so made her suddenly sad which was hardly a natural condition for Aimée so, before the mood could deepen further, she hoisted herself up, brushed down her dress, and emerged from the shadows.

"I wonder if you will be needing assistance, Doctor?" she asked, approaching McIver.

"I'm merely a surgeon ma'am," the man reminded her affably, "but yes, an extra hand is always welcomed. Perhaps you could accompany Mr Drew, my assistant? He will advise you of the basics."

McIver nodded towards a short, slightly balding man in his early middle age who was cutting a large sheet of canvas into strips, presumably for dressings. Aimée had never considered such work before and for a moment felt slightly afraid. But then her mother was an expert, so perhaps some of her skills had been passed on.

* * *

"Enemy appears to be turning," Kelly, one of the midshipmen, reported although everyone on the quarterdeck could see as much.

Casey, standing respectfully behind his captain, watched in silence. There was an hour to go before sundown and at such latitudes dusk would not last long. But the rain had already started to spot in heavy drops and, if the black mass of approaching cloud was anything to go by, they might expect a deluge.

"Two are breaking away," the lad continued, his voice cracking with excitement. "The smaller ones: they're preparing to tack!" Still Casey remained static although his thoughts were definitely on the move.

On a previous trip to the East his ship had been laid up for several months in Bombay, and he had used the time to explore the nearby Sorath region. There he had watched the local lions as they hunted in packs and could now see many similarities. The frigates to leeward were the seniors solidly blocking their prey's obvious path of escape while the younger adults, effectively the corvettes beating to windward, aimed for the tail of the group. Even if they could not immediately close, the warships should remain in contact and dawn, a bare twelve hours away, must surely see at least one of the Indiamen taken.

But that was ignoring the heavy weather that was almost upon them. A decent downpour should change matters dramatically; once darkness fell it would be relatively simple to alter course in the midst of a storm and leave their predators many miles behind. That meant waiting, of course, and Casey was experienced enough to know it would be midnight or beyond before the bad weather was at its worst. But they must prepare now; it would be no good deciding to change headings in the midst of a tempest and expect their charges to follow.

A movement from behind caught his attention and he turned to see their Royal Navy passenger approach from the growing shadows. Casey had a lot of time for King; the young man could be sharp with his tongue on occasions, but was undoubtedly a professional seaman, which was more than could be said for his own captain.

"I thought I had ordered you below!" Johnston snarled as he also noticed King's presence.

"Indeed you did, Mr Johnston," King replied, apparently amazed. "Yet now I find myself on deck once more."

The assertiveness, combined with an absence of logic, confused the already befuddled Johnston who gaped openly before turning away.

"Night is falling fast," King continued, addressing Casey as if he was his own second-in-command.

"Indeed, sir," the older man agreed. "They can't draw much closer before then and soon the storm will have broken properly. Belike we shall shake them off in the darkest hours."

Johnston had withdrawn and was now staring out at the frigates; both ships still lay a good five miles to larboard and were steadily fading in the dimming light. Further astern, the taut sails of the corvettes were more easily seen as they powered the lighter craft on at a credible speed. Either one was large enough take any of the merchants with ease and would be more than a match for the *St. George* but, even at such a pace, it was becoming increasingly obvious they would not come into range before nightfall.

"If we are intending to take evasive action later, it might be prudent to signal our intentions now while some light remains." Again King spoke directly to the mate. "A little preparation will avoid confusion and too many night signals later."

"So you feel we should be planning for a change of course?" Casey's voice was loud enough for all nearby to hear.

"I should say so," King confirmed, equally clearly. "Once we are in the thick of the storm you might consider turning northward for a spell and then to the east, but better to plan any move in advance if it is to be kept from the enemy."

Casey nodded emphatically and, such was the relief at having his own thoughts confirmed, was about to make an overt suggestion to his true captain when he saw Johnston had indeed been listening.

"There will be no need of that." The man spoke to the deck in general. "A course of action has already been decided upon without assistance from the Royal Navy. And I have no intention of waiting until midnight."

King and Casey watched him warily as the rain increased.

"You may think you know all about managing a ship, Mr King, but might not be so experienced in organising a convoy," the captain continued, his eyes now sharply focused on his passenger although the voice remained as thick. "And believe me, sir, expecting lubberly merchants to behave like men-of-war is asking for trouble."

King made no reply, Johnston was actually correct in both instances although the chance of temporarily losing touch with one of their charges was surely preferable to any being taken for certain.

"No, it is bold tactics that will see this battle won," he continued, now with a hint of bravado. "Mr Selby, prepare a night signal. I'll have a Bengal fire set at the mizzen top if you please, and be sure there is a reliable hand to tend it."

The young midshipman saluted smartly before calling for one of his signals team.

"But there is still a little time before dark," Johnston muttered. "You will excuse me, gentlemen, if I go below to take some sustenance."

Casey and King watched as the man slumped off towards his quarters, then the mate drew closer.

"If you'll pardon me, sir, suggesting a northerly heading may have been a mistake."

King considered him quizzically in the half light.

"You see, time is paramount in our trade; the longer a ship is at sea, the more she costs the owners. Deviations are acceptable but no merchantman chooses to turn back on his intended course unless truly forced and Captain Johnston might not have been in the most receptive of moods."

"I see." As King spoke the rain started to fall in earnest. "And the relevance of a Bengal Fire?"

The mate sighed. "Well, that'll be the signal for a general turn to larboard." He turned up the collar on his oilskin. "Perhaps he's thinkin' of heading south once more and trusting in the dark to see us past the warships."

"That would be a bold move."

"Bold indeed, sir," Casey agreed softly. "And I don't mind saying, not the wisest."

"Perhaps a little food might change his mind?" King phrased his words carefully.

"Maybe so," Casey grunted. "Though it will take more than a dish of lobscouse to make the man a seaman." He paused, considered, then continued in a softer tone, "Or if it comes to it, a decent officer."

* * *

When sunset finally came the cloud had increased to the extent that few stars shone and darkness was almost complete. But the wind still blew strong and constant while heavy rain had flushed the last trace of the French warships from even the keenest lookout's gaze. King was still on deck; when last seen Aimée had been comfortable enough on the orlop and there seemed little point in disturbing her, although he had a more important reason for not going below.

By remaining on deck, the enemy's position could stay imprinted on his mind and even adjusted slightly to allow for each vessel's individual progress. It was a knack learned over many years of serving aboard a man-of-war and, because of it, King had no intention of seeking shelter. He would stay for as long as the danger persisted despite his borrowed watchcoat now being heavy with rain. Casey and Scott were with him; the three had become united in the common purpose of saving both ship and convoy while also sharing less public thoughts of the captain dining in warmth and comfort on the deck below. But when Johnston did finally return it was doubtful if anything solid had passed his lips; even as he approached the scent of spirits was strong and, as salutes were exchanged with his second in command, the man was grinning like a child.

"There were no change as we lost the light, sir," Casey reported stoically. "Nearest enemy was over three miles off the *Earl of Dalkeith's* larboard quarter."

It was a measure of Johnston's state that he chose to peer out into the night, even though nothing could be visible other than the occasional glimpse of the nearest merchant's prow.

"And the frigates?" he enquired.

"About five miles to the south-west." Casey pointed over their larboard bow. "None of the French slackened sail so I signalled the convoy not to snug down with the last of the light."

"Quite right, Mr Casey." Johnston scratched at his chin. "It will do them no harm to experience a little bad weather."

Praise from a captain would usually be well received but, such was Johnston's state, Casey barely acknowledged it.

For a moment the senior man stared aimlessly into the night, then appeared to take control. "I feel it is time to make a move," he announced. "Let us hope our man remains alert in the mizzen top. Have him make the signal."

"Now, sir?" Casey found it hard to hide his surprise. "The storm's still building an' there are several hours of night ahead."

"Now, Mr Casey," Johnston confirmed.

The order was passed then a flame spluttered into life above their heads and soon much of the *St. George* was bathed in an eerie, red glow. Casey and King exchanged glances; despite the appalling conditions, the enemy must surely see such a light. It might not remain long enough to guide them in but they would now know exactly where the convoy's escort lay, and guess she was proposing to manoeuvre.

"That will do," Johnston announced after a few seconds, adding, "if they don't see that they deserve to be left behind!"

"Belay the light!" Casey ordered more sternly and all was plunged into darkness once more. Seconds later a more gentle glow could be made out from the bows of the nearest merchant.

"*Bodiam Castle*'s responding," one of the midshipmen reported.

"Then we need wait no longer." Johnston gave an ecstatic grin. "Take us to larboard – I want to pass by the smaller ships with room to spare, while not venturing too close to the frigates. Set me a course, Mr Scott!"

"Steer sou-west by south, sir." The second officer's voice rose up in the darkness. Clearly he was expecting such an order and had already worked his figures, which were roughly in line with King's own thinking.

"Light the stern lanterns!" Johnston ordered.

"Stern lanterns, sir?" Now Casey was truly amazed. "But the *Bodiam Castle* is aware of our intentions."

"Just for the turn, Mr Casey, just for the turn." The captain gave an emphatic sigh. "The enemy will make out little on such a night and I shall strike them as soon as we are properly on course." He paused to stare myopically at his first officer. "Frankly, Mr Casey, I would appreciate it if you exhibited a little more trust."

* * *

The change of course increased the sloop's speed considerably and soon the *St. George* was positively thrashing through the heavy waters. Glancing back, King could see nothing of any following ship although, such was the night, he doubted his vision could reach beyond half a cable. Then, as if to oblige him, flashes of distant lightening were added to the storm and he did make out the shadow of at least one tailing merchant, although there remained no sign of the enemy to leeward. For a moment he wondered if the atrocious conditions had been enough to turn them away and Captain Johnston had been right all along. King glanced surreptitiously at the man as he slouched unsteadily beside his officers.

The gun crews that had been stood down when darkness fell were now back at their stations and it was unfortunate that those at the larboard broadside, the one most likely to see use, were receiving the worst of the storm on their backs as they huddled about the readied weapons. But most were probably unconscious of the weather; all could guess at their current predicament and knew the next hour or so would either see them in safe waters or the midst of an all-out engagement with a far superior enemy.

But as the minutes ticked by and the bell rang for the second time since their turn, the tension began to ease. King found himself exchanging glances with Casey and Scott while Johnston slumped against the binnacle and began to doze openly. Beyond, the darkness was as relentless as ever although the storm had yet to increase and all were privately wondering if they had misjudged the captain. Whatever they thought of him, the drunken fool appeared to be leading the ship and her three charges to safety. Then a shout from the foretop lookout crashed into their hopes, smashing them completely.

"Sail ho! Sail off the larboard bow! She's beatin' towards us less than two cables off!"

Johnston let out a string of slurred oaths but Casey reacted more positively.

"Larboard battery stand to; run out your guns!"

"Belike one of the corvettes," King remarked when the mate's attention returned.

"I'd say so," Casey grunted. "And all we needs on a night like this."

Only the nearest gun crews could be picked out in any detail but the rumble of trucks was unmistakeable despite the noise of the storm. The sloop carried nine-pounder long guns – light metal that was only intended to see off privateers and other predators smaller than herself. But she was facing something far more substantial now; a French national corvette would be built from stronger timbers and carrying more and heavier weapons. There was no time to consider further, though, as whatever they had spotted should equally be aware of them.

By the time the last gun had been signalled ready there was still no target visible from the deck while those at the mastheads had also lost sight. King stared desperately into the blackness; by his reckoning the corvette should be almost alongside and, if the lookout's estimate was correct, at point-blank range. The temptation to fire into the void was strong although there could be little chance of a significant hit and doing so must only signal their own position. Then the night was split by the bright flash of nearby cannon and it became clear the enemy had no such inhibitions.

The first shots passed by at the same time as the sound of their discharge and, as King had predicted, were poorly laid. Only two came anywhere close while the rest expended themselves in the very teeth of the tempest. But the broadside had served a purpose if only by alerting the remaining French to the British warship's presence and all would now be aware that Johnston had gambled and lost. Despite the terrible conditions, the enemy squadron must inevitably round on them and the convoy was as good as taken.

But there was still no reason why they should not reply and King could see the hand of the nearest gun captain as he continued to signal his weapon ready.

"Open fire!"

For once the captain had the right idea but his voice was no match for the screaming wind. Casey took up the shout and soon the *St. George* was sending an erratic broadside into the night. Only those laying the guns knew how good their aim might be although King thought he caught flashes of what could be hits as he strained into the darkness. But whatever their success or failure, there would be no second try. With the wind almost on her quarter, the *St. George* was travelling at speed while the corvette must also be setting a fair pace as it clawed into the gale. Were they alone, the British ship might easily slip by and become lost in the depths of the night; it would have been a tempting prospect were there no convoy to protect.

As it was, the odds might be stacked against them but, with three merchants in company, some show of defence was called for and the first Indiamen should be close on their heels, just where the enemy would expect. Instinctively King glanced across at the captain although Johnston's attention was set forward rather than back at his charges.

"Shall we turn sir?" Casey asked. The older man was clearly of the same mind as King, and both waited for the reply. But when it came, they were disappointed.

"Turn?" The captain seemed appalled. "Turn? Why should we turn?"

"*Bodiam Castle* is hard on our stern, or should be," the mate explained awkwardly. "And the others won't be so far behind."

"Well, the French don't know that, do they?" Johnston huffed. "In any case, there is little we can do," he continued. "They must take their chances, as we did."

In the face of such an argument there was little anyone could say, although a fresh point had occurred to King.

"What of the other escort?" he asked, catching Casey and Scott's attention, even if the captain remained aloof. "There were two corvettes, have we just met with the first, or was it the second?"

It was something no one seemed to have considered; both mates registered the thought in silence but the captain was quicker to react. Without looking back, he rushed to the break of the quarterdeck and began to shout down to the officer in charge of the gun deck.

"Hurry along there, Mr Salmond. I'll have those larboard cannon ready for instant use or know the reason why!"

"Masthead, what do you see?" Casey was addressing the heavens and after a moment's pause the distant voice of the main lookout came through the driving rain.

"Nothing for'ard, an' I've lost sight of the corvette astern."

"And of *Bodiam Castle*?" Casey again.

"Nothing, sir," the seaman replied. "Not since the last stab o' lightening."

"If there's another about the captain may be right; we wouldn't do no good turning back," Casey told King as Johnston continued to berate the servers.

"Maybe so," King grunted in return. Both enemy corvettes were considerably larger than the *St. George*, although he was still surprised that Johnston was happy to leave his charges to their fate.

The storm was definitely worsening; a further flash of lightening lit the sky but all it revealed was the white-capped waves that surrounded them.

"Sail to leeward!" Clearly the foretop lookout had been more fortunate and his call was quickly echoed by the hand at the main.

"Another corvette, or something like it," the former continued. "Off our larboard bow an' about 'alf a mile distant."

"How close shall we pass?" Casey's lungs were like leather and his voice as strong.

"About a cable – if we both keeps to our headings."

"We'll be ready for them this time!" Johnston announced with something like a leer as he returned to the binnacle.

At their current speed it would not be long to wait although the night appeared just as dense. Twice King thought he caught a glimpse of white, probably scud from the driving wind but possibly something more substantial beating forward on a bowline. Then another fork of lightening banished all doubt.

The flash was far closer and seemed to hang over both vessels for several seconds giving each ample chance to view the other. And they were almost broadside on; the only question was who would make the first move.

"Fire!" The excitement seemed to have purged all traces of alcohol from his system and Johnston's voice rang out as loud as Casey's. But his order had been premature; even King could see the gun captains were not ready. A direct instruction from the quarterdeck carried force, however, and most of the sloop's guns were despatched immediately with only the less excitable releasing more considered shots some moments later.

The extended broadside had the effect of lighting up the enemy for longer and, though King noticed no actual hits, it would have been strange if at least one of the nine-pound balls had failed to make an impression. But light from their cannon fire also worked against them and when the Frenchman replied it was with far greater accuracy.

The first of the enemy's shots was taken on their forecastle and landed with a sound of tearing wood that was soon joined by screams from one of the gun crews. Their piece had been soundly struck and the weapon itself slewed sideways across several of its servers. Another hit one of the ship's boats smashing it to fragments that, in turn, sliced about the deck wounding anyone foolish enough to be in their way. More damage was caused aft; a shot came across the deck almost in front of King, but passed by and through the starboard bulwark without causing injury although a second pounded into the party standing by the binnacle.

Selby, the signal midshipman, was struck and crumpled to the deck without a sound while the ball went on to embed itself into the main fife rail sending the entire structure into splinters and releasing lengths of line and a succession of blocks that tumbled amongst them indiscriminately.

King instinctively raised his hand to protect his head but the cascade ended with all apparently untouched. Then a scream nearby caught his attention. Rushing forward he knelt beside Johnston's prone body. The captain had been injured in the chest; the poor light made it impossible to see what had caused the damage but his split oilskins were warm with flowing blood. King looked back; Casey was bellowing for the damage aloft to be attended to and Scott seemed concerned with replacing the men at the wheel, two of whom were also casualties.

"Help me here!" King roared. "Captain's wounded!"

Casey broke away and was soon beside him.

"Masters, Downs, lend a hand!" the mate bellowed adding, "Get the captain below and into Mr McIver's charge," when the two seamen arrived.

Johnston was swiftly removed and, in the darkness that hid much, it soon felt as if he might never have been.

"We've damage to the fore topmast sling though its being addressed," Casey said as he and King returned to stand much nearer to the binnacle. "An' the boatswain's rigging a jury fife rail using the chains."

"Wheel's manned and functioning," Scott added.

"You will take command, I trust." King's tone carried as much hope as question, although Casey's eyes remained set.

"I can manage the ship right enough, but have no experience of fighting battles," he admitted. "If you'll excuse me, Captain King, you are by far the better suited."

Chapter Four

It was a relatively unknown ship and manned by a crew he only knew socially but there was no time for King to think further: he had to act.

"Very well, Mr Casey, prepare to wear ship."

"Wear ship, sir – very good," the mate responded formally before addressing the crew in his customary bellow: "Stations for wearing ship!"

Scott collected the speaking trumpet from the binnacle and approached. The storm still raged and the sloop would need careful handling.

King glanced back, they must have travelled a considerable distance and there was no sign of either corvette although his senses remained fresh and he felt he had a fair idea of both ships' positions.

"Ready, sir," Scott reported.

King gave a nod. "Take her round if you please." The young man knew the vessel far better than he did and would be more able to gauge her ways. He also appeared supremely confident and King sensed they were in safe hands.

"Take her across, Mr Kelby. Lay the headsheets square – shift over the headsheets!"

For a moment they had the wind almost entirely aft, then, as the sloop continued to blast through the black waters, it began to creep along her larboard side.

"Man the main tack and sheet. Clear away the rigging. Spanker out haul, clear away the brails!"

Now they were turning in earnest and Scott's attention was equally divided between the sails and those at the wheel as the *St. George* careered through the tumbling seas.

"Steady out the bowlines! Haul taut weather trusses, braces and lifts!"

They were settling now and soon steadying on the larboard tack with bowlines tight and the sloop beating manfully to windward. King glanced forward at the compass.

"Can you make another point to windward, Kelby?" he asked the quartermaster. The man gave an elaborate sniff.

"I might your honour," he roared back. "Though would not care to hold it long."

"Do as you can," King replied. By his estimation any room they could claw back would be riches indeed and should mean the difference between passing the corvette at too great a distance and point-blank range.

"Gunfire, sir!"

This was Casey and following his pointed finger King could make out a glow that signalled the final shots of a broadside. That last corvette must have met with one of the Indiamen – it was impossible to say which. But the warship had opened fire, and King felt a moment of guilty relief when the deadly flashes placed her roughly in line with his calculations. Then he realised the greater implications and turned to Casey once more.

"That'll be *Pembroke*, I'd say," the older man bellowed. "She were second in line – reckon *Bodiam Castle* got by."

As if to confirm this, the bulk of a heavy merchant sailing with the wind on her quarter suddenly appeared from the midst of the storm to a chorus of reports from masthead and forecastle lookouts. But the ship was a good cable off so would pass in safety; King turned his attention elsewhere.

"Who has the gun deck?" he asked.

"Salmond. Sound enough for a youngster."

King nodded and stepped to the break of the quarterdeck.

"How are you set, Mr Salmond?"

A slight figure appeared from under the shelter of the weather gangway.

"Both batteries served and ready though number one is out of action."

"And what shot?"

"Single round." The lad's eyes were wide with surprise as he realised he was being addressed by someone he had considered a passenger.

"Very well, do you have any chain or bar?"

"Chain, sir, enough for one broadside in ready-use, I can draw more."

"One will be enough," King told him. "Add that to the larboard battery and have your men set their sights high."

"Shall I have the round shot drawn?" Salmond asked but King shook his head; the idea of removing charges in such conditions was too terrible to contemplate.

"No, this will be short range, but be sure to aim for the masts," he repeated, his voice now rapidly growing hoarse.

The officer touched his hat a little awkwardly then disappeared from sight while King returned to the conn. The *St. George* was making slower progress close-hauled but still the corvette would be upon them shortly. As if to confirm this another flash of gunfire lit the sky ahead; it was a further broadside, but this time far closer and the mass of a merchant to windward was briefly lit by its glare.

"That's *Pembroke*, sure enough," Casey confirmed with an indignant roar, "and the bastards have all but dismasted her!"

In such a gale it would take little more than one well-placed shot to cause such a disaster and, perversely, the act made King's job easier as the corvette must spill her wind to remain in contact.

"Can you gain another point?" King yelled at the quartermaster but the man shook his grizzled head.

"I'm doing all I'm able, Mister," he replied without taking his eye off the main topsail's leech, "and can't promise to hold what I got for long."

King gritted his teeth; the extra point would have been useful but perhaps they had already closed enough.

"Mr Salmond reports the larboard battery prepared." This was another midshipman and one who King had only spoken with at the dining table; the concept of fighting alongside men he hardly knew was frustrating in the extreme although he quickly reminded himself that so far all had gone well.

"Tell him to be ready, and fire as he will when the time is right."

The lad touched his hat and was off.

A flash of lightening lit the scene although the corvette's hull was now close enough to be made out and certainly within range, while the disabled merchant could be seen rolling off her beam. Whether the *St. George* would be noticed as she clawed up was another matter but King thought not; all eyes aboard the French ship were likely to be on their current conquest and, even if they were spotted, the leeward guns would not be fully manned.

"They're in for a surprise," Scott shouted across.

"Serve the buggers right," the mate grunted. A series of flashes from the French ship showed how her marines at least were aware of the sloop's presence, it could not be long before the great guns also came to life but King trusted Salmond would act before then.

And he was not disappointed; even as they watched, the first of the nine-pounders was discharged leading a ripple of fire that spread down the sloop's side at irregular intervals. The corvette's tophamper merged frustratingly into the deep black of night yet still King could detect some movement where shots were striking. Then there was something more positive; one of the spars had definitely been hit and soon a sheet of canvas was streaming out as line and timber tumbled down onto the enemy's deck.

"Struck 'er main topmast!" Casey's voice was rich with emotion and in no time the entire sloop was a mass of cheering.

"Port your helm!" King ordered, unmoved. Damaged or not, the corvette could be expected to reply and her heavier guns would wreak havoc at such a range. He must seek immediate safety in the darkness, even if it meant exposing the sloop's vulnerable stern. Scott ordered the braces adjusted to allow for the turn while Casey, inspired by King's level reaction, silenced the men. The bulk of the dismasted merchant still wallowed off the corvette's beam but King already knew what would be the enemy's next target. For several long moments those aboard the sloop stared back at the warship as she was left all too slowly behind; the range was increasing with every passing second although a broadside would still be hard to bear. A small fire had started aboard the Frenchman and by its light the damaged rigging could be seen with the darkened hull of the wounded merchant beyond.

"*Pembroke*'s a goner for sure," Casey told King. "But there's little a lightweight like us can do against four warships. Even if the other two are taken, they can't say we didn't do our bit."

King made no reply; he supposed honour had been satisfied and he certainly held no personal obligation to protect the convoy. But now he had command, the urge to continue annoying even so large an enemy was strong and there were surely a few tricks that might be played once they were clear of the present danger.

He continued to watch the corvette; there was still no sign of movement and they must start to become an increasingly difficult target for her gunners. King still considered it remarkable they had been able to deliver so close a broadside with apparent impunity but had never been one to question his luck. And then, just as the blaze aboard her was quenched and the Frenchman's lines were beginning to fade completely, the corvette's side erupted in an explosion of light and fire as her broadside was finally released.

* * *

"Captain's wounded," the seaman announced as he and another dragged the shapeless mass unceremoniously along the orlop deck. The protocol in dealing with injured aboard Company ships followed Royal Navy custom; whatever their rank or station, each would be dealt with in order of their arrival. But though he had more than enough to occupy him, the captain was the captain after all and McIver supposed some concession should be made.

"Can you attend, Mrs King?" the surgeon asked, as he glanced back from the splinter wound he was stitching. Aimée, who had been swabbing the deck after the previous patient, moved across to the body that had been dumped next to the pump casing.

"Get me some light then remove the shirt," she ordered briskly as the loblolly boy joined her. Drew had already recognised the woman's innate talent for their work and collected one of the lanterns without question. He placed the thing next to Johnston where it seemed to give out as much smoke as light, then opened the captain's oilskins and roughly ripped his linen shirt apart.

"We got us a gusher," he stated dispassionately.

"What is it?" Johnston demanded and, even in the poor light, his face was a study of anxiety.

"A splinter, Captain," Aimée informed him as she plunged her hand into the bloody mess. "But one we can surely deal with."

"It'll need plenty of tow." The loblolly boy passed a lump of cotton waste next to where the woman was trying to staunch the bleeding. Drew, like most of the *St. George*'s crew, had little time for their captain yet was privately proud of his own position and would treat him as well as any patient. But this was his world; he was in charge and anything he did would be on his terms. "Surgeon will 'ave to stitch it 'ventually but a good tight strappin' will sort matters f'now. Would you be seeing to that, Ma'am?"

"I will," Aimée confirmed before addressing the patient once more. "We shall see you are made well, Captain Johnston. I shall bandage and keep your wound stable; Mr McIver will attend as soon as he is able."

"Send for him now!" Johnston's tone had grown stronger. "I must be seen without delay!"

Aimée glanced across to where the surgeon had moved on to a topman with a broken leg and noticed several equally injured waiting for his attention.

"He will come soon, but first the bleeding must be stopped."

"Take your hands off me!" The man attempted to draw away. His eyes flashed to the loblolly boy. "Get me McIver and get him now!"

"But the lady will make you better, Captain. She's a wonder when it comes to bandages."

Johnston's wide eyes swept from one to the other. "I'll not have that mab touch me," he roared. "I need a proper surgeon, not some Gallic whore!"

* * *

The broadside landed seconds later and, despite being fired at long range and at a fading target, caused significant damage to the *St. George*. Most was confined to the sloop's stern although several shots passed over her top rail causing injuries further forward. Some fell to the splinters created when heavy iron smashes into seasoned timber and others to the shot itself, while there was also more material damage. Another of the sloop's guns was neatly taken out by a well-placed strike to its carriage, several balls punched holes into the frail bulwarks and the starboard main chains were struck. One of the replacement helmsmen followed the fate of his predecessor with the same shot also accounting for the binnacle which exploded into a mass of glass, matchwood and oil from the lamp. The warm fluid spread across the deck and, mixing with alcohol from the shattered compass, promptly burst into flames.

Clambering up from where he had fallen, King saw this as an immediate concern. He had no idea what damage had been caused aloft, but it was likely the *St. George* would have slowed. And if one broadside had reached her successfully, they must not give an aiming point for another.

"The fire! Douse the fire!" he yelled while flapping clumsily at the flames with his one hand. Two seamen joined him and, with the aid of rain and the contents of three fire buckets, the flames were subdued.

"Send for Mr Browning!" Casey roared to the ship in general then, on seeing King, added, "Fore tops'ls the only one drawing."

King was about to respond when the short, stout figure of the boatswain appeared.

"What sail can you set, Browning?" Casey demanded.

"Nothing to the main, not since we lost support of the..."

"I said, what sail can we set!" the mate interrupted.

"Fore m-main can be controlled," the boatswain stammered. "An' I might be able to raise the royal though I'd like a chance to inspect the..."

"See to it!"

Browning hurried away and Scott joined Casey and King in considering the enemy. The corvette's lines were now decidedly indistinct although they probably remained within her grasp.

"We still have way," Scott remarked as the wind shrieked about them.

"Aye, an' the Frogs have probably enough to deal with in taking the *Pembroke*," Casey agreed.

That was undoubtedly true and King felt his body relax as he sensed they might be able to depart in peace. But this was the end of any further attempts to defend the convoy; with the storm still raging, those aboard the *St. George* would have their work cut out saving their own ship without defending others.

* * *

"He needed a tighter bandage," the surgeon grumbled as he removed the sodden mass of cotton waste. "There is a vein ruptured and for all I know the brachial artery."

"I were aware of that, sir," the loblolly boy acknowledged with a total absence of regret. "But you know what I'm like when it comes to strappin'; I did what I could with tow an' gave him a dose of laudanum."

"Cotton waste will never stem such a bleed," McIver's reply carried more than a hint of accusation. "As it is, the captain has lost a deal of blood."

Hearing himself addressed, Johnston opened his eyes and blinked at the surgeon before releasing a faint moan.

"It's alright, Captain, I can close the wound. With time and fluids you'll feel more comfortable."

Johnston groaned again, then seemed to drift back to his slumber.

"If you could not do it yourself, you should have handed the job to Mrs King." McIver reached for one of a series of needles already threaded with horsehair.

"Oh, she could have done it in a trice," Drew agreed, nodding to where Aimée was applying the final dressing to the stump of a recent amputee. "And would 'ave, though the captain wouldn't hear of her touchin' 'im."

"Why ever not?" the surgeon demanded as the needle bit deep into Johnston's flesh. "Because Mrs King is a woman?"

"No, sir," Drew replied evenly. "More on account of 'er bein' a Frog."

* * *

"I'd say we got away with that one," Casey bellowed as the corvette finally faded into the night. King nodded in silence; his throat was dry from shouting while the excitement of action was having its usual effect, leaving him tired, listless and mildly depressed. But yes, Casey was undoubtedly right. Delivering that broadside meant they had not simply run off into the night, and damage had definitely been done to a far superior enemy so he supposed they should be pleased.

"Grateful for your help, Captain," Casey told him in a tone only a chance respite in the wind allowed King to hear.

"Would we could have done more," King replied.

"That's alright, sir," Casey sniffed. "I think we done enough."

* * *

But the first mate was wrong, at least on the last count; the earlier fire on the quarterdeck was not the only one to break out aboard the *St. George* that night. Another, initially far smaller, began further forward and on the orlop deck when the heavy handling which the sloop had been subjected to caused a lanthorn swinging outside the boatswain's stores to crash to the deck unnoticed. This time there was no oil to spill and ignite and the lamp's tallow candle was almost extinguished in the fall. But a small flame survived on its fat wick and, as the candle itself rolled out and onto the deck, soon began to spread.

Once more this need not have been a great cause for concern; even when a pile of chippings and sawdust – detritus from the clean sweep carried out prior to turning the cockpit into a temporary sick bay – caught alight, the blaze could have been controlled by the stamp of anyone with the will and a suitable pair of boots.

But none were available; all those nearby were too busy either dealing with the wounded, issuing cartridges or running them to the guns on the upper deck. And when the light began to dwindle all would have continued never knowing of the lucky escape they had been granted, except once more the flame did not entirely die.

A small glimmer continued and, as luck would have it, did so next to the deal door of the boatswain's store. Once more, this was nothing of note, and could have been readily killed but, again, was allowed to live. Live and live long enough to ignite the small pool of marine paint that had been spilled on the other side of the panel.

The paint was rich with oil and a deep red, like the flames that soon began to feed on it; in no time the inside of the storeroom was brightly lit. Then steadily, and still before anyone was even aware of its existence, the blaze grew to a size where it could no longer be so easily controlled, and finally assumed the dominant role.

Chapter Five

"Captain's injured, convoy's as good as lost, and there's an enemy squadron to windward," Casey stated flatly. "Must say, I've known better nights."

It was four hours since they had escaped from the corvette and in that time the storm had abated somewhat. But even though the rain might have eased it was still blowing a gale and the night remained as dark. With the sloop's tiny wardroom filled with the more able wounded, the senior officers were borrowing their captain's quarters with Casey seated rather awkwardly at the head of the dining table. Scott and Salmond were further down and King, through his own insistence, very much at the foot.

"First light is at a quarter after six," Scott announced. "We'll know more then. It's possible *Bodiam Castle* or *Earl of Dalkeith* escaped."

"Possible but unlikely," Casey growled. "If none are in sight we may as well say goodbye to the lot of them and make for The Cape." As he said the words he realised they had not been phrased in the manner expected of even a temporary master. In fact, this entire meeting was in danger of becoming a general discussion, which was not how a ship should be commanded at all. But then he was not a captain, nor ever had been, and rather resented having been pressed into the post on this, his last voyage before retirement. His eyes fell upon King, sitting mute at the far end of the table. The man knew so much more about the science of command and had led them well during the brief action. Certainly the Company could not complain at the loss of their precious ships when the *St. George* had inflicted very real damage on a far superior enemy. And he supposed it reasonable that King should not wish to continue in charge; he was, after all, a passenger. But Casey had grown used to being subservient to another, even one as inept as Johnston, so it irked him that a more experienced man was content to advise, but not control.

"What of our condition, sir? Have we heard anything more from the carpenter?" This was Salmond and another sign that the meeting was not being run properly. Usually it would have been Casey's duty to report the state of the ship to the captain yet, despite his new role, he was now being asked to do so to the third mate.

"Basically we are sound," he replied, clinging to as much

authority as possible. "Carpenter reports only light damage to fixtures and fittings. However, these do include the main fife rail and our larboard chains. Our ordinance is also depleted by two pieces although that can certainly wait and Mr Browning has requested we heave to as soon as the weather moderates," he continued. "There is work aloft that will need attending to before we reach The Cape."

"Which should be in about three weeks." Scott once more. "That's a rough estimate, of course; much will depend on what sail we can muster."

Three weeks; it was a long time to remain in nominal charge of a warship, Casey decided. And unless they were fortunate in finding a Company master at Cape Town, he may have to see them through as far as Bombay.

"Did the carpenter say how long repairs would take?" Again this was the third officer and again Casey was mildly peeved to find himself answering to a junior man.

"He thinks he can repair the fife rail and channels in a day; a temporary binnacle can be set up at the same time."

"The compass was destroyed but we can take one from the launch," Scott added. "It might not be ideal but I am sure will serve, at least as far as Cape Town."

"Indeed," Casey agreed. Then, reclaiming the meeting, quickly added, "And I have spoken to Mr McIver. His duties are such that he cannot be present but reports seven killed with Mr Selby amongst them. There are also nine wounded including the captain, of which six are likely to remain incapacitated. That leaves us with just under ninety hands, which is more than adequate, I think you'll agree."

There was a rumble of approval from the rest and Casey continued.

"On that tack, I should like to thank Captain King and his lady for their assistance." His eyes rose and met those of the Navy man; someone he had barely known until that night. "Your handling of the ship was indeed admirable, sir, and I know the surgeon appreciates the help he has received. The Company will doubtless express its gratitude in due course, but I wanted to add my personal thanks."

"It is good of you, though I would rather no mention were made of our involvement." King had no wish for thanks from the HEIC and was still mildly concerned that Johnston had not progressed well under Aimée's care. The man's wound had been caused by a simple splinter, yet he was clearly ill and McIver would not be pushed into predicting a full recovery.

"As you wish, sir," Casey agreed gruffly although King's answer had come as a relief. There was bound to be an official investigation into the action and it would be far easier to present a report that gave no mention of being helped by a Royal Navy officer. "Then if there is nothing else, gentlemen, I think we should attend to our duties."

That was said with just the right amount of gravity and, as the others rose to leave, Casey felt a little better about his performance. Maybe it was simply a knack, like taking a sighting or heaving the lead; perhaps he would become accustomed to the role of master after all? Then a frantic hammering on the door made them all turn and a midshipman erupted into the cabin followed closely by the clatter of the ship's bell being rung continuously.

"It's fire, sir," the youngster gasped, "and one hell of a blaze!"

* * *

From his place at the foot of the table, King was naturally first through the cabin's outer doors where he immediately noticed the smell of smoke. And this was different from the acrid sting of spent gunpowder that still tainted his nostrils; a warmer, almost comforting aroma of log fires and only mildly tinged by the hint of burning resin. The ship was still in the throes of recovering from the action; some bulkheads were yet to be secured while there were more than a few areas of minor damage that had to be attended to although still it seemed strange the fumes had not been noticed earlier.

"It's below," the midshipman shouted. "In the boatswain's stores!"

King made for the companionway but instinctively drew to one side. Even after several years, the loss of his left arm made such things hard to negotiate and, when the others had scampered down, he followed at a more careful pace. But once on the berth deck the scent was stronger still and, as he stood over the hatch that led to the orlop, the air became so thick it seemed impossible that anything might be living below. For so much smoke to be generated in such a short space of time the fire must not only be fierce, but also fast moving and for a moment he hesitated.

He told himself this was not fear; that he had walked the deck in action a dozen times and was rarely deterred by any mortal enemy. What he was about to meet would be a different matter though and, in the confines of the orlop, every bit as deadly. And being hampered by the loss of one arm meant he could surely be of little use. The temporary sick bay would have more than enough wounded and dying, did they really need the presence of a one-armed man? Then he remembered Aimée was amongst them and dropped down the narrow hatch and into the fume filled depths without another thought.

On landing, the first thing he noticed was a deep orange glow forward; it shone with the brilliance of a dozen suns and easily penetrated the thick smoke which was steadily filling the cramped area. By its light he could see men, mostly lying on the deck, while those that stood were coughing pitifully. He drew breath and instantly felt his chest react in sympathy but once he fell to his knees the air was clearer and the next gasp less caustic.

He could also see better; some brave souls were rigging the ship's fire engine. He could see its outline as desperate hands attached the lengths of hose and began to lean on two long pump handles. And there was McIver, the surgeon; the man was all but dragging a limp body away from the flames. King could not tell if this was one injured in battle, or more recently from the effects of fire, but it was clear a lot of wounded men would have to be removed from the orlop. Of Aimée, he could see no sign, then a faint pressure on his shoulder made him turn.

She was there, behind him and looking almost comical as she held a stained apron against her face.

"We must evacuate the wounded!" he bellowed and Aimée replied with a silent nod.

It was no hardship to return to the aft hatch and, looking up into the clear air above, King shouted as loudly as his dry throat would allow. Instantly two faces appeared and one belonged to a midshipman King recognised.

"Mr Durham, tell off four stout hands." King spoke with the authority he was accustomed to. "They are to join me here. Then form a further party; as many as can be spared, to remain on the berth deck under your command."

The lad replied with a smart salute and was instantly gone. King turned to Aimée.

"You must leave," he said and was hardly surprised when his instruction was met with a curt shake of her head.

"I shall go when I have to, but first must clear the sick."

"Very well. Then we will start with those nearest the blaze."

As they made their way forward the heat increased although there seemed to be less actual smoke. With four hands at the pumps and under the direction of young Salmond, the fire engine was now sending a credible stream of water against the smouldering forward bulkhead. But there must be a furnace concealed behind and whether it could be controlled was anyone's guess. Scott had begun frantically tearing away at any loose parts of partitioning to improve their access while Casey, apparently overcome with fumes, was kneeling on the glowing deck and coughing desperately. Nearby, McIver still struggled with his patient and, without a word, King also took hold of the man. Aimée joined them and the three lugged the dead weight over other bodies to the aft hatch where four seamen had just descended.

McIver watched the man being passed up to the willing hands above, while King turned to the party Durham had sent. "Go for'ard," he directed. "Bring any man who cannot walk and see him to the berth deck."

One, who sported a set of man-of-war tattoos on his bare arms, knuckled his forehead Navy fashion and led the rest away.

"Some will need attention before they can be moved," McIver shouted. "Perhaps you will continue the evacuation of those that are fit to travel?"

"Of course," King agreed before turning to Aimée. "We'll work together." His voice was now decidedly husky but she understood.

It took less than ten minutes yet felt like an hour, but eventually the deck was clear of all but the dead. Even the captain went; McIver dosed the tightly bound figure with laudanum and Johnston allowed himself to be manhandled without protest.

"We'll have to abandon ship."

This was Casey who had recovered to some extent although, despite the deep orange glow, his face looked grey. "We're not making any headway with the fire," he added. "The launch is sound; take that for starters."

It was hardly the place or time for conversation and King was privately glad to be given a reason to quit the inferno. Clambering up the companionway he emerged into the clearer air, though relative darkness, of the berth deck. Aimée was close behind, her bright eyes taking in the bandage-swathed bodies that had been deposited apparently at random.

"We're to make for the main deck and evacuate," he announced and the men who had brought the wounded so far immediately returned to their charges. "Pass them up through the main hatch; if you can rig a block and tackle, so much the better."

One of the men waved a hand in acknowledgement, then King made for the aft companionway and clambered up. "Clear away the launch," he ordered as he emerged into the cold, dark air, adding, "and both cutters," as an afterthought.

"Red cutter's destroyed, sir," Durham, the midshipman, replied after laying the young man he had been carrying on the sodden deck.

King closed his eyes briefly. Up to a hundred to evacuate and adequate boat space for less than two thirds. Finding room would be a task in itself but one made doubly difficult by the fire that was steadily eating into the ship's very innards. "Then clear anything away that will swim," he snapped. "And be quick about it; we only have so much time."

* * *

At the fire itself, Scott and Salmond were growing disheartened; even with four sound men at its pumps, the fire engine's flow was unable to make any impression on the flames. Instead, the blaze was growing steadily stronger, higher and nearer until both officers were starting to roast in the heat. Sweat dried instantly against their clothing while a kiln-hot draught blistered their lungs and the very air they breathed seemed thin and lifeless.

Salmond drew back and turned to Scott; the man was his senior in every way but the pair had been friends for long enough and he knew the older officer would accept a sensible suggestion.

"There's nothing more we can do." Salmond was clutching at the metal end of the fire engine's hose; the thing was almost too hot to touch and the pain it gave to his already blistered hands made his voice rise. "We must make a run for it before the magazine blows!"

They were less than fifteen feet from the entrance to the filling room and already the sloop's store of powder must be growing dangerously hot within its copper-lined chamber. Scott opened his mouth to reply but, once more, Salmond was ahead of him.

"You go first," he said and it was very nearly a command. "I shall keep the fire engine in use for now and Kelly's party can continue a while longer."

Scott glanced back to the midshipman in charge of those working the adapted elm tree pump; they were further from the flames yet the canvas hose reached a long way forward. It had been fed deep into the blaze where it was sending out clouds of steam as it steadily burned. Redirecting the pump had been Salmond's idea and the additional water had done much to keep the fire from spreading even more quickly.

"Very well," Scott agreed. "But do not linger. And be sure you bring everyone when you do go."

"Yes, Mother," Salmond grinned. For a moment the pair exchanged a glance then, without another word, Scott hurried aft into the darkness while Salmond returned to directing his hose on the blinding glare of the inferno.

* * *

On deck, the storm had eased considerably and there was what might be the first glimmer of a false dawn, although King's eyes still carried a cast from the flames and he could actually make out very little. But he did know the ship was carrying the wind on her quarter; with fore topsail and driver the only canvas showing, they were barely underway and it was probably hundreds of miles to the nearest landmass. Even minimal pressure on the fore and mizzen was proving enough to keep her steady however, while it seemed they could still rely on some support from the main to see the larger boats away. With the fife rail yet to be replaced, swinging the launch out proved a slow and frustrating business, but one that was done in time and soon the craft could be made ready for the wounded. Aimée, who had been keeping close to King, drew nearer still and placed her arm about him.

"My dear, you will have to go with them," he said, his voice unnecessarily harsh, and immediately he felt her body stiffen. The last thing he needed was a protest but she quickly relaxed and moved away before clambering aboard the boat without a word or backward glance.

The surgeon then appeared on deck and, on seeing him, King also noticed a slight hint of red further forward. The glow grew as he watched; the flames must have spread as far as the berth deck and were even now trying to reach up to the forecastle. Soon the entire hull would be ablaze, although the magazine would blow long before that could happen. Officially it was a senior Company officer's job to order the ship abandoned, but King could see no point in delaying, especially when to do so might mean the loss of every soul on board.

"We're down by one of the cutters so have little space," King told the surgeon. "Take the launch and fill it with wounded, along with as many able bodied as you can manage, but it must be filled."

"Very well," McIver agreed, "but you must give me time to arrange my patients and assemble what medical supplies I am able. My assistant should be here presently."

At that moment Drew appeared with what looked like a medical chest.

"Stow it at the stern," McIver directed, then peered up at the sky. The rain was holding off but might return at any moment while the wind would bring a measure of spray into any small boat. "And fetch blankets, plenty of blankets as well as any oilskins you can muster."

"I must remind you, space is at a premium," King cautioned.

"Maybe so," McIver was unmoved. "But it will do little good to fill the boat with men only to have them die of exposure."

The loblolly boy went to leave but stopped when the bulk of Casey, the first officer, appeared in the mouth of the aft hatchway. The older man coughed dreadfully as his lungs drew in fresh air and he heaved himself up on to the deck as if twice his normal weight.

"You've done well," he told King when the spasm was controlled and he had noticed the packed launch almost ready to depart. "Progress is not so good below."

"You mean there's no sign of the fire dying?"

"None whatsoever," Casey wheezed. "We're pouring water from the fire engine and one pump but it's turning to steam; darned thing's simply too hot and, even if quenched, the frame will never stand a sea again."

At that point the flames that had been faintly licking at the base of the forecastle broke through and began to play about the base of the belfry.

"You'll excuse me, gentlemen, but we must not delay," Browning, the boatswain, interrupted. "If you're plannin' on taking the cutter an' all, we'll have to clear the launch from the tackle and that won't be immediate."

"Very well, you'd better go with the wounded," Casey spoke, then gasped as he fought to control another bout of coughing.

"No, I'll stay," King stated firmly. "A senior Company man should be present, if only to accompany Johnston, and the fumes aboard ship are doing you no good."

Casey paused. "But your good lady?"

King flashed a look at Aimée who had arranged herself in the midst of the wounded.

"I shall be following in the cutter," he spoke loud enough for her to hear and she gave a faint smile in response.

"Very well," Casey agreed before carefully heaving himself over the sloop's top rail.

"Stand away there," the boatswain called, "and be ready with that cutter tackle."

The flames were now eating through the fore deck in two places and some foremast standing rigging was starting to burn. King looked about and realised that he was almost alone. Then Drew, the loblolly boy appeared carrying a bale of tightly packed clothing.

"Coming down!" The man tossed the load into the crowded boat before clambering after it. King peered down at the dark mass barely feet away. Aimée was there and, sensing his gaze, looked up and caught his eye. Then, with a clatter of blocks, the launch was cast off and quickly disappeared into the utter darkness of night.

* * *

"We've had to abandon the fire!" Scott yelled as he appeared through the aft hatch. "How is it with the launch?"

"Left with Casey, McIver and the wounded." King's tone was strangely brusque. "Bosun's making the cutter ready."

Both men glanced at the small boat that was being brought level with the ship's side. At best, it might hold thirty which meant the jolly boat, still swinging on davits at the taffrail, must take the rest and would be equally overloaded.

"Salmond is on his way up with the remaining hands; best leave the cutter for them," Scott suggested. "But the jolly boat can go now; you and I should take it with as many as she'll hold."

"Whatever you do, you'd better make it quick, gents." Browning, the boatswain, pointed to the flames that were now licking up the forestay and shrouds. King and Scott headed aft where a seaman was starting to release the small boat that looked totally unsuitable for the mighty Atlantic. Swinging himself over the side, King felt around clumsily with his feet while clinging to the taffrail with his one hand. It was already too far down, he would have to jump yet could not see clearly enough to know quite where he would land. Sensing his predicament, Scott climbed down next to him and silently guided his body to safety. The rain began to return in earnest as the boat was lowered to the water and more hands scrambled aboard making the small craft tip alarmingly.

"That will do; we've enough!" Scott raised his hand. A final man tumbled in to jeers and laughter from those already aboard and then, following the clack of tackle and one hefty shove from a bare foot, the jolly boat was cast loose upon the ocean.

"We should make for the launch," Scott muttered as the *St. George* pulled steadily away leaving the overloaded craft to roll terribly in the swell. "Though I'll be blowed if I can see it."

"Perhaps we might wait for the cutter?" King had found a place for himself on a stern thwart and was starting to shiver. "They'll be as overloaded as us; perchance we can clap the two together and make a form of raft."

"Good thought." Scott nodded with approval as he squeezed himself alongside. "Come morning we might meet up with the launch and add them. So what's keeping Salmond?"

Both men switched their attention to the burning form of the *St. George* still relentlessly heading eastward and taking the light with her. A cluster of figures could be made out silhouetted against the ever-rising flames as they attempted to launch the cutter. The sloop carried spare yards on skids above the waist and others began removing these. The lengths of pine would float well and were soon being thrown over the side, presumably to support any non-swimmers unable to find a place in the boat. Another party began tossing hammocks into the water to the same purpose while the cutter itself was steadily filling with men. Scott pursed his lips; Salmond was keeping his head but then he would have expected nothing less. The man was made for command; it could not be long before he was promoted to first officer or even master and Scott, for one, would have no difficulty in serving under him.

Then, even as they looked, a great white light erupted from the very bowels of the sloop and grew until it reached up impossibly high into the heavens. For several seconds the dark night was made day by a painful brilliance that gradually turned to yellow and finally red as it died. Masts, spars and pieces of hull were flung into the air to vanish in the gloom and then came the deep boom of an explosion that seemed to erupt from the very ocean itself and reached them just as the *St. George*, along with all who had been aboard, ceased to exist.

Chapter Six

Morning brought light but little consolation and no comfort. Dawn broke slowly revealing a cloud-filled sky that sent a steady deluge of tepid rain, although all warmth soon departed as it soaked into the clothing and bodies of those within the tiny packed craft. And, still on his thwart and now shivering constantly, King was also battling with remorse.

If only they had spotted the blaze earlier. Aboard a Royal Navy vessel it was customary to carry out a full stem to stern inspection at the close of action, something that would have identified a lingering fire or anything likely to cause one, and he had been remiss in not insisting upon it. And what was he thinking of, allowing Aimée to be taken from him and placed in a boat with so many desperate men? Not enough had been done to evacuate the ship earlier; admittedly he had been involved with rescuing the wounded, but McIver was the only one to give any thought to taking provisions. Too much time had also been wasted on deck, a delay that finally cost the lives of all that remained. No one knew for sure how many had been expecting to escape in the cutter; maybe thirty–forty? But, whatever the figure, it was too high. King supposed there must be a measure of collective guilt although that was no consolation as he knew where the responsibility truly lay.

Despite the regular motion of the boat, all aboard were now still and seemed set in position. They were not, however, silent. A deep rumble of conversation flowed evenly throughout; men complaining, men praying, a pitiful plea and the sound of gentle sobbing. King tried to close his mind to it all as, for now at least, they were inactive. There must come a time when movement was required, food to distribute and ablutions necessary; that was when they must expect problems.

At that point he had no idea how these might appear; apart from himself, who was only a passenger, Scott and one midshipman, the jolly boat's occupants were all ordinary hands. Skilled men certainly, but not necessarily gifted when it came to the cooperation needed for survival in a small boat. Were there to be arguments as to their course, the distribution of food or who should be in charge, the majority could easily seize control.

"Still no sign." Scott was taking one of his regular scans. King had no idea what the man expected to see; it might equally be friend or foe. Either would have been a welcome sight and the lack of both served only to depress him further. The boat was riding low in the water and, as heavy cloud blended seamlessly with the dark ocean, their area of view must be pitifully small, yet it seemed strange that after such a profusion of shipping the previous night they should find themselves apparently alone.

"They might be anywhere." Scott lowered himself once more. "Launch has twin masts and is a good sea boat."

King nodded but said nothing; loaded as she was, and with so many wounded, such a craft would still not sail particularly well. And Casey, who had command, was hardly in the best condition for ocean travel in an open boat. Perhaps when this weather eased they might have more luck, but so steady was the wind and so relentless the rain there seemed little likelihood of change before nightfall.

"We've two cases of hard tack which should last us four days at a pound a man," Scott whispered although King was sure others were listening. "I'll have to ration later, of course, but feel we should give one decent day's provision first."

With all they had gone through that seemed sensible, if only to delay any future trouble, and at least they had a seemingly unending supply of fresh water.

"Give me some space, damn it!" a voice sounded out from further forward, only to be met with a barrage of equally ill-tempered retorts before general murmuring resumed.

"I left my Suzie," another struck up. "I left her in me chest."

"Ready for some scran I'm reckoning."

"Already had breakfast, and it ain't time for dinner."

"I left her in me chest."

"Make mine a lobscouse; plenty of onions and don't forget the soft tack."

"Fresh soft tack and butter: Devon butter – love-er-ly."

"Left my Suzie in me chest."

"What's with this Suzie?"

"Aye, what you bleatin' on about, Chalky?"

"Me girl. Me special girl: she gave me an oyster hull to remember her by. I calls it me Suzie. It were in me chest and now I ain't got it no more."

"Would that be Suzie Tomkinson?"

"Red-haired mot with a squint?"

"Lives in Deptford in old Ma Ransom's nugging house?"

"Aye, that's her," the seaman admitted to a chorus of jeers and cat calls. Then a mate took pity on him.

"Never mind, Chalk, she gives 'em out pretty freely – you can 'ave mine."

And so they continued, and so they would continue until wind, rain and time gradually wore them down. King glanced at his watch once more; barely five minutes had passed since the last look. How many more times? How much longer would it be before things changed, the weather altered, a ship or land were sighted? Or the first of them decided to die?

* * *

"There's a wee bit a wark needed to the caulking on the forecastle," *Mistral*'s carpenter reported. "Whatever them dockyard laddies say, it'll all ha' tae come out and be done proper and ma Jimmies will make a better job of it – as they did in the waist." The Scotsman paused to consider. "An' I'd like to see another coat of paint on the orlop an aw; it's had two but the last werenae thick enough and there'll no be the chance later. But the hull's sound, sir, I can promise you that, and I'd say they've done a fair job elsewhere."

Lieutenant Croft nodded. A fair job, not a bad assessment considering a foreign dockyard with a fool of a captain in command. But he had been hoping for more: he had been hoping to present Captain King with as near perfect a ship as he could manage and, though the current state of HMS *Mistral* was not far off, it was still mildly disappointing.

"Very well," he sighed, "I shall beard Captain Matterson yet again. How long would you say for the forecastle to be attended to?"

"If we call the cauldrons back and start directly, it should be dain by Friday."

Friday: two days. Then there was just the new mizzen topmast to fit, followed by fresh preventer stays and she would be ready for lading. The last word from Captain King had come from a fast packet that spoke with his convoy before calling at Cape Town. From that, his arrival had been expected a week ago, although nothing had been heard since and with a dozen rumours of privateers and roving battle squadrons circulating, he supposed they should be starting to worry. And, now that the ship was almost ready, it was possible to think of something else.

Once laden, *Mistral* would be ordered to sea; that was inevitable. So much time and energy had been spent seeing her out of the dockyard, she could never be left to gather dust while awaiting her true master. And though Croft thought of himself as a practical man, it would gall him to present a ship that had taken so much time and effort to someone who might not appreciate her. However capable the new commander, he would know nothing of the frigate's foibles or, if it came to it, her crew and no end of trouble could be caused by a true dunderhead. No, when *Mistral* was taken to sea it should only be by Captain King; it was what Croft and his fellow officers had been working towards for so long and anything else would be an insult.

* * *

"T'will be good to get properly aboard the old barky again," Midshipman Summers remarked as he and Lieutenant Adams made their way down Strand Street. They were starting to move their belongings from the boarding house that had been home while *Mistral* was in refit. Adams' load included a bundle of fresh laundry which he swung gently as he walked while Summers nursed a small tabby cat against his chest with slightly more consideration. He had found the creature half-starved and wandering the back streets of Cape Town some weeks before and the pair were now inseparable.

"It will be your mog's first time aboard a ship," Adams pointed out. "She'll be in for a shock; there's rats aboard *Mistral* that could have her for breakfast."

"Malkin will deal with them." Summers' tone carried more bravado than confidence.

"Keep her locked in the cockpit and she might be alright," the senior man supposed. "Though I seem to remember the middy's berth being plagued by the blighters."

"Well that's gonna change once my girl's in place. Give her a week and you won't see a rat on the orlop."

"It's fortunate we don't have to worry over such things in the gunroom," Adams sniffed. "Never noticed so much as a mouse since I won me washboards; there are stewards and the like to take care of such things."

Summers made no comment. The pair had been midshipmen together and shared several vermin-infested cockpits before Adams earned his commission. And throughout they had remained friends, although sometimes he wished the fellow would not lord it so.

"You made your mind up about the woman then?"

"The woman?" Adams exclaimed, rising to the bait. "Are you referring to Anne?"

"Aye, that's the pumpkin," Summers agreed cheerfully. "Coming aboard is she?"

"She might." Adams was cautious. "Much will depend on Captain King."

"If it *is* Captain King," Summers reminded him. "Fellow ain't been heard of for a while and unless he shows soon we're likely to get some jobbing cove in his place."

"In which case I might not," Adams supposed. "Ask their permission, I am meaning."

"Wives are usually allowed. You hold a commission after all."

"Aye, though we haven't exactly made it to the altar. As far as the Navy is concerned, Anne is just a widow."

"But a rich one," Summers grinned although Adams was less certain.

"I wouldn't call her that," he said.

"Well her husband is undoubtedly dead and you ain't short of a bob or two yourself," Summers recalled. "So why don't you wed?"

They were coming to the end of Strand Street and, after allowing a small carriage to pass, began to make for the opposite pavement.

"Well... Have you asked her?" the midshipman persisted.

"Oh yes, and we are in agreement – as far as such matters can be. But there are complications."

"Complications?" Summers stroked the cat's forehead.

"Indeed, I shall not bore you with details but her late husband hardly made provisions for their future."

"Still, if Captain King appears, you'll ask for her to be admitted to the gunroom?"   "Oh, I fully intend to."

"Might have to clear it with the Commodore," Summers supposed.

"Don't foresee any problem there, it's not as if we're sailing under Old Jack. Mr Manning told me Sir Richard let him bring his wife aboard in previous ships and I believes his own has sailed with him in the past, so Anne should be set to come along even without our being spliced."

"And if anyone says no, she still might," Summers supposed with a grin. "You'll just have to keep her locked up, like my cat."

* * *

"Pardon me, sir, but there's a middy dressed like a malkin who says he's reporting for duty."

Lieutenant Cooper looked up from the primer on French grammar that had been trying to defeat him. "A malkin?" he asked vaguely, adding, "Oh, you mean a scarecrow," as realisation dawned.

"Yes, sir," Brett, a midshipman himself, agreed. "And right old he is too, sir. Must be all of thirty."

Cooper, who was not far short of such a crime himself, closed the book and stood.

"Very well, I'll come."

Walking out of the gunroom, he instinctively cast his eyes about *Mistral*'s berth deck but all seemed in order, or as much in order as was possible aboard a ship still shaking free of the dockyard. At every station he could see small tasks that needed addressing while the grit beneath his feet – an annoyance that returned the moment any deck was swabbed – irked him in a manner that was quite out of proportion. But Cooper had been a commissioned officer long enough to close his mind to such things, especially as there were problems of far greater magnitude that were equally unsolvable.

The main one was time; despite all their efforts the work was overrunning. These were just the finishing touches; final paintwork and setting small matters to rights, but all were dragging on far longer than anyone expected. So in some ways it was good that Captain King had yet to return; Cooper, like all *Mistral*'s officers, wanted nothing more than to present a workable ship and the reality still lay some days in the future.

On deck the situation was no better; a boatswain's party was assisting riggers from the shore in setting up fresh shrouds while McPherson, the armourer, was being noisy with hammers on the forecastle. And there, in the waist as Brett had reported, was a strangely mature yet decidedly scruffy midshipman standing next to a worn sea chest.

"Mr Midshipman Martin," Brett announced as if it were something of a joke.

Cooper stepped forward to shake the man's hand, for he was

indeed a man: if not as old as Brett had intimated, Martin was certainly well into his twenties.

"Welcome aboard, Mr Martin. I'm Cooper, second lieutenant. You are to join us for our sea trials I understand."

"Indeed, sir," Martin confirmed.

"And your history?"

"I have been serving at the Castle on Sir David Baird's staff."

"But the call of the sea were too strong?" Cooper guessed before adding, "I assume you have served at sea afore?"

"Oh yes, sir, I were aboard *Athena,* under Captain Granger when I opted for transfer ashore."

Cooper nodded; he too had been unlucky in promotion and had spent far too long in the midshipmen's berth before eventually reaching his current rank. After being passed over aboard ship, Martin could hardly be blamed for assuming service with the Governor's office would be a possible route to a lieutenant's commission although the fact that he stood before him now was proof of his mistake.

"Well you are welcome aboard, though the work will be more taxing than clerical duties."

"I am aware of that, sir," Martin grinned and Cooper noticed his clear eyes seemed unusually attentive. "To be honest, I were getting a mite stale in Cape Town."

"So this transfer is at your request?"

"Oh yes, sir."

"And why *Mistral?*"

"I heard she were a lucky ship and frankly could do with some good fortune."

"I see." For a moment Cooper held the midshipman's gaze. There was so much he wanted to ask the fellow, the foremost being quite what quirk of fate had kept him in the cockpit when most capable officers would have been commissioned years before. It was not impossible that this Martin would turn out a fool, in which case it would be discovered soon enough, but what concerned him more was he might be a fool who had learned to disguise the fact, which was a far more dangerous prospect.

And then there was his dress. Midshipmen were not known for their immaculate appearance. A few, like Brett, with a private income might be reasonably smart much of the time though the vast majority erred to the borders of shabbiness. But Martin had gone beyond that; his tunic, though clean, was patched and faded while flesh showed through the worn fabric of his shirt. There may be reasons for this apparent slovenliness and, for all Cooper knew, fresh uniform may lie concealed inside the battered sea chest, although it was also possible the chap had an addiction to any number of vices. If so he would have reason enough to be on short commons. But this was hardly the time to enquire further as Brett was close by and clearly listening.

"Well, I am sure you won't be bored while with us, Mr Martin," Cooper told him. "Do your duty well and a permanent position surely awaits. You'll find us a happy ship as well as lucky, ain't that the case, Mr Brett?"

"Oh, indeed it is, sir," Brett agreed. "And the midshipmen's berth especially so."

* * *

The rain stopped during the night and the sky began to clear but when dawn finally broke on their third morning the mood aboard the jolly boat was at its lowest. They had now spent so long crowded into the tiny craft that all were suffering from cramp and chronic stiffness while, even though it had ceased to pour and there was no longer the need to bail, their clothes and bodies remained thoroughly sodden; a condition no bloodless sun could address before nightfall. But though they remained hungry and Scott was now having to consider rationing their two breakers of fresh water, there had also been good news.

For just as the sun started to show, the topmasts of another vessel had been spotted. It was on the horizon – another thing seen for the first time since boarding the boat – but few hopes were raised. All were seamen and knew the chances of being spotted at such a distance were negligible and the vision came and went in almost the same hour. But the sighting gave them hope; no one had seriously considered themselves alone on the ocean but there had been tangible proof of at least some company. Besides, if the mystery vessel – warship or merchant, friend or enemy: they cared not which – had missed them it might have found the launch and could be providing their former shipmates with all that they so desperately missed themselves. Things such as food, warmth, shelter, fresh clothes and the chance to properly stretch or simply perform the usual bodily functions beyond the gaze and comment of others.

"I'm sending out hard tack," Scott announced when the sun was fully up and he reached for one of the cases stored beneath the thwart shared with King. "It'll be half, as before," he added. "Which means we have enough for a while longer."

"Beggin' y'r pardon, sir, but couldn't we 'ave an 'ole one this time?"

This was from one of the topmen, a slender lad of less than twenty and usually as loyal as they came. Scott considered the biscuit he had been about to break. It could not weigh more than five ounces and originally two had been issued to every man twice a day. But that was when the prospect of rescue seemed far more realistic. Hard tack remained their only source of nutrient and there was little alternative but to ration it as a small amount of food over a longer period must surely be better than feast followed by famine. Without the prospect of something to chew on, the men could grow truly restless and then the trouble might really start.

"Half for now," he temporised. "I'll consider more at the next meal."

Partially placated, the men distributed the food with only a minor squabble when one refused to pass another's share. Scott carefully brushed the crumbs from his lap over the open case before closing and setting it back beneath his feet. King watched in concern. It was the second case and he had caught a glimpse inside; the thing had been barely half full.

But despite his personal needs, King's mind continued to stray to Aimée and how she might be faring. Since their separation so much might have happened; another ship – one of the raiders or even a passing merchant – may have collected them. Or they could have foundered in the storm; with that much rain and a cargo of wounded, the launch might so easily have flooded and now be several fathoms under. He closed his mind, and eyes, to the thought so it came as a double shock when a tired voice suddenly let out a husky shriek.

"There's another, and dead ahead!"

Glare from the sun blinded King for a moment, but the vessel in question was actually far closer than the previous sighting. Less than a mile off, in fact, and it was probably a measure of their state that all aboard the jolly boat had allowed it to approach so near without detection.

A schooner; two masts and obviously fast – with the wind just abaft her beam she was making good progress. And, more importantly, she was steering almost directly for them and must pass within half a cable.

"What think you?" King asked. "American?"

"She has the look of a Baltimore," Scott agreed, "though I could hardly care less were she French." He paused and his salt-caked face cracked into a rare grin as he looked King in the eye. "And I think we might offer another round of biscuit."

Chapter Seven

"The fact is, Mr Croft, we had expected the convoy carrying Captain King to be here long before now," Commodore Banks told him bluntly. "There has been no news and no sighting reported since the monthly packet spoke with them; at that point they were less than seven hundred miles off so are now considerably overdue. Consequently, we have to assume they have run into trouble."

"I understand, sir," Croft replied stiffly. He rarely felt comfortable in the presence of gold lace and the current interview contained not only Commodore Sir Richard Banks but Matterson, a senior post captain. The latter was the fool who had charge of the dockyard and someone he had fallen foul of often during *Mistral*'s refit.

"You have done an excellent job in seeing your ship through her repairs," Banks continued. "And I am sure Captain King would have been delighted with the result." The use of the past tense sounded a note of doom that none in the flagship's great cabin could have missed. "But, as she is now in most senses ready for sea, we have to make use of her."

Croft rocked back in his seat; during the months of supervising *Mistral*'s rebuild, the possibility of her captain not returning had never occurred to him. It was only when King failed to appear in the past few weeks that his concern began to grow.

"Therefore I am handing the ship over to Captain Matterson who will be taking her in hand, at least until more definite news is received of Captain King." Banks indicated the older and slightly portly body next to him.

Croft's eyes switched to Matterson; in his position as commissioner of Cape Town's dockyard, the man had been a major obstacle during *Mistral*'s refit. Government stock had been doled out as if it were his own property, in fact Croft often suspected he had an actual interest in the goods. Of Matterson's seamanship or ability to command he knew nothing, yet the plump and balding officer was not the archetypal frigate captain.

Mistral remained a valuable ship however, and one which could not be allowed to stand idle. And with a lack of suitable senior captains on hand, he supposed the appointment was more or less inevitable. Yet still he could not credit Captain King's replacement with the verve necessary to carry a thirty-six gun frigate into action, let alone lead and inspire her crew.

He was also vaguely surprised the man should wish for such a posting when he seemed to have landed his perfect job as dockyard commissioner. The work was minimal and, whenever a deficiency in quality or quantity of supplies forced Croft to pay a call, he had found him to have dined well. Such an indolent existence might not appeal to everyone, but it clearly suited Captain Matterson.

Then again, this return to command may equally have been forced upon him although that mattered little for, whatever the reason, Croft sensed he would be a hard man to serve under and probably require a good deal of subtle coaching.

Captain King had been a very different prospect; after a series of poor commanders, Croft had welcomed his mature and capable approach like a cool breeze in the doldrums. In addition to having all the attributes of a born seaman, King was a natural leader; one with an innate feeling for his men as well as the ship he commanded. Before his arrival, Croft had been considering retirement and the prospect of once more having to support an officer he could not respect was awakening many old feelings.

"Doubtless you will wish to show Captain Matterson about *Mistral*," the Commodore supposed with what might have been forced bonhomie. "I might say that Captain King always spoke highly of his first officer," he added turning to Matterson.

"You will pardon me if I make my own mind up about that, Sir Richard," Matterson replied in that well-remembered nasal whine while eyeing Croft with the same dispassion a slaughterman might give a cow. "He caused me such problems in the past; nothing the government provided was ever good enough."

"Of course, I was aware of Mr Croft's observations," Banks conceded with slightly less good humour. "Though in truth felt the majority to be valid. Not that you were at fault, Captain," he added quickly. "The Dear knows we are mightily stretched as far as materials are concerned. But then neither should an executive officer be criticized for wanting the best for his ship."

There was a pause while Matterson digested this, then Banks began again.

"Besides," he added more gently, "as *Mistral* is to be yours, I trust you are now grateful for Mr Croft's efforts, while his performance in bringing her up to such a splendid state of readiness would seem to confirm Tom King's good opinion of him."

"Thank you, sir," Croft murmured. They were indeed kind words and from a man not known for such things. But then he reminded himself that Commodore Banks and Captain King had been good friends, which probably accounted for much.

"Be that as it may, he shall have to mend his ways if he wishes to progress under my command," Matterson snorted. "Tell me, Sir Richard, when I am confirmed as *Mistral*'s permanent captain, will I be allowed some say in the choice of my executive officer?"

"I see no need for that," Banks had now abandoned all trace of civility. "Mr Croft is an excellent officer and shall remain your first lieutenant for as long as he chooses. Frankly, sir, I consider it harsh that you should view his previous concern for the ship in such a negative light."

"Oh no, not at all." Matterson was unrepentant. "It is simply that I feel a vessel of *Mistral*'s undoubted qualities will require a slightly younger man as second in command."

* * *

Mr Midshipman Martin had not been entirely honest. Though straightforward in most matters there was one which inevitably forced him off the narrow path. This was partly associated with his career and partly his health; both subjects Martin took extremely seriously and was equally sensitive about. So, although the brief history related to Lieutenant Cooper was broadly accurate, it had omitted a few important details. For a start the reason he had left *Athena*, along with his other seagoing appointments.

Martin had been unlucky in many ways, but did regard himself fortunate in one; so far his health problems had been kept more or less to himself. The incidents that plagued him were infrequent and commonly associated with a life at sea. And they had mainly occurred in private or amongst friends who, along with those he was obliged to advise, had generally been sympathetic and encouraging.

And he knew himself to be an otherwise reliable officer, one with an instinctive feel for seamanship, a good head for figures and the all-important ability to command respect from the men. Accordingly, a good deal of leniency could be allowed for what was truly an occasional problem and one the Navy usually coped with quite well. But however infrequent the episodes, they did not stick to the usual rules so could not be ignored entirely while, for as long as they continued, Martin knew he could never sit an examination board or walk a quarterdeck in any other capacity than as a junior warrant officer.

For what Martin suffered from was very different from simple seasickness. To begin with, the condition did not necessarily present when leaving harbour or with a change in weather and, as he had recently discovered, was equally likely to occur on land.

The exact nature of the ailment remained a mystery both to him and the various medical men he had consulted. One moment he could be well and active, then a slight hint of giddiness, usually accompanied by a heavy feeling in the ears and strangely enhanced hearing, would signal the start of another attack. He then had an hour at most before all sense of balance and dignity were lost and he was reduced to a miserable wretch left clinging pathetically to the deck while the world steadily rotated about him.

Such a condition was so closely associated with the effects of drink or bad weather that it could be tolerated in a world where both were common, although he still became the target of japes from some shipmates. And when the attacks continued long into a voyage they became especially tiresome, robbing Martin of both confidence and self-respect as well as blighting all chances of promotion.

And so he had taken to changing ships on a regular basis in the hope that the motion of one would prove more agreeable. But when no difference was noticeable, Martin had finally opted for shore duties, and it was then that the problem was fully revealed.

During the six months he had lived on solid ground, Martin experienced three further episodes which were disconcerting in themselves, but he was also quick to discover that an ailment tolerated on the ocean was viewed very differently ashore. He remembered lying prone on the floor of the Castle's clerical office and digging his fingers into the very boards in an effort to regain stability while a circle of faces stared down in wonder and disgust.

A normal attack lasted roughly an hour and, after passing through the various stages of dizziness, nausea and vomiting, finally resolved itself in deep sleep, following which normal life could be resumed. But each left him more disconcerted, a little less confident and increasingly unpopular with his colleagues. The medics he consulted were equally baffled and inclined to attribute his condition to more recognised ailments, so Martin was treated for everything from sunstroke to falling sickness. Most cures proved ineffectual although one particular patent medicine did seem to make some difference. After discovering *Dr Simmond's Elixir* the attacks still occurred but appeared less intense while Martin was also becoming more expert in predicting their arrival. And so, armed with a considerable supply of the amber bottles, he had decided not to continue suffering where such things were regarded with alarm and caution, but return to the element he loved, and volunteered for *Mistral*.

The frigate was starting her sea trials; a period when she would be put through her paces following refit. Small defects were anticipated and Martin knew he might be one. An episode at the start of the voyage was likely to be excused but, should his disorder return in too great a frequency, he must expect to be unceremoniously removed when they returned to harbour. But if not, if he were able to avoid or disguise any major attacks or if, incredibly, they decided not to reoccur, he would be taken on strength and could resume what had once been a promising career.

And that was all Martin wanted. The past few months on land had taught him the difference between fighting a war with reports and despatches as opposed to physical effort. Whatever damage he could do the enemy with pen and paper must surely be outweighed by *Mistral*'s magnificent cannon while land-bound officers with their pale faces and tailored uniforms seemed particularly insipid when compared to the rugged, practical men he was once more serving alongside.

The return to shipboard life had also increased his confidence and he secretly hoped that, assisted by *Dr Simmond's Elixir*, he might see a place on the next lieutenants' board. Ten years of being confined in the midshipmen's berth had given him the knowledge and experience to almost guarantee success and, even though she lay moored to a quay and still lacked a permanent captain, *Mistral* remained a crack frigate. And one he immediately felt at home aboard, if only his health would hold out long enough for him to stay and hopefully prosper.

* * *

"Well there it is," Adams told her sadly. "With no news of Captain King and some jumped-up dockyard matey appointed in his stead, we've been sold up the river."

The boarding house room was dark and cramped yet there remained sufficient light for him to realise the woman was regarding him with total incomprehension. Though technically an American, Anne Callahan had been born in the low countries and, despite her English being excellent, it still fell short of the young lieutenant's more obscure colloquialisms.

"I mean I cannot have you on board," Adams explained. "The new man is causing no end of trouble for Croft and Cooper, and is definitely not the type to sanction a woman's presence – unless, of course, she were to share his quarters..."

"I see," Anne replied softly. "Then there is nothing I can do; I must simply face my creditors."

The possibility of her sailing in *Mistral* had been their last hope. When Anne's husband died and the full extent of his financial affairs was discovered, her being taken aboard a government warship seemed the ideal solution and should have seen off most of those eager to call in their stakes. But now there appeared little to prevent her being seized and, as the shipping season progressed, it must only be a question of time before the first bailiff arrived.

"I am so sorry," Adams declared. "If there were anything I could do I certainly would." He said the words with a hint of guilt; his share of the spoils from *Mistral*'s recent victories had left him moderately well off but the sum would hardly cover a third of what Anne owed. And while he was willing in principle to give all he had, there seemed little point when doing so would not solve the problem.

"I know, John," she agreed easing slightly. "And am sorry if I spoke harshly; it is simply not a situation I expected."

"You are certain it would not help were we to wed?" he asked.

"Rather it would make matters worse, besides being a terrible start to our married life."

"Are you sure of that?" he insisted. "For I would marry you tomorrow."

"And I you," she assured. "But it seems my late husband's debts would then only fall upon yourself."

The realisation that he might truly be sharing her predicament hit Adams hard and he struggled for a suitable reply. But fortunately a tap at the door came to his rescue and, after a call from Anne, Greta, the boarding house owners' daughter, entered.

"There is a gentleman to see you madam," she announced.

"Fellow by the name of Fallon, says he has business with your late husband's estate."

Anne looked at Adams in horror.

"I think we must assume him to be a catchpole," the young man muttered.

"A catchpole?"

"Some bully sent to collect a debt," Adams explained before turning to the girl. "Greta, Mrs Callahan has some financial problems but they need not be of your concern; I will meet any account she has with your father."

"Oh, indeed, sir," the youngster agreed. "Room's paid for until the end of the month as it is, an' we know you'll be right for it afterwards." The young widow had been late in meeting her rent in the past and advance payment was one of the conditions insisted upon before being taken back as a guest. "In any case, I know well what a catchpole might be and have no time for the devils."

"Then tell this Mr Fallon Mrs Callahan is not here," Adams directed. "If you will, say she has gone and you know not where, though I will leave that to your nature. But do not send him up here I implore you."

"Very good, sir," the girl agreed. "I'll do what I can though his ain't the sort to be put off."

When she had gone Anne rested her face in her hands. "Oh, why did David have to do this?" she mumbled through her fingers. "All that work to raise his business, only to be wasted on foolish plans that came to naught and were always bound to."

"I cannot say, though we must address matters as they are," Adams declared in an effort to appear in control. "If that truly is the first bailiff there will be others following. I shall simply have to pay him what you owe."

"And encourage the others?" she exclaimed. "Once they scent money the rest will be down on us like a pack of hyenas."

"Then you shall have to go into hiding," Adams suggested, carefully hiding the relief in his voice.

"But for how long?" she asked, looking up. "And where? Cape Town is not so large and soon you will be gone. I shall be totally alone – is there nothing we can do?"

*   *   *

Some things had not altered during Midshipman Martin's time ashore; the junior warrant officer's mess aboard *Mistral* differed little to that in *Athena*, or any other warship he had served aboard. There was even the same distinctive smell, one that lacked no single source and was at once both comforting and repugnant. The occupants were much the same as well. Summers, though by no means the eldest, was senior due to his length of service aboard ship – Martin could see him as a lieutenant as soon as a board came his way – while the others were the usual selection of youngsters whose abilities varied as much as their attitudes and backgrounds.

One was a former hand, Sennett, an amiable lad who had been promoted from the lower deck a year or so earlier and now also seemed destined for greater things. Others were the sons of sea officers and equally bound to make the Navy their career although the rest were not so likely. Most may have chosen the life as an alternative to the church or land forces and would probably have been equally happy in either. But there had been no talk of anyone else having to serve a trial period; instead all seemed confident of their place which, Martin supposed, was hardly surprising. Young men, many still in adolescence and eager to progress, were a very different proposition to someone of his great age who had apparently stagnated.

But that would change, he was strangely certain. Despite having to adjust to the new conditions, his health had stayed strong and he was starting to enjoy being part of a ship once more. And it was really where he belonged; from the earliest of days, Martin had felt an affinity with the sea and wanted nothing more than to make it his world, especially as he soon proved to be a natural seaman. In fact, everything had been in line for him to make a quick progression to commissioned rank, until his personal devil appeared to disrupt matters.

And that was another thing which would alter. Armed with a new found confidence as well as six bottles of patent medicine, Martin felt able to take on the challenge of establishing himself as one of *Mistral*'s midshipmen. In truth he was positively determined to settle and progress; it was just a pity that other members of his mess were proving so annoying.

It had begun with the allocation of hammock space; officially the ship remained in the hands of the dockyard and some men had been sleeping ashore. As the berth slowly filled, Martin found his place moved more than once as long-term members of the mess resumed their previous positions. This hardly mattered although the practice continued after the berth was full and was now starting to irritate.

And there were further equally petty annoyances; one day he opened his sea chest to find it filled with straw from the ship's manger, while his own personal cutlery regularly went missing, to be discovered later inside a lanthorn or some other unlikely hidey-hole. Brett's initial description of Martin as a malkin also had taken root, and he was regularly referred to as such by all. Nicknames were very much a part of cockpit life and such trivialities must not be given too much importance, even if it was especially galling as the name also belonged to the berth's cat. But age, experience and the objectivity that was one of the better side-effects of his particular condition had taught Martin patience; things would doubtless improve when the captain came on board and they could finally put to sea. Once general routines were established there would be little time for petty japes and they could all get back to managing a ship of war. At least that's what he hoped.

* * *

"I'll do it," Anne declared. Adams regarded her with a mixture of surprise and admiration while Greta, who had returned with the suggestion, merely looked smug.

"Are you sure?" he questioned. "I mean..."

"I am certain beyond doubt," she confirmed, rising. "We need only fix time and place; why I wish someone had suggested this before, it will cost very little and should see the end to all our problems."

"I can give you the address of a suitable church an' all," Greta announced proudly. "Father Coleson has been known to be helpful in the past."

"But Anne, do you really want..." Adams tried again.

"What I want to do and what I must need not be the same. You said yourself, you wished you could help me and so far that is what you have done while I have contributed little. What money I had is spent and, though I know you would meet them if you could, my debts are well beyond the means of a Navy lieutenant. Besides, it is my problem and now I have found a way by which I might solve it. And I shall; if you are still willing and agree to take me in marriage, then all will be set."

"Oh, I am willing." Adams nodded as his mind began to race. "In truth there is nothing I should like more. Though perhaps not in such a way..."

* * *

Nathan Daniels had recently changed a lifelong perception. And it had been a reasonably long seafaring life, one that started on the cod banks off New England and continued through a series of fishing and trading vessels until he found himself, as if by accident, master and owner of a hack trader. Throughout this turbulent period, one that had seen kings deposed, countries invaded and alliances made and broken, the British Navy had been a constant and annoying presence and the aggravation had increased of late. Barely weeks into his current voyage, one of King George's impertinent little frigates, a ship commanded by a prim and equally priggish sop of a captain, had seen fit to seize his vessel in open waters and relieve him of five men. And if that wasn't enough, one was his mate; someone Daniels had sailed with for several years and a far better navigator than he would ever be.

The *Nancy Jane* had been released but with a crew substantially reduced so, when they first sighted the overcrowded jolly boat adrift and discovered the occupants to be British, Daniels had thought twice about stopping. To take on so many of what were at best belligerent neutrals was a risk many would have refused and, had there been another officer with which to discuss the situation, Daniels might have been persuaded to leave them to their fate. But he was not a heartless man, which was the main reason why he ignored a far more lucrative trade in human flesh further north, and the sight of fellow mariners in peril finally overcame his doubts. Then, when they drew close and discovered that, rather than men-of-war, the majority of the small craft's occupants were traders such as himself, he knew his trust had been well placed.

And strangely it was that single exception, a one-armed Navy captain and the only fighting man amongst them, who had changed his mind about the British. Though initially wary of each other, the two soon became friends to the extent that Daniels even diverted from his schedule. The *Nancy Jane* had brought fish from New England to the Canaries and was heading in the general direction of Whale Bay where she was due to deposit a mixed cargo of clothing, medical supplies and rum to the traders stationed there. But with his level of navigational skills, the loss of a day or two was quite usual and, appeased by King's story, the five rescued seamen who volunteered to make up his numbers, and some assistance in setting a course, Daniels agreed to a brief search for the missing launch.

They spent six days on the exercise which was only abandoned when two French corvettes appeared on the horizon. Daniels had scant reason to fear Napoleon's Navy but was disinclined to make close acquaintance with warships of any nationality and the schooner's bows were finally set for his next port of call.

The *Nancy Jane* then lay for a spell in the huge natural harbour of Whale Bay and would normally be waiting still as no immediate cargo had been forthcoming. But partly due to his passengers' presence and partly his own good nature, Daniels decided to try his luck further south at Cape Town and so took the relatively empty craft there.

And now, as the grey bulk of Table Mountain lay in plain view, he supposed that particular part of the voyage was coming to an end. He would be saying goodbye to both the Navy captain and the younger HEIC officer who accompanied him. It would mean more space in the sloop's cramped aft accommodation but he would miss their companionship and conversation as well as the confidence which sailing with two more competent navigators gave him.

"I trust you will find luck here, Tom," Daniels said as he approached the two Englishmen on the sloop's small quarterdeck.

"I trust we all shall," King replied smiling. "Though I can see no sign of India ships at anchor."

"News may yet have been received of your woman," Daniels suggested.

"Aye, Nat, it may," King agreed philosophically. "And if not, I shall always be obliged to you."

Daniels shrugged. "I were glad of the company," he admitted. Then, turning to the younger man, "And I still cannot persuade you to join me in my venture?" he asked. "Quarter share in all profits, a modicum of cargo space and your meals provided. And I don't stick to no set trading routes but take what's coming at whatever port I finds myself. If there is nothing at The Cape I've a mind to head further east and see what may be there. They are waters I have yet to sail and someone who can point a sextant would be mighty welcome."

Scott smiled. "No, Captain; if there's a chance John Company has a place for me I'd be wise not to turn it down."

Daniels' eyes flicked over to King, who grinned openly.

"And I am also committed, Nat," he laughed, "with a command

of my own to take up."

"Ah yes, a frigate, as I recall." Daniels sighed. "And doubtless a deal larger than the *Nancy Jane*."

"Indeed," King agreed easily. "Though you have a sound ship and one I shall keep an eye out for on my travels. Especially if I find myself running short of hands."

* * *

Mistral had yet to put to sea but Martin was already hard at work. Almost as soon as he woke in whichever part of the cockpit had been allocated, he found himself fully occupied and the demands did not cease until lights out, when he finally returned to his hammock's firm embrace. And he was not alone; every other young gentleman – a term Martin privately held still applied to him – was similarly swamped under a myriad of menial tasks. For there was simply so much to do and the more mundane jobs inevitably fell to the most junior of the quarterdeck officers.

First they had to assist the purser. The ship had yet to take on her deep-sea victuals but preparations for their arrival had to be made, and those hands already aboard must be fed so a daily supply of petty warrant provisions was required. These must be seen in, listed, taken aboard and properly stowed; then, when the cook and his mates had had their fun, a note made of what had been used and fresh supplies ordered for the following day. With the steady increase in mouths to feed, the task had grown proportionally until it was almost a full-time occupation in itself.

But a growing crew meant there was no such luxury as exclusive jobs. Every day a fresh batch of men appeared which had to be divided into divisions and, although each had an overall lieutenant responsible for their care, the actual task of seeing to the men's needs fell to the midshipmen.

Some of the new intake were old hands who were used to their former messes and resented having them supplemented with the fresh faces needed to augment *Mistral*'s lower deck. And many of the latter had come from the merchant service so knew little, if anything, of sailing a warship. There were inevitable disputes that led to complaints and, in some cases, physical violence; something the midshipmen were expected to quell and an instance where Martin's age and experience became a distinct advantage. But to make matters worse, the ship was still in the final throes of her refit; entire sections of deck might suddenly be cordoned off to allow for caulking or the interminable wait while marine paint chose to dry. And it was always easier to instruct a midshipman to chase up wayward consignments of slop clothing or rosin than trouble a mighty lieutenant.

However, the volume of work at least meant he had not been worrying about health issues; with so much to occupy him, Martin could truly immerse himself in his duties while there had also been less opportunity for adolescent chiding from the others. He was still referred to as Malkin but, so used had all become to the term, it had long ceased to carry weight. Besides, even the better-off youngsters were unable to appear immaculate at all times. Some continued to taunt but they quickly became the minority as he did have one small advantage over them all.

Having served so long as a junior warrant officer, Martin had already learned most of the duties a midshipman would be called on to perform. This soon became obvious and some of the younger lads were now regarding him more as a sea daddy. And not just content with dealing out information, Martin was also increasing his own knowledge; whenever the purser mentioned a novel way of assessing cheese or the boatswain demonstrated some new and exotic hitch, he was the first to take note.

He was also determined to improve his navigational skills. *Mistral* still lacked a sailing master but even when one had been appointed, regular classes in the science would not start until the ship was at sea. But, once they did, Martin was ready to make up for time wasted ashore.

All that was in the future, however, for the present he had enough to do keeping up with current demands while trusting the condition that had trapped him in the cockpit would not return. Then, when the work finally died down, continue trying to get on with the lads who shared his mess.

Some, like Summers and Sennett, were sound enough and those there on sufferance could mainly be tolerated. But others, the sons of rich officers like Brett, were another matter. They were obviously bound for better places and regarded their current position as a temporary annoyance. In time – probably before Summers or Sennett – they would achieve commissioned rank along with an easier life and, until then, intended to enliven their present situation in whatever way they could, so still found time for a little subtle teasing.

And Martin was such a splendid target; older than all yet obviously a failure when it came to promotion, while his need for expensive medical consultations and treatment had made him by far the shabbiest. But the taunts of young men could do little actual harm and were something Martin was prepared to tolerate. For the worst they could dole out in ridicule was nothing to what he must expect were they to discover the true reason for his lack of funds and position.

* * *

"Married?" Summers questioned, although the smile was already starting to spread across his face. "But that's splendid, John, truly splendid!"

"I am indeed very happy," Adams confirmed soberly. "As you know, we have had an agreement for some while but think it now time to do the deed."

Adams had summoned his friend to the otherwise empty gunroom on the pretence of work but lost no time in delivering his news.

"Splendid," Summers repeated yet again with a grin.

"It is all I could want, all I could ask for, and Anne is definitely willing."

"And why ever should she not be?"

He shrugged, "I am a mere lieutenant."

"And I a mere midshipman," Summers sniffed, "but that is just rank; it don't mean a thing really."

Adams considered this for a moment; there were times when Summers came out with the most amazing statements and this one definitely needed explanation. But the lad had more to say.

"It is clear you care for her better than that fool she married the first time."

At the mention of Anne's late husband Adams winced. "He were a man of business," he protested.

"And what a business it turned out to be! Left her with a half-baked scheme that were doomed to fail and nothing but a mountain of debt to fund it. You would never do such a thing I am certain, so tell me which is the better man?"

"You may be right," Adams conceded. "And she is willing to take a chance on me."

"Then why the Friday face?"

"There are complications," he explained. "It won't be the regular service most expect."

"And what of it? Sailors are a tolerant bunch and will chance a Papist ceremony if that be the issue. Or any other, providing there be scran and fuddle after. With *Mistral* yet to commission you can be sure of a fine crowd!"

"No!" Adams shook his head emphatically. "It will not be a public event – not in any way. No one must know – no one. That is vital!"

"No one to know?" Summers' expression froze. "You are to be spliced yet wish it to remain a secret?"

"Very much so."

The lad shook his head in disbelief. "If funding's your problem, I'm sure that can be accommodated, though I had thought you well set after our prize court pay-out. And all will be sorry to miss such an event."

"Well they shall have to," Adams insisted. "No one is coming, no one at all. Just the parson and the minimum number the law requires." He paused and considered his friend. "Not even you, and I shall hear your promise that this will not be mentioned elsewhere."

"Not me?" Summers' eyes fell further. "Well, if that is your choice, John, I shall honour it to be sure. Though I..."

"It is complicated," Adams insisted, his face reddening, "as I did already state. You of all people know of Anne's finances; she is deeply in debt and in danger of losing her liberty."

"So I gather," Summers agreed. "And you fear a marriage will see these debts inflicted upon yourself?"

"It is the law," Adams had adopted his lofty tone. "Were she to be wealthy, her money would become mine and the same applies to liabilities."

"Then I do understand, though fail to see how keeping your marriage secret will help."

"The marriage need not be secret, just the ceremony," Adams explained. "You see there's a way Anne can be wed and leave all she owes behind."

"There is?"

"It has been practised for many years," Adams continued.

"Though not common law, the English courts respect such a procedure and it is now our only option. Anne must come to be wed without possessions; only then may I take her for my wife without debt."

"Totally without possessions?" the lad repeated doubtfully. "You mean..."

His friend nodded once more. "There can be no doubt," he confirmed. "It must be manifestly plain that she is without assets."

Summers' eyes grew round. "Oh, Lordy!" he said.

Chapter Eight

The return of Captain King came just as Croft was about to resign his commission. *Mistral* had yet to put to sea and was only partly laden when he first fell foul of Captain Matterson and the confrontations increased with each meeting. The man obviously bore a grudge and, despite the ship being better for Croft's care, seemed determined to argue with and humiliate his second in command at every opportunity.

And the opportunities came readily enough. With the crew being taken aboard, Croft had station bills and watch lists to compile, something that should be done with an eye to avoiding potential problems of men not happy with berthing or messing arrangements, while the boatswain, sailmaker and purser were constantly complaining about the general lack of supplies. Cooper and Adams, the divisional lieutenants, had been invaluable on the first point and Croft had foolishly assumed Captain Matterson, with his undoubted contacts ashore, would assist with the latter, but it was not to be. For, other than taking an hour or two each morning to pick holes in his officers' work, their new commander spent much of his time in the great cabin where an almost constant feast was in progress. This was attended by a stream of Matterson's acquaintances; well-dressed gentlemen and their ladies who would stroll about the decks at will, then leave some hours later in a dishevelled state and often with different partners.

Such goings on could not be concealed from the crew who, still raw from the denial of their wedding garland, grew steadily more surly, while with no final sailing date in sight even some junior officers started to show similar tendencies.

The last straw came when *Mistral* was almost ready to begin proper victualling. A date was set for them to receive their deep-sea provisions and appropriate preparations made aboard ship, when the victualling yard manager suffered a sudden change of heart. The man, who had been a regular attender at Matterson's soirées, left early and without his partner the afternoon before work was to begin and that evening a terse note was delivered. Apparently there had been an oversight: another ship had priority. They must wait a week at least before the first wagon would be drawing up on the quay, and Croft was in despair.

But if there were to be a delay, he decided to take advantage of it and instigated a regime of exercise for the crew. This would begin with topman drill aloft and continue through every department until all were in a better state of readiness. Accordingly, topmasts had been set up the night before but, as he emerged on the main deck the following morning, Croft was amazed to see a boatswain's party in the midst of blacking the yards. It was a procedure normally only carried out when a ship was expected to remain in harbour for some time and even then reserved for the eve of an important inspection. For a moment Croft stared in disbelief while his precious spars gleamed with a mixture of coal and vegetable tar that would take an age to dry. Then he turned to the boatswain.

"What's about there, Jennings?" he demanded.

"It were the captain, sir," the warrant officer replied sadly. "He came up firs' thing an' tore me off; said our tophamper were a disgrace."

"I see," Croft remarked crisply.

"Also said for the scuppers to be painted this af'noon," Jennings added. "So there'll be no gun drill neither. Nothing I could do, sir, as I say, captain's orders."

Croft closed his eyes. How often had that explanation been given and how often had it signalled another instance of Matterson's bloody-mindedness? All might be minor matters but together they combined to create a problem he was simply unable to confront. He told himself he was being foolish, that it was nothing more than an old man's reluctance to turn his precious ship over to a new owner, but inwardly knew different. Then, as his anger mounted, he made his way to the quarterdeck.

Matterson was there when he arrived. It was early, the first of that day's guests had yet to appear and the man was waiting by the binnacle in glorious full dress, to all intents the perfect ship's captain. Croft eyed him cautiously; was there something in his stance that announced him ready for confrontation? Or, worse, might he even be looking forward to it?

"Your pardon, sir," Croft gasped: his breath was coming with difficulty although this had nothing to do with the short journey from the waist. "You will remember we were to exercise the hands aloft this morning."

"Indeed, Mr Croft?" Matterson replied with apparent concern. "I have no recollection."

"But you agreed yesterday even', sir, after we heard there was to be no victualling. We spoke at the end of the second dog."

"And today I have decided otherwise," Matterson countered smugly. "You may have charge of the ship, Mr Croft, but you do not command her and I shall thank you not to question my orders in such a public manner. Now, if you will excuse me, I am awaiting important visitors."

To have been confronted with yet another needless irritation proved too much and Croft found himself retreating to the relative privacy of the taffrail to settle his thoughts. He knew Matterson was provoking him and had long since decided the man must have a favoured officer in mind as a replacement once he was persuaded to resign. Until that point the thought had actually served as an encouragement to remain but now, with his true captain unlikely to return and nothing but further frustration to look forward to, Croft decided enough was enough. And it was then that his eyes inadvertently swept the nearby quay and a very different officer caught his attention.

At first he thought it just another of Matterson's cronies, then an illusion – a trick of the light brought about by wishful thinking. But as he continued to stare, Croft knew there could be no mistaking and Captain King was indeed striding purposefully along the hard. Watching him, the elderly lieutenant felt such a surge of relief that he almost shouted out loud. Then years of self-control took charge and he was able to channel his emotions into nothing more than a dignified chuckle.

* * *

"It's the captain!" The roar came from a voice less inhibited further forward and, as if waiting for such a signal, all on deck immediately responded. Jennings, the boatswain, leapt onto the larboard gangway and let out a loud whoop that was hardly appropriate to the dignity of his station, while his team in the yards followed the lead with loud cheers that echoed about the stunned quayside.

Moving from his position aft, Croft returned to the binnacle just as the master's mate who had the anchor watch approached Captain Matterson with ill-concealed glee.

"Captain King 'as been sighted on the wharf, sir," the warrant officer reported.

"So I understand," Matterson replied coldly, then his eyes found Croft's and this time there was no hint of cunning. "Were you aware of this?" he demanded, the smug smile also absent.

"I was not." Croft's tone betrayed no emotion although few could mistake the look of triumph that even he could not conceal.

"Well, I shall allow him aboard," Matterson announced grudgingly, "though no more. *Mistral* is my ship now; I did not choose to become her captain but have come to find the position very much to my liking. And it is one I have no intention of giving up."

* * *

Despite the exercises planned for that day, Adams was not required until the afternoon's great gun drill and Croft had reluctantly granted him four hours' leave. So there was time enough to make arrangements and, holding Anne firmly by one hand and with a scrap of paper in the other, he led her down the narrow streets of an unfamiliar part of Cape Town. The quarter was poorly kept with none of the wide, smooth pavements or welcoming shops of more salubrious areas. Instead, a number of houses had been turned into makeshift stores by the removal of their front windows while several thin, nervous dogs scampered away as Adams' boots made sparks on the rough stone walkways. He glanced again at the address Greta had scribbled out and looked about in desperation.

"This cannot be right," he panted. "The girl must have made a mistake."

"It has to be," Anne insisted. "She was so certain and has not let us down so far; we must at least go on to the very end."

Moving off, they passed yet another line of run-down houses and were forced to turn a corner before their goal suddenly came into view.

It was a small church and matched the area perfectly in its squalor. Years of neglect had allowed the white clapperboard to grow weary and grey, the roof was more moss than slate and several panes set next to the crooked front door were yellowed and cracked. But Adams' knock was answered immediately and he knew at once the elderly man who greeted them was Father Coleson.

"So it is to be a wedding," the cleric remarked after they had been led to a small curtained alcove set beside an equally miniature altar. The church itself could hardly have held more than seventy and the pair had struggled to walk side by side up its narrow aisle. As they squeezed past the pews it seemed impossible that soon they would be making the return journey as a married couple. But once safely installed in what Father

Coleson referred to as his vestry, the prospect did seem more likely. Neither wished for a large congregation after all – anything but. As far as both were concerned, the fewer that attended the better. Father Coleson indicated a couple of frail wooden chairs and, seating himself behind what looked like a child's desk, regarded them both with a benign expression. "And Miss Greta did say there was some urgency..."

"We cannot delay," Adams confirmed. "This week if possible, or might you even do it now?"

"Now?" the soft brown eyes registered mild concern. "My son, I can do nothing today; indeed, most marriages take a month at least to arrange. There are procedures to follow, banns to be read and such things may only be dispensed with in truly exceptional circumstances."

"But we cannot wait, Father!" Anne pleaded. The cleric appeared surprised.

"I see, my dear, and am I to suspect you are perhaps with child?"

"Certainly not!" she shivered visibly.

"That is good news indeed, though were it the case, I should have less difficulty in marrying you more quickly."

"But we do have other reasons to rush," Anne implored.

"My child, I shall help if I am able, though cannot be sure of accommodating you with any urgency."

"My ship is due to sail," Adams chanced. "She currently awaits victuals but, once aboard, only powder and water shall be needed. I might be at sea within the week and have no way of knowing when I will return."

"And you really cannot wait?" Father Coleson was addressing the girl once more and this time Anne released a heartfelt sigh.

"My husband died some months back," she explained. "He left me over twelve thousand pounds in debt: I might be arrested at any time."

"Then I do understand." The cleric nodded seriously. "And think I know the procedure you will be requiring. But, forgive me for asking, is that the only reason for the ceremony?"

Adams went to speak but Anne was ahead of him. "We are in love, if that is your meaning," she replied stiffly.

"That is enough," the old man smiled. "And all I truly wished to hear."

* * *

When King joined them on the quarterdeck matters did not appear quite so straightforward. Standing respectfully to one side, Croft was determined to remain silent and had been careful to give King only the most perfunctory of salutes in greeting. Yet, though he worked hard to conceal his pleasure at the younger man's return, he was also concerned.

For his former captain had changed much since their last meeting; in addition to unusual clothing – an undress tunic and battered bicorne hat being the only obvious signs of uniform – he had visibly aged and bore a look of obvious strain unusual in one returning from a spell of leave.

"I allow you aboard my ship as a guest, Captain," Matterson's tone carried obvious defiance, "but ask that you state your business."

"Perhaps we might speak in the great cabin, sir?" King suggested.

"I have no intention of opening my private quarters for your use, now kindly tell me why you are here."

"It is of a delicate nature." King glanced about the crowded quarterdeck. "And I repeat, this is hardly the place for private discussion."

"There is nothing to discuss," Matterson huffed. "I have been appointed to this ship and am making arrangements to take her to sea. Now, as you refuse to reveal your business I shall have to ask you to leave; I am expecting guests and can waste no further time on past commanders."

"Sir, I have hardly been given leave..."

"You've had ample opportunity," Matterson snapped. "Speak with your former officers on your way off if you will, but do not detain them long; they have their duties to attend to."

"But surely you are still to be read in," King reminded him softly.

"Of course; *Mistral* has yet to be officially commissioned," Matterson barked. "Though Commodore Banks appointed me to her and it is too late now for a change of heart!"

"I come straight from speaking with Sir Richard, and he is of a different opinion. In fact the Commodore was pleased to confirm my command; if you are in doubt, perhaps we should visit him aboard his ship?"

Matterson hesitated.

"Or might you prefer to simply leave, Captain Matterson?" This time the suggestion was no more than a whisper. "And retain a little dignity?"

For several seconds the two men locked eyes while the sounds of a busy dockyard apparently fell silent. Then Matterson broke the spell and turned away.

"This is a blighted ship and has been so from the start!" he roared. "Would that I had never come across her, or the imbeciles what form her crew!" And with that he stormed from the quarterdeck.

"I shall see his servants clear what possessions are aboard, sir," Croft said as they watched the portly officer stamp down the waist towards the entry port. Both were aware of a strange tension and knew it would only ease when Matterson finally left.

"I'd be obliged if you would." King spoke equally formally. "Then you might show me about the ship. I have heard much, of course, but would wish to see what has been achieved."

"There is still a measure to be done." Croft's voice still lacked emotion. Captain Matterson had reached the end of the gangway now and was talking to two well-dressed gentlemen who had just drawn up in a carriage but, for as long as he was in sight, the atmosphere would remain. "We are still on petty warrant rations, no deep-sea supplies will be available for several days."

"The Commodore has spoken to the victualler," King announced equally guardedly. "Provisioning shall start sooner than that. If all goes well I intend to warp us to the powder quay by Friday and take on water the following morning."

At this Croft allowed himself a faint smile. "Then you have already achieved more than Captain Matterson, and he was aboard for over a week!"

"He did not have Sir Richard Banks behind him," King pointed out while they watched the carriage depart with all three inside.

"Nor, perhaps, the will," Croft sighed as the strain finally lifted.

"Whatever the case, we are to begin sea trials as soon as possible," King turned to beam at his second in command. "And I for one cannot wait to be back at sea. What say we fill the time before the first supplies arrive with some exercise?"

"Indeed, sir," Croft agreed, returning the grin.

"Excellent," King declared, placing his hand affectionately on his first officer's shoulder. "And I must say, James, it is good to see you again. Though I could wish you had chosen a different time to black the yards."

But enough could be done without encountering the tophamper and by the time Matterson's cook, stewards and personal possessions had also been cleared, *Mistral* was already ringing with the sound of bellowed commands and the rumble of gun trucks. And while the servers were involved in a lengthy dumb-show gun drill, Cooper formed the stewards and holders up for small arms exercise on the berth deck, Jennings and his mates took the opportunity to reorganize the contents of the cable tier and the carpenter's team put the finishing touches to the forecastle's caulking. So it was, that when Up Spirits was piped and the first scent of dinner began creeping from the galley's cauldrons, all were starting to cast off their shore-bound habits and behave like true men of war.

The activity continued immediately after their food with the arrival of a wagon carrying the next day's provisions. Until her holds could be filled with regulation casks of salted meat and hard tack, *Mistral* would remain on petty warrant rations. The regime boasted a diet that included fresh meat, vegetables and soft bread although in reality proved very different. Instead, victuallers were inclined to foist old deep-sea provisions on unsuspecting seamen; the final casks from ships returning from long commissions or even food that had been refused or condemned by others. Being economical, the practice received unofficial blessing and Captain Matterson had certainly shown little interest in questioning the men's fare. But when Foil reported that afternoon's delivery to be of the same poor standard, he met with a different attitude.

"Then they must take it back," King told the purser. "And if they give argument, tell them I'll have the whole lot sent to the governor's office and see what Sir David makes of it."

"Very good, sir," Foil agreed before setting off to see right was done.

"I can only repeat, it is good to have you back," Croft remarked when the purser had left the great cabin. "Though we shall need food for the morrow."

King sat back from the scratch meal of bread and cheese the pair had been enjoying. "We'll get it," he said. He had just finished recounting his experiences since the St. George went into action for the second time that day, and Croft had proved as receptive an audience as Sir Richard. "I remember the victualler here well, he pushes matters as far as is able, though clambers down just as smartly when confronted."

Croft bit into his last piece of cheese; it truly was a relief to see Captain King in his proper place, although there were still some points that worried him.

For a start his initial assessment of the man's health had been born out. He might appear as active as ever and there was no sign of physical fatigue, but still those dark shadows under King's eyes could not be ignored, nor the fact that his right cheek occasionally exhibited a nervous twitch. He supposed time spent adrift in an open boat was never relaxing, and neither would be the lack of news regarding his companion who must surely now be considered lost. Croft had never found time for such relationships and secretly despised any sea officer who indulged in them, yet did appreciate they caused a degree of worry. It was something he might bring up with Mr Manning, the surgeon, even if the captain appeared to have other matters on his mind.

And at that moment it was their marine contingent.

"It is to be the usual," he told Croft. "A lieutenant, two NCOs and forty or so privates."

"And shall they board after the sea trials?"

"No, before; they're expected tomorrow." King was emphatic. "As far as I am concerned, marines are as much a part of a fighting ship as any Jack. I shall be glad of the chance to test them out, as well as their new officer."

Croft nodded in silent approval.

"So tell me about the rest of the people, are we up to complement?"

"Currently twenty-five down. I would they could be filled and with able men but we have sufficient to sail and fight the ship if not."

"Very good. And officers?"

"I have been fortunate in securing midshipmen." Croft gave a wry look. "It seems the recapture of Cape Town brought the settlement to public notice and it has become the place to send the youngest boy."

"Then I suppose we have a collection of gentlemen's sons?" King sighed.

"One boasts a member of parliament for a father," Croft agreed. "Though others are from seafaring stock. And another, an oldster, is more experienced and might be trusted to stand a watch on his own."

"Has he seen a board?"

"I am not aware," Croft admitted. "But would think him likely to pass should he do so."

"Then that is an advantage, at least while we keep him. And senior men?"

Croft shook his head. "All we truly require is a sailing master."

"Ah yes," King replied, as if remembering. "Poor Brehaut; he will be missed."

"He was a good man, and such are hard to replace."

"They are indeed," King agreed after a short pause. "Though I think we may be in luck; I might know of the very fellow."

Chapter Nine

Although brothers, Paul and Peter Samuels were not the twins many thought. Their faces, physique and attitudes might have been identical but ten months still separated them, although it was the only thing that did.

Paul was the elder, but that gave him no authority and neither did he want it. Instead, the pair were content to go through life as equals, each looking to and after the other. No score was kept, but both were sure the incidents of one rescuing his brother from a beating, the press or a peppered doxie, roughly balanced although it mattered little if not. So when presented with a six-month unpaid wait while their current vessel, an elderly Indiaman, was taken in for repair, each were of the same mind and equally open to a spell aboard a warship. As one pointed out – neither could remember who – in a place the size of Cape Town no seaman can avoid the press for long, so they may as well claim the bounty and be sure of staying together.

Which was how it turned out. Early one afternoon the pair approached Jennings, *Mistral*'s Boatswain, during one of his frequent trips to the ropery and by the first dogwatch both were comfortably installed in their new home. And despite a reputation for being something of a prig, the first lieutenant recognised their attachment and saw to it that they messed together.

"Not a whole lot different from John Company," one murmured as they surveyed the berth deck from the comfort of their new mess table. The ship was at anchor watch so more were below than was usual and its dark underworld seemed alive with bodies. Some were yarning or playing cards, others mending clothes or carving scrimshaw. To the stern a group of marines, strangely scruffy in seamen's clothing, polished uniform leather and metalwork with pipe clay and brick dust, while forward Harris, the ship's barber, was at work under one of the few lanthorns they were allowed. Snatches of conversation floated on the air; a sudden protest or the rumble of laughter and occasionally the cry of what might have been a female voice quickly being suppressed.

The Samuels brothers had missed the main meal of the day but just eaten supper. Aboard an Indiaman this would have been cheese, hard or soft tack and possibly an apple, along with anything stowed over from the main meal and what their new employers provided proved little different.

"Bit more space, p'raps," the other supposed, "but the company seems straight enough."

That was undoubtedly the case; their mess captain was a boatswain's mate named Greenwood who had been with the ship some while and the rest were an eclectic mix that included topmen, holders and afterguard as well as an unusual number of junior petty officers. Despite their diverse abilities, on beating to quarters the ordinary hands would serve two cannon on the main deck. And even that should not present a problem, for both brothers had been nominated gunners for the East India Company and considered themselves experienced in their craft.

But that, like so much, was yet to be confirmed. Neither had served aboard a man-of-war before though knew enough about ships and the sea to understand that little good came from anticipation. They had a safe berth which, as one of them had said, hardly differed from what they were accustomed to. When the ship began her sea trials they wouldn't be the only fresh hands aboard and both were confident of earning their provisional rating as able seamen. They might not be headed for the East, but there had been numerous rumours about *Mistral* ashore. She was generally regarded as a lucky ship; certainly her people had been fortunate when it came to prize money. The Samuels brothers only needed that luck to continue a while longer and both would be content.

* * *

Martin opened the light deal door to the midshipmen's berth and stepped inside. He had spent most of the day with Foil, the purser. Fresh accounts were needed for the new commission and a complete record of all remaining stock had to be made. This had involved Martin working with Jack Dusty, the purser's clerk, and together the pair had counted and recorded everything from the residue of slop clothing to three crocks of butter that had been rancid for several weeks yet still must be accounted for. Once that was done, a fresh ledger needed to be drawn up and Martin, who had a fair hand, was an obvious candidate for the work.

He had noticed his name being called for many such tasks as he was junior enough to take direction yet showed more initiative than many of the other midshipmen. And in truth he preferred bookwork although, now it was finished, did feel unusually tired.

The working day was not officially over but, as he had skipped his midday mealtime and was no longer required, Martin had been allowed to stand down early. With luck he would find the cockpit empty and could continue reading a pamphlet describing a novel method for defining longitude, so it came as a disappointment when he entered the berth to discover Midshipman Brett, his chief irritant, seated at the table.

"What cheer, Malkin?" the young man enquired by way of greeting.

"All good," Martin replied genially although his face must have betrayed disappointment.

"Well there's no need for the horse phiz. Can't expect to have the place to yourself – I live here an all, you know."

"Oh, I am well aware of that." Martin made for his sea chest and extracted the slim booklet.

"Finished early, have we?" Brett asked as he fed a piece of ration cheese to the berth's tabby.

"Indeed; Foil, Dusty and I worked though dinner."

"Well I took my meal with the captain," Brett announced with an air of conceit.

"Did you so?" Martin seated himself opposite and opened his book. "And I trust the food was to your liking?"

Brett considered this for a moment. "It were good enough," he said.

Martin looked up from his reading and eyed the youngster carefully. In his long career he had dined with numerous captains and even a few Admirals and usually found the food served in the great cabin to be of a high standard when compared with shipboard fare. "Only so?" he questioned.

"I've tasted better."

"I have no doubt." Martin returned to his pamphlet.

"Tell the truth it were ration scran," Brett admitted after a while. "I were drafted in to copy indents under the captain's clerk and took my meal in the coach. And it's a banyan day, though it were fresh enough tommy."

Martin looked up but made no comment.

"And of course the captain didn't actually eat with us," the boy continued. "He spent the day with old man Croftie in his dining room."

"I see," Martin said as he laid the booklet down. "So why say different?"

"It were a story," the boy shrugged. "You know, to pass the time."

Martin considered him again; of all the midshipmen who routinely ragged him, Brett was undoubtedly the most annoying. Yet now, on what was probably the first time the two of them had spoken privately, a different personality might be emerging.

"Lots of things pass the time," Martin mused. "But not all are entirely wholesome."

"You mean how we take your measure?" the lad suggested with a grin. "They're just japes, Malkin, you needn't take 'em seriously."

"Indeed?" Martin raised an eyebrow.

"If you didn't, we wouldn't keep on so," Brett assured him. "You really can be a sour puss at times – it's one of the reasons we named you after the cat."

To hide his confusion, Martin glanced down at his booklet but did not read. Though it felt like a lifetime ago, it was truly little more than ten years since he had also been just another young lad fresh to the Service, and there had been some foolish enough tricks played then.

He remembered especially a mess steward with a lisp that all the boys would imitate and the schoolmaster who regularly drank himself to oblivion and one day awoke to find his prized queue mysteriously missing. Such was the manner of cockpit life, he supposed; anything outside of the norm would be pounced upon and he was probably the one out of line by remaining too long in such an environment.

The realisation brought a measure of comfort even if it was mildly depressing to realise he was now a figure of fun. But then there was no shame in being old, or poor, or suffering from illness. If the lads discovered exactly why he remained a midshipman, it would be a different matter; then they would truly have something to taunt him with.

* * *

The ship came alive at first light and, from the first squeal of a boatswain's pipe, all aboard found themselves fully occupied. With almost a full crew embarked, the berth deck was now quite crowded, with lines forming to use the heads and pissdales. The first two hours were spent in general cleaning; those parts of the upper deck where the caulking had fully set could be holystoned while swabs and brushes were used on the lower to produce a dust free, if damp, environment. The small amount of brass *Mistral* boasted was burnished with brick dust while copper cauldrons, cleaned the previous night, were filled with fresh water and secured over a newly lit galley stove. Once these had boiled and oatmeal added for burgoo, breakfast could be taken. Thirty minutes was allowed for this and then the proper work of the day could begin.

Some were still involved in the final finishing of *Mistral*'s refit, though, with the ship remaining secured to the service quay, little was officially required of the rest. But no frigate destined for active service can afford to remain idle and Croft had devised a further series of drills to bring the people up to scratch. That day's included further work aloft for the topmen with general exercise using all the ship's weapons for the rest.

And *Mistral* was well armed; her heavy cannon were by far the most important and demanded the largest share of manpower although she also carried small arms: muskets, pistols, cutlasses, tomahawks and half-pikes for close action. Instruction in their use traditionally fell to the Royal Marines, their newest recruits, who proved more than ready for the task.

Marine Lieutenant Kingsley was an eager young man with jet black hair, a lantern jaw and what Croft feared might become side whiskers. Together with four non-commissioned officers and forty privates, *Mistral*'s marine contingent made a colourful addition to the ship's complement. Kingsley formed groups of seamen on the berth and upper decks then, under the instruction of himself or an NCO and with enough privates to lead by example, each were taken through the fine art of rough-house fighting in the constricted space of a warship.

Every member of the crew received this training and practice was clearly needed. With an agreeably high proportion of skilled seamen in their number there could be few doubts about *Mistral* being handled properly, but a sweet-sailing ship-of-war was of little use if it could not deliver a punch when required. The exercises were not just intended to bring old hands up to scratch but also introduce the newly arrived merchant seamen to yet more mysteries of a fighting ship.

And two of the latter were the Samuels brothers. They had spent the greater part of their lives afloat and much of what was demanded of them came naturally. In addition to the hand skills of a seaman they could set to the capstan, launch a quarter boat or roust out cable and set a spring, while anything unfamiliar was quickly assimilated. But when they finally returned to their mess at the end of the working day, both were thoroughly exhausted.

"If that's the Navy's way with weapons drill, I wish I'd stayed with John Company," one mumbled while the other examined a blister on his right hand that had come from hauling two tons of long gun about for three hours.

"You'll get used to it," Greenwood assured them gruffly from his place at the head of the table. "An' it ain't normally quite so rushed but we was one officer down."

"That don't make no difference," Swain, a holder who also worked the gun tackle, grumbled. "Everyone knows officers don't do no work; they leave it to chubs like us."

"Don't you believe it," said Daines, one of the gun captains. "No point spouting out instructions if no one's ready to carry 'em out. Officers are needed to keep order, and they got to have eyes everywhere else folk'll get hurt. With Adams working with the sailing master, Cooper 'ad to rely on the middies an' most of 'em know a darn sight less than we do."

"Well, I've never been drilled like it," one of the Samuels brothers snorted.

"Thought we was pretty up to scratch," the other agreed.

"An' never come across pieces like them long eighteens neither," his brother added. "Tip top."

"Na, them's French," Swain gave a scowl of derision. "Came with the ship when she were captured. Give me a British Bloomfield any day."

"Them pieces have seen us all right," Greenwood countered, adding, "An' don't you worry over where they comes from," for the Samuels' benefit. "We've set 'em on their own kind often enough and turned a fair penny into the bargain."

Both brothers nodded in respect; they had already heard much of *Mistral*'s past glories.

"So what did you make, then?" one asked.

"Aye," the other agreed. "How much was prize money?"

"It were good," Swain stated with an air of reverence. "An' all down to the captain – the proper one – we weren't never going nowhere with Matterson in charge. Now Old Tommy's back we'll be flushed again afore you knows it."

"You mean it's all been spent?" the elder Samuels was amazed.

"We heard it were more than fifty beans a man," Peter added.

"That an' more." Swain again. "An' most of it's now lining Ma

Buckley's pockets."

"Ma Buckley?"

"Cat house keeper in Queen Street," Jackson, a quarter gunner, informed them.

"Most of yours might be," said Greenwood. "Others 'as plans for the future."

"Who knows the future?" Swain scoffed.

"With Old Tommy at the conn, there'll soon be more afore we knows it." Jackson had taken a bite from an apple and continued to talk as he chewed. "You India Johnnies might think you make a mint on the China run, but with a good captain it's the Navy what rules the roost."

"Mind, you have to work for it." Daines again. "Plenty of drills like today, and a deal more stowing."

"Stowing?" one of the Samuels asked.

"Aye, stowing," Greenwood confirmed. "We carries more men than any of your India tubs and all have to be fed and watered. That means shifting stores about regular to keep a level trim and that's no Saint Monday."

"An' it ain't the half of it," Swain, who spent most of his time in the holds, agreed. "There's little in the way of fancy tackle below so most of the shifting is done with brawn rather than brains."

"Which is why Swain here is so suited to the work." Jackson had now finished his mouthful and his words were spoken with such transparent sincerity that even the holder agreed.

"So how are you lads fixed?" Greenwood asked quickly.

"Most of the hard tack due in tomorrow," Swain replied after a pause. "Then meat's supposed to be comin' the day after. Powder, shot and water'll be last of all but the new sailing master's a hot one; we're likely going to be movin' stuff about till world's end."

"Well if it takes forever, it will still be done; you won't find no King's ship sailing down at the bows." Greenwood spoke directly to the Samuels brothers. "Nor with a list to starboard. We does things different in the Royal Navy; we does it proper."

* * *

By the end of the week *Mistral* was indeed ready to take on powder and shot although the latter proved a problem that even Sir Richard Banks could not solve. Her French-made long guns required a slightly larger ball to the standard British eighteen-pound shot, and supply was limited.

"We have barely seven rounds for each great gun, plus a small amount of canister and bar," Croft informed his captain at their regular morning meeting. "Ordinance have been promised more with the next convoy, but that isn't due for a week."

"That might be worse," King sniffed. "Though I would have preferred to have changed the cannon during refit."

"I did try," Croft assured him, "but two full broadsides of Bloomfields are not so easily obtained this far south."

"Of course not, James," King said softening. "Forgive me, I have a deal on my mind at present."

"Of course," Croft agreed. "Though I must say the new man is settling well."

"New man?"

"Mr Scott. He would appear to be a fine sailing master; we are lucky he agreed to join us."

King nodded. His mind had indeed been elsewhere; there was still no news of Aimée and he was coming to the conclusion there never would be. "Yes, a valuable addition to the ship," he agreed.

"And I have perhaps some further news," Croft added. "One of the officers has applied for permission to be married."

"Married?" King found it almost hurt to say the word. "Who might that be?"

"John Adams. The woman in question is the Callahan widow, from our previous commission."

"That surely is a turn up."

"Indeed," Croft agreed with a total lack of enthusiasm; anything connected with matrimony was of little interest to him. He knew others found such things fascinating and was rather relieved to discover his captain just as blasé.

"Do you have any objection, sir?"

"No. No he is welcome, and good luck to him," King answered after a moment's thought.

"He did say he wished it to be kept secret," Croft continued.

"Did he?" King snorted before adding. "Thinking of the cost of the wedding breakfast I have no doubt. Well he won't hear of it from me and I shall not be attending."

* * *

Actually, Adams never did discover who let the secret out. And, with the days before his wedding being so filled with seeing the crew trained and their ship properly victualled, he had little time to prepare for the ceremony himself. His responsibility had been to assist Mr Scott, their new sailing master, and the man had proved to be more than a perfectionist when it came to anticipating the ship's trim. Twice *Mistral*'s holds and storerooms had been emptied, only to be re-filled then rearranged again, while the task was made that much harder by having to allow for the several tons of powder, shot and water they still awaited.

It was done in time but such an undertaking meant working from dawn to dusk, and there was enough for any junior lieutenant to do at other times to ensure he had no chance of slipping ashore and meeting up with Anne. They had communicated, of course, but little could be said through notes which might be read by the messenger so, when he finally took his seat in the small church, he was more than a little apprehensive.

And the feeling grew with the realisation that he was not to be alone. By law there had to be two witnesses; Summers was grudgingly allowed to fulfil one of these roles and the girl, Greta, had agreed to stand as the other. But as he sat in the first pew and awaited Anne's arrival, Adams was becoming increasingly uneasy.

First a group of seamen had rolled in. In the poor light he could not be sure if they were from *Mistral* and assumed they would only be staying a while, so paid them little attention. After the intense activities of the last few days and with the ship only awaiting shot and water, a final shore leave had been granted, although Adams would hardly have expected any of *Mistral*'s people to spend time in a run-down church. But when the crowd grew steadily until most pews had been taken and by men he definitely knew well, his anxiety increased.

"Where have they come from?" he hissed when Summers finally joined him.

"Blowed if I knows," the lad replied easily. "Though there are more outside and I sighted Foil and Jennings arriving in a carriage."

"Foil and Jennings?"

"That were all I could see but there were others; reckon our entire lower deck's aiming to be here."

"But that's terrible," Adams exclaimed. "Can't you make them go – this is a private occasion."

"Nothing I can do," Summers shrugged. "I'm surprised they even know there's a wedding planned and must be unaware of the style. No one's here to see either of you shamed. You might look on it as a compliment; your average Jack only turns out for a popular officer."

Adams shook his head; the whole thing had got out of hand. It was bad enough Anne being pursued for debts she had no part in acquiring, but when the only solution was to be humiliated so, it was surely too high a price to pay. But that was it, they had both known the terms for the wedding. Were she truly to cast off all encumberments from her first husband it had to be obvious to all present, even if that included his entire ship's company.

* * *

"We ought to have found ourselves a decent nugging house b'now," Swain complained. "Or be half-seas over in a tavern."

"An' not the one by the Castle," Harris, the ship's barber, interjected. "Them's waterin' the beer, I'm sure of it."

"We've leave till the end of the second dog," Greenwood reminded them firmly. "An' if we can't spend an hour of it showin' support for a decent officer it's a sad state of affairs."

"Well, I hopes she shows soon, I've a thirst on me that will take a brewery to..."

"Hey up," Daines interrupted him with a sharp dig from his elbow. "That sounds like the mot now."

* * *

Adams glanced at his watch and swallowed. It was nine; the time Father Coleson had stipulated and the church was positively heaving. Behind him he could hear mutterings from men supposedly accustomed to confined spaces as they grumbled about the cramped conditions, while a constant squeak from the old church door told how more were regularly being admitted. But he did not turn around: not only did he want to avoid making eye contact with so many shipmates, Anne was due to appear at any moment and, for once in his life, he had no wish to see her.

Then, with a swish of the dusty curtain, Father Coleson appeared from his tiny vestry adjoining the altar and gave a silent nod in his direction.

"The old cove couldn't have seen his place so full in ages," Summers muttered on Adams' right. "Maybe he'll consider holding this sort of kick up more regular in future?"

Adams glared at him. "Where did they all come from?" he whispered, only to receive yet another shrug from Summers.

"Who can tell? There're no senior officers present but we seem to have most of the starboard watch."

"But how did they know?" Adams persisted. "Did you tell anyone?"

"Certainly not! Though you know ships as well as I do; sound travels and a secret ain't a secret unless you keeps it to yourself."

"You don't think they're here..."

"To see a naked woman?" Summers shook his head. "We've been ashore too long for that to be a novelty. My guess is they've heard one of their officers is getting spliced and thought they'd come along. Apart from cat houses and taverns, Cape Town hasn't a great deal to offer; I'd judge this is simply today's distraction."

Adams made no reply although he could feel his insides burning and guessed his face to be red. Then there came a collective gasp from way back in the congregation and he knew Anne had arrived.

The noise soon dwindled until there was silence but still he did not turn. Only when he felt a presence close by and the cleric signalled for him to stand did he take a glance to his left.

Anne was there and as lovely as ever. And she was mercifully decent; not well dressed, perhaps, but her heavy linen shift was sufficient to give some modesty. Greta, from the lodging house, stood alongside and appeared especially protective of her charge in a room so crowded with men. And then, even before Adams realised, the girl began to lead Anne away.

Both made straight for the vestry and slipped behind the velvet cloth. Adams switched his attention to Father Coleson, who seemed to have been expecting the move and beckoned for Adams and Summers to step forward themselves. Then, when the two men were standing directly before the altar, a hand threaded itself past the curtain and reached out to him. Accepting the naked limb cautiously, Adams felt a slight squeeze and looked to his left. There, deep inside the vestry, he could see Anne's face staring anxiously out at him. Adams smiled and instantly relaxed, then gave a reassuring squeeze in return before Father Coleson started to speak and the ceremony began.

Chapter Ten

Less than a week later and fully provisioned at last, *Mistral* was finally at sea. Standing in his accustomed place on the windward side of the quarterdeck, King felt it might have only been weeks since he guided the frigate in against a far superior enemy. It had been at the end of an action that briefly became the talk of London before apparently being forgotten forever although his memories remained fresh. Then his thoughts moved on to what had happened next; there had been the frustrating trip back to England followed by a stifling English summer spent trooping from one solicitor's office to another. It was a time made bearable only by Aimée's constant presence and now, with no news of her or the crowded boat that had whisked her off into the night, he was coming to accept the rest of his life would be spent alone.

But that did not mean there was nothing to live for, he told himself firmly. Some things had not changed, he was still an officer in the British Navy and now seemed sure to remain one for as long as he breathed. And even before Aimée, there had been the consolation of close friends; men like Robert Manning, Richard Banks and, more recently, James Croft. All had very different personalities but were similar in some respects; with each he could be certain of mutual trust, regard and, if not love, at least an understanding that probably equalled the affection felt by many sailors for distant spouses. As they continued to serve together such empathy could only grow and, King supposed, would be sufficient to see him through to the end of his Service career. It must, for after having known and loved Aimée, he already knew no woman could ever take her place.

Once such a conclusion had been reached it was easier to close his mind to that particular aspect of his life and concentrate fully on the ship, which was a far more attractive subject. In *Mistral*'s repair and fitting out, Croft had exceeded all expectations; she was undoubtedly on the top line and the man had done equally well in other areas. Despite enticements that ranged from discreet offers of bounty to outright physical force, the majority of *Mistral*'s people had stayed with the ship. And Croft had also arranged for fifty-three experienced East India Company hands to be added, bringing them up to almost a full complement. King's contribution had been to invite Scott, the former second mate from the *St. George*, to volunteer as their sailing master. After realising the number of Company officers lying idle ashore at Cape Town, Scott had jumped at the chance and King was quietly confident the move would benefit all. Scott had already distinguished himself in planning *Mistral*'s provisioning; after taking on several tons of shot and water, the ship had sailed with hardly any adjustment to her trim and King was confident the young man's navigational abilities would prove as good.

Others had settled equally well in their existing roles; Cooper, the lieutenant who joined them towards the end of *Mistral*'s last commission, was turning out to be exceptional both in his seamanship and ability to command respect; attributes that were almost of equal importance. And Adams, until recently a midshipman, was also faring nicely. Privately King had wondered if the young man would prove suitable commissioned officer material but, after a poor start, he was taking to the role as if born to it. Even from his detached position, King was aware of the most outrageous stories circulating about the man's recent marriage but, whatever the truth of it, no harm seemed to have been done and their junior lieutenant may even be benefiting from a degree of notoriety.

Mistral had now officially begun her trial period and was expected to remain at sea for as long as was necessary to ensure both men and materials were working correctly. But already King felt certain of both and truly wanted nothing other than to return to harbour and be despatched on a mission of real importance. Only then could he fully immerse himself in his work and, closing his mind to any distracting thoughts of what might have happened to Aimée, put the weapon he had helped forge to proper use.

* * *

Martin placed his hand to his forehead and took a deep breath. His ears felt unusually full and there was a high-pitched sound that came from nowhere and was steadily growing. They were symptoms he knew only too well, while other signs were making themselves known that were equally familiar. He looked about in desperation; he and several other midshipmen were in the gunroom where the new sailing master was conducting a class on defining longitude. Martin had taken to Scott immediately; the man knew his subject thoroughly and was obviously keen to pass the knowledge on while also being alert enough to identify the oldster's own talent for navigation. But quite how he would cope with this current difficulty was another matter.

"Are you well, Martin?" Scott asked doubtfully and the midshipman knew he had the undivided attention of all present.

"No, sir," Martin replied thickly as he felt his entire body sway.

"Malkin's seasick!" Brett's comment was followed by a ripple of laughter from the lads.

"Don't be a gaby, we're hardly in a swell," Scott snapped. "What's the trouble, Martin?"

"A headache, sir." Even to him the words sounded slurred while the small room had now started to spin.

Scott considered him. "If it be a bad one you had better report to the surgeon," he said.

"Surgery's over for the day," Brett announced proudly.

"I'm not talking about surgery, present yourself to Mr Manning," the sailing master directed. "Tell him I sent you."

Martin rose from his seat and staggered slightly. He probably should be in the sick berth even though it would mean the end to any hope of staying aboard *Mistral*.

"Brett, go with him," Scott ordered and Martin was vaguely conscious of the young man's arm steadying him as they squeezed through the gunroom door.

Outside Martin paused for a second. The noise in his ears had begun to fade but that would not be the end of matters.

"You're really crook," Brett said as he regarded him with a hint of awe. "Want me to find a couple of hands to carry you?"

Martin shook his head and immediately regretted the act as his world began to spin faster.

"No," he said faintly. "No, I shall be alright; just give me a moment."

"Think you can make it for'ard to the sick berth?"

Martin did not reply. He had left it too long; trusted too much in that foolish medicine and now was truly in a fix. And it hardly helped that Brett of all people was with him, not that it mattered much as he would be thrown off the ship as soon as they raised harbour.

"I'll be alright," he lied, as another wave of dizziness began. And then the deck rose up to claim him.

* * *

Aimée's captors had treated her surprisingly well, even after learning that, despite being as French as any of them, she was as good as married to an officer in the British Navy. Following a day and two nights that none of the launch's occupants cared to remember, they had sighted the French squadron at first light and were taken aboard what Casey declared to be one of the largest frigates he had ever encountered.

Léopard, as she had come to know her, certainly felt palatial when compared to the sloop she had so recently quitted. Wider decks, higher masts and bulwarks that looked capable of keeping more at bay than simply a rising sea – Aimée had stared with open wonder as she was courteously helped aboard. The ship also felt more solid with none of the *St. George*'s pitch and toss, a motion she had never truly become accustomed to, while the line of smiling officers looked far smarter than those aboard her previous vessel.

And they were her people; despite the affection she felt for King, some of his countrymen left a lot to be desired, while the sound of her own language being spoken correctly, a subtle difference in attitude and demeanour, even the scent of the coffee they offered, revived feelings long forgotten.

Their wounded were brought aboard and she naturally followed them to the surgeon. This turned out to be a serious young man named Moreau. Aimée noted the dark hair and somewhat sad eyes along with the fact that he seemed unperturbed by the sudden arrival of so many injured. She was later to learn there was little that disconcerted him medically and, while he and McIver, *St. George*'s surgeon, assessed each patient in the luxury of a modern sick berth, she and the HEIC loblolly boy assisted. With the exception of one topman, an amputee who had died during the first night, and Captain Johnston who, although ostensibly recovering, remained surly and determinedly mute, none seemed the worse for their time in the open boat and, when Casey returned from speaking with the ship's officers, all wounds had been freshly dressed.

"We're to stay aboard, at least for the foreseeable future," the elderly officer announced and Aimée remembered the look in his grey eyes and how confusion seemed to overpower his exhaustion. "But the captain seems a reasonable sort for a Frenchman. Any fit hands will be given the chance to volunteer for the Frogs, though he assured me those preferring otherwise will be well cared for. An' it ain't as if they're short of men," he sighed. "Ship's carrying a deal more crew than usual, officers as well as men. To be used to man prizes I have no doubt, but still there'll be cabins for us; you and I shall have to share," he told McIver, "an' we'll probably need to take in Captain Johnston once his injuries permit. But Captain promises you'll have your own, miss."

"For that much we can be grateful," McIver supposed.

"For that an' a deal more," Casey added. "We weren't going nowhere; if the Frogs hadn't stopped there's no tellin' what might have become of us."

The three considered this for a moment, then Casey began again.

"We're to berth on the orlop and don't expect more than a bed an' a bucket." He gave a discreet cough. "But, as I say, it could have been worse."

Aimée was sure that was the case and wondered if the deference being shown was on account of her condition. Some things had been impossible to keep secret aboard an open boat and Casey would certainly have mentioned it when speaking with the captain. But McIver had doubts.

"Do you think we can trust them?" he asked.

"I do." Casey was positive. "For a start, they're willing to trust us. In their position I'd see all prisoners secured, but they're prepared to allow free passage about the ship for as long as we don't abuse the privilege. Besides, they've no reason to lie and I think would have sent us off with one of the captured Indiamen if they weren't already on their way to France. One of the smaller ships has trouble with her tophamper; something I think the old *St. George* might be responsible for though didn't think it fitting to bring the matter up. Once that's sorted the squadron will continue south, then separate and hunt for more Indiamen. When they think they've found enough, the idea is to head home where we'll be landed as prisoners. At least most of us," Casey eyed Aimée cautiously, "I didn't answer for you, miss."

At the time Aimée had wondered if she might be treated as a traitor as her countrymen were inclined to show little mercy to anyone not fully committed to the national cause. But as the days wore on and she became more accustomed to both the ship and those aboard her, her doubts began to dwindle.

Although a warship and many miles from home, *Léopard*, felt like a part of France. And it was the old France; the one she remembered when young. The ship was undoubtedly overcrowded and many of her seamen brutal by any standard, but the officers were generally genteel with none of the nervous officiousness displayed by bureaucrats in her home country. They also organised the hands, set drills and even supervised punishments with a greater degree of compassion than she had encountered aboard British vessels.

And she soon came to know the frigate's captain. Claude Adenis was a mellow man in his middle fifties with daughters of her age and a never-ending stream of reminiscences that would make an afternoon meal last well into the evening. Then there were others; a young and earnest *aspirant* who was keen to improve his English and the *lieutenant* who, having acquired a bolt of silk from one of the Indiamen, was teaching himself to embroider a scarf for his wife. But most of Aimée's time was spent with Moreau, the *Léopard*'s surgeon.

Before long, most of the regular hands were well enough to join their fellows in a communal area forward and Captain Johnston, disgusted with both his fate and present surroundings, had taken to his cramped shared cabin and the bottle. But as was common aboard any sailing ship, there continued to be a regular stream of minor injuries to keep the department busy.

And she was busy with it, while McIver took the sun on deck and the loblolly boy, Drew, yarned with his mates forward, Aimée quietly adopted the duties of sick berth assistant under Moreau. She found him to be a patient teacher and soon learned more of her duties along with a little about herself.

For not only had Tom been her first true love, but also the only man she had come to properly appreciate beyond her family. And as time went on and her condition gradually progressed, she began to realise he was not unique in having a degree of compassion and understanding.

* * *

"It's not seasickness, at least not in the accepted sense," Manning told him. "Our motion is slight and there have been no other cases whereas I am often swamped at the start of a voyage."

Martin said nothing; he was in the sick bay and lying in a bunk, rather than a hammock. The rough woollen blanket was clean and he felt the unusual sense of calm and restfulness that was common after one of his attacks.

"Yet neither does it present as a form of falling sickness." Manning scratched at his head. He was perched on a stool and seemed to be looking down on Martin as if he were an object of particular interest. "You appeared conscious throughout."

"I was," Martin agreed thickly. "I always am; it's later I need to sleep."

"So you have suffered such attacks before? Why did you not mention them?"

Martin shrugged. "I supposed you would not have taken me aboard."

"Probably not," Manning agreed. "But now you are here, why not tell me more?"

"They started some years ago, when I was preparing to take my first board. I had three more in a short space of time and they were treated with ginger."

"As if seasickness." Manning nodded.

"They have continued since and there has been no better cure."

"And you feel giddy?"

"Very," Martin confirmed. "There is pain in my ears and I can either hear very well, or little at all."

"Interesting," the surgeon pondered. "Anything else?"

"At the start there is a strange sound, as if an insect is trapped within my head; it's one of the warnings of an attack."

"And this only happens at sea?"

"No, on land as well. It can be at any time, any place."

Manning sat back on his stool. "Interesting. I shall have to do some reading but would judge the ears to be a major factor."

Martin swallowed. He had consulted many medics on the subject and several had been ships' surgeons, but this was the first to treat his condition with any degree of gravity.

"Though I am still unsure if we can discount the falling sickness," Manning continued. "We truly have a lot to learn in that area; it is only recently such a condition was being put down to the work of spirits. What have other medics said?"

"Mainly they claim it to be seasickness," Martin admitted.

"Understandably." Manning nodded. "Though that would hardly account for the episodes ashore; did you seek medical advice at Cape Town?"

"On several occasions and have taken a number of cures."

"Which I assume proved ineffective."

"One not so, there is a bottle in my tunic."

"I shall look at it later, though frankly do not hold out much hope. And sadly can do no better, for I doubt there is anything further I can prescribe. But I cannot allow you to remain aboard a warship, you must understand that."

"You'll tell the captain?"

"I should."

"That I was seasick?"

"There is more to it than that, as I think we both know."

Martin rested back on his pillow and closed his eyes. To fail his trial period aboard *Mistral* would probably spell the end of all future employment at sea. He may secure a shore posting but the work was hardly the same and there was no guarantee he would be welcomed at the Castle, where his condition was known. Although his major concern remained that his Royal Navy career was to end, and just as he had been getting used to life at sea again; for a moment the injustice felt immense.

"If it is any consolation, you were well looked after by Mr Brett," Manning added. "He all but carried you here himself."

Martin opened his eyes. The early part of an attack was always indistinct but for Brett to have helped was not what he would have expected.

"Very well, I shall let you sleep." The surgeon rose. "If all is well you may be fit to return to the cockpit later."

"I'd prefer it if you did not inform the captain," Martin called out and Manning stopped.

"I have little option," he said.

"But the attacks are rare and that could even have been the last."

"We are only expected to be at sea another week," Manning pondered. "Should you avoid a further instance, I suppose there might be reason for me to keep the information to myself. Though I cannot recommend a permanent posting, you must see that."

"I get good warning," Martin reminded him.

"That is so," the surgeon agreed. "And you haven't been dealt the best of hands, so are probably due a little consideration."

"If another attack seems likely I shall report straight to you," the midshipman promised. "And undertake to go ashore when we return in any case."

"If you're leaving the ship what difference shall it make if the captain is aware?"   Martin shrugged again. "I simply wish to see out the sea trial," he said.

"Very well," Manning sighed. "I doubt if anything so very dramatic will occur before then."

* * *

But before they had even contemplated turning for home and while *Mistral* still rocked to almost constant exercise, the thoughts of all aboard were suddenly diverted. Predictably, the first inkling of change came at dawn and from the main masthead; a time and place known for revealing both danger and opportunity. And such was the news that, even before the sun had properly risen, all knew there would be no more exercise that day.

"What do you see there?" Chance had dictated Croft was on the quarterdeck and he bellowed the question for the third time in as many minutes.

"No change, sir." The lookout's tone might have held a hint of reproach. "Sighting's hull down and well to the west; all I can make out is tops'ls, though I still say she's a warship."

Croft sniffed and turned away in frustration. The captain had appeared at the masthead's first call and, although the pair stood barely feet apart, no words had been exchanged other than the briefest of acknowledgements. For a moment Croft considered making some comment before rejecting the idea. The recent fright when Matterson had taken command only emphasised how good it was to be serving under a true captain, yet King was not without fault. On occasions the man welcomed suggestions while at other times they were treated with disdain and Croft had no wish to start the day on the wrong foot. Yet it was frustrating in the extreme; with every passing second the sun crept higher, highlighting *Mistral* for anyone stationed to the west to examine at their leisure, while it would be ages before they, to the east of the sighting, would be granted the same opportunity.

"It's a shame we are not in their position," King remarked unexpectedly.

"Indeed, sir," Croft replied formally.

"And they have the wind," the captain continued, adding, "though that does not mean we cannot take a closer look. Mr Scott!"

King's last words had been directed at the sailing master currently studying the ship's rough log by the binnacle. "Sir!" Scott responded instantly.

"I'll have t'gallants on her if you please; then we shall see about the royals."

King and Croft watched in satisfaction as the topmen swarmed up the ratlines. The north-westerly wind was constant but light and they had barely been making steerage way under topsails, forecourse and jib. But *Mistral* had always been a strong sailer; once the additional canvas was in place they knew she would show a good turn of speed. And it was equally good to know that, whatever the sighting might turn out to be, there was no need to fear it.

Chapter Eleven

Fifteen minutes later, with royals raised and staysails added, *Mistral* had turned closer to the wind and was bearing down on the sighting with true purpose. Still on deck and standing nearer to the binnacle, King felt his spirits rising; it was a change to feel the ship move for a reason other than exercise and he always found the first hour of the day, when the sun was rising and breakfast could not be far away, particularly enjoyable. The chances were strong that they had come upon a British ship, either heading back from South America, where Popham was rumoured to be doing great things, or perhaps one diverted from their course south and now making for Cape Town. With luck, he might share a meal with the captain who could well be carrying news.

This was one of the most valuable commodities to be exchanged between ships mid-ocean although King wasn't concerned with developments in the military or political situation. The only news that truly interested him was that of Aimée. Or even the woman herself, he chanced, allowing his imagination free rein. He might have been wrong, she could still be alive and it was not impossible for her to be aboard the sighting. Whatever they were heading towards may well have passed through the area where the *St. George* was lost and it was surely not stretching possibilities too far to suggest they could have collected her, along with the launch. Then, before his thoughts totally lost control, he checked them; some things were simply too good to hope for.

"Deck there!" Yet again the call came from the masthead but this time it was the voice of Sennett, the midshipman sent to report. "I have the sighting properly now. She's sailing with the wind on her quarter and making directly for us. And I'd guess her to be a frigate right enough."

King and Croft exchanged glances; it was hardly a revelation. The course had been reported on first sighting and a frigate was one of the more likely classes of ship to be encountered sailing alone that deep into the Atlantic. And there still seemed good reason to believe her to be British, even though none of the force regularly stationed at Cape Town were expected to be within a hundred miles.

"What think you?" King asked softly and Croft raised an eyebrow.

"I think we should wait and see," he replied. "But if you'd like a vague guess, I'd say she is the enemy."

King nodded; that had been his impression as well, if one he had been trying to suppress. The force that met the *St. George* had contained two frigates and two corvettes; but the squadron may have divided since. In fact, such a move would make perfect sense. Either of the frigates would have no difficultly preying on an entire India convoy, and the two smaller ships should prove as successful working together or even alone.

"I think you are right, Mr Croft," King agreed. "And that we should clear for action."

* * *

Within an hour there was no doubt. In that time *Mistral* made herself ready for combat and the two ships had closed to the extent that they now lay less than three miles apart. The sighting had revealed herself to be a trim frigate, certainly no larger than *Mistral* and possibly slightly smaller. She had an elegant hull, a fine, if over-sparred, rig, and looked to be faster and more nimble in stays. But there was no reason to doubt the tricolours that flew from her jack and mainmast; no other country would fly such a flag on encountering an armed British vessel. This was a French National warship and proud of the fact, and it was also blatantly offering action.

The enemy still held the windward gauge and, positioned as they were off *Mistral*'s starboard beam, continued to bear down under all plain sail.

"Strike royals and t'gallants," King ordered calmly. The reduction in sail may as well be done now as later; the pair were closing far too quickly: he would prefer to have all his men at the guns and the minimum amount of canvas exposed when it came to actual combat.

"She's holding her course," Croft murmured. The sun had been climbing for some while and by its ever-growing rays the oncoming ship looked particularly stark as she ran towards them, a cloud of spray rising high from her stem and the steady wind now only just off her larboard quarter.

"She is," King agreed, then glanced down to his gunners in the waist. Cooper and Adams were there, standing as firmly as the gun crews waiting by their pieces. At that moment the servers were evenly distributed between both broadsides; if he had a plan in mind, now would be the time to reinforce one or other battery but, until the enemy made a move, he had no idea which. And it would be for the enemy to decide, of that he was certain.

The art of naval warfare had hardly been neglected; there were books and pamphlets by the score devoted to the subject. These had been produced by an eclectic selection of writers that ranged from crusty old Admirals through successful frigate captains and ended rather notably with an amateur who had produced what many claimed to be the finest on the subject. But King had not read any for years and neither did he wish to. His career as a commanding officer had included more than its fair share of action; the majority had not been planned yet mainly proved successful and he had no intention of altering his method now.

Mistral was losing speed and had started to settle, yet still the enemy came on. If both kept the same heading, the pair would pass within a cable of each other; excellent range for considered broadsides, yet King was certain his opponent would do no such thing. And he was right; just as the two ships closed to roughly a mile and the first shots had been despatched from their forecastle mounted chasers, the French frigate made a sudden and violent turn to starboard.

"Follow him!" King directed, adding, "And man the starboard battery!"

"Starboard your helm!" Scott's order rolled out. "Take us hard to larboard!"

The ship bucked at the harsh handling and one of the transient servers sprawled headlong as he rushed to the opposite battery. But *Mistral* recovered quickly – more quickly than the enemy, King decided; the Frenchman was under a far greater press of canvas and took over two minutes to regain equilibrium. Once the hull had steadied he expected the first broadside; the range was long but not impossible and a lucky hit on the British ship's tophamper would make a considerable difference to the rest of the action. But the French captain held his nerve which, when combined with the fact that he still offered combat, told King much about the man he faced.

Now they were heading on nearly parallel courses, both ships with the wind almost on their beam although the Frenchman continued to show a full suit of sails and was drawing ahead. Which was fine, King decided soberly. He was covering his adversary for the time being with enough distance between the two to react should it be necessary. And once more he would be reacting: he still had no intention of initiating the next move, even if inwardly certain what it would be.

And he was soon proved correct. Just as the enemy frigate had pulled ahead to the point when both ships would shortly be out of the other's arc of fire, the Frenchman put his helm across once more. This time it was to steer for *Mistral*'s bows and, for a moment, King wondered about turning also. But not to follow – if he steered to starboard, and headed closer to the wind, he might take his opponent's stern. Such a move would require an increase in sail, of course, and, even then, his would remain the slower ship. He swallowed then decided otherwise. The Frenchman was proving a wily opponent; it would be better to play his game and let him make the first mistake.

"Starboard the helm," he ordered softly and, once more, *Mistral* turned to larboard. But, as both ships recovered and began to run before the wind, the gap between them started to close considerably. King had no idea what weight of cannon his opponent mounted, but even a relatively light shot would cover the distance with reasonable accuracy while his own eighteen-pounders were almost guaranteed a fair number of important hits. For a moment the temptation was strong, but something made him stop; whatever the French captain had in mind, he was prepared to risk a broadside to obtain it and King had no wish to oblige him.

The chance was not offered for long though; even as King made up his mind to wait, the frigate moved again.

"Port the helm, man larboard battery!" King gulped as his opponent seized the moment.

"Port the helm, hard to starboard," Scott recited stoically as the ship lurched into yet another tight turn.

Once more the Frenchman had turned to larboard with the intention of creeping up on their bows; if King had released a broadside earlier, *Mistral* would have been in the midst of reloading and unable to react as quickly. As it was, their equally sudden starboard turn had been not only possible, but seemed likely to swing matters decidedly in favour of the British. For now the enemy's vulnerable stern was open to him, and all he need do was fire upon it.

"Mr Cooper, you may..." King began, but the man had noted the turn and, just as *Mistral* was passing the Frenchman's stern, her larboard broadside was released and the first shots sent flying towards the enemy.

"To larboard once more," King ordered before the barrage could strike. However badly the Frenchman might be wounded, he must prepare his next move before the first had taken effect. But as the shot finally landed it seemed such precautions might be unnecessary.

The broadside hit the Frenchman as if in a single blow; at one stroke the stern gallery crumbled as several eighteen-pound round shot descended upon it while, directly above, the mizzen was also taken. From such a distance it was impossible to see if it had been struck on the chains, or a chance ball had found the mast itself, but the end result was the same. With a frantic flapping of canvas the entire structure collapsed to leeward and was soon dragging the ship stern on and into the wind.

Mistral had straightened now and was running down the enemy's starboard broadside. King drew breath; their larboard battery was still being served, yet the Frenchman's guns remained unused; if they missed the chance of firing now he had seriously misjudged his opponent.

But no, though his ship was damaged King's opposite number was obviously keeping his head and, even as the French seamen struggled to free themselves of the sea anchor that had been their mizzen mast, their gunners despatched a full broadside.

"Secure yourselves!" Croft ordered gruffly and King found himself fidgeting awkwardly as those who were able sought what shelter they could behind stanchions, bulwarks and gun carriages. Denied such consideration, the officers stood tall but all waited with equal anticipation and fear as the iron shot flew towards them. And then, after the brief warning of an early splash, the remaining barrage arrived in force.

The enemy must have been distracted by their damage for no specific part of *Mistral* had been targeted and most areas were affected. A twelve-pound ball shattered the foretop and topmast chains, while the forebitts were partially struck, though proved stout enough to deflect the shot with minimal damage. Three men at number five gun fell. They, along with nearly every other server stationed at the larboard battery, had taken no notice of the first lieutenant's warning and continued to load their piece, while the frigate's hull received several eye-watering belly blows that sent shivers throughout her timbers. But apart from the inevitable splinter injuries and a foretop man who broke a leg falling to the deck, *Mistral* emerged from the onslaught relatively unscathed.

"We've lost support from the foretops'l." Croft's remark was almost conversational. "Though the forecourse seems unaffected and is drawing well."

King nodded; *Mistral* might not be making dramatic speed but it was more than the Frenchman, who still had to shake off the wreckage trailing behind, while the lack of balance expected when losing a mast had yet to be corrected.

"Larboard battery is almost ready," Scott added. As sailing master, such matters should not concern him, but King accepted the man was relatively new to the post and obviously had the ship's interests at heart.

King glanced at the enemy; he guessed it would be three or four minutes before their guns were loaded once more, time enough for what he had in mind.

"Very well, we may take her further to larboard," he grunted and again the ship heeled as she swept into a steep turn.

Damaged foremast or not, *Mistral* was far closer to the enemy frigate now and when using the battered hull as a guide, seemed to be positively steaming in. Even as he watched, King could see Frenchmen desperately hacking at the remains of their mizzen rigging as the mast still held them as securely as any drogue while, further forward, figures could be seen taking up position on the ship's forecastle. These might be marines, soldiers or seamen but were equipped with muskets; clearly the French felt *Mistral* would draw close enough for such weapons to be of use. King glanced down to where his own marines stood in measured ranks along the bulwarks and was quietly confident Lieutenant Kingsley's men would give as good as they got.

And now the larboard servers had grown silent; King considered the line of raised hands that signalled their pieces ready. All guns had been slewed as far forward as possible, which was a strange thing for Cooper to have ordered, considering they were intending to rake the enemy. Then he saw the sense in the young lieutenant's actions.

"Prepare to turn once more, master," King told Scott. Cooper really had been very clever; the hint was plain enough for anyone to comprehend, yet he had not called attention to it and King wondered if he would even acknowledge the ploy later. "But this time I want her back on the reciprocal course," he added, and the sailing master smiled as he also realised the wisdom of the manoeuvre.

For indeed there was little point in fully crossing the enemy's hawse when to do so would only make them vulnerable to the unused guns on their larboard side. Far better to release their load now, then turn back and engage to starboard once more. "Very well, Mr Cooper!"

"Fire!" The order rang out and *Mistral*'s guns were despatched as one but, yet again, King did not pause to consider the damage.

"Take her about, Mr Scott!"

"All hands wear ship!" It was a mark in the sailing master's favour that he used a speaking trumpet to combat any temporary deafness caused by the broadside. *Mistral* was immediately thrown into the confusion of a speeding turn which gave few the chance to view their enemy. But, once they were on course and creeping back, it was clear considerable damage had been done.

The Frenchman's dolphin striker hung drunkenly from the bowsprit while her starboard forechains appeared weakened. There were also numerous holes in the bulwarks that held little significance in themselves though were probably an indication of internal damage. But it was also clear the French had not been idle during *Mistral*'s manoeuvre; in addition to finally casting off the trailing wreckage, cannon were starting to reappear from her gun ports.

"We'll add this broadside, then send another loaded with canister," King bellowed to the waist and was acknowledged with a salute from Cooper. He switched his attention further aft. "Mr Kingsley, I should be obliged if you would organise boarders."

"Very good, sir," the marine lieutenant replied before calling to his sergeant.

Cooper had seen the starboard battery was also trained forward and, with another broadside planned before the two hulls collided, there was little point in delaying further; after a glance at his captain, the second lieutenant released the long guns in a ragged broadside.

The reply came almost simultaneously and for a moment there was true confusion as shot and splinters flew about *Mistral*'s upper decks. A helmsman was felled by debris tumbling from the tophamper and a particularly unlucky shot passed through the boarding party forming on the forecastle and accounted for several in one stroke. Smoke from both barrages then added its own brand of misery but, when the wind finally cleared the air, King realised they were considerably nearer the Frenchman and the starboard battery was close to being ready. Their masts had also been unaffected and now surely nothing could stop a collision with the enemy. Then there would be yet one more broadside, and they could take them by boarding.

"Ready forward!" the marine lieutenant called hoarsely from the forecastle as he raised his sword dramatically.

"And aft!" the younger voice of Adams was far nearer.

King waited as the two ships inched closer. There were snaps of musket fire from *Mistral*'s marines yet it seemed as if a strange silence had come upon the waiting Frenchman. Beside him, King could feel the tension from the men manning the quarterdeck carronades, at any moment they would be called to send their loads of shot and scrap metal to shred the enemy's deck and the deadly charges would be followed in person by *Mistral*'s heaviest seamen, many of whom were already fingering their evil weapons with something close to love. And then, mercifully, Croft spoke.

"Damn it, sir, I do believe they've struck!"

King opened his eyes wide and breathed again; his body was rigid but he was still in control. And yes, the man was right; there was an officer on the Frenchman's forecastle with hat held high and waving, as if in greeting, while the tricolour that had been flying from the main had been released and was snagged against the fore topmast in its bid for freedom. Others aboard *Mistral* had also noticed and an expectant rumble rose up until cheers were ringing out throughout the ship.

"It might be a ruse," Croft remarked suspiciously, but King knew otherwise; there was little doubt in his mind that the French had no stomach left for the fight and he, for one, was in full agreement.

Chapter Twelve

The feeling of anti-climax was a familiar one; King had rarely felt the sense of elation claimed by most at the end of a successful action and usually wanted nothing more than peace and solitude. Both were in short supply, however, and, backed by years of experience, he forced his mind to focus on matters in hand. Fortunately his officers responded readily and set to, securing the capture as if taking an enemy frigate without significant loss was an everyday occurrence. Within two hours of the last shot being fired the warship had been boarded and pronounced safe, her crew contained and work on the more basic damage begun. King ordered the commanding officer to be brought to *Mistral* and it was there, in the great cabin which had hardly suffered in the recent action, that he now faced him.

The man was relatively old for frigate command; King would have placed him well into his fifties which, coming as he did from a country where so many senior men had been removed, made him more unusual still. And he spoke no English, or claimed not to – a fact that caused a degree of concern.

King's time in Verdun and latterly being close to Aimée had given him a reasonable command of the French language. To his knowledge the only other commissioned man with such familiarity was Adams, but to conduct such an important interview with just the third lieutenant present would almost be an insult to the other two. He might allow Croft to attend through courtesy, but it would appear strange to have Cooper there also and King had no wish to offend his second lieutenant; the man had performed particularly well in the recent action and had the makings of a fine officer.

And then Cooper had surprised him yet again by modestly admitting to a basic knowledge of the language, something that pleased King on more than one level. He had every respect for James Croft but in some matters his age and temperament were against him. For organising the ship and regulating her crew the first lieutenant could not be bettered, but when it came to dealing with an enemy officer, King would prefer a younger man's opinion; one without the trappings and prejudices of the old Navy.

But as King began to speak he sensed the Frenchman would not prove an easy subject. His initial politeness had been met with curt grunts and scowls while every attempt to discover more about the man's ship or her mission brought utter silence.

"You will be sent back to Cape Town and confined, although it might be possible to arrange your exchange at a later date," King's stumbling words were made more clumsy by the look of growing disdain on the Frenchman's face.

"The Emperor does not condone such things as exchange," he all but spat in reply.

"The Emperor is many thousands of miles away," King countered swiftly. "As is my Sovereign. So what is decided at the outposts of their empires is between those who command them and I feel the Governor of Cape Colony would look kindly on an arrangement."

"Then perhaps, when my squadron has captured this ship and you are my prisoner, such things will be remembered."

"I hope they shall," King replied levelly. The fact that a squadron had been mentioned might be nothing more than a ruse, although it could mean he was speaking with the captain of one of the ships responsible for the attack on the *St. George*. He paused and looked across at Croft and Cooper. The latter was following their conversation with rapt attention whereas Croft had the look of bemused amazement common when close associates communicate in apparent gibberish. King turned back to his prisoner and decided on a change of tack. He had an idea and, though it might have little chance, still felt it worth pursuing, especially as they had made scant progress elsewhere. But as he braced himself to begin there came a bellow from the marine sentry posted outside the great cabin door and Adams was admitted.

"Beggin' your pardon, sir, we've a problem with some of the prisoners; they're objecting to the scran."

"I think I might deal with this, sir," Croft announced, rising, and King felt a sense of guilty relief. There was no doubt that Croft had been contributing little to the interrogation and he was strangely eager to move to the next stage without his presence.

"I am certainly aware of a squadron active in this area," King began when the first lieutenant had left. "For one has already accounted for some merchant shipping."

The Frenchman saw fit to acknowledge this with what might have been a nod.

"That was to the north though, and a fighting officer such as yourself would be expected to move southerly as the shipping season develops." He eyed his opponent carefully; to give away too much might be a mistake but, as he was now their prisoner, there surely could be little harm in the Frenchman knowing something of their intelligence. "That would be the sensible path for sensible men, as would dividing such a force to make it more effective."

"You must not expect me to comment on such matters," the man sniffed haughtily, even if King was aware of a small degree of softening. "I will say nothing that could harm my countrymen."

"And I would not expect you to," King confirmed. Then, taking the plunge, "But perhaps we might speak together as gentlemen?"

That was certainly a risk; many French officers would object to being referred to in such a way, but King guessed the man opposite to be of a different ilk.

"Let me be plain," he continued when no reaction was obvious. "A force of three merchant ships accompanied by a small escort was attacked by a French squadron not two months past."

The Frenchman remained silent but was clearly listening.

"To the best of my knowledge, they consisted of two corvettes and two frigates; one of which may well have been your own ship."

"Captain, I repeat, I shall not tell you anything that will betray my country."

"And I repeat, I am not asking you to," King stated with equal force. "I speak as a person, not an officer, and it is a personal favour I wish to ask."

Now there was perhaps a hint of interest on the Frenchman's face.

"Someone close to me, a lady, was present on the convoy and took to the water when her ship was destroyed. It is possible that you know something of her fate; if so, I should be greatly obliged if you would inform me."

For a moment silence hung over *Mistral*'s great cabin. Only the distant sound of bellowing orders and a steady beat of hammering broke into their sanctuary and nobody moved. And then the French officer relaxed slightly; his shoulders lowered and he gave a sigh.

"I may know of the woman to which you refer," he murmured.

* * *

"Kind of you tae offer, Russell, but do you not have responsibilities elsewhaur?" the Scotsman asked. *Mistral*'s carpenter had two ships to repair, both had recently seen action and his team would be sorely stretched. Yet he still felt reluctant about borrowing men from other departments.

"Is it because I'm a cook or lacking a leg you don't want me?" Russell demanded.

"It's neither, laddie," Anderson told him patiently. "I ken yer joinery to be guid though I'd hae thought you'd be needed in the galley. There'll be men tae feed, and probably a deal more than usual."

"The hands've just eaten. And the French have their own slushy to look after them. 'Sides, Dale, my mate, knows the duties as well as I do – some might say better."

"Very well, you can support Skinner with the forebitts." Anderson nodded towards the battered structure forward. "They'll likely need a new upright."

"I can do that!" Russell exclaimed with delight.

"Ye may think otherwise when ye get started. It'll mean cuttin' and planin' a fresh length o' oak, an' most of our spare ain't green."

"It'll be a pleasure," Russell assured him, "and make a change from working with salt horse."

* * *

"We discovered the small boat several days after the action," the French captain told him. "It had several wounded aboard as well as a doctor and his assistant. They were collected in my commandant's ship and his surgeon was able to give further treatment."

King swallowed. "And where are they now?"

"I know not, they may have been transferred," he seemed wary. "But it will be a place of safety."

That might be another ship, a regular port, or some less official place ashore where the French had established a temporary base. But wherever, King knew it would be stretching matters to enquire further and the fact that Aimée could be presumed alive was far better news than he had ever dared hope for.

"And you should not worry," the older man continued, softening further. "Your lady is healthy. I spoke with her myself not three weeks ago and all are aware of her attachment to a British officer. But even if that were not the case, she will be well cared for, as would anyone in her condition."

Now that the news had been fully digested, King found himself breaking into a rapturous smile and one that was mirrored by Cooper.

"That is indeed good new, sir, and I thank you for it," King exclaimed. "But you will excuse me, my French may not be so good. What do you mean by her condition?"

"I mean that she is with child, sir," the captain told him simply.

* * *

"We got the bitts sorted in a couple of hours, spent the rest of the watch sealing holes in the bulwarks."

"Sounds like you've had a rare old day," Greenwood mused. "As I recall you've helped Anderson's lot in the past – enjoy the carpentry, do ya?"

"Right enough," Russell grinned. "Never so much as touched a chisel afore I joined, but chips says I'm a natural."

"Surprised you can tell," Swain grunted. "I can't understand a word the bugger says."

"So why did you decide to become a cook?" one of the Samuels brothers asked – Russell wasn't sure which.

"A Frog round shot took off me leg," he tapped his peg against the mess table nonchalantly. "It were the only way of stayin' aboard ship. Can't say I cared much about scran before and can't say I do now."

"Explains a lot," someone muttered, but Russell was used to such comments.

"Hurt, did it?" Billy, the mess boy, had been wanting to know more about the slushy's missing leg for a while and it was only now, when an adult had broached the subject, that he felt able to ask.

"A bit, when it happened. Though I don't notice nothing these days."

"What, nothing?" the lad was wide-eyed with wonder.

"Nothing." The cook tapped the leg once more. "'Cause it's made of wood, see. And wood don't feel no pain."

* * *

"Mr Cooper will command the prize," King announced; it was something he had decided upon some time before and purely because the man spoke excellent French – or so he assured himself. Cooper, with his natural competence and command, would handle the task with ease with the only obvious downside being King might miss his reassuring presence aboard *Mistral*. But there had been something more to his choice, something that King was inclined not to admit even privately.

"Mr Cooper would seem an excellent candidate," Croft agreed. It was their regular morning meeting; the two of them were seated in the privacy of the great cabin and King felt unusually glad there had been no discussion. In the past Croft may well have wanted the post for himself, although now seemed far too devoted to *Mistral*.

"And I'll send Kingsley along with the marines," King added.

"All of them?"

"Yes, they will be of more use guarding the prisoners; besides, their presence will mean I can retain more seamen aboard *Mistral*."

"Yes, yes, of course." Croft nodded. "I see that now. And I assume we will be accompanying the prize?"

"No," King spoke quietly. "We are still officially on our working up exercises and I wish to see them completed."

"But the ship has taken damage."

"Which can be dealt with." King was adamant. "I have spoken to Mr Anderson and he is confident of having us back in full sailing trim by tomorrow morn'."

"The ship has performed well so far, surely we have done enough?" Croft persisted.

"Possibly, though there remain some areas in which she could be improved, and her sea trial is the best place to address such matters."

"I see," the first lieutenant replied, although King was sure he did not. Croft had been absent for much of the interview with the French Captain and had no way of knowing what was learned about Aimée. The only man who did was Cooper, and he had been sworn to secrecy.

Of course, King had no special reason to keep the news of his companion's fate to himself. But, since learning she was alive and probably on the same ocean, he felt reluctant to debate the issue or head straight back for Cape Town. And if his time at sea were to be extended it was better done for an official reason rather than on some personal whim.

And it would be a long shot by any standards but, if he didn't make some effort at finding Aimée, King knew he would never forgive himself. She might be many hundreds of miles away or just over the horizon and, apart from knowing it to be a heavy frigate, he only had a vague idea of the vessel that could be carrying her. But as he was at sea and in a ship eminently suitable for the task, it would be foolish not to take advantage of the fact. And time was certainly important; enough had already passed since her rescue and he had no intention of wasting more. Then there was the added factor that she appeared to be carrying his child, which raised the stakes even further.

"How long do you intend for us to remain on our trials, sir?" Croft asked as if following his line of thought while King was also conscious of the honorific that had crept in and was rare between them during these morning meetings.

"I should say a week," he replied. "No more."

A week was a considerable period, especially when the ship had already spent more than that on her working up exercises and taken part in a significant action: King would have quite a bit of explaining to do when he finally returned to Table Bay. But a week was nothing when it came to searching the South Atlantic, especially as he had no true idea what he was looking for.

* * *

By the following morning Anderson and his team had performed miracles. Assisted in no small way by the boatswain and most of *Mistral*'s topmen, the French frigate now sported a fore topmast spar that had been secured to the stump of her mizzen and was carrying sufficient yards to see her safely back to Table Bay. Basic repairs had also been carried out to the hull and, though the lead patches were unsightly and no one could call her rig elegant, she was perfectly seaworthy. *Mistral* had been similarly attended to and, if not as slick as the day she left Cape Town, her working up exercises could certainly continue.

"I have to say how grateful I am for such an opportunity," Cooper told his captain in the great cabin. "You are putting a deal of faith in me, sir, and I appreciate it."

"It is but a few hundred miles to Cape Town," King shrugged. "You should handle that within a week if all stays fair. Would that I could lend Mr Scott, but think you might be trusted to find your way."

"Indeed, sir," Cooper beamed. "I foresee no great difficultly."

That should surely be the case as there were few navigational hazards: all Cooper had to do was head east until he raised the African coast, then make his way down to Table Bay. But supervising that number of prisoners would be a different matter.

He would have Kingsley, the entire marine contingent and the further twenty-five trained hands King had allowed to manage the ship, along with two midshipmen and a master's mate. But it still meant Cooper's force was vastly outnumbered and it would not be the first capture to be retaken by its original crew.

"I intend to follow within a week," King added. "And have said as much in my report."

"Which I shall see is handed in promptly, sir," Cooper confirmed before adding, "but may I ask where you are intending to head?"

King looked at him doubtfully. "I shall continue with the sea trials," he replied in as level a tone as he could muster, "so will remain in this vicinity. Why should you ask?"

"Forgive me, sir, but I was thinking of what the Frenchman said."

"He gave little away, apart from there being several enemy ships in the area." King's tone remained flat. "And that was something we already suspected."

"Yes, sir," Cooper agreed, although there was an air of awkwardness about him. "But your good lady – my French is not so good but I gather it likely she is being held aboard ship, and probably the larger frigate that met the *St. George*."

"That is possible."

"Forgive me, sir, but we know little about the man holding her, though he must be aware of her potential value should his vessel be captured."

"You mean, if caught we might trade his liberty for her return?"

"And possibly that of his officers." Cooper nodded. "Bonaparte only instigated his ban on prisoner exchange at the start of the current war, until then the practice was customary."

"So you think her unlikely to have been sent ashore?"

"Very unlikely, sir. Though you will forgive me mentioning the matter."

King shook his head. "No, in truth I value your view and, have to admit, appreciate the chance to talk on the subject with another – you have told no one else I am assuming?"

"No one, sir, and neither will I if that remains your wish."

"I should appreciate it," King confirmed, "and welcome your opinion. But if you suspect I will be spending the next few days searching for a ship that is likely not even to be in the area, you may relieve yourself of the notion."

"Yes, sir," Cooper agreed with a smile.

"A week, no more, then *Mistral* shall return to Table Bay where news may already be waiting."

"Indeed, sir." Cooper appeared relieved.

"And one more thing," King added cautiously, "you will not follow my lead but head straight for Cape Town. I wish for no deviations even to speak with another vessel and if a Frenchman is sighted you must not linger but do all you can to run."

"Oh yes, sir," Cooper confirmed. "They shall not even sight my wake."

* * *

The prize made her departure at first light, leaving those aboard *Mistral* to resume their working up exercises. By the end of the day they had pumped ship, fought several imaginary fires and despatched five live rounds from each cannon after a three-hour dumb-show gun drill. And, despite what King had told Cooper, the ship continued heading west throughout, while carrying slightly more sail than was perhaps wise.

The hands performed well with noticeable improvements from the merchant seamen amongst them and every divisional officer reported themselves more than satisfied, yet King was only reasonably content. For the news that most interested him was not of crew or ship but could only come from the masthead, and his disappointment at the lookouts' lack of performance was quite unreasonable.

Despite *Mistral*'s speed, and her ability to sweep a horizon nearly twenty miles off, she might have been sailing on an empty ocean. He knew he was taking a chance by heading west, when a raider hunting for Indiamen could be expected to patrol waters nearer the African coast, but for that very reason more merchants chose the deeper passage after rounding the Cape of Good Hope. Many even avoided Cape Town altogether and made straight for St Helena, trusting their safety to the anonymity of such a vast space. A convoy intercepted so far from land, and presumably help, could be captured at leisure with less fear of interruption and it was just such a target that a larger ship – one such as the frigate that may be carrying Aimée – would be hoping for.

Nevertheless, as the afternoon of the second day drew on, the weather closed in and a faint mist started to shield the horizon, King began to have doubts. He supposed there might be three more days before they need turn back, then perhaps two further weeks at sea before raising the African coast again, yet still his frustration grew.

The hands were mustered in the waist while Manning, his assistant surgeon and the loblolly boys demonstrated the use of a tourniquet. Adams had the watch and Scott was below instructing the midshipmen in navigation, but their captain was apparently deep in thought and remained head bowed against the rising wind as he determinedly paced the quarterdeck.

King knew that to effectively remove himself so was the act of a coward. Sending *Mistral* to the west must have created comment amongst the officers although even Croft would hardly dare engage his captain in conversation while he appeared so intent. Yet just before eight bells, when the first dogwatch was due to start and the second issue of spirits made, the sailing master appeared on deck and cautiously approached him.

"If you'll pardon me, sir, I think we should put a reef in the t'gallants."

King paused from his own personal exercise and realised that, not only was he uncomfortably hot, his main meal of the day had been missed.

"T'gallants?" he repeated distantly, before staring up at the straining canvas. They had struck the royals shortly after the hands' dinner, but Scott was quite right; though still coming from the north, the wind had gathered considerably and looked likely to grow further. "Very good, Mr Scott," he said at last and, with an air of relief, the sailing master touched his hat before turning to call for topmen.

King supposed it might have been better to strike the topgallants completely; the breeze showed no sign of abating and the hands currently swarming up the starboard shrouds could be needed again within the hour. But *Mistral* would travel further in that time under reefed topgallants than without so the extra work would not be wasted. And then as Up Spirits was called, and most of the lower deck were relaxing with their second issue of grog, he finally received the news he had been waiting for.

"Sail ho! Sail off the starboard bow!"

The call caused a rumble of interest from all, but King seized upon it as if it were meant for him alone.

"What do you see there, and where away?" he bellowed in a tone more suited to an excited midshipman.

"She's square-rigged and hull down," the lookout reported. "Steering roughly our course but under tops'ls and stay's alone. I'd say we was gaining on her."

King pursed his lips and caught Scott's eye.

"We might carry the t'gallants a while longer, sir," he said, as if reading King's mind.

"Then I think we should," King replied. It probably wasn't the ship he craved – chances were high it wouldn't even turn out to be an enemy. But it was a sighting and a chance, and King was determined to take all the chances he was offered.

* * *

Two hours later the light was starting to fade although *Mistral* had closed considerably and all was definitely falling in her favour. The chase, as King now considered the sighting, was hull up and remained in constant sight of the masthead while those on deck could catch the occasional flash of topsails on the darkening horizon. Half an hour before, the midshipman sent aloft with a glass had chanced their quarry to be a single-decked warship; news that had stirred interest in all and almost driven King to a frenzy. There was no such British vessel expected thereabouts and, while a neutral was always possible, neither was it likely. And even when a subsequent report suggested she might only be the smallest of frigates, a jackass or possibly merely a corvette, his interest remained high. Either would be an easy conquest for *Mistral* and, if she had been part of the original battle squadron, there was a very real prospect of learning more of Aimée – if only they could close before sunset.

But despite the wind continuing to blow hard, the chances for that soon started to fade and, as the sun finally touched the western horizon, it signalled the start of heavy rain that had the air of permanence. As the first drops fell, King forced himself to relent. They had struck the topgallants an hour before, yet were still closing. No one could tell what the next few hours would bring; it was likely his prey would alter course as soon as darkness became complete, although he remained confident that dawn would not reveal a totally empty ocean.

"Chase is changing her heading, sir!" This was the masthead once more, and the young midshipman had the entire ship's attention. "Turning roughly three points southerly."

King exchanged glances with Croft. The smaller craft would know herself pursued and be keen to shake off the warship that hunted her. And in his haste, the captain may think his ship already invisible so could have been just a little too prompt in ordering a fresh course.

"We'll keep her as she is, Mr Croft," he said firmly. Only a fool would reveal the gambit had been noted; far better to let the sun disappear completely, then order *Mistral* to follow and spend the night in silent pursuit. And even if they did not meet in darkness, it was now almost certain that dawn would reveal the enemy within easy striking distance.

For the first time in what seemed like months, King felt himself relax. The distant warship was unlikely to be carrying Aimée, but at least he might receive further word of her. And, if not, he now had an even stronger reason to remain at sea a little longer. So really things were beginning to pan out rather well.

Chapter Thirteen

Although it might not have been the best move financially, Scott had been glad to transfer to *Mistral* and the Royal Navy. For a start, his contract with the Honourable East India Company was only valid for the voyage aboard the *St. George* as far as Bombay, after that he would have been back to seeking seagoing posts, probably as a mate but possibly a midshipman once more. Bombay was also not as good a hunting ground as London but, following the sloop's spectacular end, he discovered Cape Town to be far worse.

His new employers would also pay him a reasonable salary; the British government allowed eight guineas a month to anyone prepared to navigate a fifth rate, which was over three more than his previous masters. But when the HEIC tonnage allowance was taken into consideration he would be considerably worse off, while prospects for advancement in a King's ship were poor indeed. With sailing master being the highest warranted rank, there was no obvious progression and if he wished to apply for a commission as lieutenant, he would have to stand a board alongside midshipmen and master's mates. It remained a respectable position however and, more to the point, would allow him to truly practice his craft away from the security of sailing within a convoy on formally prescribed routes. But it was that very point that was currently worrying him as, after searching in vain for the faintest sliver of moon for his evening sighting, Scott had ruefully taken refuge in his cabin.

It was there that he kept his own personal chart which was an exact copy of the official version currently laid out in the captain's quarters on the deck above. But both were sadly lacking as far as detail was concerned. Scott had intended to purchase better from his own pocket and already owned more modern examples for the approaches to Table Bay, False Bay and The Cape itself, but after that his funds had run dry. When they sailed this did not seem so great a problem; *Mistral* was unlikely to venture very far on a simple working up exercise and soon he would be able to draw on his Royal Navy pay to supplement the library. But all that now seemed a very long way away and, as the ship continued heading west-south-west with the brink of a gale blowing on her starboard quarter, Scott was feeling decidedly ill at ease.

The noted navigational hazards were few and all a good distance off. Even though it had been impossible to take a lunar sighting that evening, he had shot the sun perfectly at noon and, when checked against chronometers that were yet to disagree, the results were encouraging; Tristan da Cunha lay many leagues to the north-west while Gough Island, though slightly nearer, should also be a long way from their path. But it was only relative safety; that part of the South Atlantic had yet to be comprehensively surveyed and being an active volcanic region meant even quite substantial landmasses could erupt almost overnight. Scott didn't think a modern chart would tell him anything more but it was a sailing master's responsibility to take every precaution and he would have preferred to be absolutely certain.

* * *

Evening on the berth deck and, though *Mistral* remained cleared for action, mess tables had been rigged and benches set in place to give those off watch a modicum of comfort.

"It's not as if the Frog's a liner," Billy, the boy of the mess, remarked for the third time.

"Wouldn't make no difference if it were," Swain was dismissive. "*Mistral*'s fought liners in the past, and won."

"As I heard, you had a couple of meaty frigates to back you up in that," the older Samuels remarked.

"Aye," his brother agreed. "And one were a cut-down sixty-four."

"Well we ain't facing a liner this time," Jackson pointed out. "She's naught but a corvette and you know how mastheads like to puff up a sighting to make 'emsleves look bright. Belike we'll find her barely more than a sloop and a darn sight smaller than the frigate we dealt with a few days back."

"That's assuming we even see action," Russell, the cook, pointed out.

"So, either way, none of you have a thing to worry about," Greenwood added sagely. "As Jacko said, we've already accounted for a fifth rate, an' that weren't no real bother were it?"

Greenwood was right; the frigate action, though dramatic, had not been so very terrible. But it had taken place in daylight and was more or less predictable with little preamble and absolutely no storm. *Mistral* currently had what felt like a full-blown gale on her quarter which was driving her through the black waters to goodness knew where at a speed that was hardly comfortable.

"Whose worrying?" the Samuels brothers asked simultaneously.

"Aye," Greenwood agreed as he grinned at the faces clustered about his mess table. "Who indeed?"

Even when a topman, Greenwood had been the head of a mess, and with his recent rise to boatswain's mate, he saw no reason to change. He might have chosen to berth elsewhere, it being common for junior petty officers to mess with others of their rank. But most of those present had been mates for some time and as Russell was now a cook and Jackson a quarter gunner, there were enough senior men for his liking. Besides, Greenwood took a genuine pleasure in bringing newer hands on.

The Samuels brothers were a case in point. Though skilled seamen who could hand, reef and steer with the best of them and despite a working knowledge of ordinance, they'd known nearly nothing about how a warship worked. Both were learning, of course, and he'd continue to help them – they all would. That was the benefit of being in a decent mess, a newcomer could rely on guidance from those about him. They had already been in one action and survived; a couple more would make them true men-of-war.

"So how come we've not been beaten to quarters?" Billy, the boy, asked.

"Captain don't see the point," Daines told him. "You know what it means – we done it enough times over the past week or so. If we were at quarters now there'd be no watch below. Most of us'd be gathered round the cannon and getting soaked with those that weren't like as not miserable elsewhere."

"Not me, I'd be snug in the grand mag. with the gunner," Russell muttered. "That's if chips don't need me."

"Captain reckons we'll fight better with a few hours' sleep inside us," Daines continued. "And if there's cause, he can call us up at a moment's notice."

"And do you think that's likely?" Billy again.

"Na," Swain told him confidently. "Chase will carry on throughout the night. We'll stand the middle watch with the rest of the starbolins and likely get a few hour's further caulk afore first light."

"You sure of that?" One of the Samuels brothers was doubtful.

"Sure? I'm bleedin' certain."

"Aye," Daines agreed. "Ain't nothing gonna happen tonight and, if it does, we can deal with it."

The newer members of the mess grinned at each other in relief and one of them even went to speak when there was a gut-wrenching shudder that ran through every timber and the ship felt as if she had suddenly been thrown backwards.

Throughout the berth deck men, benches and equipment were tossed into a score of untidy heaps while, higher up, hands crashed into cannon, tumbled from the gangways or simply fell headlong onto the unforgiving strakes. And aloft Ackerman, the forecastle lookout, described a graceful arc as his body plunged downwards and, caught by the wind, disappeared forever into the thrashing waters below. Which might almost have been a punishment for, of all aboard *Mistral*, he really should have seen what was coming.

* * *

On deck, Adams had the watch and was one of those who sprawled spectacularly with the impact. For a moment he lay face down as he gathered his thoughts, then quickly began to rise.

"What the devil, John?" Summers, midshipman of the watch, asked as he also righted himself.

"We're beached," Adams gasped. "And on my bloody watch."

"Let go the sheets there!" It was the voice of the boatswain and hearing it brought Adams back to reality.

"Thank you, Mr Jennings," he mumbled then, in a louder voice, "Topmen aloft and take in canvas!"

"Foretops'l's split an' we might have sprung the mizzen topmast," Jennings informed him gruffly, "though we was lucky to keep our tophamper."

That was undoubtedly true, but Adams had other things on his mind and made for the larboard bulwark. The night was dense and starless while even the dim glow from the binnacle had momentarily stolen his night vision. But even as he waited, the blackness remained impenetrable without the faintest flash of spray to show where shoals may be lurking. He paused and looked further forward; there was perhaps something just off their larboard wale but hardly significant and surely not enough to have halted a fifth rate so comprehensively.

"Mr Adams!" The voice of Croft, the first lieutenant, made him turn.

"We're aground, sir."

"I am aware of that," Croft snapped. "Kindly have a light rigged off the larboard beam."

Summers grabbed at one of the ready-use dark lanterns and scrambled off down the larboard gangway.

"I assume the enemy was still off the larboard bow when last sighted?"

"Yes, sir," Adams replied, "though that were before my watch began. Neither lookout reported anything for the past hour."

"That much is obvious," Croft snorted then, turning to look Adams full in the face, added, "Perhaps you had better tell me exactly what happened?"

* * *

Below, Anderson was one of the first to react. Though snug in his hammock, the carpenter was wide awake by the time his feet hit the deck and running aft even before his conscious brain had fully taken in what was about.

"Orlop, now!" he shouted, passing Russell. "And bring all who c'n help wi' ye!"

The cook raised a hand in acknowledgement before stumping manfully in pursuit. But the carpenter was too fast and, by the time Russell reached the aft companionway, had disappeared.

"Skinner!" he yelled, seeing one of the carpenter's crew. "Chips is below, we're to follow."

"I'm there!" the lad, a lanky youth from Sussex, shouted in reply before pushing past and throwing himself down the companionway leaving Russell to follow more cautiously in his wake.

On the orlop it was darker than ever as one of the mounted oil lamps had crashed to the deck, leaving a puddle of fluid that warmed any with bare feet.

"See to that, Russell," Newton, the carpenter's mate, directed as he also pushed past. There was a line of fire buckets rigged by the companionway; Russell grabbed one and tipped its contents over the spillage.

"What's about there?" a young midshipman demanded as he emerged from the darkness.

"Ship's aground," Russell replied smartly while collecting

another bucket.

"Aground?"

"Aye, aground – best look it up in one of your books, Mister."

Though young, the boy was still an officer and entitled to respect although this was hardly the time for niceties and Russell stumped on forward into the darkness without another thought.

"Larboard frames seem sound, but we've sprung several strakes," Newton was reporting as he arrived.

"But there'll be more belaw ahm thinkin'," Anderson grunted, "and uir main water's stowed beneath."

"With most in leaguers," Skinner agreed. "Filled, they weigh in at over a ton a piece an'll be the very devil to shift."

"Well, we're going to hae to, or send a wee laddie in." Anderson glanced about at his surroundings, strangely static after many days of constant motion. "Ship's beached as solid as a rock by the feel o' her."

"A lad won't know what he's lookin' at." Newton again. "Needs someone with an eye for timber. Ask me we'll have to get a fair number of them leaguers drained and out just to take a look."

"Anyone ken the state o' the tide?" Anderson's demand met a line of blank faces.

"Make a difference, does it?" Russell asked.

"I'll say," Newton snorted. "If we're on a low and badly holed beneath, there won't be much we can do anyways; ship's as good as sunk."

"Aye, it'll be th' end of *Mistral,*" Anderson agreed gloomily, "and little we can do abit it".

* * *

The same thought had been in King's mind as he made a more measured descent into the frigate's bowels. He had been enjoying a late supper with Croft and Manning and knew exactly what was about as soon as the ship struck. On deck, all had been relatively contained; apart from the loss of their foretop lookout there had been no major injuries and when he left, the boatswain had just begun a systematic check of the tophamper. But his major concern lay below. *Mistral* was a well-found ship and relatively new, but no vessel can meet land at speed without sustaining some damage.

Exactly what, and where, would depend on the ground beneath

them. Mud or soft sand was the best option but there was little likelihood of either; if they had come across an uncharted rock or some small landmass, as must surely be the case, razor sharp edges of volcanic pumice were almost guaranteed.

On the berth deck he could hear the shouts of junior officers as they raised and organised the watch below. Taking advantage of the confusion, King was able to make his way unnoticed down the aft companionway and land cautiously on the orlop.

Ahead, a series of lights showed where Anderson and his team were gathered about the forward hatch. King walked quickly, his head bowed to dodge the deckhead, and approached the group.

"What do you see there?" he demanded on arriving.

"Nothing tae speak of on this level, sir." Anderson showed no sign of surprise at his captain's sudden appearance. "Slushy's just dropped intae th' hold to check doon lower."

"The cook!" King questioned.

"Aye, sir," Newton confirmed, only slightly abashed. "It's Russell – him with the peg. Knows a fair amount about carpentry and has helped us out in the past. Reckons being a leg light will see him past the leaguers."

"Very well," King grunted. "Then tell me what he discovers and I need to know immediately, is that clear?"

"As soon as we do, you will," Anderson assured him. "Though I should say now, y'r honour, ah'm nae expectin' good news."

* * *

Since losing his leg, Russell seemed to have spent all his time trying to be as useful as a fully able person. Becoming a cook had helped; what work he did was easily carried out and it was supposedly a respectable position. But for many years the post had traditionally been allocated to injured Jacks and now carried, if not an element of shame, then at least condescension. The time he spent as an unofficial member of the carpenter's team was different; there he was valued for what could be achieved with his hands and the missing limb was hardly noticed. Consequently, when a lithe body was needed to slip between the immense water casks that filled part of *Mistral*'s hold, he had immediately volunteered. After all, he was slim, strong and knew a fair amount about carpentry while this was one occasion where the lack of a left leg might even be an advantage. But once he was alone in the darkness of the ship's nether regions he began to have doubts.

For a start he was standing ankle deep in water; there was no current as such, but *Mistral* was undoubtedly leaking from somewhere and steadily filling. The thought chilled him more when he considered the mission ahead and it was a sensation that became physical as the cold liquid slowly began to creep up his right leg. But there was no going back; Russell had committed himself to the task and was determined to see it through.

"Lamp's a coming down," a voice announced from the hatchway and a glowing lanthorn began a slow descent on the end of a line. Russell caught hold and turned the light on the wall of horizontal casks that lay to either side, with only the slimmest of passageways running between. Both stacks reached almost to the deckhead; hardly enough space for a child to slip through while to either end there was an equally narrow gap between the end of the pile and a bulkhead. But he had thought to slip through that crack and, as he looked further, decided he could.

His peg came off in seconds and was left on a suitable cask, then, collecting the lanthorn with one hand and holding fast to one of the casks with the other, Russell hopped his way clumsily through the water. Reaching the end he set the light in front, before inching his body forward. Both bulkhead and casks were equally solid and, as he eased his bulk between the two, Russell sensed the air being squeezed from his lungs. There was a moment of panic as claustrophobia set in; the water was still rising and he was in danger of becoming wedged. Then, taking control, he edged the lamp forward to the next tier of barrels and continued, crabwise, after it.

After gaining a couple of yards he reached an obstruction; a leaguer on the lower tier had been set slightly closer to the bulkhead. It was only a matter of inches although the obstacle would have defeated any able-bodied man. But not him; he needed only the space for one limb and was able to pass by relatively easily. The small victory was enough to bolster him and soon the light was shining on the ship's inner hull. Seeing this, Russell quickly dismissed the thought that he must now be all of fifteen feet into the stack with the corollary that, were the pile to shift even slightly, he must be slowly and steadily crushed. Instead, he pulled himself in deeper with his hands, and finally reached the equally narrow gap between the last row of leaguers and *Mistral*'s inner scantlings.

And now it was time for the task he had agreed to undertake. The frame that supported the bulkhead was sound and, as far as he could see, so was the next. But he had to make a thorough examination of all if everything already endured was to be worth a candle.

Easing himself round the edge of the casks, he once more blessed the space allowed him by the lack of a leg. The lanthorn was serving him well, he could see the solid strakes of the inner hull and noted a lack of weeping although the water he stood in was continuing to rise. Moving on, the space became tighter still and he found it harder to inspect the lower timbers although he could at least move as far as the next frame.

But there he found a problem; he had come a good distance down the length of the pile and, considering the time spent in getting to that point, would be more vulnerable than ever. There was also the now not inconsiderable fact of the rising water. Still, the frame looked like being the major obstacle as it encroached by several inches and was actually touching some stacked casks. There remained a small opening, however, and one possibly large enough for a man to slip through were he so determined.

Reaching forward, Russell placed the lanthorn through the hole where he might reach it later then, hoisting himself up, began to thread his body through the gap. It was far tighter than he had expected; both shoulders were constricted by casks on one side and scantlings the other while the gravel used to bed each huge leaguer in place scraped at his skin. But soon he was through, and even able to breathe a little easier as he edged forward. And then, by the light of the flickering lanthorn, he saw what he had come for.

The damage lay ahead and could just be made out. Several of the inner strakes were disrupted and water flowed steadily through a small gap. It would need a sizeable repair, but should be manageable, especially as the puncture was several feet up the side of the hull. But unless steps were taken to clear the ingress, the ship would be flooded. He paused and listened; there was no sound from either pump and he quickly guessed the reason. *Mistral* had foundered on what was probably a single rock; she may well be balancing and the last thing anyone would want – the last thing he himself wanted – was for her to move. Anchors may even have been set and it would be sensible to allow a fair amount of water in simply to maintain stability. But not too much he hoped because, at the current rate, he would be lucky to be clear of the casks before it reached over his head. As it was, to reverse out from his present position would take some time. But luck had been with him thus far and he saw no reason for that to change. And at least his journey had not been in vain; he would come back with news – vital news that might conceivably save the ship and all aboard her.

Russell had never sought acclaim for acclaim's sake, but it would be good to glory briefly in a little admiration – to be acknowledged for something achieved rather than an injury which many regarded with an element of humour. And then his luck did run out. There was no time to linger and, as he reached for the lamp in the cramped space, he might have been a little hasty; the thing was hot, it slipped easily through his chilled fingers and, when it fell into the water with a gentle hiss, Russell was left in total darkness.

* * *

"Well it's good news and bad, sir," Scott announced and King noticed the sailing master's face appeared incredibly pale in the great cabin's candle light while his hands, currently holding a tightly rolled chart, were shaking slightly. "By my reckoning we struck at about two hours after high, so can expect some time before any leak increases significantly."

King nodded seriously. That could indeed have been worse although, if *Mistral* were perched on an outcrop of rock, a falling tide could do further damage. That was a point best kept to himself, however; Scott was clearly shaken by the night's events and right now King needed the very best from his officers. "So in time there will be four hours of a high tide which we might use to refloat the ship?" he asked instead.

"Yes, sir," Scott agreed. "Providing repair work can be undertaken."

King was still awaiting the carpenter's report but Anderson had not been hopeful; unless absolutely no damage had occurred, and the rising level in the well rather repudiated that, *Mistral* would have to face being partially flooded twice a day.

A lot would depend on exactly what they had grounded upon; if it turned out to be an island, or there was land close by, it might be possible to lighten the ship considerably and transfer some of the crew ashore. But if rocks, or a single point jutting proud, the prospects would be far worse.

"And you have no clearer idea as to where we are?" he spoke as gently as he could.

"No, sir," Scott replied miserably while unfolding the chart and laying it out on the dining table. "As you are aware, dead reckoning places us about here," he said stabbing the paper with his forefinger. "And by all accounts there shouldn't be a promontory within a hundred miles."

"It cannot be helped," King assured him. "This is a volcanic region; hazards can be raised in no time and there is a fair possibility we are the first passing this way in a while."

But as he said the words a cold feeling ran down his spine. The enemy corvette had been ahead of them; perhaps her captain already knew of the peril and had lured them to it? Worse, maybe what King had taken for a foolishly premature change of heading at nightfall had been carefully planned. If so he had been taken for a prize chub, and the thought was not a pleasant one.

"But at least we may get the chance to record the spot so others will be aware," Scott continued and King eagerly seized the point.

"Indeed so," he agreed, ignoring the fact that first they would have to fix the ship, then see her refloated and at that moment neither seemed likely.

The door to the coach opened and McNamara, his steward, entered. "Pardon me, sir, but the carpenter wishes to speak with you."

"Yes, of course, send him in," King directed before exchanging glances with Scott.

"I must repeat how sorry I am, sir," the latter mumbled. "Especially after the opportunity you gave me."

"And I shall say again, you are not to blame," King told him firmly. "I offered the post of sailing master on account of your obvious abilities as a navigator and nothing you have done since has caused me to change that opinion."

Scott nodded silently, but it was clear the words had gone unheeded. The man was set on punishing himself and, as Anderson entered with another in tow, King realised he was not the only one.

Even before the Scotsman crossed the room he had flashed a look of contempt in the sailing master's direction. But the identity of the second visitor was enough to bring all thoughts back to the immediate matter for, stumping behind, was Russell, the ship's cook.

He was clearly soaked through although, with the rain continuing to pour on deck, that hardly made him unusual. But there were deep gashes to his chest and forearms, his shirt and trousers were also badly torn and his face bore the marks of one clearly exhausted. "Get that man a seat," King ordered and Scott was first with one of the dining chairs which Russell gratefully slumped onto.

"Mr Russell hae made a thorough examination of our inner hull, sir," Anderson announced. "So I thought it best you hear his report personally; fur he hae surely placed hemself at great risk."

"Of course," King agreed. "What did you find, Russell?"

"Lower hull is holed to larboard," Russell stated softly. "I could see a knob of rock which is also blocking the opening, your honour, though water's still comin' in."

"I see, and would such damage be repairable?" King's eyes flashing to Anderson.

"In the right conditions, sir. Though we shall hae tae lighten the ship and lay her over tae some extent."

"You mean on her beam ends?"

The Scotsman shook his head. "Nae fully, sir; even a wee angle ma' be enough. But a lot wi' depend on our exact position and we'll only ken that fur certain come daylight."

"Of course," King agreed. Earlier the coxswain had attempted to launch a boat but, despite the fair degree of lee provided by *Mistral*'s hull, the weather was simply too harsh and there had been no sign of moderation since.

"Well, we shall have to wait for first light. In the meanwhile I appreciate your efforts," King told the cook. "Perhaps you will see the purser issues Mr Russell with some fresh dry clothing and a tot?" he added to Anderson.

"I weel indeed, sir," the Scotsman replied. "It were a brave thing yon laddie did, though 'tis a pity it were necessary."

Anderson's last statement was made directly at Scott. The sailing master opened his mouth to reply but King was ahead of him.

"I'll thank you not to cast aspersions against my officers," King growled. "Whatever we have struck is not shown on any chart and Mr Scott is in no way responsible; do I make myself clear?"

"Ye do indeed, sir," the carpenter replied a little sulkily.

King considered them both. Whatever his powers as captain, he was unable to control men's thoughts; if others held Scott responsible for the grounding he could hardly order them not to. But Scott would have to look after himself; with dawn still several hours away, *Mistral* vulnerable and an enemy warship in the vicinity he felt the night already held enough problems without looking for more.

Chapter Fourteen

But morning did bring some reprieve. As the sun made a cautious appearance in the east, both rain and wind began to falter and, when it had risen to the extent they could see their immediate surroundings, King supposed things might have been worse.

Mistral was wedged on the very edge of a short outcrop of rock that ran directly out from a small island to larboard. No one could say how long the place had existed, or quite how such a landmass could have been missed by cartographers, but its presence would at least allow the possibility of repairs to be thoroughly investigated. And Anderson had already begun work; even before the sun was fully up, two of his team were being lowered over the side on whips and, by the time the island had been fully revealed, the Scotsman was ready with a report.

The ship would need to be both secured and lightened; that much King had expected. After that, Anderson intended attaching stays to the lower masts which in turn were soundly anchored to the nearby shore. Then they would begin shifting stores to allow the ship to list slightly to starboard when the next high tide lifted her. She would settle again on the ebb and it would be a question of making repairs before the following high water raised her once more. Although pressed for an answer, the carpenter would not estimate how long such an operation would take, but King suspected they must remain marooned and vulnerable for at least a week.

And in that time much could happen; the storm, or the enemy, might return and either could spell their end. In the first case they had been relatively lucky with the recent tempest; though strong, the wind had been constant. Were they to be struck with a gale that fluctuated, changing points with every bell and varying from gentle gusts to a full-blown hurricane, an already weakened hull would soon be ground to pieces. And if the corvette made an appearance it might be equally bad. Stranded as she was, *Mistral* could only strike within the limited arc of her guns; it would take no great feat of seamanship to manoeuvre a small warship to bear on her bow or stern, then the French might knock her to pieces with relative impunity. But though he would take precautions, King knew better than to dwell on the dangers when it was infinitely preferable to make positive moves and, if these could also avoid further trouble, they would be doubly valuable. Which was why he had summoned the sailing master and one of the more responsible midshipmen as soon as the situation was fully revealed.

"You are to take one of the cutters," King told them. "I want a survey of the island with regular soundings and any natural harbours duly noted – have you done such a thing before?"

"I have not, but am familiar with the procedure," Scott replied.

"And I can learn, sir," Martin added after the shortest of pauses.

"Good, then choose your men." King was now speaking directly to the midshipman who would have a greater knowledge of the hands' abilities. "Take those you can trust and provisions for two weeks; that will have to include grog which will be up to you to ration and administer."

Martin had performed well in the brief time he had been with them. And whatever his initial doubts – King had once noticed straw sticking to the man's uniform – he could definitely be presented at the next lieutenants' board so it would do no harm for him to have some experience of independent command. And a competent survey might help Scott regain an element of self-respect while also cementing his appointment with the Admiralty, even if it would probably take longer for the hands to fully trust him again. As captain, King was isolated from the general sentiment of the lower deck, yet he remained uncomfortably aware that Anderson was not alone in blaming the sailing master for their current predicament.

"Very well, go as soon as you are able."

"And how long shall we have, sir?" Scott asked.

"I'd say at least a week; record as much as you can in that time. If we are able to leave before I shall signal with cannon fire; basically, should you hear guns, make straight for us. Other than that, it will be up to you."

King considered them both; Scott appeared relieved and Martin cautiously excited. An accurate chart of a previously unknown hazard would be of immense benefit although, to King's mind, the main advantage lay in the young sailing master's absence. In a week, *Mistral* should be made sound again and any resentment ought then to gradually fade. But what lay ahead for the rest of the crew would be a taxing enough time without having to worry about personal disputes.

* * *

It wasn't the first time *Léopard* had cleared for action during Aimée's stay aboard; twice before the call had come when the frigate's guns were run out and all made ready for combat. But on previous occasions the sight of the warship preparing to give battle had been enough and their adversary – if such a term was appropriate when applied to scantily armed merchants – had given in without a fight. This time would be different though, even as she made her way from her tiny cabin to the sick berth she knew that from the grim yet determined looks of all about. They were preparing for battle, but this would not be a simple matter of going through the motions; whatever they faced was expected to fight back.

"We can leave Monsieur Talbot to sleep," Moreau, the surgeon, informed her with a slight rolling of his dark eyes. The *quartier-maître* had been a regular patient for all of Aimée's time aboard the frigate. Ten or twelve days of sobriety were customarily followed by one almighty drinking bout that only ended when the man was totally incapable. He would then be reliant on the medical team to nurse him back to health so that the process could begin again. Talbot had been delivered to them the evening before and was still deep in a sleep that might last until the following day. Not even the prospect of a forthcoming battle could be expected to wake him, nor even the battle itself, if it came to it.

"Very well," Aimée agreed. "Shall I attend to dressings?"

"Do that, if you please. I know not what is keeping Devall; he should have the instruments and medications on the lower deck by now. Mr McIver and his assistant are already there and making preparations."

Bonded by the universal cause and language of surgical practice, it had become usual for the British medics to assist whenever necessary and Aimée sensed they would be especially useful on this occasion.

"Do you know the situation?" she asked, reaching for one of the brown paper packages that held a supply of ready-use bandages.

"A sighting has been made," the surgeon replied. "We had the news first thing in the wardroom and thought it to be a lone Indiaman but as we closed it seemed otherwise. I know nothing else."

Aimée pondered for a moment. "A ship sailing so, might that also be a warship?"

"It might," Moreau agreed. "In which case it is likely to be an enemy. We have few so large in the area and Americans are usually based further to the north."

"So we are likely to be facing an English ship?"

"I believe so."

The last Aimée had seen of Tom King was that hurried farewell aboard the *St. George*; since then there had been no news. No news, that is, apart from the devastating explosion that must have told the end of the small warship. Yet still she could not wholly convince herself he was dead. It might be nothing more than a young girl's fancy, but there was an air of indestructibility about a man who had already gone through so much yet survived. Then she sensed Moreau close to her and all thoughts of her former lover were banished.

"I don't want you to be concerned." He laid a hand on her shoulder. "English or not, they are unlikely to be more powerful than this ship. And *Capitaine* Adenis is a fine officer; he will ensure either victory or a safe escape. Believe me, I have served in many ships and have never felt so confident as I do aboard *Léopard*."

"I know," Aimée agreed; indeed the young man had already revealed much about his earlier life to her, as she had to him.

"Then perhaps you are thinking is your Tom King aboard?" He raised an eyebrow quizzically.

"There is no reason for him to be," she laughed. "As far as I am aware, Tom is dead and I think should be forgotten."

The young man nodded seriously. "Then that is another thought we both share," he said.

* * *

Martin was in a rush; he had done all he could to prepare for his adventure with Scott and now needed only to grab a few personal items for himself. Most of the junior warrant officers' possessions had been moved to the boatswain's storeroom when their berth was requisitioned by the surgeon and he was fortunate that his sea chest was not one of those currently being used to form a makeshift operating table – fortunate because at that moment he had no wish to run into Mr Manning.

Entering the stuffy room he found his chest and collected a change of shirt from the meagre collection within. Small boat work meant the likelihood of wet feet but Martin lacked any spare trousers and only one extra pair of socks, so he would pass by the purser's store and claim more from the slop chest. But apart from that, and a few necessities from his housemaid, he was ready and went to close the chest, when he noticed one of his bottles of patent medicine.

He picked it up briefly and peered at the label; *Doctor Simmond's Elixir for the Falling Sickness* purported to be an infusion of St John's Wort and other valuable medicinal herbs. The physician himself peered out from its label looking the very epitome of learning and respectability while there were numerous testimonials from apparently satisfied patients. *Mistral*'s surgeon had been dismissive but the stuff cost Martin good money so he had continued to take it. The door opened and he stuffed the bottle into his ditty bag just as Brett entered the storeroom.

"I hears you're set for a cruise with the sailing master." The midshipman gave a derisory smirk that seemed essential in all cockpit conversations.

"Aye, I thought I'd leave the real work to you," Martin replied in a similar vein.

"Oh, you can trust us to sort the ship out, and have her ready for when you deem to return." Brett had found his own chest and was sorting through its contents.

"I shall expect nothing less." Martin turned to leave.

"But you're sure you'll be square?" the lad asked looking up and suddenly serious.

"I'm sure. It were only a bout of seasickness."

"It were more than that," Brett insisted. "We were hardly in a swell, and the sawbones don't keep you in sickers for a simple case of flashing your hash."

"Manning was just being careful," Martin assured him although the youngster was not convinced.

"Maybe you should drop by and check afore you go?" he suggested. "Just to be on the safe side?"

Martin appeared to consider this for a moment. "I'll do that," he replied, equally serious. "Just as soon as I've bothered old man Foil for an advance on a couple of pairs of trousers."

* * *

The island was similar to many volcanic outcrops that Croft had seen in the past; a black sandy beach stretched out from *Mistral*'s current resting place to shallow cliffs which, in turn, stepped up to a central pinnacle towering many feet above them. From there it should be possible to sweep a horizon up to thirty miles away although Croft doubted if even the skills of a topman would be sufficient to scale such sheer sides. He made a mental note to check although first must investigate the possibilities for shelter.

The tide was currently rising; soon he would know for certain how far up the beach the waters reached. With luck there should be a backshore large enough to house any ordinance and stores they needed to remove. At that moment he was considering some of their larboard broadside; each of the eighteen-pounder carriage pieces weighed roughly two tons and moving them would be easier than raising a similar weight of stores from the hold.

Anderson had already explained in detail how he hoped to cant the hull to starboard in order to reach their damage; to that end he, the boatswain and a party of topmen were currently rigging stays from the far edge of the beach that would eventually attach to *Mistral*'s lower masts. Once she had been lightened to larboard, these would prevent the frigate from laying over too far when the waters rose once more.

But it would not be this tide; Croft already knew there was too much to do in the remaining hours and the next would take place in darkness when only a fool would attempt such a feat. No, it would be the following day at the earliest before anyone could contemplate starting on the lower hull and even that would be fast work.

A muted rumble told him how the ship's twin chain pumps were in use; they would continue for the next four hours and should prevent the ingress rising too high, while still allowing the ship to remain firmly lodged. He had organised teams so that no trick lasted more than twenty minutes, with a maximum of four in any twelve-hour period, but still the work would be exhausting, especially when a deal more manual labour was required elsewhere. *Mistral*'s lower deck hands were made of solid stuff and none were strangers to physical effort but he could expect a few to fall by the wayside.

He began to pace across the frigate's sloping quarterdeck as he considered further complications. If they were to erect any form of shelter ashore it must be without the help of the carpenter's crew, who would be fully occupied with the major damage to the hull, as well as any less vital repairs required elsewhere in the ship. He supposed something could be achieved with spars and canvas and the average Jack was not averse to turning his hand to most things. Still, it was another consideration, especially as at all times he must retain enough gunners to man the starboard battery in case an enemy were to return.

He stopped and looked out to sea as he thought further. The sky was crystal clear with a well-defined, and thankfully empty, horizon while a liquid sun continued to gain strength as it rose. With such a view they could be confident of starting work without fear of interruption from the east, although if their chase from last night – and was it really only last night? – were to chance upon them, *Mistral* would be the proverbial sitting duck.

Forward he could see Scott and Martin supervising the launching of a cutter – a procedure made more awkward by the ship's current angle. They had chosen good men to accompany them and all seemed to be working together, although some of the hands were continuing to view the sailing master with caution, if not contempt. And that was surely a shame; had *Mistral* been steering a few yards to starboard she would have passed by the island and the current line of rocks that held them without noticing their existence, although a similar distance to larboard may as easily seen her a total wreck. If anyone were to blame it was the lookouts although Ackerman, at the foretop, had already paid heavily for his inattention. Besides, Croft had been at sea long enough to know such things could happen and were rarely the result of a single man's carelessness. He supposed the trick lay in not looking for fault but solution. And it was the same with his current problems; none were insurmountable, it was just a question of how each were tackled.

Which was his job and, though the prospect now seemed daunting, Croft knew himself equal to it and secretly rather relished the prospect.

* * *

They had been at action stations for over two hours but, apart from some tight manoeuvring, something the captain seemed especially keen on, no guns had been fired aboard *Léopard*. The enemy also seemed silent, although such a thing was hard to gauge on this, the lowest deck in the ship. But no casualties had been sent down to the temporary sick bay and Aimée was starting to grow restless.

"How much longer do you think?" she asked Moreau. The two were seated side by side on the oak platform that would become their operating table if the need arose.

"I cannot say." The surgeon gave a characteristic shrug.

"Whoever we are fighting seems determined to drag matters out to the very end."

"That is assuming we are fighting. There may be more than one: we might be running from a fleet."

"We might," the man accepted with a smile. "But if *Capitaine* Adenis chose to flee we would not be turning so. Besides, I have seen this ship at speed and there are few who can catch her."

Aimée sighed and glanced about. When cleared for action and without many of the lighter bulkheads in place, the deck looked almost spacious. Behind her, in the bows, Captain Johnston and those seamen who had remained loyal, were locked inside the storerooms that became temporary cells on such occasions. Then there was the entrance to the forward magazine; the *St. George* had only needed a single powder store but more would be required aboard a larger ship. A few days back she had been invited to enter one of *Léopard's* and stared in silent awe at the stacks of impending death stored within.

Great care was taken, of course; the magazines were always well guarded and she had needed to replace her shoes with others made of canvas before entering. But even without the precautions Aimée had realised the danger of such places and how vulnerable a ship must be because of them.

Then, further aft, was the second operating table; this was for Moreau's two assistant surgeons while a third platform, one that had been made especially, was used by Mr McIver and Drew. Beyond that was cabin space that included her own small home, although the surgeon had promised to see she was moved to better quarters with more access to light.

Reminded of her condition, she rested her hands on the small bump that was now becoming noticeable; it would be several months before she gave birth but already some movements were less easy.

Moreau had noticed the movement. "You are in pain perhaps?"

"No, just a little tired of waiting."

"For the battle or the baby?" he asked with a flash of white teeth and she smiled in reply.

"Both, I should think."

"Well you need not worry for either," the man insisted, placing a comforting arm about her shoulder. "The battle will be over within the day, you can be certain of that, as you can that we shall be victorious. As for the baby, perhaps not quite so quickly, though the outcome will be as good. And I will be beside you throughout."

She rested her head against him; they were indeed comforting thoughts.

But then a deep rumble from the ship's very fabric banished all mundane fancies. Somewhere, several decks above their head, things were progressing and at least one of their great guns had been fired. In the dim lantern light all exchanged glances, then the ship moved again, more suddenly than before, and another grumbling of thunder echoed about the dark space.

"We have developments it seems," Moreau muttered as he removed his arm and the pair drew apart. The noise of firing had been replaced with the sounds of heavy objects being wheeled across the deck. A faraway whistle blew and there was a chorus of shouting. And then came another sound, every bit as stimulating as the gun fire.

"The men are cheering," the surgeon added with a smile. "So we were victorious, just as I predicted. You see, Aimée, you may depend on everything I say."

* * *

Once they were clear of the ship, Scott's party settled to the task in hand. Despite his brief time aboard, Martin was evidently an efficient officer and had chosen the hands well. They were five seasoned Jacks who handled the small boat with total competence while seemingly content to leave him to his instruments with none of the snide remarks the last few hours aboard *Mistral* had contained. And with the prospect of nothing more than a little undemanding boat work, the chance to sleep on a beach and possibly hunt for game, the entire excursion was starting to take on something of a holiday atmosphere.

Scott had decided on a northward start from the outset; then they would round the tip of the island and begin work moving steadily down the westward side as they made the scientific survey Captain King had ordered. The result might not be greeted with anything other than mild interest by the Admiralty, but should establish him as a cartographer while he secretly wondered if he would be allowed to name the landmass.

"That would appear to be it," Martin remarked, and Scott shook himself free of his dreams to inspect the land to larboard. They had indeed reached the island's northern shore and he was pleased to see his predictions had been correct. The central hill, which must surely be of volcanic origin, was every bit as prominent while the lower levels of sheer rock that ended in a short beach were as he had observed from the eastern aspect. He glanced at his chronometers; essential tools if he were to make an accurate survey, then collected his sextant.

"Very good. Mr Martin, can I trust you to take an accurate bearing?"

"You can indeed, sir,"

"Then that shall be your responsibility." Scott handed a small wooden box across. "And who is able with the lead?"

Two hands shot up and the sailing master was amused to notice both belonged to the Samuels brothers.

"Very good, you shall have charge of depth – there is a sounding rod also if need be. I assume the management of the boat may be left to you three?" he asked the remaining men who grinned confidently in return. "Then bring us closer to the shore and we can begin our work."

The cutter heeled slightly as Martin pressed her helm across and soon they were running for land. There seemed little if no vegetation, so the likelihood of fresh meat was low, and probably an equally scant chance of any natural shelter. But the next few days should be enjoyable none the less, and definitely less of a strain than repairing a beached and vulnerable warship.

* * *

The first of the wounded had been delivered and now there was no time for anything but work. Seven men made it as far as *Léopard*'s lowest deck, but one was quite dead when they laid him down. The others exhibited the mixture of wounds expected when iron balls are fired at men aboard wooden ships. Few troubled the others although Aimée, still relatively new to such injuries, had to brace herself on several occasions. But it was the last, an officer, that caused her the most concern.

He was British and from the Royal Navy; the sight of his uniform caused her to draw breath as much as any injury – Tom had worn one so very similar.

"It is a splinter wound to the shoulder," Moreau announced. "We will have to remove any foreign matter then stitch."

That was obvious and she wondered why Jean was telling her something so simple, before realising she must have been staring at the wounded man for far too long. Swiftly the tunic and shirt were removed, then Aimée started to wipe down the bloody torso. It was a long, but fortunately shallow, incision and the cause, a black sliver of pointed wood, was evident above the patient's shoulder blade. Grasping this firmly in his stained fingers, Moreau eased it out and Aimée immediately swabbed away the surge of fresh red blood.

"Is it bad?" the man asked in halting French. The surgeon glanced at Aimée.

"Bad enough," she told him in his own language. "But we will make you well again."

The officer gave a nod, then winced suddenly as Moreau made the first incision with his needle.

"It will only be a few stitches," Aimée lied as the surgeon tied and cut the gut.

"I did not seek action," the man muttered softly.

"Do not concern yourself with that now, everything can wait until you are well."

"But I did not seek action," he insisted. "I tried to run, and not fight." There was a faint smile. "I could hardly have fought if I had wished to – there were not the men."

"He is rambling," Moreau spoke softly. "Give him some laudanum. When we are done he can sleep and will be the better for it."

Aimée reached for one of the bottles that always lay close by and, ignoring the tin cup sitting next to it, poured a trickle of the thick fluid onto the man's lips in the way she had been taught. He licked at it instinctively and, while his mouth was open, she allowed a little more to drizzle in. The surgeon was right, yet it seemed the young officer was determined to tell them something of importance. A brief cough, then the eyes opened again and he gratefully accepted more of the drug.

"Don't let them think I tried to fight," he insisted once he had swallowed and this time barely flinched when another stitch was thrust deep into his flesh. "Tell Captain King. Tell him I intended only to run. Only to return to Cape Town."

"Who is this Captain King?" she exclaimed, drawing back and suddenly turning cold. But there was no reply; the man had already lapsed into a deep stupor.

Chapter Fifteen

By the fourth day progress had been made on every front. Still marooned off the island's eastern shore, *Mistral* had been lightened by the removal of barrels from three larboard carronades along with two from her long guns and, with the aid of securing lines and an equal amount of cursing and praying, now lay tilted slightly to starboard, her wound at last exposed.

And, once a proper examination was possible, things did not look quite so bad. Although denied access by the leaguers that still filled her forward hold, Anderson announced himself willing to effect a temporary repair from the outside. The result might not meet dockyard standards, and must rely on support from fresh copper covering the patch, but should see them back to Cape Town and possibly last a good deal longer.

To the western side of the island, Scott's party had also been successful. Almost half the landmass was now accurately recorded with special attention having been given to one small bay that might provide, if not a harbour, then at least temporary shelter for a future ship in difficulties. The evening excursions ashore proved less satisfactory. Martin led the men in two hunting expeditions but, although they stumbled about inland with much enthusiasm and a good deal of shouting, no wild boar presented itself as game and neither did any sea bird prove cooperative. But as Scott spent his evenings copying that day's rough draft to his master chart, he was more than satisfied. From what they had seen of the western shore of the island, the major features had already been recorded and, once the southerly point was rounded, they would be in sight of *Mistral* once more.

But it was on the morning of the fifth day that their idyll finally came to an end. It had begun like every other; a scratch meal of hard tack accompanied by cocoa boiled up on the previous night's fire before their boat was loaded and launched into the gentle surf. As with every other day, it had been Scott's intention to be surveying by the time dawn broke, with the cutter remaining at sea until nightfall; an arrangement that suited all in the group. But the sun had only just risen and was yet to be visible above the island's single stark peak when something far more sinister came into view.

"It's the Frog corvette," one of the Samuels brothers declared as the vessel emerged from the shadows of night. For several seconds all were shocked into silence; the warship was under topsails and forecourse and sailing gently with the wind just off her starboard beam, three miles from where their own craft lay wallowing in the offshore slop.

"Steering to pass the island," Scott remarked at last, his voice little more than a whisper.

"Do you think her to be looking for *Mistral*?" Martin asked in equally low tones.

"Unlikely," Scott replied. "Unless she knows her to be there."

The corvette was certainly showing no sign of haste and had several points in hand as she headed to clear the southern tip of the landmass.

"So what do we do?" Martin again. "If we hoist sail and try to warn the others we will be seen."

That was true and something Scott was already considering. It was possible the Frenchman would continue past and not notice the vulnerable frigate beached further to the north while his own small force might remain where they were, stay undetected, and even continue with their work. He knew it to be a choice only he could make and was equally aware of the naval tradition for ignoring inconvenient truths. But stranded as she was, *Mistral* would be hard to miss and, if caught unawares with guns unmanned and in the midst of repair, might well be taken.

"We warn the ship," Scott announced. "Stredwick, raise the masts and show some canvas."

That had been another decision quickly reached; they could have begun under sweeps until sighted and, so powered, may have reached the southerly point in reasonable time and undetected. But in order to give those aboard *Mistral* sufficient warning, speed was vital. Even close-hauled they could travel several knots faster than any oar could propel them and, though a risk, it was one he knew they must take.

The spars were swiftly rigged and as her sails drew tight the boat came to life. Soon she was slicing through the shadowed waters with a gentle hiss sounding far too loudly from her stem. Scott swallowed as he considered the oncoming craft; for the time being he and his men would be all but invisible against a backdrop of grey rock face but it would not be long – a few minutes at most – before the sun was over the ridge and shining down on them. Then a small boat speeding under lateen sails would be only too obvious.

Of course, they would have the heels of a corvette, but the enemy were also slightly to the south and could draw nearer when his cutter rounded the island. Even if caught unprepared, it would not take long for the warship to rustle up a broadside, and only one shot from the lightest of carriage pieces should account for their boat and all aboard her.

* * *

On the eastern shore, all were continuing in ignorance of any danger. Anderson and his men had worked throughout the night and, though they had yet to cover the fresh wood with a layer of sheet copper, were quietly confident the hull would be watertight for the forthcoming high tide. The news had come at the right time as far as Croft and King were concerned; both pumps had been needed for longer than either of them had anticipated and with the work necessary seeing the guns removed and the ship secured, little else had been achieved. But now at least they could make a start on recovering the ordinance, so it had been with a feeling of relief that Adams' party was sent ashore to prepare. If all went well, they could start fitting the copper sheeting as soon as the tide began to ebb once more, then begin taking on cannon with the next rise. By dusk, they should have three or four sheets secured and, if they worked on under lamplight as before, may even see the ship loaded and seaworthy by the following day.

In which case he would have no hesitation in signalling for the cutter's return, King decided. Nothing had been heard of the small boat for several days, but Scott must have completed a good deal of his survey. And if it were only half done, what had been achieved would still be of use, even if greater value had been served by separating him from the crew. He stood on the quarterdeck, now angled slightly to starboard, and looked out towards the rising sun. They had been lucky so far with no sign of the storm returning and repairs turning out simpler than expected, *Mistral* could be at sea by the following evening. There would be little point in continuing his search for Aimée; the ship would be patched for the time being but must be taken in for proper repairs and had already seen more action that most in what had only been a working up cruise.

"Four hours until high." The first lieutenant's comment broke a silence that had lasted for some time.

"Indeed," King agreed, wondering vaguely if it were an indication of their strengthening friendship that each could remain within feet of the other yet not feel obliged to speak.

"Adams is making progress with the carronades." Croft glanced towards the shore. The junior lieutenant was intending to make full use of the rising water by having his ordinance ready to load as soon as their launch could reach them. Once the tide made its way up the black sand of the beach, his working party would begin and, judging by the time it had taken to remove them, the lighter barrels should be back aboard *Mistral* when it began to ebb.

A loud thumping noise came from within the ship as one of Anderson's party secured an outer strake while a squeal of tackle blocks from above told how Jennings and his team were setting about replacing several lengths of running rigging. But on the quarterdeck, silence had returned. Then King gave a sudden start.

"What was that?" he asked and Croft blinked in confusion.

"I heard nothing, sir."

King shook his head. "Probably my imagination," he sighed, "but I thought it to be cannon fire."

* * *

The last shot from the corvette's bow chasers had passed directly over their heads, missing both masts by a matter of feet. Scott and Martin exchanged glances; they had already done all they could. With both sails set and drawing well the small boat was making a good speed, but the Frenchman was less than a mile off their stern and they must remain within range for some while, certainly as long as it would take to fully round the southern point of the island.

The sound of another shot passing by made them duck down once more, but this time it cleared them easily and sent up a brief splash about fifty yards off their larboard bow. They knew from recent experience there would now be a reprieve of perhaps two minutes before the process was repeated and both sat more upright in the sternsheets.

"We'll signal *Mistral* once there's a chance they can see us," Martin said, adding, "that way it should come as less of a surprise when chummy here turns up," as he glanced back at the pursuing warship.

The corvette was now under all plain sail and rigging stunsails, which almost pleased the more dispassionate Scott; extra canvas would make his pursuer marginally faster, but also a good deal more visible to a distant frigate.

"Small arms ready, men," he ordered quietly. "There's no point in waiting to clear the point, I want a volley from all, then reload as swiftly as you can."

The hands acknowledged his words with nods or brief knucklings of foreheads before they attended to their weapons. There were five muskets aboard the small craft and both officers were armed with pistols; it would hardly be a cacophony, but hopefully enough to alert those aboard the ship, even if their boat was missed by the lookouts.

And then came the familiar sound of a distant six-pounder long gun as the first of the corvette's bow chasers spoke again.

* * *

"That's small arms fire and no mistaking," King insisted, staring out over the stern. "Masthead, what do you see there?"

"Nothing in sight," the lookout, perched way above on the maintop, replied. "Though I might have heard muskets an' maybe a cannon jus' now."

King glanced at Croft in triumph and the older man looked back blankly. "I regret, I can only hear Mr Anderson at work," he said.

"Begging your pardon, sir, but I thought I heard guns an all." This was Sennett, one of the midshipmen, and Croft appeared to accept defeat.

"Shall I signal Mr Scott's party to return?" he asked.

"No, they will have to look to themselves for now," King replied. "I want nothing that might draw the enemy's attention. And you can ask Anderson and his men to cease their racket."

A sharp order brought silence that made all aboard the frigate feel yet more vulnerable, but there was still more that King could do.

"You there, Jennings, bring your men down." Then, turning back to the first lieutenant, "I want all starboard guns manned and ready; boarding netting rigged and small arms issued."

Croft stepped away and began organising those on deck while topmen slipped down backstays and took up positions at the cannon. Again King looked astern, there was nothing in sight but, even as he looked, the sound of another barrage of small arms fire echoed from afar. The first lieutenant's words came back to haunt him; four hours until high, that meant for probably the next two *Mistral* would have to remain static on the rocks and an open target for any enemy who cared to take advantage of the fact.

* * *

Martin gritted his teeth as he held the cutter on course; they had rounded the island and were now flying before the wind with sails goose-winged and taut while a constant cloud of spray steamed back from their stem. And, so intent was he, there was no chance to look back for even a second, although the regular passing of shot told him the French had turned also and were still in hot pursuit. But then he could also see the stark outline of *Mistral* not so very far ahead.

Her trim had altered and she now lay more inclined to starboard but it was obvious the frigate remained as set as before. Martin was not certain what angle her guns might manage but sensed that, carefully handled, the corvette could manoeuvre off her unprotected stern. And, once so positioned, she might begin a raking fire that would eventually cause the larger ship's destruction.

But before that could happen, he and Scott must consider their own safety. To some extent they had been lucky; if the enemy had kept their course on rounding the island, they might have despatched a full broadside and it would have been strange if at least one shot had not struck the small boat. The French captain was in no apparent hurry, however, and why should he be when there was time aplenty to catch them as well as close with the stranded frigate? And, as his bow chasers were continuing to fire off two shots at such regular intervals, there was every chance he might achieve both without unnecessary delay.

Scott was hunched next to him at the stern sheets while Stredwick, Burchett and Veness huddled together in the bottom of the boat. The Samuels brothers worked so perfectly in concert that they had long since taken over the sailing of the cutter. They sat far more upright and to either side as they gripped the sheets. Another shot passed, this time a good way off to starboard and Martin wondered if they were reaching the limit of the enemy guns' accuracy. Certainly a twenty-five foot cutter should be faster than any full-rigged ship, and they had been running for what felt like most of the morning.

But at least there was now no need to worry about alerting *Mistral*; even from such a distance it was clear the ship was aware – he could see what looked like the launch heading from the shore and guessed all aboard were preparing for action. He gauged the distance once more; with luck they would arrive in time to join the defenders. His only doubt

157

was if they could avoid the corvette's shot for so long.

And then, suddenly, there was no question. Martin felt the passage of air against his face, a sensation that was instantly followed by the crack of iron smashing into wood and a muffled groan. Startled, he took a tight grip on the tiller but already the boat's motion had changed. Rather than the firm, lithe thing he had been controlling, the craft was suddenly sluggish while both sails began to flap impotently and white water streamed in through the ragged hole that had appeared close to where one of the Samuels brothers had been seated.

"Steer for the coast!" Scott ordered, but Martin had already pressed the tiller across and, using what momentum remained, the boat began a leaden turn to larboard.

"You there, Burchett, commence bailing – help him Veness," the sailing master continued. "And Stredwick, clap on to the foresheet there!"

Scott himself rose up and grasped the mainsheet and slowly the boat was brought under control, although they were now broadside on to the corvette which was continuing to bear down on them.

"Make for that beach!" Scott pointed at a break in the nearby rocks. Martin gauged the distance; it was a good cable off and they would have to endure several more shots from the bow chasers at what would be an ever-decreasing range.

The injured man was rolled into the bottom of the boat where his brother, who had no eyes for distraction, attended him while the remaining hands continued to bail. With the change of course, less water was being driven through the jagged hole but still it could not be contained and Martin silently watched its progress as the level steadily rose.

Then there came the sound of another pair of shots from the corvette, almost simultaneous this time and sooner than any of them expected – the recent hit had clearly encouraged the French gunners. But now the shore was in plain sight and almost attainable.

"Can you steer her through?" Scott asked as Martin noticed two outcrops of rock that barely broke the surface and were probably a continuation of the ridge which had accounted for *Mistral*. There remained the smallest of passages between their jagged edges and he carefully aimed the cutter at the gap.

Their speed must have been greater than he had thought as the promontories seemed to flash by and then, just as another shot passed overhead, they were approaching the beach itself. But the single ball was not alone, another followed and another after that. Even though he had yet to bring the boat safely in, Martin found himself glancing back at his pursuer and it was not an encouraging sight.

The corvette had yawed and, in an effort to finish them off, drawn closer to the shore. Even as he watched, fire from her larboard broadside was running steadily down her hull, with each shot being considered, deliberate and aimed directly at him.

* * *

Aboard *Mistral*, the fate of the cutter and her crew had been noted, although there was too much on King's mind to consider it for long. Adams had returned with the shore party and much was already being done to prepare for the corvette's approach. All starboard guns were loaded and run out, with their carriages slewed aft to cover as much of the frigate's stern as possible. A pair of larboard long guns were also being moved and mounted to fire directly aft in King's own quarters. Two eighteen-pounders would do little against a full broadside from even a minor warship but at least some fire might dissuade the enemy from venturing close. In the French captain's position, King would have taken his ship further out to properly assess the situation, although there was little to be seen from there that could not be learned from their current perspective. Nevertheless, after firing that one broadside on the beached cutter, the corvette had indeed gained some sea room and was now bearing down on them off their starboard quarter. Adams, who was in charge of the improvised stern battery, had reported his pieces almost ready and the enemy must surely be nearing accurate range. The lieutenant was under orders to open fire as soon as there was chance of a hit, and King was almost holding his breath until he did. But here was Anderson to bother him and he wondered what fresh mischief the carpenter had discovered to plague him.

"You'll pardon me, sir, but it wud seem ye intend firing yon broadside cannon."

"If we are given the chance," King retorted. "Does that present a problem?"

"It is likely, sir," the Scotsman told him dolefully. "We're still groonded an' I would prefer nae tae put the hull under fuver strain."

King bit back the instinctive reply that, perhaps Anderson would rather they simply surrendered to the enemy; the man must surely know their predicament and was not seeking to annoy.

"Very well, what do you suggest?" King asked sharply.

The Scotsman pursed his lips. "Perhaps a few shots, individual ones, sir, an' spaced weel apart. Nae broadsides, the vibrations would only cause th' ship tae grind on the rocks and see her bottom scraped awa'."

King sighed; he supposed that was a consideration and one he had overlooked.

"Perhaps when th' tide lifts us?" Anderson suggested. King flashed a look at Croft who had been listening throughout.

"High water is in a little over three hours, sir," the first lieutenant reported. "Though, if it proves sufficiently watertight, the hull should lift well before then."

"How long?"

"Maybe ninety minutes," Croft replied as if the information had been forced out of him.

Ninety minutes. With a spring attached to one of the anchors and the speedy release of all shore lines, he would then be able to swing *Mistral* about. And with such manoeuvrability as well as the full use of their starboard broadside they should account for the corvette with ease. Except King knew he didn't have ninety minutes.

* * *

The cutter was beyond any immediate repair and a good mile of rock-strewn beach separated the stranded seamen from where *Mistral* lay prone upon the rocks. But the enemy corvette was still in sight and apparently considered them dealt with. They watched as the ship altered course and began to make for the stranded frigate.

Scott pursed his lips. They had done their part in warning *Mistral* of the danger and were unlikely to be of further use. But to stand and witness their ship being systematically destroyed was not a pleasant prospect.

"We have to keep moving!" he said.

"But Peter!" the surviving Samuels brother protested. "Ain't we gonna see to him?"

"Poor bugger's dead," Stredwick told him harshly. "There ain't nothing we can do."

"We can see he's decently buried," the remaining brother insisted.

"Maybe later," Scott temporised. "Our first concern is to regain the ship." He glanced across to Martin. "You have the chart?" he asked, but the midshipman looked back at him vacantly.

"The chart?"

"Our efforts for the last few days," Scott snapped. The man's face was deadly white, which might be understandable in the circumstances, but there was also an odd look in his eyes which the sailing master didn't care for at all. "Get back to the cutter and collect our workings," he directed. "And the instruments; bring those as well."

"What about Peter?" Samuels again.

"Cover him with a sail if you must," Scott retorted. "But be quick, both of you."

He might be fresh to the Royal Navy but it was a universal rule that, when his ship was in danger, a seaman's duty was to rejoin her immediately. But there were more reasons to be going; Samuels' death had to be reported while, if *Mistral* did end up a wreck, they might still give assistance from the shore. And then there was what he had seen in Martin's eyes, a look that chilled him more than he could say.

Suddenly the novelty of independent command had lost its allure and, whatever some might think of him, Scott wanted nothing more than to be back amongst his shipmates.

* * *

Minutes later *Mistral*'s stern mounted long guns came into use. The first shots were ineffective but must have disconcerted the enemy to some extent as, after exchanging a couple of volleys from her bow chasers, the corvette came no closer. Instead she put her helm across and presented her larboard broadside. The move had been made when the smaller ship was a little less than a mile off their counter and King could not blame the French captain for being cautious. However vulnerable it might be, a fifth rate remained far more powerful than any corvette. Besides, for all the Frenchman knew, *Mistral* was not stuck fast and might be simply trying to lure his ship closer.

The first broadside was badly laid, with only one shot striking. But that landed soundly just below *Mistral*'s taffrail, sending splinters that found three men at the sternmost carronades as well as shattering their flag locker. Still it was poor shooting, although the enemy could be expected to improve with practice.

King turned his attention to his gunners in the waist. "Can any of your pieces bear, Mr Summers?" he bellowed, but the young officer shook his head.

"Not at present, sir, though the enemy is bound to be blown off shore slightly," he replied. "And it won't need much before she's in reach."

That was definitely the case; the corvette had reduced sail and was lying hove to and in a position where she could rake *Mistral*'s stern. However, in order to avoid the frigate's broadside cannon she was close to the shore and the steeply shelving sea bed meant it would be difficult to anchor. No unsecured sailing ship can remain totally stationary however, and any drift would surely be directed away from danger.

As if to punctuate his thoughts, one of their own stern mounted cannon was fired from the deck below and King felt the vibrations through the soles of his boots. Anderson had been right in his warning; a full broadside would have caused significant damage, yet it hardly seemed as if they were to be granted the opportunity.

"Level but well to seaward," Croft reported mournfully. If the stern mounted guns were to make an impression they would have to do better than that.

"Mr Sennett, my compliments to Mr Adams and request he raises his aim," King said, turning to the midshipman. "It will do little good to strike at the hull, we must wound them aloft."

The lad scampered off with the message just as the Frenchman fired another full broadside. This time two shots were received low on *Mistral*'s stern and might have affected those at the cannon mounted in his own quarters. King gritted his teeth. It was a bad situation and one that could only deteriorate: as soon as the French captain realised they were truly stuck fast, he was bound to creep closer.

Another of Adam's cannon fired and this time the result was more promising; it might have been a trick of the light, but King was sure he caught a glimpse of the shot in flight as it passed by the Frenchman's tophamper barely feet from her mizzen. The second piece followed a few seconds later but its path was lost completely as the enemy chose the same instant to release their third broadside.

This time true damage was caused. Frigates were designed to inflict rather than receive punishment and lacked the solidity of a line-of-battleship while much of their upper works were more intended to deflect wind and weather than enemy shot. *Mistral*'s stern bulwark was hit for the second time and instantly separated into individual planks, leaving those on the quarterdeck feeling even more exposed. Further hits were received below and the mizzen itself was also struck, although mercifully low enough for the shot to glance off. King withdrew his watch; it was still more than an hour before they could hope to turn the ship, and the corvette was staying obstinately out of reach of even their starboard carronades. He glanced towards Croft, who appeared as resolute as ever. King knew the man would remain so while the ship was knocked to pieces beneath his feet although he, as her captain, could not be quite so detached.

In such a situation, men would soon start to die and King knew the responsibility of losing even one unnecessarily would accompany him forever. He had surrendered a ship before, although that had been to a superior force; to yield to a smaller vessel went against every instinct in his body. But there was nothing else for it, the enemy's next broadside was due at any moment and, hard though it must be, he must act immediately.

And then one of the stern mounted cannon spoke again and, this time, took away the corvette's main topmast.

* * *

"She's hit the Frog!" Stredwick shouted.

They had covered roughly half the distance to *Mistral* and the heavy rocks that had slowed their progress were starting to give way to more manageable sand. It would still be several minutes before they reached the frigate's stricken form however, and all were starting to tire. But what the seaman had said was correct; the corvette – almost level with them, although a good way offshore – had definitely taken a hit to her tophamper and the party watched in fascination and relief as the enemy tried to cope with the damage aloft.

"Have to sort that lot out afore they sets to on the barky again," one of the hands muttered with evident satisfaction.

"Like old Ma Riley's washing," another agreed.

Scott considered his group properly for the first time since they had abandoned the cutter. The men had made good progress with even

Samuels seeming to have forgotten about leaving his dead brother. But though he had kept up as well as any, the midshipman was still causing him concern. His skin had not lost its pallor and there was no change in that ghastly look to the eyes.

"Are you well, Martin?" Scott asked. They were close enough to *Mistral* now and, with the immediate danger postponed, he felt less tense.

"All-a-taunt-o thank you, sir," the midshipman's voice was indistinct and he paused to swig from a small amber bottle.

Scott supposed the last hour or so had been especially taxing and everyone reacted differently under pressure. But soon they should be back to the ship and normality; then everything would appear so much clearer.

"Very well then, we should continue."

But though Scott and the others turned to go, Martin remained; a fact that went unnoticed for some while. And when one of them did look back it was to see the midshipman had fallen to the ground and was lying face down and quite still. And strangely his hands seemed to have dug deep into the black sand for support.

Chapter Sixteen

King regarded the officers he had summoned to the remains of his quarters. Behind them, at the stern gallery, the two eighteen-pounder long guns still stood in silent sentinel while impact from French round shot could be seen in several neat holes punched in the ship's stern. On noting the damage, the carpenter had reported worse had been caused by *Mistral*'s own cannon. The timber that checked the weapon's recoil had proved nowhere near strong enough and the lower counter rail was now cracked. Nevertheless, their injuries were more than balanced by what had been doled out to the French.

On losing part of her main, the corvette had withdrawn before making slow progress seaward where Summers had managed a few inconclusive pot shots with the quarterdeck carronades. And, though now invisible from the deck, the masthead still had her in sight; she was hove to once more and probably effecting repairs. Quite what she would do next was anyone's guess, and the reason he had called this meeting.

"Mr Anderson estimates we should have our copper attached and be ready to sail with tomorrow's high," King announced. "It will mean our working throughout the night and not just the carpenter's team; Mr Adams, I believe you still have ordinance to load?"

"Yes, sir," the young officer agreed. "One of the long guns and a larboard carronade."

"Then that can continue when we are afloat on tonight's high." King nodded, "And I do not wish for any of those attending the hull to be involved in your work."

Anderson's men would be busy enough while the tide was low, while Adams' needed water beneath the launch's hull to bring the heavy cannon barrels alongside. Normally the working parties would have been combined, but King had other ideas.

"In fact, none of us will be getting any sleep. Those not actively involved in repairing the ship or replacing her ordinance will stand guard and form a defence."

King glanced at the faces that sat to either side of the dining table. To his left, Croft and Adams showed no surprise while Scott, freshly returned from his escapades ashore, seemed equally nonplussed. The sight of the sailing master reminded King of another matter; he had heard that Martin was sent straight to sick bay after rejoining the ship, though strangely not through injury in action. King knew no more and, with everything else to consider, had not found chance to call upon him. But Summers, Sennett and several other midshipmen were present and currently viewing him with ill-concealed interest.

"A beached frigate must surely be a great temptation," he mused, "and frankly, gentlemen, I do not think the Frenchman will leave us be."

Now there was a definite muttering between the younger members, but King continued.

"To strike their main topmast at such a range was undoubtedly fine shooting by Mr Adams' team although we have to allow that a fair degree of luck might also have been involved."

A ripple of good-natured laughter greeted this but King carried on.

"However, I feel they will be unlikely to try the same mode of attack again." He paused. "Instead, I am expecting a land action."

This time the discussion was louder and more general: even Adams and Scott exchanged a word or two.

"So in the absence of marines, I want all not actively repairing the ship or returning ordinance to form a defence against seaward attack under Mr Scott's command." Although strictly a sailing master, Scott had already proved himself a capable fighting officer and King did not have the manpower to be selective. "And I mean all; each of our serviceable guns are to be loaded with an additional charge of canister on top of round shot and there are to be enough men set aside to serve them. Then, apart from masthead lookouts, which are to be changed half-hourly, and Mr Manning's medical department, everyone else, including those of Mr Adams' and Mr Anderson's parties not currently working, must be available for combat. While we remain aground, some will need to be stationed ashore as the French may choose to beach their craft further off and make a landward attack, but during high water most must be aboard ship. And they will be wide awake and ready, do I make myself clear?"

It seemed he did; all nodded keenly and there was even a hint of excitement from the younger men. Noticing this King had to hide a frown; this was to be no party and neither would there be glory. Of the two, *Mistral* remained the larger ship and, even though stranded, would be expected to defend herself. Should she be captured, King's career would be his last consideration, although it must be finished nevertheless.

"Let me make it plain; the French are inclined to over-man their vessels and a corvette can be expected to contain more than one hundred men, ignoring any additional carried for prize crews. To balance that we are severely depleted and lack marines while the work on repairs and replacing cannon must continue. So, although we might muster slightly more on paper, remain at a disadvantage. And please don't think we will be facing a token force; in the enemy captain's position I would have no hesitation in sending the majority of my people on such a mission, so we must expect stiff opposition."

His statement only fuelled the discussion further although Croft, it seemed, had a question.

"I wonder if I might make a suggestion, sir?" he asked, hand raised slightly like a schoolboy's. King nodded.

"In addition to the launch, there is one cutter and the jolly boat left serviceable. We might row a guard further out to sea?"

"We might," King conceded. "Though the cutter fully loaded would do little to dissuade such a force and, even if an alarm were raised, it would take valuable men away from the ship's defence."

This was greeted by knowledgeable nods from all, including Croft and, as he sat back in his chair, King was strangely reassured. However desperate the situation might appear, it was almost countered by having such a band of officers to back him. *Mistral*'s lower deck were equally solid and he realised then that, by some quirk of fate, he had acquired the crew every captain yearns for. And, despite the circumstances, with such men at his side he felt he might do anything.

* * *

Martin appeared to have made an enemy. The surgeon had been brusque and to the point; he was far too busy coping with the physical injuries of battle to deal with one apparently contemptuous of his care and trust. Besides, apart from Martin's own bottle of *Dr Simmond's Elixir* – which seemed to have mysteriously disappeared – the only remedy he could offer was rest. That was something the midshipman had been glad to take advantage of although, now he was awake and back to reality, it was time to think more of his future.

Throughout his naval career Martin was regularly overworked and often under pressure, yet had never felt himself indispensable. However demanding any particular task might be, there were always others ready to take his place and always those above to supervise what he had done. But while they had been away, and certainly in those desperate minutes as he struggled dizzily up the beach from the wrecked cutter, it had been different. He was one of only seven men; more than that, one of only two officers, so much had depended on him alone.

And he had let them down; however much he might excuse himself by claiming his particular condition was not of his making, that remained an undeniable fact. As soon as the wrecked cutter grounded he had known an attack was coming, known that shortly he would become incapable of caring even for himself, yet had been unable to warn the others or avoid what was to come in any way. And, again, there was no vindication in saying it was something that could not be avoided, for he could have done so by not placing himself in such a situation in the first place.

Besides, what would have happened if he had lost balance earlier, when they first sighted the enemy corvette or while running from her guns? With all so dependent on one another, the entire party would have been lost – *Mistral* might even not have been warned and, though he might take chances with his own, he had no right to risk the lives of others.

So, even if he never fell ill again, he must now accept there was no place for him aboard a warship. As soon as they dropped their hook in Table Bay he would be knocking on the doors of the Castle and pleading for his former position. Shore service might lack the magic of being at sea, but was apparently his only option while at least he would not be directly responsible for anyone else. As he came to this conclusion a strange weight seemed to lift from his shoulders, and Martin became the only one aboard *Mistral* to succumb to a peaceful night's sleep.

* * *

They had done all they could; the launch, already loaded with the last of the carronade barrels, was at the high water mark waiting for the tide to claim it while, a little higher up the beach, the business part of the final carriage piece was lying equally ready. It would be two hours at least before any further work would be possible; until then, and against the sound of distant hammering as Anderson's party worked, there was little for any of them to do. Consequently, Adams had allowed the majority of his men to find what comfort they could in the black sand and rocks of the backshore, while a line of sentries, carefully hidden amid the scrub and occasional boulders, kept a careful watch over the short distance of beach separating them from their stranded ship.

"Swain was trying to light a pipe," Summers reported as he returned from his rounds.

"You stopped him?" Adams enquired, and the younger officer handed over half a perique of tobacco and a tinderbox.

"He can be dealt with in the morning," Adams said, although the prospect seemed as distant as Christmas.

"No sign of anything from the ship?" Summers asked as he seated himself next to his friend against a convenient rock.

Adams shook his head. "Or the enemy for that matter. But then I wouldn't expect there to be. With no moon to speak of till later and chips and his team making enough noise to wake the dead, the first we'll hear of the French is when they start firing on us."

"I'd chance we might see a bit more from back here." Summers gazed down at the shallow beach.

"We might," Adams agreed. "Though still not much."

The ship was only sparsely lit by the occasional lantern but vast stretches of empty foreshore reached out to either side and were totally encased in darkness.

"But it should not be for long," the midshipman continued. "If Anderson does all he intends, *Mistral* will rise on the tide for good. Then all we has to do is send on the last of our cannon, warp her out, and we can square away. With a bit of luck we'll be back in Cape Town by the end of the month."

"Aye," Adams agreed brightening slightly at the prospect. With Anne's debts effectively cancelled and further prize money due for their recent capture, she should be able to move from the boarding house and set up home for them both somewhere more respectable. A previous idea for resigning his commission had returned and, with the change in their circumstances, now seemed viable once more.

"When do you think they'll be coming?" Summers asked as he rested his foot against a rock.

"It'll have to be soon," Adams replied. "Weather looks like staying clear and if they waits too long there'll be something of a moon."

"Reckon the lookouts will be seeing much?" the lad persisted.

"Aboard ship?" Adams clarified. "No way of telling. You know how a mist can gather offshore; the French might get within pistol range before we knows they're about. But that's assuming they're coming at all."

"And you don't think they are?"

Adams shrugged. "That's another thing we can't judge; captain seems convinced of it, but that's only one man. Personally I think we've given them one bloody nose and they won't wait around for another. *Mistral*'s a darn sight bigger than any corvette and they don't know us to be undermanned."

"We're still obviously stranded, though," Summers reminded him. "And still vulnerable."

"If Anderson does his work properly she'll be afloat within a few hours; then, with a working starboard battery, the old girl will see off any number of landing parties." He sighed. "I tell you, Michael, unless they come soon, it won't be worth their bother. And if their ship's in sight when dawn breaks they'd better watch out else we'll have another prize to add to our collection."

Adams sat back duly satisfied although Summers remained anxious. The French ship had not headed away; when darkness fell she was still in sight from the masthead and apparently seeing to her rig. Even another all-out assault was not out of the question; if her repairs were successful she might creep in as before and, carefully handled in the darkness, prove a very difficult target while the vast and stationary bulk of *Mistral* would be a hard mark to miss. But he supposed his friend was right; Adams was older after all and more senior and, as if it made a difference, married. Yet though he knew all this and could see sense in the argument, still he remained concerned. And then he saw a reason to be so.

* * *

"Two more sheets wull do it, sir," Anderson told Croft in the flickering lamplight. The first lieutenant glanced up at *Mistral*'s hull. Those fresh plates already in place were noticeable only by the slight change in colour; the light was poor and his was an inexpert eye but it appeared Anderson and his team had done a superb job, and one that only lacked a few pieces to make it complete.

"And you can have that done by high water?" Croft asked, glancing briefly at his boots that were already awash.

"Ah believe so, sur." The Scotsman was reassuringly positive.

"It'll be close, but my mates ur fair getting the hang o' coppering."

That seemed to be the case, even as one of the sheets was being secured a party was raising another into position. Croft watched as they manoeuvred the heavy metal between them on a pair of extra-wide ladders that had been especially constructed for the job. It was quite possible that, until a day or so ago, none had been faced with sheathing a ship before, yet were now performing the task like experts.

And not all were carpenters; Croft noticed several topmen and members of the boatswain's team at work while even the cook, a man who lacked a leg, was making himself useful by drilling securing holes in the copper. It was just one more example of the seaman's innate versatility and he was about to comment on the fact when he heard a strange sound. It came between the regular beats of the workmen's hammering and, if he hadn't known better, Croft would have said it was musket fire.

He turned in the direction of the noise but even the poor lantern light was enough to make little visible in the darkness beyond *Mistral*'s stern. A movement close by made him look back; Anderson had a look of wonder on his face but the expression swiftly changed to one of blank resignation as his body slumped to the ground. For a moment Croft stared stupidly at the space where the Scotsman had stood; nothing else was altered, the men were continuing to work with two determinedly pounding the current plate home. And then reason took hold.

"Look alive there, sentries!" he bellowed but his order was redundant. Though lacking marines, a line of musket men had been stationed on *Mistral*'s larboard gangway and, as the group of charging Frenchmen came into view, began firing down on them. And then more British appeared; men who had been waiting patiently in the lee of the vessel's hull rose up and laid in to the enemy with cutlasses and pistols. Croft reached for his sword and drew it but delayed in joining the fray; in the darkness chaos reigned and friend could be injured as easily as foe. Then a sound from behind alerted him and, turning back into the carpenter's lights, he saw another group emerging from around the ship's bows.

"Musket men!" He pointed at the fresh danger, but those stationed above had already been sent down to join in the foray on the ground. A ball whipped past his head and another plopped into the ground close by. Croft instinctively squatted down next to Anderson's body as more shot followed.

Some of *Mistral's* men must have noticed the new threat and, turning from the battle behind, were now running back to take the enemy head on. Croft rose to follow but there were more musket shots and two of his group fell to them. He raised his own sword and bellowed for others to close up. The crowd before him was substantial while the flow of French continued and suddenly he knew there were far fewer British to see them off. He glanced back; where were those on deck? The larboard sentries had joined the fight, but there were gunners stationed at the starboard battery. Without their help the ground party would soon be overwhelmed and *Mistral* destroyed as easily as if she had been knocked to pieces that morning.

More figures gathered next to him; men from the other fight which was probably over. But they were still not enough and, as the enemy bore down on them, Croft sensed it could only end one way.

* * *

"To larboard!" Adams shouted as he stumbled forward. Summers' young eyes had noticed the first boat the moment it beached half a cable from *Mistral's* stern and the lad had rallied the men immediately. But it became clear even as they charged that this force was smaller; what must have been a larger boat had grounded forward of the stranded ship and was carrying far more.

Adams tripped and almost fell before recovering himself although the delay meant him dropping back in the pack of running seamen. But looking forward he could still see Croft under the work lanterns, along with what might have been the boatswain and master-at-arms as they gathered together, only to be smothered by a throng of charging Frenchmen. For a moment Adams wondered if he should order his force to join them but instinctively decided against it. A surprise attack on the enemy's flank would do more good while the sight of another group physically joining the fight ahead of them should encourage the others.

"Larboard, larboard I say!" he screamed again. If he had considered joining Croft's force others might have the same idea and Adams was suddenly desperate that they made a concerted and separate attack. The flash and pop of a pistol to his right told how some fool had fired early and may have warned the enemy but it soon ceased to matter as the bulk of his men fell upon the French.

It was a brief and bloody fight that few could later remember in any detail; Adams joined when he was still only midway in the group and flayed out almost indiscriminately with his hanger, barely noticing others as they fought, or fell, to either side. But soon the French were turning in retreat and it was then that a further group of British appeared from around *Mistral*'s bows, effectively blocking any attempt by the enemy to regain their boat.

Adams could see Allcorn, the ship's bullock-bodied master-at-arms, as he wielded an axe above his head like a child's toy. "Steady, steady there!" the beast was yelling in a tone that commanded attention.

"You will surrender!" Adams added as loudly as he could manage although his voice cracked and much of his breath was gone. But the message was conveyed well enough and, before anyone had fully realised what was about, individual men began to toss their weapons to the ground and were thrusting their hands up high.

"Times like this we could use the marines," Scott, who must have led the last group, remarked casually before calling for a seaman to collect the fallen arms.

"Get that lot lined up an' in the light," Allcorn continued as he strode forward. In such a situation age and experience, backed up by seventeen stone of solid muscle, gave the petty officer a natural authority no scrawny lieutenant could hope to emulate. Soon the bemused prisoners were being herded towards the lanterns where Anderson and his men had so recently worked and, following meekly in their wake, Adams caught sight of more familiar faces.

Most were shouting instructions or physically guiding the French into one solid mass that could be guarded more effectively, and then for the second time in what was probably as many minutes, he saw the first lieutenant.

Croft had sheathed his sword although Adams noticed there was a tear across his uniform tunic and what might be blood on his shirt. "Very good, Mr Adams," the older man told him as he approached. "Assist Mr Allcorn in rounding up the prisoners, I suspect a French speaker will be of use. And you did well," Croft added as an afterthought. "Your attack on the enemy's flank was well placed and perfectly timed."

"Thank you, sir," Adams mumbled before heading for where Allcorn was continuing to berate the bemused French. Then Summers appeared at his elbow; the lad seemed mercifully unhurt and even more animated than usual.

"It were brilliant, John, brilliant!" he gushed. "The way you took on the enemy's tail like that – it saved the day!"

"No, it were Scott's men coming from round the bows," Adams muttered quietly. "They're the ones what won it."

Chapter Seventeen

He had no idea where the plan had come from, but it was a good one, Adams allowed as he settled himself in the sternsheets of the unknown cutter. When it was decided upon he had been seeing to the prisoners but, only minutes after defeating the landing party, it seemed they were to continue the attack, using the enemy's boats for an all-out assault against their own ship. Summers was wriggling next to him at the tiller and there must be another twenty-five ordinary seamen wedged into his craft and more in the larger launch Croft commanded to his right. With one fight already won, everyone's blood was up and Adams' main problem would probably be keeping his force of fire-eaters quiet while they located the enemy warship. Then they must approach it in such a way that no suspicions were aroused, before boarding quickly with as much noise and confusion as they could muster. With most of her fighting men ashore and now held prisoner, the ship should be easy meat – at least that's what Adams hoped because, even as he returned Summers' confident grin, the young officer knew himself near to the end of his own personal tether.

* * *

Croft was not so disheartened. Despite having once sworn never again to involve himself in physical combat, the counter attack had been entirely his idea; a snap remark so apposite that all immediately jumped on it and command had rather been thrust upon him. But then his recent experience of hand-to-hand fighting had somewhat bolstered him.

Rather than disgrace himself with clumsy moves and fuddled thought as in the past, he had not fared too badly. No enemy had fallen to his blade and he could still feel the sting of a cutlass slash across his own chest that might have been so much worse. But the fact remained, the group he nominally commanded had been victorious, and against a considerable force; a quick count revealed just over sixty men taken prisoner – a number that, when added to the list of enemy casualties, had been a major factor in making this present venture appear viable.

And he truly was the natural choice to lead; there had been no discussion or apparent thought. The lack of a left arm obviously excluded Captain King but Adams could have been given overall charge, or one of the senior warrant officers. As it was, he had command; an antiquated officer who, just a short time ago, had been the only lieutenant in a washed-up brig with an equally worn-out captain. To his mind it demonstrated that no cause is ever totally lost.

* * *

Watching them go, King did not regret staying behind. Since the loss of his arm, physical combat had been almost impossible, although he no longer regretted the fact and now secretly welcomed it. Certainly no one had expected him to take part in repelling the landing party, which was very much to the good as far as he was concerned. In the past, when fully able, he had involved himself in hand-to-hand combat and even regarded himself as being something of a master of the art, yet now realised such action appeared very different to the casual observer. For he had indeed witnessed the brutal fighting from *Mistral*'s canted quarterdeck and, although he would have never admitted the fact, was heartily sickened by it. Some might find a science in such brutality but those few minutes of close action appeared as no more than a glorified pot-house brawl and, terrible though it might be for a fighting officer to admit, the only emotion it evoked in him was one of disgust.

There hadn't even been room for fear; if the French had won he, along with all who survived, would simply have been taken prisoner. Such a thing had happened before and the experience hadn't killed him while some might say the chances of meeting up with Aimée again could improve with them both in enemy hands. And in any case, he was starting to doubt who the enemy truly were; the French, Dutch or Spanish he had encountered during his career had turned out as agreeable, or not, as an Englishman, while plenty of his countrymen were far easier to hate than any official foe.

The fact that the French had not been successful, so were now prisoners themselves, was something he could only credit to those about him – the officers and men he had come to know and respect – he had had little to do with the matter. And neither was he particularly involved when it had come to taking the fight back to the enemy; the plan had been entirely of Croft's making. The lieutenant offered the suggestion in his customarily impassive manner while the prisoners were still being rounded up but, despite only having just emerged from another fight, the firebrands seized upon it immediately. And King supposed they would do well; taking a small ship with both surprise and a heavily armed boarding party was a relatively simple matter especially as it seemed their target would be all but bereft of crew. But even if they failed and were repelled, *Mistral,* would soon be afloat again and, despite the work still needed to her hull, should be able to make for Cape Town where news of Aimée may even be awaiting him.

And that was another matter King was keeping secret. For, whether his men were successful in capturing the corvette or not, at that moment the fate of one young French woman mattered more to him than anything else.

* * *

The night seemed darker still as they drew away from *Mistral*'s beached hull and it was only when a pusser's moon rose cautiously above the eastern horizon that the enemy corvette was finally sighted. Hove to and drifting slightly in the rolling mist and a gentle north-westerly, Adams and Summers could just make her out as she stood about a mile off their larboard bow.

"We might continue under oars," Croft said when he had ordered his own boat alongside, "though doubt we will get close enough to catch her sleeping."

"No, sir," Adams agreed, "and however poorly manned she may be, there'll be a good lookout kept."

"Then we shall continue under sail. It may actually be of help as they will know the look of their own craft."

"What when we are challenged?" Adams asked. "Do you have any French speakers?"

"You speak it yourself," the older man reminded him. "As does Mr Summers."

"But not like natives; we need a Frenchman."

"Any with the lingo?" Croft asked, addressing the crew of both boats in general, but there were no takers. "You'll just have to do your best," he said, returning to Adams. "And we discovered a blue-glassed lantern in the bows; it might be for some form of signal."

"We have one as well," Adams confirmed.

"Then have it ready to light, but shield it as soon as you can," Croft replied. "I intend closing on the enemy's stern, which will probably be the easier way aboard. But there are bound to be sharpshooters; the last thing we need do is give them a mark."

"Can I make a suggestion, sir?" Summers' cautious voice chimed out in the darkness.

Croft was inclined to discourage junior officers from showing initiative, especially when, as now, it was in front of the people, but then neither could he dismiss such a public request.

"Might we divide our force?" the midshipman continued.

"To what end, Mr Summers?"

"We could close on their stern as you suggested, sir, while your boat boards at her prow. One of us is bound to arrive before the other and will take the enemy's attention, allowing the second to gain a foothold even if the first is unsuccessful."

Croft paused for a moment; it seemed a worthy enough proposal, especially as only so many men could board a ship simultaneously. Summers' scheme would allow the Frenchman to be comprehensively filled with attackers with far less chance of injury to their own, while the recent shore action had shown the value of a two-pronged attack.

"Very well," he grunted finally. "We shall separate; you close under sail and showing a blue light when you feel appropriate; I shall strike our masts when half a mile off and continue under oars. When you come to board, or if the French smell a rat before, make as much noise as possible; depending on the situation I shall either join in the attack or follow in retreat but, in the latter case, do not attempt to close with me."

"No, sir?" Adams and Summers asked in unison.

"No," Croft was definite. "If we're smoked the French can give chase and, however badly we think them manned, they will be sure to carry enough to send a broadside in our direction."

The cold words were enough to silence any further questions and, as Croft gruffly ordered his boat away and both craft picked up the gentle breeze once more, a sense of tranquillity seemed to overcome them, although it was one that concealed a good few racing hearts.

* * *

"She's not showing any lights," Summers muttered softly as the corvette's stern became more defined. The slender moon had risen slightly and light from a few of the brighter stars was now cutting through the mist. But of the first lieutenant's boat, presumably to starboard and on a roughly parallel course, there was no sign.

"We have to behave like Frenchmen," Adams said. "Frenchmen returning after a failed attack."

"So, shall we show a light?" the midshipman suggested, "or order the hands to chatter?"

"That might be going too far; we don't want to give them an aiming point and even one word in English could be enough to smoke us. But I take your meaning," he added before continuing in a louder voice. "I think it time we tried the blue lamp."

Adams still had the tinderbox Summers had confiscated from Swain and, after passing the thing up the boat, its original owner used it to strike a light. Soon the entire cutter was bathed in the cold radiance of the coloured lantern.

"That's enough," Adams ordered, and the glow was quickly stifled. For up to a minute the boat continued to claw towards the corvette with both officers' eyes primed for the first flash of gunfire. Then a more peaceful sight was revealed.

It was also blue and shined for barely a breath but encouraged all who saw it.

"Very well," Adams continued, addressing the boat in general. "We're going in."

* * *

Minutes later they were within accurate musket range and the tension had mounted further. The time he had already spent in the boat had settled Adams' earlier qualms to some extent but, now action appeared not only likely but imminent, he felt his mouth starting to dry and knew the hand that gripped the counter was shaking slightly. For a moment he glanced at Summers and, even in the poor light, the youngster seemed a picture of composure. Then a stark shout broke the spell.

"*Allumez une lampe et rapprochez-vous,*" it ordered curtly.

"They want us to come alongside," Summers muttered.

"I know," Adams hissed in reply. "Keep her as she is." They were heading directly for the corvette's stern although this would not be obvious until they drew closer. "The lamp, Swain!" Adams whispered forward and the instruction was passed along the crowded boat. For a moment they were lit once more by the ghostly blue glow before, unbidden, the light went out.

"*Qui est-ce?*" Again the voice came from the corvette and this time was a good deal stronger. Adams cleared his throat.

"Boucher," he half mumbled, half shouted in reply.

"*Qui ça?*" The response was immediate.

"*Nous avons des blessés à bord.*" Adams again and this time some fool in the boat giggled at the sound of his officer speaking French. For a moment there was apparent confusion, a clear lantern appeared above the taffrail and by the extra light figures could be seen gathering to peer down at them.

"Oars, men!" Adams grunted and the boat began to surge forward under the added impetus. "*Nous avons des blessés à bord,*" he repeated with more force and, even to his ears, the words rang false. Then the corvette's counter was barely feet away, both sails began to flutter as they drew into her lee and there was a clatter of steel as the men prepared their weapons.

"*Restez où vous êtes!*" a different voice all but screamed in desperation.

"Swain, the lamp – and keep it burning!" Adams bellowed. They would be boarding a strange ship and must have some light, even though it might make the enemy marksmen's job easier. "Those that can, make the deck, others enter through the stern windows," he instructed. Then they were drawing level with the corvette's counter and the small boat crashed against her rudder.

Croft's instruction about making noise had been forgotten by Adams, but as Summers reached up and swung himself onto the stern gallery, he did so with a shriek that inspired the others. There was the crash of breaking glass and soon the corvette was filled with screaming, scrambling bodies clambering up her hindquarters. Adams followed his friend, taking slightly more time than both him and the seaman to his left. But eventually he was through the smashed stern window and tumbling rather ungainly onto the deck of the great cabin.

"Come on," Adams ordered, even though he was still semi-prone while Summers had already sprung to his feet. A single candle lit the small room which was comfortably furnished and had the air of a country cottage rather than a fighting captain's private quarters. More seamen were scrambling in through the stern windows as the pair drew their swords and advanced towards the cabin entrance. A pale-faced boy in white uniform appeared through a side door and was swiftly knocked to the floor by the swipe of a seaman's pistol, then they were out of the cabin and at the main doors of the coach where they could stare out on the dark expanse of main deck beyond.

It appeared relatively clear; the glow from tubs containing lighted slow match gave pools of light by which figures could be seen gathered near the readied cannon. The French seamen appeared entranced by what was taking place on the quarterdeck above where the rest of the British boarders were presumably arriving, although none made any move to join their comrades and the impression they gave was not of fighting men. But there were also plenty of darker shadows that might hide any amount of danger and for a moment Adams drew back. Then, raising one foot, he savagely kicked at the latch, which remained firm. Another kick, harder this time but still no response and he was about to aim upwards and attempt to smash through one of the heavy panes when Summers calmly reached forward, turned the handle, and pushed both doors open.

Adams barged through, sword extended, with Summers yelling close behind. Three of the waiting gunners made a move towards them but none were armed and, seeing the screaming demons that had come from nowhere, backed off with their hands held high. More British seamen swarmed out behind and there was the crack of a pistol as one fired wildly at the bewildered group.

"Belay that!" Summers yelled, his adolescent voice cracking. There might have been twenty Frenchmen on the main deck but certainly not more. All were unarmed and most had the appearance of idlers. "You there, Swain, secure those men," he snapped in a more businesslike tone.

"The rest of you support him," Adams added. Then, as the master-at-arms emerged from the cabin, "Mr Allcorn, I want a guard mounted on each of the hatches. No one is to go below and deal with any who try to come up. We can secure the entire ship when Mr Croft's boat arrives."

Summers glanced back at the command deck above. "Quarterdeck seems quiet."

"Let's take a look," Adams replied as he made for one of the companion ladders.

The midshipman was right, as they stepped onto the deck above they found the other boarders had already rounded up a further ten Frenchmen, two of whom were dressed as officers; apart from these, the ship might have been deserted. Shouts came from forward; Adams turned briefly to see the first of Croft's force tumbling over the corvette's forecastle. He drew breath and spared a quick smile for Summers before approaching the more decorated of the two officers. How could he put this? His intention must be plain, yet at the same time he did not wish to antagonise or humiliate his opponents.

"*Bonsoir Monsieur,*" he began almost conversationally. "*J'ai le regret de devoir vous déposséder de votre navire.*"

Chapter Eighteen

Mistral lifted perfectly on the night's high tide and, even before he received news of the corvette's capture, Captain King had ordered her warped clear of the line of rocks that had both saved and almost wrecked her. All aboard knew that, despite the loss of Anderson, it would have been quite practical to complete her repairs but even a further twelve-hour delay was to be avoided, it seemed. And ships had undoubtedly sailed with worse defects than a couple of missing copper plates but the fact that their captain, until recently happy to extend their cruise apparently indefinitely, was suddenly equally keen to be gone attracted comment amongst those on the lower deck.

The seamen did not talk for long though, there being too much to do in keeping the ship secured on heavily shelving ground while continuing to load the last of the ordinance and dealing with their French prisoners. Besides, not all the ordinary Jacks were so very interested in their captain's thoughts; despite the events of the recent shore action and what they might expect when dawn finally broke, one man at least had his mind set elsewhere.

Scott's cutter had been run ashore less than twenty-four hours before yet, to the surviving Samuels brother, it felt much longer. For Paul Samuels was deep in mourning and something inside told him he always would be.

It was not the suddenness of Peter's death, or even that his brother was no longer present; despite their apparent inseparability, the two had spent short periods apart and on more than a few occasions their close association had bordered on the claustrophobic. But to accept Peter as gone for ever, that the last sight of him would be that broken body on a deserted beach, was beyond him while the prospect of a future lived alone seemed too daunting to contemplate.

But Paul Samuels did know that this was not the end; that life, for him at least, would continue, if in a different manner. The two of them – or he, as it must now become – had been aboard *Mistral* long enough to integrate into her crew and already life aboard a man-of-war seemed vastly preferable to any in a merchant. The others, the men of his mess along with those of the watch he served in, appeared reasonable sorts and were well led by a good team of officers. In time, Paul supposed he might find another tie mate, one he could look after as they would him. But not another brother; that post must forever remain vacant.

* * *

During the night the captured corvette approached amid a cacophony of cheering and catcalls from her exhausted captors, but when dawn finally broke revealing *Mistral* afloat and the Frenchman flying a union flag over her tricolour, the true enormity of what had been achieved became apparent. Men who had slept little but worked much took on new energy and, as Russell's range was lit once more and began producing food for both British and French, something close to a carnival atmosphere descended.

And no one was more conscious of this than Scott; even without having redeemed himself by warning *Mistral* of the Frenchman's presence and leading the counter attack on the enemy landing party, the lower deck's new found bonhomie was strong enough to wipe out all resentment from the earlier grounding.

"Seem a cheerful lot," he remarked to Sennett as they stood on the break of the quarterdeck while the men enjoyed their midday issue of grog.

"Aye," the youngster agreed. "I just come back from checking my division and no one complained about the morning's burgoo. And that was with Russell in charge."

"Isn't he always?" Scott asked absent-mindedly.

The boy shook his head. "Does no more than supervise," he said. "It's Dale, one of his mates, what most times runs the galley an' he's in sickers with a cut leg."

"I had no idea."

"Russell knows more about carpentry than cooking," Sennett assured him. "Ask anyone who's tasted his scran."

* * *

With no Cooper on hand, and Adams and Croft fully committed elsewhere, King had little option other than to interview the corvette's commander alone, and he proved a different prospect to the elderly officer who had captained their previous capture.

Certainly far younger: King would have placed him at no more than twenty-five, and with fine fair hair. But as he considered him, King mainly noticed the man's slight blush that looked out of place against his otherwise pallid skin and could have been an indication of either defiance or fear.

"You put up a brave fight," King began in an effort at appeasement.

"The luck was on your side," the youngster announced and was apparently ready to argue his statement.

"Maybe so," King conceded gently. "And maybe next time the luck will be with you, though do not forget this occasion. I too have been in your position and can confirm there is as much to learn from defeat as victory."

The French officer considered this for a moment, then seemed to unbend slightly.

"I expect you wish to learn of my movements," he supposed.

"I know much already," King smiled. "Yours was one of four ships in a squadron sent south to seek out and capture merchant convoys; another, a frigate, has already been taken."

The youngster swallowed but said nothing.

"Though strangely that is not my main concern," King continued evenly. "One of your first victims was a southbound convoy which you were successful in taking."

Still the officer remained silent although now was considering King with interest and a growing respect.

"And shortly afterwards one of your ships collected survivors from a small boat. It is those that most interest me and, as news of them can in no way weaken your own forces, I hope such information can be shared between gentlemen."

Now there was a definite flicker and King wondered again why, in a regime that purported to denounce all levels of status, the position of gentleman was still so plainly respected.

The Frenchman shook his head. "I cannot help you," he said. Then, sensing he might have been too brusque, added, "I cannot because I had nothing to do with the incident. But I am aware of the boat you mention, and that survivors were indeed rescued."

"And do you know what became of them?" King's voice was now slightly strained. "I ask because a woman close to me was amongst them."

"Then I will tell you all I know, sir," the youngster declared almost haughtily. "I was indeed part of a squadron, though you will excuse me if I say no more of its size. But the survivors were taken aboard my commandant's ship."

"And do they remain there?" King enquired in as level a tone as he could muster.

"That I do not know, my ship was despatched independently shortly afterwards so I can say no more. But my commandant is a good man; no harm will come to any prisoner under his care."

"So I have heard, and I trust you and your men will find me as accommodating. But tell me one more thing; do you think him likely to retain his prisoners or might an arrangement be possible?"

"I have no way of knowing that either." The young man had an air of genuine regret. "Though French officers are under strict instructions; the exchange of captives is rare and very much discouraged. So I think it unlikely that any prisoner coming into *Capitaine* Adenis' hands would be returned in any circumstances."

* * *

The thought stayed with King as he and his officers supervised preparations for getting underway and, by the time both ships were ready to start the trip back to Cape Town – *Mistral* with forty-three Frenchmen secured below and the corvette, under Adams' command, only slightly less – he was able to ponder on it further.

He had already assumed all the ships *Mistral* had encountered were from the enemy squadron that met with the *St. George,* but the corvette's captain had let slip his commander's name, which gave something of a personal slant to his thinking. The sloop and her three Indiamen charges might even have been Adenis' first conquests although that was pure speculation and he certainly could not know how long such a cruise would last. But with the shipping season underway any well-handled predator should not be idle.

Two of the enemy squadron had already been accounted for and the time must come when the remaining ships ran short of hands for prize crews. At which point they would either enter a neutral port and attempt to raise more, or make the long trip back to France to refit. And though he knew her well, the concept of Aimée being returned to her home country disturbed him almost as much as other potential fates.

They had been together for most of his stay in Verdun and during their escape to England, then almost all the previous English summer had been spent in the other's company. But he realised now that far too much of the latter time was wasted trying to sort out his own matrimonial affairs. Every effort had come to naught and it could hardly have been the ideal activity for an ardent lover. Once back in France, the lure of returning to her true home and family must seem an attractive alternative to waiting for a one-armed companion who appeared unable, or perhaps unwilling, to shake off an existing wife.

But whatever her allegiances, he had only the two weeks Scott had forecast it would take to raise Cape Town in which to find her. After that, *Mistral* was bound to spend further time in the dockyard before probably being sent on a specific mission which might take him many miles away. Other British ships were at sea and there was always the chance that the frigate holding Aimée would be captured, although the thought of her in the midst of another naval engagement was hardly comforting. And he had the absurd yet persistent feeling that, if anyone was to rescue her, it really should be him.

* * *

"So you're the captain's wife!" Cooper's surprise was very evident.

"No, I am his, companion," Aimée corrected. "In France there is a better word but I do not think it truly translates to your English."

"And my French is probably insufficient," the Englishman agreed ruefully. "But forgive me, I knew of Captain King's lady of course, though no one mentioned you were French, or not married, or..." His eyes dropped from the young woman's face, then widened as they took in the bulge at her midriff.

"I think there is a lot you do not know," Aimée stated seriously.

"In truth, I only joined *Mistral* towards the end of her last commission." Cooper lay back on his pillow. "And your personal arrangements are none of my concern..."

"Does any of it bother you?" she raised an eyebrow.

"Bother me?"

"That I am not Tom King's wife, yet carry his child? Or perhaps that I am French?"

"No, none of it," Cooper was quick to confirm as he raised himself once more. "As I have said, it is none of my business. And I am pleased beyond measure that the Captain is to be a father, though would chance no one in Cape Town is aware of the fact." Cooper did not add that the bright young girl who now knelt before him was also assumed dead but thought better of it. Like most sea officers, he lacked many social graces but prided himself on at least some sense of diplomacy.

"Well, I do not wish for you to be concerned with anything other than regaining your health," Aimée said, laying a hand on his. "It is less than a week since the surgeon removed that splinter and you are still weak."

Cooper supposed she was right and relaxed once more. Seven days ago he had indeed been in temporary command of a fine frigate, the prize of Captain King, an officer he respected more than any he had served under. Yet since then he had allowed the ship, and the prisoners she carried, to be recaptured while he himself was wounded and now in turn held captive. Cooper knew he had nothing to reproach himself for; the enemy warship that currently held him was discovered at first light and would have been a more powerful opponent even if his vessel had boasted a full crew. And though he had done all he could to avoid capture his attempts had been futile from the start. But to make matters worse, he now found himself in the presence of his captain's companion, a charming woman but one he seemed destined to insult at every opportunity.

"Captain King is a fine man," he told her awkwardly. "And lucky to have someone so beautiful to bear his child."

Aimée gave an embarrassed laugh. "Mr Cooper, I believe I am the lucky one," she said. "And so grateful to you for giving me the news that Tom is alive."

"Oh, he is alive," Cooper confirmed, then paused. Alive, and possibly close by. Aboard a Royal Navy frigate, in fact, and probably searching for the very ship that carried them.

A distant noise made the woman turn, and Cooper noticed the surgeon approach from the shadows and lay a comforting arm about her shoulder.

"*Vous ne devez pas fatiguer le patient,*" he whispered softly and she glanced up at him.

"*Ça va, je ne serai pas long. Monsieur* Cooper *va déjà beaucoup mieux.*"

Cooper said nothing; he had spoken with both his carers on several occasions but this was the first time he remembered seeing the pair together. It was also the first time he felt truly free of the drug which had made his wound bearable. And because he could finally gauge things more clearly, quickly came to a conclusion that was simply too hard to avoid. But, like it or not, there was something in the way the fellow's arm rested so, something which suggested an attachment that went way beyond friendship.

* * *

There were various similarities with the last time Adams had been given command of a prize. Summers had been his second in command then, and there were also prisoners to contend with. But that adventure had ended with the capture of his vessel along with all those on board, and he was determined not to let the same thing happen twice.

And he would not, he told himself firmly as he boarded the corvette and cast a cautious glance over her tophamper. The French had made a good job of replacing the main topmast; a slightly lighter spar stood in its place which would serve, at least until they raised Cape Town. The rest of the ship was also in reasonable order; carefully handled she should even show a good turn of speed and the nine-pounder broadside cannon were long guns – carronades might fire a heavier shot but carriage pieces were far more accurate and perfectly capable of delivering a sound punch. On gaining harbour the ship was bound to be taken onto the Admiralty list when some young officer would be pleased to captain her and, though he had barely held his commission as lieutenant a year, Adams was secretly hoping it might be him.

After all, *Mistral* was proving to be a lucky ship and accelerated promotions were not unknown, especially on foreign stations. Soon he might be a commander, with a fine ship to make his own, which was certainly a viable alternative to resigning his commission and trying for an India Company post. With a British Navy epaulette on one shoulder and a respectable wife by his side – one that would certainly be allowed to accompany him on active service – his life would be complete.

But first he would have to see the ship safely to Cape Town and, though they would be sailing in company with *Mistral*, that was by no means a certainty. There was at least one enemy frigate likely to be in the area while both British ships were lumbered with an additional cargo of prisoners. And when the shortage of officers and men was considered, as well as a complete lack of marines, Adams supposed he really should not be counting his chickens.

He had already made what provisions he could and chosen his prize crew with care. Most were experienced hands with only a few gifted more in strength than ability. For the emphasis would be very much on sailing the ship; there was very little chance of their going into action and only the need to tend the prisoners had prevented him from having an entire crew made up of able seamen.

A clatter from behind told him someone was rushing up the aft companionway faster than was advisable, then Summers bounced onto the quarterdeck, brim-filled with enthusiasm.

"Our dunnage has come on board," the boy announced with his usual familiarity. "Shall I have it stowed in the great cabin, or are you saving that for the French?"

Herding the ship's former officers together made sense; all had given their word to cooperate but would still need guarding, so the captain's quarters were ideal. But then with only Summers, a master's mate and an even younger midshipman to accommodate, there would also be plenty of room on the deck below. And if they were a little crowded, that was hardly Adams' concern.

"No, Mr Summers," he replied with overt formality. "They can mess with you and the other junior men; I shall be taking the great cabin for myself."

The lad considered him for a moment and even tried a smile as his friend had a habit of teasing on occasions.

"Is there a problem?" Adams asked, his voice now a credible imitation of Captain King's after a particularly disappointing exercise.

"No," Summers replied, before correcting this to, "No, sir," and adding a hasty salute.

* * *

And so they squared away for The Cape. Two weeks was perhaps a conservative estimate; without drawing too much attention, King felt it might stretch to three which was time enough to encounter Adenis' frigate if it truly were in the area. There was perhaps the small point that neither British ship was fit to meet a hostile opponent; *Mistral* lacked both marines and a full complement of seamen while, with barely enough aboard to tend her sails and contain prisoners, the prize would be more liability than asset. But still King felt having two ships at his command would at least confuse any opponent. Besides, since being appointed to command, he had been successful in most encounters and though the people might be few, they were inordinately experienced while the prospect of prize money they must already have accumulated had helped to create a level of morale higher than he had ever known.

No, there was a powerful French frigate loose somewhere in the near vicinity and, if given the chance, King would have no hesitation in bringing it to battle. And the fact that Aimée was likely to be aboard only made his determination stronger.

Chapter Nineteen

On the seventh day after leaving the island a ship was indeed sighted. The call came mid-morning when the watch on deck had just shaken the reefs out of *Mistral*'s topgallants and a group of twenty Frenchmen were taking the air in her waist.

"Off our larboard bow," the main masthead reported. "And not sporting much in the way of sail."

On deck, King pricked up his ears. In the past few days they had encountered little in the way of shipping apart from one distant northbound convoy that showed no inclination to linger. As they drew nearer to The Cape that was likely to change but still he thought it unusual to come across any vessel not making full use of the steady north-westerly.

"Where heading?" he demanded, briskly.

"Roughly south, though hard to say for definite," the lookout replied. "She's naught much more than a smudge at present. But I'm certain of her canvas; tops'ls but little else."

Had the sighting been showing more she would have been easier to both identify and track although, based entirely on the scant information provided, King was already drawing conclusions.

"Mr Sennett, take a glass up and tell me what you see."

The midshipman of the watch jumped to and, slinging the deck telescope over his shoulder, proceeded to race up the larboard shrouds. Watching him go, King remembered the relief of breaking a watch with a sudden dash to the top. Mr Midshipman Sennett had started as a third-class volunteer and only been promoted to *Mistral*'s quarterdeck towards the end of her last commission. But he had taken to his new duties well and would certainly progress; it was quite possible the lad currently making the difficult transfer from futtock to main topmast shrouds might end up a captain himself in time.

Croft made his appearance on the quarterdeck and acknowledged King's presence with due formality. With both Cooper and Adams absent, the man had been busier than ever but seemed to be thriving on the extra duties although his face showed concern as he took in the news.

"Can't say I like the sound of that, sir," he muttered. "Unless they're undergoing repairs, there can be few reasons why a vessel should loiter so."

"I can only think of one," King stated with more conviction.

"But if it is the enemy you spoke of, we are in no condition to meet it."

On recounting his interview with the captured captain, King had been selective in his information; the chance of their meeting with a heavy frigate was certainly mentioned but he had said nothing of any likelihood it could be carrying Aimée.

"Maybe not," King sniffed. "Though *Mistral* is sailing well despite her injuries and has enough to man her guns."

"Barely, sir," the older man persisted, his voice now almost a whisper.

"Deck there, she has the look of a frigate," Sennett's voice rang out just as the ship's bell was struck six times. Croft said nothing but his look of apprehension was unmistakeable and there might also have been an added hint of censure.

Which was almost too much for King; he turned away from his second in command, walked to the break of the quarterdeck and took a deep draught of clean Atlantic air. The man was right, of course; in their weakened state it would be futile to take on a warship of almost any significant size but, now the opportunity had been thrust upon him, it was simply too hard to resist. The sighting was almost in their path, he was hardly seeking her out; indeed they would have to deviate from their present course to avoid it. And anyway, this wasn't entirely a personal matter.

If he were facing *Capitaine* Adenis' ship, it was one that had already caused a deal of damage to the merchant trade and was liable to do more. Aimée might indeed be on board, although that was by no means certain and, whatever the case, he considered himself professional enough to place such personal concerns to one side. For he was a King's Officer and had sworn to intercept all enemies of his sovereign; intercept and destroy. To do otherwise would be a dereliction of his duty.

On the main deck the prisoners were preparing to file down after their time in the fresh air. Once back on the orlop they would be provided with their main meal of the day. It made sense to feed them before the hands although King was pleased to see them go for one particular reason: whenever there were French on deck he had the absurd feeling of being watched. But even as the last of them disappeared below, the sensation remained and then, turning slightly, he realised Croft had followed him to his place of sanctuary.

"Are you determined to fight this Frenchman, sir?" the first lieutenant asked.

"We don't know if it is a Frenchman," King reminded him curtly. "Sennett isn't even sure the sighting to be a frigate."

"That is true, sir."

"I have no intention of endangering the ship unnecessarily, if that is what you mean," King continued. "Though, if a suitable opportunity presents, neither shall I refuse it."

The older man absorbed this without comment or reaction.

"You do not agree, James, that is clear."

"Whether I do, or do not is immaterial," Croft replied. "If you think us ready to fight, I shall support you as always."

"I realise that," King conceded as finally he softened. "And appreciate it more than you know."

* * *

By the time the hands were also fed, matters had moved on. It was customary for the officers to take their own main meal of the day at that point but, such were the developments, none had any thought for food. Not only had the sighting been reliably confirmed as a frigate, she had also turned marginally towards them and was now showing more sail as she bore down.

On the gun deck, Martin was certainly not hungry. Despite having been officially relieved of most responsibilities he had continued to carry out light duties, although these were mainly confined to clerical work for the purser and sailing master. But with *Mistral* poorly manned and action imminent, such a concession could hardly remain and any officer who was ostensibly fit and capable must be used. Accordingly, he had been assigned to the forward area of gun deck where he was to assist in the management of the ship's eighteen-pounders.

Martin had seen combat often enough, and drilled the servers on many occasions, but this would be the first, and last, time he would supervise a battery in action. With Cooper and Adams absent there was no gunnery lieutenant as such and, though Croft remained in nominal command and in control of the aft section and carronades, Martin knew a lot of responsibility would be with him. The first lieutenant would be at the break of the quarterdeck whenever possible and was aware of the midshipman's condition. If he succumbed to another attack, Martin would be removed from the deck and supposedly taken to the sick bay for care, although he suspected a far more practical fate awaited. In the heat of battle, no time could be spared for one whose life was not in danger and Martin would be quite content in a dark corner of the berth deck where he might do battle with his own personal enemy.

But he was not thinking of what might go wrong and actually had a very positive attitude. Since the last attack, and his resolution to seek a less demanding position, various possibilities had come to mind. He might indeed apply for a shore posting at the Castle in Cape Town, or return to England and take up some other conventional clerking position, although either would be a waste of his considerable skills as a navigator. With his ailment being both sporadic and well signalled it was not inconceivable the merchant service might find him a post; not as a senior officer perhaps, but anyone who could reliably work a lunar and was capable of setting course would be a useful addition to most vessels. But that lay in the future, for now Martin was content to concentrate on the job in hand. For the Royal Navy had been his life for so long and, as this would be his last opportunity to serve aboard a warship in combat, he was determined to give a good account of himself.

"Expecting action are we, Mr Martin?" The use of his proper name by a voice he knew well made him pause in his inspection of number two gun.

"It is a distinct possibility, Mr Brett," Martin replied with equally formality. He couldn't begin to guess why the youngster had finally abandoned the hated nickname and had no intention of finding out. "We'll be under the direction of the first lieutenant," he continued, "who has vowed to keep an eye from the quarterdeck though I suspect we shall be left to our own devices much of the time."

"And you are happy with that? I mean, do you feel able?"

Martin considered the lad; there was no hint of mocking in his expression just simple concern.

"I am if you are," he said. "And Sennett has returned from masthead duty, he is stationed on the quarterdeck but can be on hand if need be."

"Well, let's hope he ain't required," Brett suggested. "Belike the pair of us can manage well enough on our own."

* * *

Long before the sun had properly begun to descend, the situation had developed still further. By six bells of the afternoon watch – three o'clock in landsmen's terms – the enemy was in clear sight from the deck. All could see she was a frigate and a powerful one; broadly similar to *Mistral* in fact, although definitely a forty-gunner. Both ships would be mounting eighteen-pounders on their main decks but the enemy carried more and must be stouter built into the bargain. And she could equally be expected to boast a larger number of men as convoy raiders were known to sail with an abundance of hands while it was surely unlikely she would have depleted her people to the same extent as *Mistral*, or have given up her entire detachment of marines. Indeed, as King watched her in silence he decided the only real factor in his favour lay in the Frenchman being alone. If another warship had been present, even one as small as a sloop or a brig, he would have had little hesitation in running.

Which was probably the right move even now, he privately acknowledged. In a stand up fight and with *Mistral* fully manned, King was quietly confident of beating any single-decker afloat. As it was, he had a minimal crew and was two commissioned officers short. But even if *Mistral* were at less than her peak of efficiency, there were plenty worse in the fleet. And besides, he had a definite advantage in the corvette.

King glanced across at the prize now; she might not be capable of much in the way of fighting – it would be strange if young Adams were even able to fire off more than one of her nine-pounders – but simply having another ship to face would make matters harder for his opponent. There would be two for *Capitaine* Adenis to consider, two that might force him to react; the Frenchman would have no idea how the corvette was manned and might not even recognise her as a former ally. No, if Adams responded promptly to King's signals, they might yet make a fight of it.

"Enemy's still a good three miles off," Croft remarked as he joined him. The wind was staying solid in the north-west and the French frigate, now heading roughly westerly, was taking it just forward of her beam. Meanwhile, *Mistral,* on the opposite tack and a close reach, was steering more northerly and steadily gaining the windward gauge. With the corvette to larboard, it should be possible for both British ships to turn and take the enemy with the wind on their quarter. But that would be relying upon his opponent being a fool, and from what King knew of him, *Capitaine* Adenis was anything but.

It was really quite novel to know the name and even a little of the character of the man he was to fight. And stranger still to realise Aimée was probably aboard his opponent's ship and the two of them were physically closer now than at any time since they parted. But as soon as the thought occurred he dismissed it; as far as he was concerned this would be just another engagement, one of several he had undertaken as captain of a warship and many more while a supporting officer. And it would end the same as most, with the Frenchman taken and his own ship victorious. Then, and only then, would he allow himself to think about the woman he hoped was currently sheltering well below the waterline.

* * *

Adams was less confident. The reassuring bulk of *Mistral* was close at hand but further off, and making steady progress under topsails, forecourse and staysails, lay a far more powerful frigate. It was one that must prove more than a match for the British ship and could wreck his own with a single salvo. And there would be no possibility of returning the compliment, even if chance were given. With his prisoners secured below and under guard, Adams had enough men to handle the sails, but no more. The corvette's guns were run out, of course, and to all intents the ship must appear potent yet, in reality, lacked the hands to fire a single broadside.

Obviously Captain King was aware of the situation and would not place him in a position of danger; Adams' function should simply be one of providing visible support. The enemy must not be aware of his lack of firepower and should regard him with an element of respect, for even a nine-pounder corvette could pose a threat to a frigate if it were able to cross its hawse.

So his would be a blocking role and one that required a cool head to carry off. For if he was to maintain the threat, Adams must ensure he never assumed a position where he might actually use his guns: were a perfect occasion to present, and the chance not taken, the enemy would smoke him for the fraud he was. Then, far from being an asset, Adams and his impotent little warship would become a liability. And there lay his primary fear, for such a situation could only end one way.

* * *

"Be ready to take us to starboard," King warned Scott. Then, in a louder voice, "The signal, if you please, Mr Sennett."

Mistral was now considerably to the north-west of the Frenchman and had captured the windward gauge so it made sense to make full use of the advantage. Adams, in the prize, remained half a cable to larboard; there would be an inevitable delay when they turned and the corvette might drop back slightly, but King credited the young man with enough sense to keep himself from the Frenchman's guns.

"Stations for wearing ship!" The sailing master's bellow brought every hand to attention and now all were waiting for the final order.

"Very well," King grunted and the signal was struck just as *Mistral* heeled into the turn.

"Brace up headyards!" Scott had moved forward and was supervising from the break of the quarterdeck. "Overhaul weather lifts! Haul aboard!"

With the evolution complete, *Mistral* steadied and began to take on more speed as the wind came over her starboard quarter. King glanced across at the corvette. Adams had done well; the prize was only slightly behind in the turn and had taken station astern and to starboard with both ships now making for a point ahead of the enemy. And they should arrive in time to deliver a devastating broadside into either the frigate's bow or stern, except no one was fool enough to believe matters would stay that way. Exactly how his opponent would react was another matter, however, and, for all King had learned about *Capitaine* Adenis, the next fifteen minutes would tell him so much more.

Croft returned from supervising the gun crews; the Frenchman remained out of range and King supposed he had come aft in the hope of learning which broadside would be in use first.

"The enemy has room to tack," King remarked softly. When commanding previous ships he had avoided discussing tactics with his fellow officers but in Croft's case it felt strange not to.

"Aye," the older man agreed. "In which case we shall have to look to the prize."

King nodded. If the Frenchman timed his move correctly, he might metaphorically drive a wedge between the two British ships and separate them, yet he was reasonably certain that was not on Adenis' mind. For a start, he could not know the corvette was effectively unarmed

198

and must expect his own ship to be caught in the crossfire from two broadsides. Adenis might return the compliment which would probably wreck the smaller vessel in the process, but King sensed him unlikely to take such a risk. And, as the minutes ticked by, he was proved correct.

"They're holding steady," Croft muttered. The enemy were indeed holding their course and had not struck any canvas. Instead the Frenchman was continuing to cut through the blue water with a credible cloud of spray rising from his stem. If matters continued there was every likelihood *Mistral* would enter the frigate's arc of fire before she could take up a raking position.

But, again, King thought otherwise, and again he was right. Even as he opened his mouth to reply, a shiver in the Frenchman's sails gave him the clue he was looking for.

"Now turning a point or two to larboard," he said as the inner workings of his brain began to whirl. By effectively presenting his broadside early, Adenis was drawing a line in the sand; King had the choice of steering for the stern, and facing an equally effective broadside on his own fragile bows, or wearing again and making for the enemy's hawse. And the choice was further influenced by the corvette's presence; if he took the second option, Adams would be left horribly exposed. For a moment he wondered if that were truly on the Frenchman's mind, but was quick to reassure himself. Adenis simply could not know the corvette's state – he might have recognised his former consort, guessed her to be a prize and even anticipated a scratch crew, but it was one thing to think so and quite another to risk everything on that single supposition. King could easily have sent a party of gunners aboard the corvette in which case, while *Mistral* headed stoically for the enemy's bows, the corvette could continue to take her stern. Were they successful, the French would be lucky to come out of such a position with all masts intact and more than two-thirds of her crew uninjured. For a moment King found himself regretting not having provided the men and leaving *Mistral* with just enough to serve one broadside. Then he realised he must behave exactly as if he had.

"Prepare to wear ship, Mr Scott," King ordered as he took a step closer to the binnacle and away from Croft. "Mr Sennett, signal the prize to maintain their current heading."

"But Mr Adams cannot rake the enemy's stern," Croft protested. "He has barely enough to serve his sails."

"Maybe," King agreed without turning. "But the French don't

know that. And as we draw nearer only a fool would fire on a corvette when a heavy frigate was trying to cross their bows." Then he glanced back at his second in command and relaxed slightly. "I should say Mr Adams will be safe enough. In truth, I don't envisage him closing sufficiently to come into range; our friend will move long before that can happen. And then we shall have him on the run."

* * *

Croft had noticed his captain drawing away; he was used to sharing the younger man's thoughts and, despite the explanation, still felt mildly excluded. And now, as he absorbed his words, the doubts increased.

To his mind, King had been taking unnecessary risks for some time; the very fact they were currently in the midst of the South Atlantic and not snugly moored in Table Bay was confirmation of this, while taking on a prime frigate when his own ship lacked men and was hampered by an impotent prize were hardy cautious tactics. But this must be the final straw; exposing a poorly manned corvette to enemy fire was the height of lunacy. Yet, as he considered the matter further, it might also bear the mark of genius.

For had it been lunacy when Duncan boldly patrolled off the Texel with two antiquated warships and effectively blockaded an entire invasion fleet? And what of Nelson steering out of line at St Vincent to take on the might of the Spanish Navy with a single battleship? Then other examples occurred to him; Cochrane carrying a thirty-two gun frigate with a fourteen gun brig or Pulo Aura, when Dance and his fleet of merchantmen saw off and actually gave chase to a powerful squadron of French warships. All such endeavours must have appeared rash at the start, it was only later, after proving successful, they were hailed as heroic.

Yet still he could not be sure if King's latest move would prove so. His captain's brief return to England, then the loss of his companion, had undoubtedly brought on a change. Though as resolute as ever, he appeared strangely preoccupied, while Croft now had the uneasy feeling that more had been learned from the corvette's French commander than he was prepared to reveal.

Such impressions might be pure fantasy, of course; there could be few captains and first officers who were as honest and open with each other. And with an enemy barely out of range to leeward, this was hardly the time to debate his superior's character. Croft cleared his throat, then noticed King was considering him quizzically.

"I ask you again, James," he said, moving towards him once more. "Do you think we might carry this off?"

Croft paused: he knew his own defects. Captain King could outmanoeuvre him in conversation as easily as fighting tactics and had an air of command he could never hope to emulate. Yet here he was asking for an opinion; one that could mean the difference between life and death for them all. And King clearly valued his input, which was foolish for sure as, despite their difference in age, Croft was nowhere near as experienced in combat matters. But then his age might have given him something else and, in a flash of intuition, he realised what it was.

An uncluttered perspective. If Croft was right, and there were facts his captain knew which he remained in ignorance of, they could easily be influencing his judgement. Consequently King was looking to him for a dispassionate view, one unclouded with other thoughts or considerations: confirmation that what an experienced and capable fighting officer considered possible was indeed so. Once that truth was realised, there was only one answer Croft could give.

"Yes, sir," he stated firmly. "I think we might."

* * *

Aboard the prize, Adams was less certain. His doubts had begun with the recent change of course – he had followed unquestioningly and still intended to obey his captain's instructions even though his private hope that, on discovering *Mistral* to be in company with another warship, the Frenchman would simply run was proving groundless. But now the British frigate had turned again and looked likely to abandon him to the terrors of a powerful enemy's broadside, his composure was starting to crumble.

"*Mistral*'s wearing to starboard!" Summers informed him as he returned from some private business forward.

"So I see," Adams replied in what was intended to be a strong voice although it broke horribly.

"Does he expect us to rake the Frog's stern?"

"I know not," Adams sighed. "Though if so, he shall be severely disappointed." He glanced forward; what men he had were mainly stationed at the braces. It was possible one or two guns might be discharged, but more would become a liability as a cannon fired then left unsecured could cause as much damage as enemy shot.

"*Mistral*'s on the wind now," Summers remarked, and Adams switched his gaze to the British ship which was gaining pace and drawing away to starboard. Judging by the angle, it seemed obvious the enemy would soon be able to draw a bead on the larger ship, so his own would be left in relative safety. But that didn't alter the fact he was approaching a heavy frigate's stern. If, by some wild chance, he were able to take station off it the effort would be wasted; worse, to show himself as effectively unarmed must seal his own fate for good.

But the Frenchman was showing no sign of turning; both frigates must surely have the other in range so it could only be moments before the first opened fire. And then the incredible happened.

Adams gasped as he watched, hardly realising it was the first breath he had drawn for some time. But there was no doubting what he saw.

"She's turning – the Frog's turning further to larboard!" Summers shouted while his shoes made a clumping noise on the deck as he cavorted.

"So she is," Adams agreed wearily. The French frigate had indeed thrown her helm across and, now on a similar course to *Mistral*, was beginning to gather speed as the wind came up on her quarter.

"They're on the run: Captain King has got them on the run!" Now the lad was positively screaming and even the hands at the wheel and by the mizzen braces gave rumbles of appreciation. Adams was not so sure, however; King might apparently be seeing the Frenchman off, but it was not the end of the action, only a postponement. Both frigates were fast, but the enemy carried more sail and could be expected to draw away even if *Mistral* added more. And once the French had gained sufficient distance, they would be able to yaw, leaving the oncoming British ship to face their broadside guns.

But at least a temporary reprieve had been won. With their attack now turned into a chase, Adams expected King to order him to follow and every second the prize continued sailing at an oblique angle to the fleeing warships was one that would have to be earned back later. But he was in no rush to close with enemy; he had already drawn as near to a heavy French frigate as he cared to.

* * *

"Add t'gallants sir?" Scott suggested but King shook his head. In truth he was sharing some of Adams' feelings; they had come minutes, possibly seconds, from opening or receiving fire and the prospect of either had not been pleasant. On one hand he now realised that, with a minimal crew, *Mistral* simply could not afford the casualties of even a long-distance exchange and, on the other, there remained the knowledge that somewhere deep within the enemy frigate might be Aimée.

King breathed a silent curse and took a turn across the quarterdeck. He truly had hoped to suppress all thoughts of the girl but, now they had ambushed him yet again, was forced to accept that such things were not so easily dismissed. In which case it would be better to let the enemy go. There were still several hours before night; the Frenchman should be long over the horizon by then and likely never to be seen again. It was a terrible thought yet preferable to continuing the fight with the prospect of harming Aimée hanging over him.

He swore to himself once more while looking back at the empty northern horizon. No, he had been wrong and could see that now; he had involved *Mistral* in an action that should never have started and, as his opponent seemed content to flee, it was undoubtedly better to let him do so. He turned to make some remark to that effect to Croft, then noticed the man was staring forward with a set expression. King followed his gaze and saw with dreadful clarity that *Capitaine* Adenis did not share his intentions and was turning back to challenge him.

* * *

The enemy frigate was in the process of wearing, which complicated matters further for she would come back close-hauled and probably make straight for Adams' corvette, still running before the wind off *Mistral*'s larboard quarter.

"Make to the prize: wear ship and steer sou'-west," King directed and Sennett scuttled off with his signals team. As soon as the corvette passed he would order Adams about and have him follow once more, but at least one decision had been taken from his shoulders. The French were clearly keen for a fight and he was in no position to do anything but oblige them.

"Take us hard to larboard."

Scott was by the wheel and muttered the instruction to the helmsmen before raising his voice to those at the braces.

"All hands, wear ship!"

Mistral took the manoeuvre at speed like the thoroughbred she was and soon began picking up the pace on the larboard tack.

"Two more points to larboard if you please, Mr Scott."

The enemy was off his starboard bow and making good progress; the slight alteration would bring the Frenchman more on the beam while still allowing *Mistral,* the slower ship, to close on her. King had almost given up hopes of a successful raking; his opponent having already proven himself too wily to be caught in such a way. So the time had come to see if an exchange of shot would alter matters.

"Prize has turned back, sir," Sennett reported.

"Very good, make for her to take station on my stern once she passes," King ordered. It would mean more work for Adams' hands but the corvette would be safer on his tail and her presence might at least distract the French gunners. "And take us a further point to larboard."

"Prepare starboard battery." That was Croft bellowing down to Martin on the main deck but King determinedly closed his mind to other men's concerns as he did to another matter that was even less under his control. *Mistral* was doing well, despite being under limited sail she had moved into position swiftly enough and soon would be opening fire. That is, unless the enemy decided to first, he reminded himself, before suppressing the absurd hope that immediately arose. For, if the French were to release the initial broadside, it would remove even more responsibility from him.

But no, they were saving their powder; both ships were now well within the other's reach yet both stubbornly held back as if unwilling to appear the weaker in what had become a war of nerves. King paused a second longer; time enough to take in the beauty of the sun, just starting on its downward plunge, and the blue of the ocean, surely too rich a tone to ever be recorded on canvas. He realised then that he was about to start something which might as easily cost his own life as see him effectively a widower. But there was no reason to delay further and, with the hint of a sigh, he turned towards Croft.

"Very well, James," he said. "You may open fire."

Chapter Twenty

Mistral rolled slightly as her cannon roared out. It was still long range for any fancy shooting; her guns had targeted the enemy's hull and, after a few seconds, the results became evident.

"Good work, Mr Croft," King called out to the first lieutenant who had moved forward to supervise the broadside. And his words were not hollow; one fountain had erupted considerably aft of the Frenchman, probably the product of poor aim or a badly cast shot, and two fell slightly short. But others had found the moving target and as they watched, the enemy's jib boom was struck and instantly disappeared while the jib itself billowed out like so much uncontrolled laundry. But the damage had not robbed the French of any ability to reply; even as she staggered slightly from the sudden imbalance of rig, a line of glowing red ran down the frigate's larboard side and a full broadside was returned on *Mistral*.

As the shots began to tell, King wondered briefly quite what would have happened if his opponent had not been hit for, even with the unexpected deviation caused by the loss of a spar, the aim had been exceptionally good.

Damage was caused to *Mistral*'s starboard forecastle, one of her anchors was struck, but fortunately held although a cathead was smashed into a thousand pieces. And men fell; several by the starboard bow chaser were wiped out as if by the swipe of an unseen brush while number eight cannon, nestling in what should have been the lee of the forecastle itself was struck soundly on the barrel and sent spinning round to account for three of its servers. And there was other damage to fabric and fittings that sent evil slivers of pine and oak slicing through the air to cut, maim and sever while those of the starboard batteries, who were still desperately tending their warm pieces, had both the screaming of wounded and the silence of death to distract them. Such a scene had appalled King in the past yet now seemed to sicken him for the first time and he looked away in disgust.

"We must turn further, sir!" Croft was bellowing.

"Turn?" King physically shook his head to make the thoughts flow.

"To larboard!" the first lieutenant insisted pointing forward. "The enemy is creeping ever closer to the wind, if we stay as we are, the next dose will land square upon our prow."

Yes, of course; King could see that now. "Mr Scott, take us four points to larboard!"

Mistral could manage that and still comfortably keep the wind. The alternative might have been a starboard turn, risk another broadside, then round the enemy's stern and take her with his larboard guns, but that would have left the corvette horribly exposed.

The ship began to creak into her turn while her starboard gunners continued to load and the fallen were steadily cleared from her decks. King had only a rough idea of the number injured but knew they lacked the reserves to fill many spaces. And once again there was the uncomfortable feeling he had started something that really could not be finished.

* * *

"Swain there, put your back into it, man!" Martin shouted as the server heaved the eighteen-pounder back, his feet slipping on the blood-stained deck. They were further forward and in the relative darkness of the forecastle and all were working under incredibly harsh conditions, but the midshipman knew any sign of sympathy or compassion would be positively detrimental.

"Daines, ready with that priming – look alive!" The gun captain in question had stepped away from his cannon and dropped the powder horn which now swung uselessly from his belt; something had drawn his attention and Martin feared it might be the body of Harris, ship's barber and more recently a server at the adjacent cannon, that had yet to be disposed of.

"Carter, Gibson – see that cleared!" Martin ordered, indicating the corpse. His ears were ringing with the sound of their recent broadside and a growing pain was making itself known in his head, but all that had to be set aside. His presence was the only thing keeping the men working as a team; unless he remained as hard as his surroundings all control would be lost. The hands sprang forward to heave the seaman's remains upright and Martin suppressed a retch as Harris seemed to revive with the movement.

"To the surgeon, Mister?" one asked but Martin shook his head; whatever life Harris appeared to possess was long gone and his empty body was unceremoniously fed through a gun port.

And then he noticed Brett, bareheaded and watching aghast by the bulwark.

"Lost your hat, lad?" he asked, but Brett seemed not to hear and, as he glanced at the lad's eyes, Martin could tell the boy was many miles away.

* * *

"Starboard battery ready!" Croft reported and King considered the enemy once more. Closing fast, the Frenchman was becoming a better target with every second but the sooner they despatched their second broadside, the sooner they could send another. A curt nod to the first lieutenant brought yet another explosion of gunfire and King's reddened eyes peered through acrid smoke as he attempted to gauge the result.

This time it was not so gratifying; more shot had fallen short and, though the Frenchman appeared otherwise bracketed, there was no obvious damage. But blows taken to the hull were rarely spectacular, King reminded himself. For all he knew, his opponent had been struck low and hard: even as the two ships continued to close, they might be starting to take in water.

The thought shocked him as he remembered exactly who could be suffering as a result, and he dug the fingers of his hand into his palm in anguish. This had to stop; there must be a way. He might surrender, of course, although *Mistral* had only received one broadside and not taken anything like the punishment expected for such a drastic action. Or he might turn away, except that would only encourage the enemy to give chase, as well as abandoning Adams in his impotent corvette.

"Here comes another!"

The gun captain from one of the quarterdeck carronades gave the warning and King looked up in time to see the end of the enemy's ripple of fire. It was a ripe red row of flashes that might be signalling his own destruction; a concept that even sounded momentarily attractive. But as French shot landed about his ship, cutting deep into men and material as it did, King – and his dilemma – remained unscathed.

"Jennings – get that preventer stay spliced or replaced!" Though a relative stranger to action, Scott appeared to be keeping his head. The man stood next to the binnacle with all the aplomb and assurance of a lieutenant while Croft, elderly by anyone's gauge, was further forward and roaring at *Mistral*'s gunners as if the sweating bodies were nothing more than dumb beasts of burden.

"Prize 'as not responded to my last signal, sir." This was Sennett; the youngster was also keeping his head and reporting as coolly as any seasoned officer. And this was important information; the corvette was indeed not following *Mistral* into battle, instead it lay almost a cable astern and was continuing to head directly away. Such confusion was not unusual in the heat of battle, as King was well aware. "Make, 'take station on my stern'," he ordered, and Sennett touched his hat in response.

Thoughts of the enemy drew him back and King realised his own last turn had not been tight enough; consequently *Mistral* had gained marginally and was drawing closer to the Frenchman. And he would be able to deliver another broadside shortly; already some quarterdeck carronades – always faster guns to service – were being signalled ready. Soon they would be fired, sending further death and destruction on a closing target that was sure to return the compliment shortly afterwards and for a moment King wondered at the futility of it all.

"Starboard battery's prepared!" Croft shouted back from his station. Then, as his expression changed slightly, the older man asked, "Is something the matter, sir?"

"No, nothing," King replied smartly as he pulled himself together. "Carry on, Mr Croft."

* * *

The fact that they were out of immediate danger was not lost on Adams although having to watch two frigates exchange such murderous blows was almost as troubling. In his experience it was rare for any foreign ship to be as slick in their gunnery as a British man-of-war, yet the Frenchman was matching *Mistral*'s broadsides in both timing and accuracy. And this was probably the purest form of naval combat with anticipation and manoeuvrability being as important as raw fire power. Two ships of the line might slug it out and pound the other to pieces, but frigate captains had to think beyond simply firing off their cannon. It was the nautical equivalent of duelling with sabres and victory would go to the one who moved faster whilst also dealing out more, and deadlier, blows. Should either be wounded, lose a mast or a truly significant spar, they must surely be defeated, and if that happened to *Mistral*, Adams would be left in an unenviable position indeed.

Consequently he had not missed Captain King's signal; Summers reported it as soon as he acknowledged the hoist and now the lad was visibly sulking after his own refusal to comply with the instruction. But whether the corvette could fight or not, the last place Adams wanted to be was within range of such an onslaught and, though it meant disobeying a direct command, he had no intention of following *Mistral* into action.

He glanced aft once more; the British frigate was holding up well and appeared to be giving and receiving in equal measure but knowing how poorly manned she was only increased his concern. And, of the two, the French was undoubtedly the larger – larger and more powerful, with stronger timbers and almost certainly a bigger crew. So truly it was better for him to run. Run and leave his captain and the men they had come to know so well to the mercy of the French. King was not the type to surrender straight away; probably several minutes would pass while the French manoeuvred into the perfect position before beginning a telling bombardment that could only end in *Mistral*'s destruction. And in that time he knew a more intelligent officer would do something positive. But Adams' mind had never been the sharpest and was currently set solely on self-preservation. And he would survive; even if the enemy remained sound enough to give chase, they had already lost the support of their jib boom. It was not the most vital piece of tophamper, perhaps, but his corvette should still have the heels of them.

Yes, that must be his plan; after all, a captain's duty was to place the safety of his command above all else. Besides, an effectively unarmed corvette seemed almost superfluous; he could take no active part in the action other than to pose a minor threat which was truly no more than a bluff. And without *Mistral*'s support, that bluff would soon be called so there would be no ignominy in retreat; nothing to berate himself for afterwards and surely no man should face court martial when his actions had saved his ship.

The realisation that, despite his confusion, somehow, magically, he had reached a decision was reassuring. He would maintain his current heading and stay under minimal sail, at least until *Mistral* showed signs of defeat; then pile on the canvas. And though much that he held dear would be left in his wake, it was undoubtedly the right move. In time he might even come to think of it as brave.

* * *

But there was no room for abstract concepts like courage or cowardice aboard *Mistral*. All had a job to do and most were doing it to the best of their ability and beyond. They had despatched two more broadsides only to suffer the same and the fact that their enemy's gunners were continuing to keep pace would have been worrying if any had the time to consider it. Instead, every able hand was fully engaged in the many tasks necessary aboard a ship of war in the heat of action.

The servers at the starboard battery had been augmented by most from the larboard, leaving only the second captains to stand by their silent weapons, yet so many had fallen that still more were needed to tend those guns in use. But their regular reserves, the forty or so marines the frigate normally carried, were absent while those detailed to care for the wounded found themselves more than usually occupied. And so it was that idlers such as the ropemaker, armourer, coxswain and yeoman of the sheets were being called in to assist at the great guns while others attended to the wounds *Mistral* had already suffered.

Which, to that point, were not so very terrible. Shot had been received low on the hull but none, so far, had penetrated beneath the waterline and, though much of the frigate's tophamper lay in tatters, the basic spars and a fair amount of standing and running rigging survived. Those topmen who could be spared were aloft rigging fresh line while treating the regular passage of enemy shot as yet one more distraction in an occupation already fraught with danger.

And below, in the darkest part of the ship, the darkest of works was underway. Manning, in his makeshift sick berth, was treating the casualties with the speed and dispassion he had acquired over many years of combat surgery while those in the grand and forward magazines dispensed a constant stream of cartridges to the ever needy, yet steadily diminishing, team of ship's boys. Even Scott had been called in to replace one of the injured helmsmen and was carrying out his own orders while stoically ignoring the warm stickiness that covered much of *Mistral*'s wheel. Only King appeared unoccupied although, considering the volume of conflicting thoughts that rushed continually through his brain, that was probably unfair.

So accustomed had he become to victory that the Frenchman's ability to maintain a steady and high rate of fire had come as a shock. Usually a few well-laid barrages would be enough to slow an enemy's pace yet, as the two hulls drew closer and both ships' broadsides became more effective, he began to wonder if *Mistral* would be the first to tire.

And however bad their own position, he was uncomfortably aware it might have been so much worse. If that one lucky hit had not weakened the enemy's bowsprit, the Frenchman would have been across their hawse by now and pounding shot after shot down the length of the British frigate's hull.

Which was still a fate that remained likely for, even without the support of the jib boom, the French were starting to pull ahead. Unless King did something they would be drawing out of his own frigate's arc of fire, and be free to tack across her bows. Then *Mistral* must surely be at the mercy of their broadside cannon and with little chance of reply. He glanced about, taking his eyes off the enemy and his immediate surroundings for the first time in what felt like an age. Over the taffrail he could see the prize and was surprised to note that, rather than following him, Adams was continuing to head away from the action.

"Mr Sennett!"

"Sir!" The response came from close by and King realised that, such were their injuries, the midshipman and his signal's party had been assisting at one of the quarterdeck carronades.

"Did the prize respond to my last signal?"

"There was an acknowledgement, sir," the midshipman confirmed, before glancing back and noticing with horror that the corvette was now considerably out of station.

"Repeat it," King snapped. "And add 'most immediate'."

The lad and his assistants immediately deserted their cannon and soon black balls of bunting were rushing up a mizzen halyard. King watched them go and the colourful flags break out. He had no idea what Adams was about but, once the fellow saw sense and turned, he would signal for him to increase sail and pass on their larboard side. With luck the threat of a corvette crossing his own bows would deter *Capitaine* Adenis from continuing further and such a message was certainly worth the loss of one cannon in the next broadside.

* * *

"*Mistral*'s signalling again and it's the same message," Summers reported on the corvette's tiny quarterdeck. In direct contrast to the larger ship, those aboard the prize were remarkably idle. Nothing had been required of them for some while and most were taking the chance to watch the action over top rails and through gun ports.

"Very well," Adams acknowledged and even to him his voice sounded tense.

"Shall I order the helm across?" the midshipman enquired more gently. The pair had been friends long enough for him to know when something was wrong, and this was definitely such an occasion. "John," he added, in even lower tones, "John, we have to turn *Mistral* needs our support."

"There's nothing we can do. We are unarmed, I must look to the safety of my own ship."

"But the captain needs us," Summers was almost pleading. "We must respond."

Chapter Twenty-One

By the time King's attention returned from the corvette, *Mistral* had despatched, and received, another broadside, yet still both ships were avoiding serious damage aloft. But the Frenchman was undoubtedly drawing ahead; soon each would be beyond reach of the other's main guns, although the enemy had the advantage and must shortly be in a perfect position to tack across the British frigate's prow. He might increase sail, although doing so meant robbing men from the cannon and, were the gun crews depleted further, weapons would start to fall silent. Or he might turn sharply to starboard and risk facing an early raking in an effort to capture the Frenchman's stern with his unused larboard pieces. To make the most of such a manoeuvre called for a perfectly sound tophamper along with a full and fit crew, whereas those he had left were starting to tire. If Adams would only get a move on all should be well but, as he looked back once more, King realised the corvette was still solidly sticking to her original course.

"What the devil?" he muttered momentarily confused. Adams had no reason to delay and might be placing himself in danger; were *Mistral* forced to strike it would not take much for the Frenchman to turn and even a long-distance barrage from a forty-gun frigate could spell the end of a corvette. Then he felt a wave of relief as the small warship finally put her helm across, her sails were released, and she was thrown into as tight a turn as any captain might wish for.

"Prize has worn, sir," Sennett reported.

"Yes," King agreed. "Make for them to forereach; they are to pass and take station off our larboard bow. And they must do so immediately, do you understand?"

"Aye, aye, sir," the lad agreed as he made for the flag locker once more.

* * *

Adams watched in silence as Summers brought them about and the corvette gathered way on the opposite tack. They had also shaken out more sail and were generally doing everything to be up with *Mistral*, currently slogging it out with the Frenchman less than half a mile ahead.

"Captain's signalling for us to pass him," Summers reported in a firm tone that Adams had never heard before. But then he had never known the lad take the initiative so, for the recent change of course was in no way down to him but all the junior man's doing. And now that they were being called in to support *Mistral*, he supposed Summers would be ordering that as well.

* * *

Mistral trembled as another broadside rumbled out but, before the smoke had fully cleared, Croft was already shouting back to King.

"There'll be one more from the long guns – after that they won't bear!"

King moved to the starboard side of the quarterdeck and peered across at the enemy frigate. For some while she had been pulling ahead whilst gradually edging closer to the wind and *Mistral* had been matching broadside with broadside while she turned also, but now all had grown eerily silent aboard the Frenchman. That must mean they expected him to try and take their stern or were holding fire in order to tack across his bows. But either way it seemed *Mistral* was in line for a raking.

"Mr Scott, can you bring us closer to the wind?"

The young officer considered the sails as he tried the wheel hesitantly. "I might gain half a point, sir – no more."

King cursed openly. Behind he could see the corvette adding more canvas as she gamely tried to catch up although Adams had left it too late; it would be all of fifteen minutes before his ship was in a position to head the enemy off and by then the Frenchman should already be installed off King's prow. Whatever happened, his opponent held the upper hand.

"Bring her as close as she will hold," he ordered, his attention still fixed at what was proving to be an unbeatable enemy. The dreaded chill of defeat had started to creep up his spine and it was a sensation he knew only too well. But though he had undoubtedly failed in the past it had always been an honourable beating by an opposition that was demonstrably stronger. This Frenchman was only marginally larger than *Mistral* and should have been handled with ease, especially as King had the support of another vessel. Even the excuse that his ship was undermanned crumbled to nothing when it was remembered who had chosen to start the fight. The only mitigating factor was one he had kept to himself: that a woman – not even his wife – was likely to be sheltering within his opponent's ship.

Mistral creaked closer into the wind and her cannon trucks squealed as the heavy weapons were heaved into position. He supposed they might try a boarding; even without marines, King could raise a fair number of fighting men. But from the way she had been handled, his opponent appeared well manned and was commanded by a true professional. Whoever this *Capitaine* Adenis might be, he surely had a rosy future ahead of him, and one that would hardly be sullied by the capture of a prime British fifth rate.

The deck vibrated again – this was the first broadside *Mistral* had sent without an intervening reply but must also be the last; King decided. And there would be no point in waiting for the inevitable; for the French to tack, then present their broadside to *Mistral*'s bow. He might continue to fight, but even one sound raking should be enough to knock the stuffing out of his ship and much of her crew. No, he would strike long before the enemy took up such a position.

* * *

Mistral's guns had been firing continuously for some time and Martin's head ached from the sound while his ears had grown so numb it was impossible tell if one of his damnable attacks were imminent or not. But, for once in his life, he truly did not care. If the worst happened and he suddenly found himself clinging to the deck with all sense of balance lost, he would still be better off than the poor souls who had already fallen beside him. And, despite an earlier resolution to avoid such things, fate had cast him into a responsible position so he felt obliged to see it through.

Mistral's store of fresh hands had never been large to begin with and now was running desperately low; Martin had robbed every last man from her larboard battery and disbanded the parties clearing the injured, yet still some starboard gun crews remained light while an ever-growing number of dead or badly wounded lay waiting to be cleared. Morale remained high however, and his gunners were continuing to send regular broadsides, despite the French shot that rained about them and was steadily reducing their numbers. And Brett, still hatless but now in control, was performing equally well. He had given the lad responsibility for the powder supply and the midshipman had risen to the task, urging the boys on with threats and curses in a manner not so very different from Martin's own. But once *Mistral*'s final broadside was despatched and her servers secured their pieces for what many knew would be the last time, the mood began to alter.

While there had been a task to perform and only by working quickly and efficiently could they hope to survive, the men were relatively simple to control. But once idle, they soon showed signs of restlessness.

Many were experienced men-of-war and knew exactly what the French were about while being equally aware little could be done about it. The mutterings grew until some were demanding the chance to board, while others began looking towards the quarterdeck for some indication that *Mistral* would strike. Brett, who had called his team of powder monkeys to a panting halt, approached Martin for direction.

"There is nothing to be done." The older man had to bellow to overcome the ringing in his own ears. "The enemy have trapped us by the wind; we can only tack, though that must surely make the situation worse."

"But might we not steer to starboard?" Brett, equally deafened, roared in return.

"To what end? It would merely present our bows to the French the sooner."

"Then do we strike?" the boy asked, wide eyed and in a lower voice although few on the gun deck could have heard if they had wanted to.

"I suspect we shall," Martin agreed. "But if not, you and I will have to secure the hands."

Now the younger midshipman's expression turned from fear to confusion.

"At my word see that every man takes shelter," Martin continued, now shouting directly into the boy's ear. "There might be little, but gun carriages will suffice. The enemy will cross our bows; see every man is aft of their piece and remains so."

"But what of Croftie?"

Martin glanced up and back to the quarterdeck but there was no sign of the first lieutenant.

"I have charge in his absence," he yelled in reply, "and shall issue small arms should we be ordered to board or repel. But there will be a broadside first, and the men must be protected."

"And what of ourselves?" Brett asked doubtfully.

"Aye, what indeed?" Martin grunted.

King noticed Croft coming aft. With the long guns now unable to bear, the first lieutenant could still command the quarterdeck carronades; the shorter barrelled weapons being equipped with carriages that gave a wider arc of fire.

"I could load with canister," he suggested, and King noted how the streaks of powder and dust on his skin made his friend appear decidedly aged. "We might still carry her by boarding."

"It will not do, James," King sighed. "I fear we are done for."

"You may..." the older man began but something made him stop. Then King was struck again by the first lieutenant's face although now it appeared positively rosy while what had been tired eyes had grown wide and were fixed on something terrible in the near distance.

Turning back to the enemy, King was in time to see an immense column of white flame as it changed to yellow, then red, and then fade to a thick pall of rolling smoke as the air was rent by the roar of an almighty explosion.

* * *

Summers saw it from afar. He was by the corvette's binnacle having unconsciously taken the place usually occupied by the commanding officer. The prize had been preparing to pass *Mistral* so exact details of the enemy's destruction were obscured by the British ship, yet still all aboard knew what had happened. He turned back to Adams who had relegated himself to the taffrail.

"The Frenchie's blown," he said and the older, and supposedly more senior, man simply nodded in reply.

* * *

In *Mistral*'s waist, where Martin and Brett had been shepherding the servers into taking cover, the explosion came as a massive reprieve. So intent had the two been in their work they missed the initial flash and, as the roar reached them, merely thought it the start of a particularly close and deadly broadside. But the reaction of those nearby said otherwise and, rushing for a gun port, Martin was in time to see the last scraps of debris falling into the sea. For a second he peered out at the murky waters where so recently a proud and deadly enemy had sailed, then turned back to meet the eyes of Brett. And, despite the certainty of what had just occurred, the lad was looking to him for explanation.

* * *

But the Frenchman's destruction needed no clarification. When wooden ships did battle with gunpowder that needed to be moved between decks, fire or explosion was an ever-present threat with consequences that were frequently devastating. This was by no means the first action King had fought to end so and his recent experience in the *St. George* only increased his appreciation of the danger. But that had been at night; now, in the light of a dying sun, he was able to witness the awfulness that remained when a ship was blown to pieces and such detail gave the horror a totally new dimension. As did the fact that this time he was far more personally involved. He had known men caught up in the loss of the *St. George*, but had loved Aimée and that placed matters on an entirely different level.

"It must have been one of the magazines," Croft muttered as the pair continued to stare down on the flotsam-strewn waters. But King did not reply, indeed, he did not hear, although that had nothing to do with the din of explosion that still echoed in his ears. The reason was far more simple: he had simply ceased to listen.

Chapter Twenty-Two

"Mr Martin has returned in the cutter," Croft announced as he entered the great cabin. This was the last of the ship's boats to have been sent to trawl through the scattered remains of the Frenchman and probably King's final hope.

"Anything?" he demanded, but the first lieutenant shook his head.

"I fear not. A deal of wreckage and plenty of human remains, but no sign of life."

It was not to be surprised at, although King had still been nurturing the hope that, if not Aimée, someone might have been thrown clear of the explosion who would be able to tell him more.

"Very well," he grunted. "There seems little point in delaying further; are we fit to sail?"

"Mr Jennings wishes to replace some standing rigging and Mr Newton still has work to undertake on the lower hull though both believe they can be finished relatively quickly."

"Newton?"

"The carpenter's mate," Croft replied levelly. "Mr Anderson was..."

"Yes, yes of course," King snapped, suddenly irritated both by the earlier loss of the carpenter and that he had been seen to have forgotten the incident.

"Shall I signal Mr Adams to stand by? It might be better if we continue to The Cape in company?"

King eyed his first officer doubtfully. "If you think fit," he said. "Though Adams is perfectly capable of making the journey alone."

"I would consider it wise, sir." The first lieutenant seemed adamant and King was mildly surprised that he should choose to address him so formally in the privacy of his quarters. And for that matter, why was he regarding him with such apparent concern?

"Was there something else?" he growled.

"Not exactly, sir, though I was wondering if you would be speaking with Mr Adams – perhaps while we await repairs?"

Now Croft was definitely behaving strangely; of all the subjects on King's mind, Adams and his wretched prize was probably the least of them.

He shook his head. "Why this preoccupation with Adams, James?"

"He was hardly prompt in responding to your orders, sir."

King thought back but it was like trying to recall the name of his grandfather's dog while wrestling with a tiger. Nevertheless, Croft was obviously determined to pester him with trivialities; there had been Martin's report, boatswain's problems, guess the name of the carpenter, and now the cove was fussing about the third lieutenant of all people.

"Your signal for the prize to turn was all but ignored," Croft reminded him.

"As I recall, it were acted upon eventually," King snorted as the memories returned.

"After several minutes," the older man persisted. "In which time Mr Adams might have taken up his correct station. With the corvette threatening their prow, the enemy would have been unable to cross our own."

"The prize was effectively unarmed."

"But there was little risk. Mr Adams need only have faced whatever chasers the Frenchman carried while it would have appeared the corvette was offering a full broadside, something even a heavy frigate would have wished to avoid." Croft paused and lowered his eyes for a moment. "If I may say so, sir, your plan was inspired."

King sighed. From a man like Croft, such praise meant much, yet hardly helped to clear his mind of other, more personal, thoughts. Thinking back, he supposed Adams had been lax and briefly recalled his own frustration. Then he remembered the event had actually taken place barely two hours before.

"If Mr Adams had acted correctly, all would have been very different," Croft continued relentlessly. "And I am not saying we would still have been victorious; no one will know what caused that explosion – a cartridge igniting close to the magazine perhaps or some small fire we failed to detect. But without it, and with no support where support had been ordered, our goose would surely have been cooked. So I must maintain that, when young men are lax, they should be brought to account – if only as an example to others."

"And perhaps to present their side of matters?" King suggested.

"Of course," Croft was quick to agree.

"I suppose you are right," King sat back in his chair and sighed. "I shall have him come across when convenient, though there is much to see to before then."

More to the point, there were a myriad of tasks that only he, as captain, could address. He had yet to visit Manning on the orlop and really should make a personal inspection of the ship to encourage those attending her repairs. The captured French officers must be visited as well; probably they would know something of the action but it would be polite to pass on what he personally knew. Yet to realise all had taken place so recently – a few hours ago Aimée had been alive yet now ceased to exist – only added to his grief. And all he truly wanted was solitude: peace and quiet and a chance to mourn someone he had already lost and then found.

But Croft's comment about Adams' action had struck a chord. Certainly if the prize had been off their larboard bow as he directed, the enemy would have been forced to yaw. And it was quite possible the action would have continued longer and ended in quite a different manner. Without that terrible explosion, *Mistral* would certainly have been beaten and at that moment he might have been exchanging pleasantries with *Capitaine* Adenis in the French frigate while the dull ache of failure ate away at his marrow.

The thought was at once grim and beguiling for, though defeated and a prisoner, Aimée should still have been alive and possibly alongside him. That single fact would have made everything right and was all he longed for at that moment.

* * *

"So what are we to do?" Summers asked. "Stay hove to and wait on the captain?"

"You are asking me?" Adams snorted. "That's a rare change I fancy!"

Summers glanced at him. Darkness had fallen and they were on the quarterdeck with the hand at the wheel the only other living being nearby. The man was apparently dozing on his feet as the ship gently nudged the slight swell, but still it was hardly the place for delicate conversation.

"I am asking because you are my superior officer," the younger man declared softly before adding, "and my friend."

The last statement seemed to penetrate Adams' resolve and he visibly relaxed.

"I could see no point in following the command, Michael," he said, drawing back from the binnacle. "We were being sent in to fight yet had no weapons – or none that might be used."

Without acknowledgement the pair turned away in the search for privacy. "But it was the captain's instructions," Summers insisted as they approached the taffrail. "He would never have endangered us; there must have been a plan, even if we did not know of it."

"Possibly," Adams allowed as he stared aimlessly towards an invisible horizon. "But I could not be sure he were giving the orders. It might have been Croft, or Scott; either would have sent us to our doom without another thought."

That was something Summers had not considered; if he had, it might have made a difference to his own actions.

"The French frigate was a powerful ship – bigger than *Mistral* and far, far bigger than us," Adams continued. "We wouldn't have survived a single broadside. And frankly, Michael, I have been forced to surrender a prize in the past so had no wish to do so again."

That was understandable, though still did not alter the original point. Adams was given a direct order and in the most public way possible. Yet it had been ignored or, to be more accurate, only obeyed because Summers himself had overruled his superior officer. Furthermore, he could not dismiss the fact that his friend's disobedience must ultimately reflect on him, when it was due to his efforts that they had responded at all.

"Do you think there will be an enquiry?" Adams' question broke a silence that had lasted for some while.

"You mean a court martial?" Summers shook his head. "I truly could not say. But think Captain King will want an explanation. And, were I you, I would start to think of one sharpish."

* * *

The trip to the orlop was all King had expected. His first call had been on Robert Manning, although the surgeon was a shipmate of many years standing and little needed to be said. The man was obviously busy and King felt in no mood to linger, but a brief glance at the butcher's bill showed *Mistral* had been far worse off for men than King realised.

"That's the list of those that reached me," Manning told him as he returned to wrapping a bandage about a topman's lacerated arm. "I cannot speak for any that fell and were disposed of on deck while there are always those who take their time to present."

King nodded, that was frequently the case after an action; in the haste to carry out repairs it was common for seamen to ignore or roughly patch up minor injuries. Then, often days later and when the wound was turning septic, they would appear for treatment, with the medical department receiving the blame if a limb needed to be removed.

"I'll see the divisional officers check their men," King promised as he considered the scrap of paper. Thirty-three injured and nine dead; the latter was a low number but must refer to men who had died of their wounds in Manning's care. He could expect more, probably at least another twenty, which meant roughly a third of *Mistral*'s company had been major casualties.

It was a high proportion but little good would be done by commenting further; Manning had his work cut out for the next few days and King would be better moving on and talking to the Frenchmen confined in the forward pens.

That had been an even briefer visit; the captured officers must have been expecting release and to learn the details of their countrymen's fate came as a shock. King left them and was about to ascend to the berth deck, using the forecastle companionway rather than inconvenience Manning, when a thought occurred.

He was close to the filling room for *Mistral*'s forward magazine. The copper-lined chambers held a good proportion of the ship's high explosives and it would have been some form of ignition in just such a place that accounted for the enemy frigate. King paused with his foot on the first step; Aimée was likely to have been on the Frenchman's lowest deck, probably caring for the wounded or at least taking shelter. And, for all he knew, she might have been aware *Mistral* was the ship being engaged and probably about to be defeated. Despite every precaution, powder stores remained vulnerable places and it would have taken little effort for her toss a lanthorn through an open door or start a small fire in some other way. King bit his lip as he thought; a bold move for sure but one she was quite capable of. And then he refused to think further as he stamped determinedly up the wooden steps.

* * *

All had been working continuously since the action's abrupt ending but, as the night drew on, any with skills not so desperately needed could return to their messes and Paul Samuels fitted that category. During the action he had worked hard to serve his cannon, keeping his place within the team with barely a thought to the one member missing. Then later, when memories of his brother returned, he had quietly volunteered for one of the least popular tasks following combat.

This he had carried out in conjunction with the sailmaker who truly bore the responsibility and, using hammocks, round shot and help from the occasional tie mate, turned the ugly remains of any dead not already disposed of into presentable packages that might receive a respectable send off the following morning.

It was not a duty he had carried out before or wished to undertake again, but Samuels did find it mildly cathartic. The regret he felt at Peter's loss remained as vast and would only dwindle slightly with time, but at least there was now less guilt to carry over leaving his brother's body on that deserted beach. And with the task finally completed, he walked in a daze along the length of *Mistral*'s berth deck before slumping down in his accustomed place at the mess table.

"There's scran," Daines told him curtly. "Cheese if you'd like, and hard tack."

"Got some onions an' all if anyone's interested," Billy, the boy, suggested.

"And someone mentioned a duff," Swain added, with a pointed glance towards Russell.

"Aye, that's in hand," the cook replied. "Though you needn't fear; I've been assisting chips so dug Dale out of sickers to bend on a few puddings."

The others laughed gently but Samuels remained silent and no one objected.

"Reckon we'll be squaring away on the morrow." Daines had spent the evening replacing carronade tackle with the gunner's mate and, though he was physically tired, lacked the psychological exhaustion of Samuels.

"Aye, as soon as burials is over," Swain agreed, adding, "How many you got for us, Samuels?"

"Too many." The seaman's reply was brusque and did not convey his true feelings. For though he apparently remained aloof, Samuels felt anything but distant.

His brother was gone and would never come back; the pair had seen each other through much and he could never know a partnership like it again. But now Samuels sensed he had found something else; something, if not better, then almost as valuable.

He had only been a part of the mess a matter of weeks, yet already the difference between shipmates aboard a merchant and a man-of-war was obvious. Friendships had been made that would last a lifetime and, as he grew to know more about the ship, Samuels sensed she would become more important to him than any bluff-bowed Indiaman. And, as he glanced surreptitiously at the faces crowding around his table, he decided they were good enough. There might be a measure of gentle banter now and then, but it was generally accepted that everyone would support each other. None would ever be left to brawl alone and all were prepared to pop whatever they held dear to lend to a messmate. In fact, each would carry out the duties of what he and Peter had expected of the other and, though one was now gone and could never be replaced, Samuels knew he had found comradeship almost as strong.

* * *

Three days later much of her damage had been attended to and *Mistral* was considered sound enough to withstand quite a substantial storm. But rather than bad weather, the sun shone brassy and bright amid a crystal sky while the steady north-westerly kept both ships on course for an early arrival at Cape Town. And a measure of routine had also become established so that, with all else attended to, there was nothing to stop King speaking with Adams – at least nothing he could think of.

For really he had no interest in the meeting; whether the young lieutenant had misunderstood his signal or simply been slow in responding was of little concern; he had already decided the delay had been insignificant and might even have worked in their favour – if such a concept was appropriate considering the outcome. But Croft remained insistent and King felt he owed it to his second in command to formally investigate the matter.

He would do so alone, however; James Croft might have won his respect and friendship but King was not blind to the man's faults. He was as tenacious as a bulldog and, once an idea formed, would cling to it until proved correct or so disparaged that only a fool would consider it further. And, however little King cared about the outcome, it would be a sensitive interview, as any enquiry that questioned an officer's performance must, so the last thing he wanted was his first lieutenant chipping in.

But when the appointed day arrived, King did have a distraction, and one that was totally self-inflicted. He had woken with a headache which was undoubtedly the result of taking too much drink the previous night. And this was not an isolated incident; before the action King had hardly touched alcohol for many years, yet was forced to accept that recent meals had been accompanied by an increasing amount of wine. Now it was recognised, the trend would end, King assured himself as he downed several draughts of strong dark chocolate; from that day on his previous sober ways would definitely return.

But, despite the resolution, his headache remained and continued throughout an hour of pacing on the quarterdeck. And it was just as firmly entrenched at the appointed time so, when he took his place in the great cabin, the last thing King felt like was an intensive discussion with a young and able officer eager to avoid court martial.

Nevertheless, there was no avoiding it and, at four bells in the forenoon watch, King stood while McNamara showed Adams in.

The lad's greeting was formal and reserved while the hand he extended felt just as cold, but King had been in a similar position in the past and was prepared for just such a reaction.

"It's a pleasure to see you, John," he said, indicating the seat usually taken by Croft at the otherwise empty dining table. Despite his state, King had carefully chosen the surroundings; an interview conducted across a desk was far more confrontational and could never have the informality possible at a table more associated with pleasure than work. "I trust all is well aboard the prize?"

"Indeed, sir," Adams replied cautiously. "Though the French officers have complained about sharing quarters with their men."

"That is hardly to be surprised at," King smiled. "And rather gives the lie to any wishes for equality."

Adams stared back, stony faced. "Yes, sir."

King closed his eyes and momentarily placed a hand on his temple; very well, if that's how the lad wanted it...

"I wished to speak about your conduct in the recent action."

Adams made no comment and remained as impassive as before but the tension had definitely risen.

"I was concerned to note you did not immediately respond to my signals, and require an explanation."

"I have nothing to say, sir," Adams declared.

"Nothing to say?" King questioned. "It is a reasonable request and you shall surely meet it, either now or at a subsequent court martial."

"On reaching Cape Town I shall be resigning my commission," Adams announced abruptly.

King paused and considered the lad again. "Resigning?"

"Yes – yes, sir," Adams hurriedly corrected himself. "I want no more of the Navy and seek a different life ashore."

King nodded. "Then that is a decision you must make, although it might not be so simple. You are currently committed to *Mistral* and will remain one of her officers until told different. And I might further add that, should I decide to send you for court martial, your resignation will mean little and may be interpreted as an admission of guilt."

Adam's expression had turned to one of affront, although King chose not to notice.

"But enough of that for now, we must still address the current problem," he added quickly. "If it is indeed a problem. I am going to ask you once again; why were you slow in responding to my signal?"

"I did not respond," Adams declared with more than a hint of defiance. "It were Michael Summers who ordered us around. Without him the prize would have continued sailing south and out of danger."

"I see." King sat back in his chair.

"You only provided a small prize crew; I had barely enough to sail the ship let alone account for the prisoners," Adams continued with slightly less magnitude. "Yet we were ordered to engage a large fifth rate."

"I ordered you to block her," King corrected. "That is a very different matter."

"Maybe so, sir," Adams allowed. "But it felt different at the time. And I wasn't sure it were you doing the ordering – *Mistral* had been in action a good while and…"

"I understand," King assured him and, indeed, he truly did. As far as he was concerned the matter may as well be finished. More could be made of it, of course, and Croft would undoubtedly be on his hind legs by now had he been present. There was also the not insignificant matter of Summers taking charge of the prize, which some might argue was tantamount to mutiny. But King had no heart for that either.

"So tell me now why you intend to quit."

The lad paused. "I feel it best, sir. I am recently married and have not progressed sufficiently. The men do not take to me and neither do other officers – in short, I am poorly suited to the life."

King closed his eyes again; the headache was just as great but now at least he had a true distraction.

"Well, that must surely be a personal decision, but I would point out that you have only recently achieved commissioned rank. Commanders are not made overnight, yet you are well on your way to such a position. And I have received no complaints from fellow officers – rather the reverse – while I also understand your recent wedding was well attended by the people when they had every reason to be elsewhere."

"I am aware of that," Adams declared primly and it was his tight-lipped, pompous expression that finally made King see red.

"I don't know what you think we are about, here, Mr Adams, but the Navy is not a seminary for young ladies."

The sudden outburst took him by surprise and the lad blinked in astonishment; but more was to follow.

"We wear the King's uniform, which means our loyalty is to him, rather any personal concerns."

"Yes, sir," Adams replied automatically.

"Frankly I feel if you are harbouring feelings beyond the Service it is better that you do go; I for one have no use for an officer who cannot keep his mind solely on his duty and am certain others shall agree with me."

Now the young man was staring at his captain with a look made up of shock and wonder.

"But enough of that for now; you can give me your decision when we make harbour. I may as well tell you, I have no wish to pursue the earlier incident; as far as I am concerned, it is over. But remember my words, Adams; the British Navy has no room for those with their minds set elsewhere."

Chapter Twenty-Three

"Two frigates and a corvette," Scott marvelled. "I'd heard *Mistral* were a lucky ship, but that truly is an exceptional haul."

"Exceptional indeed," Manning agreed wearily. "Especially when this was to be nothing more than a sea trial."

After running before a steady wind for a little over a week they had finally sighted the African coast just before sundown. All knew the following day should bring them close to Cape Town and possibly into Table Bay itself so, for the first time since *Mistral* set sail, Scott was starting to relax. Manning also could finally rest having disposed of many of his patients with only the more awkward, or determined, hanging on for the hospital place that awaited them. The pair were in the gunroom and, having taken a light supper, were now sitting back and enjoying a rare glass of port.

And they were not alone in unbending slightly; with land almost within reach a spirit of lethargy had spread about the entire ship. It was as if all were aware they had given much and soon should need to give no more. For they would be back in harbour, back to the constraints of land life; mundane tasks and swinging the odd spree ashore for the hands and fighting with crooked suppliers or spotting crank workmanship for the officers as *Mistral* spent yet more time in the dockyard.

As Scott had stated, it had been a remarkably successful voyage yet there remained an unaccountable feeling of failure in the air. It was as if all their victories might not have been fairly earned and they were effectively the losers. And there was another sensation that was equally unexpected; one of infinite sadness. Any ship that returns with so many of her people missing can never be truly called happy, yet this was something else, something undefinable, but present nevertheless.

But nothing quite so ethereal bothered Scott that evening. His original statement was correct; *Mistral* had performed well and lived up to everything expected of her, although not all aboard had been as successful in passing their personal appraisals.

"You've sailed with the captain a fair spell, I'm told," he remarked, cautiously broaching the subject.

"Much of my time at sea," Manning agreed.

There were just the two of them at the table. Foil, the purser, was in the stewards' room bringing his accounts up to date and Croft was standing watch – a rare event for any first officer but essential with so many senior men absent.

"So you think you know him well?" the sailing master persisted.

"As well as anyone I should chance," Manning allowed, "though probably no better than you."

"Hardly," Scott protested. "We first met at Leadenhall Street earlier in the year."

"But have gone through much together since. And did you not follow him into the Service?"

"I did," Scott agreed. "And yes, we spent some time in an open boat where there are few secrets and little pretence. Though the man I see now is a very different specimen."

The surgeon rubbed at his chin in thought. "There is equally no room for rank in such places," he said. "Tom King is now your captain and, as I have long since learned, however close a friendship you cannot expect the same understanding when such a situation endures."

"No, but there is something more," Scott insisted. "When we first met he was indeed a passenger and I had been expecting a change when serving under him. But he treated me considerately and went out of his way in my defence over the grounding; in truth I was proud to have him as my captain."

"And now?" Manning asked, more alert.

"Now there is a definite change. Since the last action he has been almost unapproachable."

"It has been an especially taxing time," Manning reminded him. "And you have to allow for the loss of his companion. The pair were as close as any married couple yet, unless there is news on reaching Cape Town, she must surely now be considered gone forever."

"Indeed, but Miss Aimée went missing some time ago; much has happened since and..."

"And you feel he should have dismissed all thoughts of her?" Manning smiled. "The workings of the human mind are beyond the scope of any simple surgeon, yet I know grief to be not so simple. I will however grant that, after a little initial melancholy, Tom did seem to be coping and it is only of late a change occurred."

"Since the last action," Scott agreed. "That proved the turning point. Yet it was a battle won, and won at a time when defeat seemed inevitable."

"Perhaps it was the way in which it was won?" Manning fingered his glass reflectively. "Neither of us are fighting men yet spend our lives alongside those who are, so probably know their ways better than most. And for them an enemy is to be beaten, not annihilated; few look for such total victory, especially when it could be considered unfairly earned."

"You may be right. But is that enough to change a man so? Perhaps it is something that could be discussed with a friend?"

Manning shook his head. "Again, I cannot say, and neither would I think it wise to enquire. But I do know this much: if Tom King wishes to talk over any matter, he will be first to start the conversation. And when he prefers to keep a secret, nothing with tear it from him."

Scott nodded and picked up his glass once more. "Yes, I am sure you are right and I am probably speaking out of turn. For it is only an impression; I simply felt I should share it with someone who knew him a little better."

"As you say, an impression," Manning agreed, "and one that is best left alone, especially when we have good wine to finish." So saying the two men simultaneously downed their drinks.

For a number of reasons the surgeon was glad the conversation had come to an end; it was never healthy for officers to discuss another in their absence and especially so in the case of the captain. But he had indeed known King a good while and through testing times for them both, yet never before had he encountered the withdrawn and slightly bitter individual that now inhabited the great cabin. It was a change that had been concerning him for some time, both on a personal and a professional level. Manning suspected his friend was not eating well and had considered enquiring further of his servant although the hollow cheeks and persistent gaunt expression already told him much. But what he had said to Scott remained correct; if King needed help he would ask for it. Until then it was better to play the matter down, certainly when speaking with fellow officers. Whatever he did he must never admit to being equally concerned and harbouring very similar worries.

* * *

"Then there are just a few matters of personnel to address," Croft said as he collected a sheet of paper and studied it for a moment. Their morning meetings had become brief affairs with King adding little to his suggestions and this one, probably the last before they raised Cape Town, was following a similar pattern.

"Mr Martin has been declared physically unfit," he announced, "and is not recommended for permanent service."

King looked up. "Martin?"

"Yes, sir. Oldster midshipman..."

"I know who he is," King interrupted, "but what the devil's the matter with him?"

Croft pursed his lips. "Surgeon states chronic seasickness," he replied. "Though I believe it to be something more sinister and wonder if Mr Manning is not of the same opinion."

"But we've hardly seen white water."

"There was, perhaps, one significant storm," Croft reminded him gently, "though it seems the condition is liable to present even in a calm."

King shook his head. Seasickness was common in the Navy and no respecter of rank or position although it did obey other rules. "Is this why he was in sick bay after the cutter was destroyed?" he asked.

"I believe so." For several reasons the older man had been hoping his captain would not probe too deeply.

"Then I think we can assume something different," King stated with apparent satisfaction. "And if he is not suitable for combat duties, it is indeed better he were gone."

"Yes, sir," Croft agreed and referred to his list again. He supposed the pair of them were still on relatively good terms although the old rapport was definitely missing. "And then there is the question of the carpenter," he continued quickly. "A replacement must be found for Mr Anderson; we may recruit in Cape Town or there is always Mr Newton."

"The carpenter's mate?" King questioned, glad to have remembered the name.

"Yes, sir. He performed well in supporting the late Mr Anderson and with running repairs following our recent action. I consider him worthy of the post."

"Better the devil you know I suppose," King grudgingly agreed. "Especially as any appointed from the shore are likely to be dockyard trained and with a similar attitude."

"Then Mr Newton will have to be replaced as mate," Croft continued, "There are a number who might fill the post; Skinner would be my recommendation though that still leaves the carpenter's department a man light. And I was wondering about Russell joining them."

"Russell? Isn't he the cook?"

"He is, sir, though it is more an honorary position, certainly as far as Russell is concerned." Croft raised an eyebrow. "Some might look on it as a demotion, though I feel he will jump at the opportunity, and predict there will be others equally glad of the move."

During their short time at sea there had been several complaints about the quality of *Mistral*'s food, although the first lieutenant had no intention of bothering his captain with the details at that moment.

"But doesn't he have a wooden leg?"

"I believe he has several," Croft chanced, "and made each one himself for specific occasions."

In the past such a remark would have drawn a smile or even laughter from his captain and, though the first lieutenant would never have considered himself a humourist, they were occasions he used to enjoy. But now the man stared back at him with that same empty expression and he could not help but feel sorry.

"So he is skilled as a carpenter?" King confirmed.

"As I understand, sir. And his efforts were invaluable in identifying our damage when we took the ground." Croft was about to add more; in his view Russell's appointment would also be welcomed by others of the carpenter's crew, although he doubted if his captain was in the mood to care much for that aspect.

"Will he be easy to replace as a cook?"

Russell could have been replaced by one of the ship's cats with few noticing the difference, but Croft had learned his lesson and wasn't about to make another attempt at levity.

"Yes, sir. His mate is very experienced. I think the change of roles would be a popular move all round."

"Very well," King grunted, and the first lieutenant duly made a note. That was the last issue and he had no intention of remaining in the great cabin any longer. Quite what had brought such a change in his superior officer was a mystery but of one thing he was certain; popularity was no longer one of Captain King's concerns.

* * *

"I wanted to thank you properly for helping me through the action," Brett announced.

Once more he and Martin were alone in the midshipmen's berth and, once more, seated opposite each other while the cat, more confident now and heavy with young, lay solidly on the table between them. Martin looked up from his current pamphlet, a thesis on predicting currents in uncharted waters, and considered the lad.

"I did nothing that requires thanks," he said.

"Oh, but you did," Brett corrected. "I were adrift and would have foundered were it not for your presence."

"My presence?" Martin asked, surprised.

"Aye, strong and firm, like nothing would shift you. And you gave me a task, one I were capable of; it distracted me though all I truly had to do was follow your example."

The older man shrugged. "Any officer would have done the same."

"Any commissioned officer maybe. But few midshipmen."

Martin searched for words but it seemed the youngster had enough for both of them.

"I know Croftie were supposed to be supervising the guns, but it was you who had true control in the waist, and you who noticed me aback."

"Maybe so," he agreed reluctantly, although the words had heartened him greatly. He had just been advised by the first lieutenant that there would be no permanent berth for him aboard *Mistral*. It was a decision Martin had been expecting but the disappointment was almost offset by Brett's words.

"You know I shall be leaving at Cape Town," he said, and the youngster nodded.

"I heard as much and am sorry."

"And are you aware of the reason?" Martin added.

"I am, though it seems unfair. What will you do?"

"I'd like to find a ship," the senior man rested back in his chair. "It would have to be a merchant of course though I am relatively skilled as a navigator and can stow a cargo as well as any."

"And you do not feel your ailment will be noticed?"

"I shall not seek to hide it," Martin stated firmly, "so the Honourable Company won't employ me. But I do get good warning and Mr Scott feels an independent master might think differently."

"I could go with you," Brett suggested, and Martin gave a short laugh.

"No, you have a future in the Royal Navy," he declared. "How would your father feel if he heard you had taken berth in a trader?"

"He'd be furious," the midshipman admitted with a youngster's lack of concern. "But I don't mind telling you, some aspects of our cruise did not suit me at all."

"You must not judge any ship by her sea trials; few see as much action as we did in the time."

Brett looked doubtful. "Perhaps, though it feels as if I'd be better off in a merchant. We could try for a place together," he continued with growing enthusiasm. "Be a team; I could care for you when crook and be taught navigation in return."

"You lost your nerve for an instant, no more," Martin told him gently. "These things happen, a momentary lapse cannot be allowed to alter your life."

"But it were not my first time in combat."

"It need not be; no one can say when a man might forget himself in action, but the chances are strong such a thing will not happen again. And, if it should, you now know your demon can be conquered."

"I still think myself more suited to the life of a trader," the young man sighed.

"Sailing the same route year after year with one eye always turned for privateers?" Martin laughed. "Believe me, if I could choose between a merchant and a man-of-war, I know where I would ship."

"Yet you are to opt for a merchant?" Brett reminded him.

"Only through necessity. For there is another choice, and any place at sea is a thousand times preferable to one on land."

* * *

And so, on the afternoon of the following day, it was a quiet and thoughtful ship that eased gently into Table Bay and made her number.

"No sign of our earlier prize," Croft commented as the sailing master brought them up to the anchorage.

"I was thinking the same myself," Scott agreed as he prepared to take the first bearing. "The dock seems to have a ship in place with others moored at our previous wharf and a deal more in the roads."

"But only the warships are known to us. And none appear to be

Cooper's frigate."

Scott made no comment. There was one merchant he did recognise: *Nancy Jane*, the American schooner that had plucked them from the ocean. Daniels must be back in Cape Town touting for a cargo and the sight of her sent his thoughts racing.

"But then she needed repair," the first lieutenant continued, still thinking of their prize. "Maybe they've progressed with the facilities at St Helena and Cooper has been ordered there?"

"Or she could be on her way home," Scott suggested.

"I truly hope not," the first lieutenant snorted. "I've no wish to lose a good officer, nor any of the prize crew if it comes to it."

"Might that be a prospect for us? Being sent back to England, I am meaning."

Croft scratched his nose. "It might," he replied at last. "We've just gone through one major refit and the next need not be as extensive though a recall is always possible."

Scott had heard much about *Mistral*'s recent docking and knew of the considerable efforts made by all to see her put to rights. Croft especially had worked hard, yet much of what had been achieved must inadvertently be down to their captain.

Though away for much of the time, his officers and men had been loyal enough to prepare the ship in his absence, which was surely a testament to his popularity. But since their last action the man's morose and unpredictable behaviour had undoubtedly undone much of the good built up and, wherever she was attended to, Scott sensed *Mistral* would emerge from her next refit in a poorer state and probably lacking several of her officers.

The men would be different and have less choice in the matter but for as long as King remained remote, Scott doubted *Mistral* would ever return to the happy, and lucky, ship she had once been.

"I'll have the quarter boat prepared." The captain's voice was sharp and came from behind making both officers jump with surprise that, in Scott's case, was mingled with guilt.

"Quarter boat; yes, sir," he repeated while snapping to attention and saluting. But King ignored the compliment and collected the traverse board from the binnacle instead.

"And see the crew are properly rigged," he grunted without looking up. "Get Foil to release some of the slop clothes he's been hoarding."

"I'll speak to the purser, sir," Scott promised. The captain turned back to consider him for a moment and the younger man was struck by the look of vacant misery in his eyes.

"Well don't just stand there," King snapped, "get on with it!"

* * *

Mistral had been directed to an anchorage some distance from the official quay and the lack of wind meant a lengthy row for the men at the oars. Cape Town was now also firmly into spring; a relentless sun burned in an otherwise empty sky and King could see the sweat running freely down the men's shirts. But there was no room for sympathy in his soul; all such nonsense had been banished in that one devastating explosion which turned defeat into victory yet spelled the end of Aimée. He was aware of this, as he was his increasingly monstrous behaviour since and even had some insight into how the sudden change of mood was causing doubt and concern amongst his officers. Yet, so overwhelming was his desolation, he lacked both the will and ability to change matters.

Whilst Aimée had simply been missing the pain was bad enough and later matched almost exactly by joy and relief on discovering her to be alive. Yet all that emotion had been obliterated, literally before his eyes. And even the subsequent realisation that she was probably to blame, that Aimée had almost certainly sacrificed the French ship, her own life and the life of their child to save him only increased King's torment. Such an act was so like her; generous, impulsive and foolishly wise. Traits that had made him love her so much then and miss her so desperately now.

It was a pain he was coping with, but only just. Once more his head ached from drink taken the night before although he had now graduated from wine. The small supply of brandy taken aboard for entertaining guests was long gone and, with a pang of shame, he remembered last night's bottle had been all but begged from the gunroom by McNamara.

As the boat moved forward in the sunshine, King knew this most recent humiliation must also be the last. The prerogative for a ship's captain to do and say very much as he pleased had been abused dreadfully; he had allowed himself a generous measure of space to grieve, but all that should now end. Within an hour he hoped to be speaking with Sir Richard Banks and possibly the colony's governor;

neither would take kindly to the bouts of ill temper he had allowed himself of late. On returning to the ship he really had to make amends; Aimée's loss was a private concern and had nothing to do with anyone else, especially as he was the only person truly to blame. For there had been every reason to avoid action with the enemy frigate; if only he had allowed the Frenchman to slip though his fingers, she would be living still.

They were approaching the quay; King could see civilians as they walked along the hard looking characteristically smart, if slightly wooden, and wondered for a moment about his own appearance. He was wearing a full-dress uniform but should have seen that McNamara spent longer brushing down the nap while he was equally aware of his own inattention with that morning's razor.

But Sir Richard would understand and might be someone he could finally share Aimée's loss with. The two other candidates would normally have been Croft and Manning but, as with all aboard *Mistral*, both knew nothing of her presence in the enemy frigate. They were, however, aware of his determination to engage the Frenchman, as well as how close *Mistral* had come to being beaten. Sir Richard Banks would see his actions in a more dispassionate light and deal with his personal loss in the same way; for at that moment the last thing King needed was sympathy.

Now they were alongside the landing stage and he stood uncertainly as the boat was made fast.

"I shall be calling at the Castle first, then may need you to take me to *Relentless* if the Commodore is not ashore."

"Aye, aye, sir." Sennett, in the sternsheets, responded automatically although King could detect reserve in his tone. The midshipman was one of his favourites yet also appeared to be treating his captain with caution and again King resolved to make a change.

And then something caught his eye that banished all such trivial thoughts. It was a person – a man – standing amid a group of civilians yet dressed in a uniform he knew well and without another word King found himself stepping clear of the boat and clambering onto the quay.

On gaining solid ground there was the initial giddiness usual after a spell at sea but even that was ignored and, staggering only slightly, King began to half run towards the figure. As he drew closer he knew this was not a dream and neither were his eyes deceiving him: the person standing nonchalantly on the road was indeed someone he had thought long dead. But there was still a trace of doubt in his bewildered brain and as he called out it was with every expectation of being disappointed.

"McIver!" For a moment the figure remained unmoved. "McIver," he repeated slightly louder. "Doctor, is that you?"

* * *

"Sam Scott as I live and breathe!" the American exclaimed.

"Good morning to you, Nathaniel," *Mistral*'s sailing master replied with mock formality as he touched his hat. "I wonder if we might step aboard."

"To be sure!" Daniels beamed enthusiastically as he held back the hinged top rail that blocked *Nancy Jane*'s gangplank. Two men boarded and one was the British John Company officer they had plucked from the ocean all those months back. He now wore a Royal Navy uniform but the grin was the same and the American never forgot a face. The other, possibly slightly younger, was another Navy man, although his garb was far less grand and even comfortably shabby.

"As you can see, I joined with Tom King," Scott explained when they were aboard.

"And would that be his frigate?" Daniels asked, nodding towards *Mistral*.

"It is," Scott admitted with obvious pride, "and I her sailing master."

"A fine craft to be sure; I see now why my offer weren't good enough," the American laughed. "Though I had thought Tom's ship to be freshly out of refit, whereas yonder looks more in need of one."

"Aye, it were a sea trial to remember," Scott reflected with a glance at his companion. "But what of the *Nancy Jane*?"

Daniels shrugged. "I've been carrying coastal stuff mainly, including a few cargoes its best you don't know about," he added with a wink. "But have just missed out on a load of timber for St Helena."

"So you still lack a deep-sea navigator?" the sailing master assumed.

"I do, though have been coping well enough by clinging to land. But if you've had a change of heart I should welcome it and pay you well."

"Not me, Nat, but I do know of a fine fellow who would be a worthy substitute." Scott indicated the midshipman. "Martin here can shoot the sun with the best of them and has the neatest hand into the bargain."

"So you know your figures?" Daniels asked.

"I do," Martin confirmed.

"The two of us carried out a survey together," Scott added. "Never have I known better support."

"Then I'd say your passage is booked," the American exclaimed.

"I do have something to tell you first," the midshipman confessed. "At times I suffer from episodes of near oblivion..." Martin faltered and his face grew red.

"Episodes?" Daniels' grin faded.

"Yes, I do not lose consciousness but am sorely distracted..."

"Would you be meaning the falling sickness?" the American interrupted.

"It is similar," Martin blinked, "though perhaps not as bad. The symptoms are likened to seasickness and do not last for long."

"You poor bastard." Daniels' tone had lost all humour and he regarded the man with obvious concern. "What with that and being a lobsterback, the Good Lord sure treated you rough."

"Are you familiar with the condition, Nat?" Scott enquired.

"No, but the falling sickness has blighted my folks. Both Ma and sister Katie suffer."

"It is of a similar nature," Martin confirmed. "Occasional and I get good warning."

"Martin, my boy, I should not care if it were every week and twice at Christmas," Daniels grunted. "Can you keep me on a course to hit St Helena along with any other place I might need?"

"Oh, he can do more than that," Scott interjected. "Martin can also stow a cargo and most times will stand a watch with the best of them."

"Then I'm more than happy," the American beamed once more. "And can already see we shall get along famously."

* * *

As King drew closer there was no doubt. The man had turned in response to his call and, though more weather-beaten than before and wearing better clothes, he was indeed the same person last seen aboard the *St. George* that terrible night.

"Why, I had thought you dead," King announced clumsily as he approached.

"Then I am glad to disillusion you," McIver replied extending a hand.

"But I heard the launch rescued and taken aboard *Capitaine* Adenis' ship."

"Which I was," the surgeon confirmed. "Along with our wounded and several from the *St. George*. I stayed with the *Léopard* some months."

"Yet are now in Cape Town," King continued while his weary brain battled to make sense of the situation. He had assumed the medic blown to pieces with the Frenchman, yet here he was and clearly alive.

"Do you know of *Léopard*'s whereabouts?" McIver asked.

"If it is the ship I met a week or so back I do," King confessed. "She is sunk: I destroyed her myself in *Mistral*."

McIver closed his eyes and nodded. "It is the way of things I am sure, though she were a good ship and you will have killed some gallant Frenchmen."

The last piece of information was almost too much for King to take in and for a moment he struggled for thought.

"Her captain, Claude Adenis, released me on account of my work for his countrymen," McIver explained as he rubbed wearily at his face. "Oh, do not get ideas, any services I performed were purely medicative though there are those in Cape Town keen to brand me a traitor. I saved lives, which is what I trained for and could hardly care less about their country of birth."

"So you knew *Capitaine* Adenis well?"

"I did; there are few I respect more and am grieved to hear of his death. He took a number of merchants and did so without unnecessary loss of life," McIver continued. "Then, latterly, recaptured one of his own warships."

"Would that have been a frigate?" King asked as realisation began to dawn.

"I believe so," McIver confirmed. "And understand she had previously been taken by yourself. She were fair knocked about so had to be returned to France and should be on her way there now."

"And my prize crew?"

"They went with her."

"All of them?"

"As far as I know. There was a lieutenant, fellow by the name of Cooper I believes. He was wounded but not badly so."

King nodded; that explained the absence of *Mistral*'s prize in the harbour.

"Adenis was good man," McIver repeated firmly. "Many would have dropped their prisoners over the side or found a likely spot to see them marooned – which would have amounted to the same thing."

"But you are here now," King insisted.

"I am," the surgeon agreed. "My efforts were appreciated and I was not forced to France. We raised Cape Town a few weeks back and were landed offshore in the old *St. George*'s launch."

"We?" King questioned.

"Myself and my medical team, including your companion, Miss Aimée."

King made no response; his already fuddled brain had reached capacity and seemed incapable of absorbing more. But something of the surgeon's meaning did get through and he found himself physically reaching out to the man.

"Do you mean Aimée is alive?" he asked as he gently shook McIver's shoulder.

"She is," the surgeon confirmed and added a tired smile. "And well, though indisposed at present which is understandable. That were another reason for my release," he continued. "Adenis had no mind to send a pregnant woman back to France against her wishes though I sensed there was another reason to let her go that I were not privy to."

"She could have gone back to her home?" King repeated stupidly.

"She could," McIver agreed. "Cooper would have seen her safe, if such a thing were needed. But she wouldn't hear of it, and I gauge there to be only one reason for that."

"Then she came with you, and is now in Cape Town?" King spoke the words carefully, as if expecting them to be contradicted at any moment.

"She is," McIver repeated. "I have just returned from attending her. The birth is not expected immediately but I have advised rest for the remainder of her term." The surgeon eyed him cautiously. "Which means no undue excitement," he added firmly.

"I must see her." Now he was almost pleading.

"You shall." The medic gave the same smile. "But do you not have business here in Cape Town? I noticed your ship is freshly in; there will surely be matters to attend to."

McIver was right and King took a grip on himself. He was a professional sea officer with a duty to perform; Sir Richard must hear of the recent action and may have further news of Cooper and the prize crew. Then there was the captured corvette to consider along with the French they were currently holding prisoner. Now he knew Aimée to be alive, it was strangely easy for him to revert to Service matters. He would need at least the morning with Commodore Banks and Governor Baird then perhaps as long speaking to the dockyard superintendent – with luck they would have found a more suitable replacement for that fool Matterson. But the evening would be free to spend with Aimée, and it should be the first of many.

With *Mistral* once more needing repair, he would be stranded in Cape Town for some while. There was no telling how long the work would take but must surely allow him to be with her through to the birth of their child. And it was then that the barriers finally broke and he found himself awash in a wave of emotion.

"No, now," King insisted as he gripped McIver's shoulder tighter. "I want to see her now – everything else can wait."

Selected Character List

(positions and ranks are as they first appear in the story)

S *St. George*

Johnston	Master
Peter Casey	First Officer
Samuel Scott	Second Officer
Salmond	Third Officer
McIver	Surgeon
Kelly	Midshipman
Selby	Midshipman
Durham	Midshipman
Browning	Boatswain
Kelby	Quartermaster
Drew	Loblolly Boy
Tom King	Passenger
Aimée Silva	Passenger

HMS *Mistral*

James Croft	First Lieutenant
Cooper	Second Lieutenant
John Adams	Third Lieutenant
Kingsley	Marine Lieutenant
Michael Summers	Midshipman
Sennett	Midshipman
Martin	Midshipman
Brett	Midshipman
Foil	Purser
Jennings	Boatswain
Greenwood	Boatswain's Mate
Anderson	Carpenter
Newton	Carpenter's Mate
Allcorn	Master at Arms
Russell	Cook
Dale	Cook's Mate
Daines	Gun Captain
Jackson	Quarter Gunner

McNamara	Captain's Steward
Stredwick	Able Seaman
Burchett	Able Seaman
Veness	Able Seaman
Harris	Ordinary Seaman and Ship's Barber
Swain	Holder
Billy	Volunteer (Third Class)

French National Ship *Léopard*

Claude Adenis	Captain
Moreau	Surgeon
Devall	Sick Berth Attendant

Also
Nathaniel Daniels	Master of the *Nancy Jane*
Greta	Boarding House Worker
Paul Samuels	Merchant Seaman
Peter Samuels	Merchant Seaman
Anne Callahan	American Civilian
Captain Matterson	Commissioner, HM Dockyard Cape Town

Author's Notes

Although they had no true value in law, **Smock Weddings** were an accepted way for a woman, usually a widow, to relieve herself of inherited debt in both England and America during the late eighteenth and early nineteenth centuries.

Midshipman Martin is depicted as suffering from **Ménière's disease**, a condition that would not be identified for more than another fifty years. In 1861 Prosper Ménière published a paper on the subject, although the combination of symptoms has been noted throughout history with many well-known figures including Jonathan Swift and Martin Luther thought to be sufferers. Current research suggests that between 0.03 and 0.19 percent are affected and, despite symptoms that can be truly life changing, there remains no specific cure. In most cases the condition continues for five to fifteen years, after which the sufferer is considered to be in remission and usually left with mild disequilibrium, tinnitus and hearing loss in one or both ears.

The turn of the nineteenth century heralded a general change in medical thinking with some conditions such as **Falling Sickness (epilepsy)** being reconsidered. Until then spiritual possession had been suspected with sufferers subjected to any number of religious 'cures'. True progress was slow, however and confused by a profusion of patent remedies containing often harmful chemicals and herbs such as copper, mercury, belladonna and foxglove. Unsurprisingly, none showed any beneficial effect. Later and it wasn't until later in the nineteenth century, when John Hughlings Jackson and his contemporaries placed research on a more scientific basis, that effective drugs were developed for its treatment.

John Clerk of Eldin (1728 – 1812) was a successful merchant and owner of a coal mine although it is as an amateur naval tactician that he is now most remembered. Clerk's interest in naval tactics was aroused through close association with a former sea officer, and he began to study past campaigns and the memoirs of those who took part. In his *Essay on*

Naval Tactics (published 1790) Clerk broke new ground by advocating a more aggressive stance, something that was quickly seized upon by notable commanders including Duncan and Nelson, and he can be credited with the concept of 'cutting the line' in fleet actions.

Alaric Bond
Herstmonceux 2019

About the Author

Alaric Bond has had a varied career, writing for various periodicals, television, radio comedy as well as the stage. He now focuses on historical nautical fiction with fourteen published novels, twelve of which are in his acclaimed 'Fighting Sail' series.

Set during the Revolutionary and Napoleonic wars, these have no central hero but feature characters from all ranks and stations; an innovative approach that gives an exciting and realistic impression of life aboard a warship of the period.

Apart from writing, Alaric enjoys sailing, cycling and playing an assortment of musical instruments rather badly. He and his wife live in Sussex, they have two married sons.

www.alaricbond.com

Selected Glossary

Able Seaman One who can hand, reef and steer and is well-acquainted with the duties of a seaman.

Aspirant The French equivalent of midshipman.

Back Wind change; anticlockwise.

Backed sail One set in the direction for the opposite tack to slow a ship.

Backstays Similar to shrouds in function, except that they run from the hounds of the topmast, or topgallant, all the way to the deck. (Also a useful/spectacular way to return to deck for a topman.)

Banyan Day Monday, Wednesday and Friday were normally considered such, when no meat would be issued.

Barky *(Slang)* Seamen's affectionate name for their vessel.

Bead (to draw a) To take aim.

Bean *(Slang)* A guinea.

Binnacle Cabinet on the quarterdeck that houses compasses, the deck log, traverse board, lead lines, telescope, speaking trumpet, etc.

Bitts Stout horizontal pieces of timber, supported by strong verticals, that extend deep into the ship.

Board Before being promoted to lieutenant, midshipmen would be tested for competence by a board of post captains. Should they prove able they would then be known as passed midshipmen but could not assume the rank of lieutenant until appointed as such.

Boatswain *(Pronounced Bosun)* The warrant officer superintending sails, rigging, canvas, colours, anchors, cables and cordage etc., committed to his charge.

Braces	Lines used to adjust the angle between the yards, and the fore and aft line of the ship. Mizzen braces and braces of a brig lead forward. **Block** Article of rigging that allows pressure to be diverted or, when used with others, increased. Consists of a pulley wheel, made of *lignum vitae*, encased in a wooden shell. Blocks can be single, double (fiddle block), triple or quadruple. The main suppliers were Taylors of Southampton who, at their peak, produced over 100,000 blocks a year, all of which being handmade. However in 1801, Marc Isambard Brunel took out a patent for machinery to manufacture ships' blocks that could be used by unskilled workers and offered the production to Taylors. They refused, but the Navy adopted Brunel's system which turned out to be the first form of mass production.
Brig	Two-masted vessel, square-rigged on both masts.
Bulkhead	A partition within the hull of a ship.
Bulwark	The planking or woodwork about a vessel above her deck.
Butcher's Bill	*(Slang)* List of dead and wounded following an action.
Canister	Type of shot, also known as case. Small iron balls packed into a cylindrical case.
Carronade	Short cannon firing a heavy shot. Invented by Melville, Gascoigne and Miller in late 1770's and adopted from 1779. Often used on the upper deck of larger vessels, or as the main armament of smaller.
Cascabel	Part of the breech of a cannon.
Cab	*(Slang)* A brothel, also Cat House and Nugging House.
Cat House	*(Slang)* A brothel, also Cab and Nugging House.
Caulk	*(Slang)* To sleep. Also caulking, a process that sealed the seams between strakes.

Channel	*(When part of a ship)* Projecting ledge that holds deadeyes from shrouds and backstays. Originally chain-wales.
Chips /Chippy	*(Slang)* Traditional name for the carpenter. Originally from the ship builders who were allowed to carry out small lumps of wood, or chips, at the end of their shift.
Chub	*(Slang)* A gullible fool: an allusion to a fish of that name that is supposedly easy to catch.
Close-Hauled	Sailing as near as possible into the wind.
Coaming	A ridged frame about hatches to prevent water on deck from getting below.
Companionway	A staircase or passageway.
Counter	The lower part of a vessel's stern.
Course	A large square lower sail, hung from a yard, with sheets controlling and securing it.
Cove	*(Slang)* A man, usually a rogue.
Cutter	Fast, small, single-masted vessel with a sloop rig. Also a seaworthy ship's boat.
Dale	Drain aboard ship, larger than a scupper. See pissdale.
Deadeyes	A round, flattish wooden block with three holes, through which a lanyard is reeved. Used to tension shrouds and backstays.
Ditty Bag	*(Slang)* A seaman's bag. Derives its name from the dittis or 'Manchester stuff' of which it was once made.
Double Tides	*(Slang)* Working alternate watches (also watch and watch about).
Dunnage	Officially the packaging around cargo. Also *(Slang)* baggage or possessions.
Factor	An agent for the East India Company.
Fall	The free end of a lifting tackle on which the men haul.
Fetch	To arrive at, or reach, a destination. Also the distance the wind blows across the water. The longer the fetch the bigger the waves.
Fife Rail	A structure set at the base of a mast and used to secure halyards.

Flashing the Hash	*(Slang)* to vomit.
Forereach	To gain upon, or pass by another ship when sailing in a similar direction.
Forestay	Stay supporting the masts running forward, serving the opposite function of the backstay. Runs from each mast at an angle of about 45 degrees to meet another mast, the deck or the bowsprit.
Friday Face	(Slang) A dismal countenance – probably due to Friday still being a day of abstinence, or *jour maigre*.
Futtock	A lower frame in the hull of a ship (similar to a rib). Futtock shrouds run down from the edge of a top to the mast.
Gaby	*(Slang)* A simpleton, often conceited.
Glass	Telescope. Also, hourglass: an instrument for measuring time (and hence, as slang, a period of time). Also a barometer.
Gunroom	In a third rate and above, a mess for junior officers. For lower rates the gunroom is the equivalent of the wardroom in government vessels.
Go About	To alter course, changing from one tack to the other.
Half Seas Over	*(Slang)* Drunk.
Halyards	Lines which raise yards, sails, signals etc.
Hanger	A fighting sword similar to a cutlass.
Hard Tack	Ship's biscuit.
Hawse	Area in the bows where holes are cut to allow the anchor cables to pass through. Also used as general term for bows.
Hawser	Heavy cable used for hauling, towing or mooring.
HCS	Honourable Company Ship – a vessel sailing under the HEIC flag.
Headway	The amount a vessel is moved forward (rather than leeway: the amount a vessel is moved sideways) when the wind is not directly behind.
Heave To	Keeping a ship relatively stationary by backing certain sails in a seaway.
Head	A toilet.

HEIC	Honourable East India Company.
Holder	One aboard ship employed to move stores below deck.
Idler	A man who, through his duty or position, does not stand a watch, but (usually) works during the day and can sleep throughout the night.
Jackass	*(Slang)* A sixth rate frigate usually of twenty-eight guns.
Jack Dusty	*(Slang)* A traditional name for the Purser's clerk.
Jib Boom	Boom running out from the extremity of the bowsprit, braced by means of a martingale stay, which passes through the dolphin striker.
John Company	*(Slang)* The Honourable East India Company.
Jolly Boat	Smallest of ship's boats, usually clinker built and frequently stowed at the taffrail. The name may come from the Dutch *jolle* meaning small boat.
Junk	Old line used to make wads etc.
Jury Mast/Rig	Temporary measure used to restore a vessel's sailing ability.
Kick Up	*(Slang)* A disturbance. Also a hop or dance.
Landsman	The rating of one with no experience at sea.
Lanthorn	Large lantern.
Larboard	Left side of the ship when facing forward. Later replaced by 'port', which had previously been used for helm orders.
Leadenhall Street	London headquarters of the H.E.I.C. The offices fronted Leadenhall street although the Company's warehouses were usually accessed from Lime Street.
Leaguer	A long, large cask with a capacity of 127 imperial gallons, normally used to hold water.
Leeward	The downwind side of a vessel.
Leeway	The amount a vessel is moved sideways by the wind (as opposed to headway, the forward movement, when the wind is directly behind).
Liner	*(Slang)* Ship of the line (of battle). A third rate or above.
Loblolly Boy	*(Slang)* Medical assistant so called because fish *(slang, lob)* was often served in the sick bay.

Lobscouse	A dish of salted meat (originally fish but later beef or pork) with vegetables and crumbled ship's biscuit.
Lobsterback	*(Slang)* American term of abuse for an Englishman that came to full prominence during the war of 1812.
Lubber/Lubberly	*(Slang)* Unseamanlike behaviour; as a landsman.
Luff	Intentionally sail closer to the wind, perhaps to allow work aloft. Also the flapping of sails when brought too close to the wind. The side of a fore and aft sail laced to the mast.
Mab	*(Slang)* A wench or harlot.
Manchester Goods	Cotton or woollen goods, linen etc.
Martingale Stay	Line that braces the jib boom, passing from the end through the dolphin striker to the ship.
Mog	*(Slang)* Cat (from the Welsh).
Nugging House	*(Slang)* A brothel, also Cab and Cat House.
Old Jack	*(Slang)* Nickname for John Jervis, 1st Earl of St Vincent (1735 – 1823). He was also known as Sour Crout, Hanging Jervis and Jarvie.
Oldster	*(Slang)* One considered old for their current rank. Usually used in connection with midshipmen or occasionally lieutenants.
Orlop	The lowest deck in a ship.
Ordinary Seaman	A reasonably experienced hand who has usually served at sea for between one and two years.
Perique (tobacco)	Tobacco was issued or sold to the people in short, tightly bound, lengths commonly called periques after a type of tobacco grown in Louisiana. These were also known as plugs and (somewhat inevitably) pricks.
Phiz	*(Slang)* Face.
Pissdale	Urinal.
Point-Blank	The range of a cannon when fired flat. (For a 32 pounder this would be roughly 1000 feet.)
Pop	*(Slang)* To pawn.
Prig	*(Slang)* A thief, a cheat: also a conceited coxcombical fellow.
Pusser	*(Slang)* Purser.

Pusser's Moon	*(Slang)* Also Purser's Moon. Usually applied to a crescent moon – i.e. not full (a mean portion).
Quarterdeck	In larger ships the deck forward of the poop, but at a lower level. The preserve of officers.
Quartier-maître	*(French)* Quartermaster.
Queue	A pigtail. Often highly prized by the wearer and tied by his best friend (see tie mate).
Ratlines	Lighter lines, untarred and tied horizontally across the shrouds at regular intervals, to act as rungs and allow men to climb aloft.
Reef	A portion of sail that can be taken in to reduce the size of the whole.
Rigging	Tophamper; made up of standing (static) and running (moveable) rigging, blocks etc. Also *(slang)* clothes.
Running	Sailing before the wind.
Saint Monday	*(Slang)* A religious holiday usually observed by the lower classes. To work on such a day can be punishable by a fine.
Schooner	Small craft with two or three masts.
Scran	*(Slang)* Food.
Scupper	Waterway that allows deck drainage.
Sea Daddy	*(Slang)* An older seaman who teaches a youngster his craft.
Sheet	A line that controls the foot of a sail.
Shrouds	Lines supporting the masts athwart ship (from side to side) which run from the hounds (just below the top) to the channels on the side of the hull.
Slushy	*(Slang)* The cook. It was one of the perks of the position that he was allowed to skim the fat from the boiling cauldrons of meat. This 'slush' could later be sold to the boatswain for greasing blocks, or the men to spread on their biscuit; the money made was known as his 'Slush Fund'.
Smoke	*(Slang)* To discover or reveal something hidden.
Soft Tack	Bread.
Specie	Gold or silver coin.
Spirketting	The interior lining or panelling of a ship.

Spring	Hawser attached to a fixed object that can be tensioned to move the position of a ship fore and aft along a dock, often when setting out to sea. Breast lines control position perpendicular to the dock.
Stay Sail	A quadrilateral or triangular sail with parallel lines hung from under a stay. Usually pronounced stays'l.
Stern Sheets	Part of a ship's boat between the stern and the first rowing thwart and used for passengers or officers.
Strake	A plank.
Tack	To turn a ship, moving her bows through the wind. Also a leg of a journey relating to the direction of the wind. If from starboard, a ship is on the starboard tack. Also the part of a fore and aft loose-footed sail where the sheet is attached, or a line leading forward on a square course to hold the lower part of the sail forward.
Taffrail	Rail around the stern of a vessel.
Thumper	*(Slang)* A third rate or above.
Ticket Men	Hands employed aboard a pressing tender to replace those crew seized, and see the vessel safely to harbour.
Tie mate	A seaman's best friend; the two would mess together, tie each other's queue and generally be supportive. A tie mate was also responsible for seeing to the body if his friend died while aboard ship.
Tommy	*(Slang)* Fresh bread (or soft tack).
Tophamper	Literally any weight either on a ship's decks or about her tops and rigging, but often used loosely to refer to spars and rigging.
Tow	Cotton waste.
Trick	*(Slang)* A period of duty.
Veer	Wind change, clockwise.
Waist	Area of main deck between the quarterdeck and forecastle.
Wale	A reinforced section of hull that runs from bow to stern.

Watch	Period of four (or in case of a dogwatch, two) hours of duty. Also describes the two or three divisions of a crew.
Watch List	List of men and their stations, usually carried by lieutenants and divisional officers.
Wearing	To change the direction of a square-rigged ship across the wind by putting its stern through the eye of the wind. Also jibe – more common in a fore and aft rig.
Wedding Garland	An actual garland that would be raised when a ship was expected to remain at anchor for some while. It signified the vessel was not on active duty and women were allowed aboard. This was considered a preferable alternative to granting shore leave, a concession that was frequently abused.
Windward	The side of a ship exposed to the wind.

About Old Salt Press

Old Salt Press is an independent press catering to those who love books about ships and the sea. We are an association of writers working together to produce the very best of nautical and maritime fiction and non-fiction. We invite you to join us as we go down to the sea in books.

www.oldsaltpress.com

More Great Reading from Old Salt Press

Honour Bound by Alaric Bond
Satisfied that he has forged HMS *Kestrel* into a formidable weapon, Commander King is keen to take her to sea once more. But the war is not progressing well for Britain, and his hopes of remaining in Malta are shattered as *Kestrel* is moved closer to the action. And so begins a story that covers two seas and one ocean, as well as a cross-country trek through enemy territory, a closer look at the French prison system and a reunion with several familiar faces. Containing breathtaking sea battles, tense personal drama and an insight into the social etiquette of both Britain and France, Honour Bound is a story brim-filled with action and historical detail.
ISBN 978-1-943404-14-8 e.book 978-1-943404-15-5 paperback

The Elephant Voyage by Joan Druett
In the icy sub-Antarctic, six marooned seamen survive against unbelievable odds. Their rescue from remote, inhospitable, uninhabited Campbell Island is a sensation that rocks the world. But no one could have expected that the court hearings that follow would lead not just to the founding of modern search and rescue operations, but to the fall of a colonial government.
ISBN 978-0-9922588-4-9

Evening Grey Morning by Red Rick Spilman

In *Evening Gray Morning Red*, a young American sailor must escape his past and the clutches of the Royal Navy, in the turbulent years just before the American Revolutionary War.

In the spring of 1768, Thom Larkin, a 17-year-old sailor newly arrived in Boston, is caught by Royal Navy press gang and dragged off to HMS *Romney*, where he runs afoul of the cruel and corrupt First Lieutenant. Years later, after escaping the *Romney*, Thom again crosses paths with his old foe, now in command HMS *Gaspee*, cruising in Narragansett Bay. Thom must finally face his nemesis and the guns of the *Gaspee*, armed only with his wits, an unarmed packet boat, and a sand bar.

ISBN: 978-1-943404-19-3 978-1-943404-20-9

Finale by Joan Druett

This cross-continental journey had proved very pleasant, particularly considering that he was dead. Or so Timothy ironically mused...

The year is 1905, and the heyday of Thames, in the goldfields of New Zealand. Back in 1867, Captain Jake Dexter, a flamboyant adventurer and pirate, and his mistress, the actress Harriet Gray, invested the fortune they made during the gold rushes of California and Australia in a theatre and hotel called the Golden Goose, which has become an internationally acclaimed tourist venue, famous for its Murder Mystery Weekends. Guests gather, and a fake murder is staged, and it is up to them to find the killer. But this hugely successful venture is now at great risk. Timothy Dexter, an American of dubious ancestry, threatens the inheritance of the Golden Goose Hotel, and the Gray family gathers to hold a council of war, interrupted when a real murder intervenes. And a young tourist, Cissy Miller, entrusted with a Harlequin costume and a very strange mission, may be the only one to hold the key to the mystery.

B07C6627YW e.book 978-0994124661 Paperback

Rhode Island Rendezvous
Book Three, The Patricia MacPherson Nautical Adventures
by Linda Collison

Newport Rhode Island: 1765. The Seven Years War is over but unrest in the American colonies is just heating up…

Maintaining her disguise as a young man, Patricia is finding success as Patrick MacPherson. Formerly a surgeon's mate in His Majesty's Navy, Patrick has lately been employed aboard the colonial merchant schooner *Andromeda*, smuggling foreign molasses into Rhode Island. Late October, amidst riots against the newly imposed Stamp Act, she leaves Newport bound for the West Indies on her first run as *Andromeda's* master. In Havana a chance meeting with a former enemy presents unexpected opportunities while an encounter with a British frigate and an old lover threatens her liberty – and her life.
ISBN: 978-1-943404-12-4   978-1-943404-13-1

Blackwell's Paradise by V E Ulett
The repercussions of a court martial and the ill-will of powerful men at the Admiralty pursue Royal Navy Captain James Blackwell into the Pacific, where danger lurks around every coral reef. Even if Captain Blackwell and Mercedes survive the venture into the world of early nineteenth century exploration, can they emerge unchanged with their love intact. The mission to the Great South Sea will test their loyalties and strength, and define the characters of Captain Blackwell and his lady in *Blackwell's Paradise.*
ISBN 978-0-9882360-5-9

The Beckoning Ice by Joan Druett
The Beckoning Ice finds the U. S. Exploring Expedition off Cape Horn, a grim outpost made still more threatening by the report of a corpse on a drifting iceberg, closely followed by a gruesome death on board. Was it suicide, or a particularly brutal murder? Wiki investigates, only to find himself fighting desperately for his own life.
ISBN 978-0-9922588-3-2

The Shantyman by Rick Spilman

In 1870, on the clipper ship *Alahambra* in Sydney, the new crew comes aboard more or less sober, except for the last man, who is hoisted aboard in a cargo sling, paralytic drunk. The drunken sailor, Jack Barlow, will prove to be an able shantyman. On a ship with a dying captain and a murderous mate, Barlow will literally keep the crew pulling together. As he struggles with a tragic past, a troubled present and an uncertain future, Barlow will guide the *Alahambra* through Southern Ocean ice and the horror of an Atlantic hurricane. His one goal is bringing the ship and crew safely back to New York, where he hopes to start anew. Based on a true story, *The Shantyman* is a gripping tale of survival against all odds at sea and ashore, and the challenge of facing a past that can never be wholly left behind.
ISBN 978-0-9941152-2-5

The Money Ship by Joan Druett

Oriental adventurer Captain Rochester spun an entrancing tale to Jerusha, seafaring daughter of Captain Michael Gardiner — a story of a money ship, hidden in the turquoise waters of the South China Sea, which was nothing less than the lost trove of the pirate Hochman. As Jerusha was to find, though, the clues that pointed the way to fabled riches were strange indeed — a haunted islet on an estuary in Borneo, an obelisk with a carving of a rampant dragon, a legend of kings and native priests at war, and of magically triggered tempests that swept warriors upriver. And even if the clues were solved, the route to riches was tortuous, involving treachery, adultery, murder, labyrinthine Malayan politics … and, ultimately, Jerusha's own arranged marriage. An epic drama of fortune-hunting in the South China Sea during the first two decades of the nineteenth century, The Money Ship is a fast-moving novel on a sprawling canvas that spans three oceans and a myriad of exotic ports. As the pages turn, Jerusha voyages from the smuggling and fishing port of Lewes, Sussex to Boston in its glittering heyday, then back to newly settled Singapore, until her quest for love and pirate treasure comes to a spine-chilling climax in the benighted lands of Borneo.
ISBN 978-0994124647

Blackwell's Homecoming by V E Ulett

In a multigenerational saga of love, war and betrayal, Captain Blackwell and Mercedes continue their voyage in Volume III of Blackwell's Adventures. The Blackwell family's eventful journey from England to Hawaii, by way of the new and tempestuous nations of Brazil and Chile, provides an intimate portrait of family conflicts and loyalties in the late Georgian Age. *Blackwell's Homecoming* is an evocation of the dangers and rewards of desire.

ISBN 978-0-9882360-7-3

Britannia's Gamble by Antoine Vanner

The Dawlish Chronicles: March 1884 – February 1885

1884 - a fanatical Islamist revolt is sweeping all before it in the vast wastes of the Sudan and establishing a rule of persecution and terror. Only the city of Khartoum holds out, its defence masterminded by a British national hero, General Charles Gordon. His position is weakening by the day and a relief force, crawling up the Nile from Egypt, may not reach him in time to avert disaster.

But there is one other way of reaching Gordon…

A boyhood memory leaves the ambitious Royal Navy officer Nicholas Dawlish no option but to attempt it. The obstacles are daunting – barren mountains and parched deserts, tribal rivalries and merciless enemies – and this even before reaching the river that is key to the mission. Dawlish knows that every mile will be contested and that the siege at Khartoum is quickly moving towards its bloody climax.

Outnumbered and isolated, with only ingenuity, courage and fierce allies to sustain them, with safety in Egypt far beyond the Nile's raging cataracts, Dawlish and his mixed force face brutal conflict on land and water as the Sudan descends into ever-worsening savagery.

And for Dawlish himself, one unexpected and tragic event will change his life forever.

Britannia's Gamble is a desperate one. The stakes are high, the odds heavily loaded against success. Has Dawlish accepted a mission that can only end in failure – and worse?

ISBN 978-1-943404-17-9   978-1-943404-18-6

HMS Prometheus by Alaric Bond

With Britain under the threat of invasion, HMS *Prometheus* is needed to reinforce Nelson's ships blockading the French off Toulon. But a major action has left her severely damaged and the Mediterranean fleet outnumbered. *Prometheus* must be brought back to fighting order without delay, yet the work required proves more complex than a simple refit. Barbary pirates, shore batteries and the powerful French Navy are conventional opponents, although the men of *Prometheus* encounter additional enemies, within their own ranks. A story that combines vivid action with sensitive character portrayal.
ISBN 978-1943404063

Britannia's Spartan by Antoine Vanner

It's 1882 and Captain Nicholas Dawlish has taken command of the Royal Navy's newest cruiser, HMS *Leonidas*. Her voyage to the Far East is to be peaceful, a test of innovative engines and boilers. But a new balance of power is emerging there. Imperial China, weak and corrupt, is challenged by a rapidly modernising Japan, while Russia threatens from the north. They all need to control Korea, a kingdom frozen in time and reluctant to emerge from centuries of isolation. Dawlish has no forewarning of the nightmare of riot, treachery, massacre and battle that lies ahead and in this, the fourth of the Dawlish Chronicles, he will find himself stretched to his limits – and perhaps beyond.
ISBN 978-1943404049

The Blackstrap Station by Alaric Bond

Christmas 1803, although the group of shipwrecked Royal Navy seamen have anything but festivities in mind as they pitch their wits against a French force sent to catch them. And all the while rescue, in the shape of a British frigate, lies temptingly close, yet just beyond their reach… Encompassing vicious sea battles, spirited land action and treachery from friend as much as foe, *The Blackstrap Station* tells a stirring tale of courage, honour and loyalty, set against the backdrop of what becomes a broiling Mediterranean summer.
ISBN 978-1-943404-10-0 e.book 978-1-943404-11-7 paperback

Water Ghosts by Linda Collison

Fifteen-year-old James McCafferty is an unwilling sailor aboard a traditional Chinese junk, operated as adventure-therapy for troubled teens. Once at sea, the ship is gradually taken over by the spirits of courtiers who fled the imperial court during the Ming dynasty, more than 600 years ago. One particular ghost wants what James has and is intent on trading places with him. But the teens themselves are their own worst enemies in the struggle for life in the middle of the Pacific Ocean. A psychological story set at sea, with historical and paranormal elements.
ISBN 978-1943404001

Eleanor's Odyssey by Joan Druett

It was 1799, and French privateers lurked in the Atlantic and the Bay of Bengal. Yet Eleanor Reid, newly married and just twenty-one years old, made up her mind to sail with her husband, Captain Hugh Reid, to the penal colony of New South Wales, the Spice Islands and India. Danger threatened not just from the barely charted seas they would be sailing, yet, confident in her love and her husband's seamanship, Eleanor insisted on going along. Joan Druett, writer of many books about the sea, including the bestseller *Island of the Lost* and the ground-breaking story of women under sail, *Hen Frigates*, embellishes Eleanor's journal with a commentary that illuminates the strange story of a remarkable young woman.
ISBN 978-0-9941152-1-8

Captain Blackwell's Prize by V E Ulett

A small, audacious British frigate does battle against a large but ungainly Spanish ship. British Captain James Blackwell intercepts the Spanish *La Trinidad*, outmaneuvers and outguns the treasure ship and boards her. Fighting alongside the Spanish captain, sword in hand, is a beautiful woman. The battle is quickly over. The Spanish captain is killed in the fray and his ship damaged beyond repair. Its survivors and treasure are taken aboard the British ship, *Inconstant*.
ISBN 978-0-9882360-6-6

Hell Around the Horn by Rick Spilman

In 1905, a young ship's captain and his family set sail on the windjammer, *Lady Rebecca*, from Cardiff, Wales with a cargo of coal bound for Chile, by way of Cape Horn. Before they reach the Southern Ocean, the cargo catches fire, the mate threatens mutiny and one of the crew may be going mad. The greatest challenge, however, will prove to be surviving the vicious westerly winds and mountainous seas of the worst Cape Horn winter in memory. Told from the perspective of the Captain, his wife, a first-year apprentice and an American sailor before the mast, *Hell Around the Horn* is a story of survival and the human spirit in the last days of the great age of sail. ISBN 978-0-9882360-1-1

Lady Castaways by Joan Druett

It was not just the men who lived on the brink of peril when under sail at sea. Lucretia Jansz, who was enslaved as a concubine in 1629, was just one woman who endured a castaway experience. Award-winning historian Joan Druett (*Island of the Lost, The Elephant Voyage*), relates the stories of women who survived remarkable challenges, from heroines like Mary Ann Jewell, the "governess" of Auckland Island in the icy sub-Antarctic, to Millie Jenkins, whose ship was sunk by a whale. ISBN 978-0994115270

Britannia's Shark by Antione Vanner

"Britannia's Shark" is the third of the Dawlish Chronicles novels. It's 1881 and a daring act of piracy draws the ambitious British naval officer, Nicholas Dawlish, into a deadly maelstrom of intrigue and revolution. Drawn in too is his wife Florence, for whom the glimpse of a half-forgotten face evokes memories of earlier tragedy. For both a nightmare lies ahead, amid the wealth and squalor of America's Gilded Age and on a fever-ridden island ruled by savage tyranny. Manipulated ruthlessly from London by the shadowy Admiral Topcliffe, Nicholas and Florence Dawlish must make some very strange alliances if they are to survive – and prevail.
ISBN 978-0992263690

The Guinea Boat by Alaric Bond

Set in Hastings, Sussex during the early part of 1803, *The Guinea Boat* tells the story of two young lads, and the diverse paths they take to make a living on the water. Britain is still at an uneasy peace with France, but there is action and intrigue a plenty along the south-east coast. Private fights and family feuds abound; a hot press threatens the livelihoods of many, while the newly re-formed Sea Fencibles begin a careful watch on Bonaparte's ever-growing invasion fleet. And to top it all, free trading has grown to the extent that it is now a major industry, and one barely kept in check by the efforts of the preventive men.

ISBN 978-0994115294

The Scent of Corruption by Alaric Bond

Summer, 1803: the uneasy peace with France is over, and Britain has once more been plunged into the turmoil of war. After a spell on the beach, Sir Richard Banks is appointed to HMS *Prometheus*, a seventy-four gun line-of-battleship which an eager Admiralty loses no time in ordering to sea. The ship is fresh from a major re-fit, but Banks has spent the last year with his family: will he prove worthy of such a powerful vessel, and can he rely on his officers to support him?

With excitement both aboard ship and ashore, gripping sea battles, a daring rescue and intense personal intrigue, *The Scent of Corruption* is a non-stop nautical thriller in the best traditions of the genre. Now available in audio format.

ISBN 978-1943404025

Turn a Blind Eye by Alaric Bond

Newly appointed to the local revenue cutter, Commander Griffin is determined to make his mark, and defeat a major gang of smugglers. But the country is still at war with France and it is an unequal struggle; can he depend on support from the local community, or are they yet another enemy for him to fight? With dramatic action on land and at sea, *Turn a Blind Eye* exposes the private war against the treasury with gripping fact and fascinating detail.

ISBN 978-0-9882360-3-5

The Torrid Zone by Alaric Bond

A tired ship with a worn-out crew, but HMS *Scylla* has one more trip to make before her much postponed re-fit. Bound for St Helena, she is to deliver the island's next governor; a simple enough mission and, as peace looks likely to be declared, no one is expecting difficulties. Except, perhaps, the commander of a powerful French battle squadron, who has other ideas.

With conflict and intrigue at sea and ashore, *The Torrid Zone* is filled to the gunnels with action, excitement and fascinating historical detail; a truly engaging read. Now available in audio format.

ISBN 978-0988236097

Printed in Great Britain
by Amazon

68350193R00163